The
Scribe
of Akrai

Enjoy this time travel
to ancient Sicily from
a Camelot writer.

jmiano@cox.net

The Scribe of Akrai: Luxo reveals the secrets of Trinacria

A Peace Corps Writers Book — an imprint of Peace Corps Worldwide

For more information, contact peacecorpsworldwide@gmail.com.

Peace Corps Writers and the Peace Corps Writers colophon are trademarks
of PeaceCorpsWorldwide.org

ISBN: 9781950444540
Library of Congress Control Number: 2022923752

First Peace Corps Writers Edition, December 2022

Interior Design: Dania Zafar
Cover artwork: Elena Cutrona (elenacutrona.it)

The
Scribe
of Akrai

Luxo reveals the secrets of Trinacria

JOE MIANO

A PEACE CORPS WRITERS BOOK

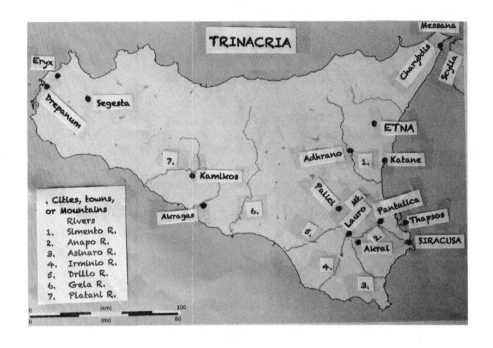

Color photos are available from the author by messaging him on Facebook account under Joe Miano.

CONTENTS

DEDICATION

This book is dedicated to two important people in my life.
First, to the memory of my grandfather,
Sebastiano Miano.
When I was just a child, he was the first to open my mind to the
landscape, people, and stories of Sicily.
Next, to my Muse, talented artist, and life-long friend,
Kay Kaiser
who encouraged and gave me the
confidence to continue to write.

BEGINNING CHARACTERS

Uncle Raffaele – *my uncle and brother of my grandfather*
Sebastiano – *my grandfather*
Enzo – *archeologist who finds the caves*
Luxo – *200 BC Siculi scribe who writes the history of Trinacria*
Anax – *the Sicani who transmits his people's history to Luxo*
The Muse – *mysterious stranger*

PLACES

Trinacria – Sicania – *old names for the island of Sicily*
Akrai – Acrae – *old names for the present city of Palazzolo Acreide*

Acrae

by Gaetano Miano

Richiamo canti
di Acrae,
sbiaditi al distacco
dei miei anni profondi.
Rimbalzano tremiti
d'Anapo,
ondoso di miti.
Rapiti al nostalgico vento
lontano,
ascolto
cangianti i colori dei Greci
nel silente Teatro.
Lesto il sospiro
mi ode in volto
del tempo fanciullo,
fragrante
di erba natia.

Acrae

TRANSLATION BY JOE MIANO

I remember canticles of Acrae,
faded by separation
from my subconscious years.
Quivering they rebound
as the Anapo
is full of myths.
Enraptured by the nostalgic wind,
I listen
to the changing colors of the Greeks.
In the silent Theater.
My breath nimbly
sings odes to my face
of childlike times,
fragrant
of native grasses.

Acrae (It.) – **Akrai (Gr.)** – current day Palazzolo Acreide, is the Greek city-state about 20 miles from Siracusa forming the northern boundary of the early city state (700 BC). It is Gaetano's place of birth.

Anapo is the river which rises in Acrae and flows through Siracusa and out near the sea at the Font of Arethusa. It is full of mythical ideas.

Acrae is known for its wonderful ruins among which is a theater in very good condition. (Palazzolo Acreide is the current town below the ruins.)

CHAPTER I

Cave 9, Innermost Cave (212 BC)

The Beginning of The End

INSCRIPTION Ω

> *I, Luxo of Akrai, a proud Siculo, have inscribed on these walls the
> history of Trinacria¹, from the time of the first inhabitants to the current
> tragic occurrence. This will be my last and most tragic inscription. Now,
> since we are conquered, the Romans will write the history as victors. I
> will retire to my homestead satisfied that I have done my best to tell the
> truth about this land and people. In these caves I have tried to weave
> a tapestry that at first seemed full of hanging threads, just like the
> Hellenic women who sit and weave for hours. But now, I hope that
> after voyaging through all the caves you see that the tapestry is complete
> and that you have found my tale a most beautiful and colorful creation.*
>
> *All praise to Adhrano, our God of Fire, and Aphrodite, whom the
> Romans call Venus, the goddess of love, whom we honor in her temple
> in Akrai.*

The Roman gave an ominous stare and yelled, "Halt! What is
your business on this beach? Do you not know all Hellenes
are to be in their homes by order of the Roman general?"

---

¹ Trinacria – Sicily.

"I am occupied with my work, let me be!"

"What are you writing? Is it a message to the insurgents? To the Carthaginian supporters? Stop immediately!"

"Noli turbari circulos meos! (Do not disturb my circles)!"

"Ah! You are being obstinate. Come, now, immediately! You are to explain to me what you are doing here. Are you writing secret messages to the Greeks? Are you a member of the rebellion? I am ordered to take any rebellious Greeks to see General Marcellus. He is now in command of the entire island. Siracusa has fallen, and all are now subjects of the Empire. Come with me now. We go to the citadel in Ortygia to see the General. We must make haste, for he is a man of many responsibilities. Do not enrage me further!"

"Noli turbari circulos meos! I am at the point of inspiration in my theorem. Go. Your general can wait!"

With that Atticus of the Roman Legion withdrew his sword and with a circular motion in the air, removed Archimedes' head from his body, leaving him in the sand.

A boy watched terrified from behind the trees in the distance, higher up, beyond the shore, his eyes filled with tears. Sevas (Σεβαζ) was overcome and afraid. Jumping down from where he was sitting, he ran home to Eleni, his mother.

"*Métēr, Métēr!* The Roman soldier. Father. He is no more! He lies on the beach!"

"Sevas, are you dreaming? What are you saying?"

"Come and see! We are destroyed!"

And so, they slowly went to the beach and retrieved his body. With tears they prepared it for burial. They placed the old man's body on a donkey and carried it to the cliffs where there were caves in which to place his corpse.

Atticus returned to Ortygia, the center of Siracusa near the temple of Apollo where General Marcellus had set up his headquarters.

"General, the one you call the Sand Writer would not come. I was afraid he was leaving secret messages to instigate more rebellion! He resisted so I could not bring in the traitor like you commanded. He lies dead on the beach."

"Atticus, what have you done? I specifically commanded you to bring him to me alive! Yes, traitors were supposed to be brought to me, or slain, but did you not recognize him? Recognize what he was doing? You have ended the life of the greatest man in all of Hellas! You are banished! You are posted to Lampedusa. You will rot there and have time to think about what you have done. This is the man who helped defend this great city against our fleet with mirrors and the chain guarding the harbor. He invented the mighty claw which sunk our great Triremes.[2] His inventions were innumerable! It will be a thousand years before someone as great as Archimedes walks upon this Earth!"

INSCRIPTION Ω

And so, the great light was extinguished as Heracleides, his close friend recounted. But this story started long before. This unique island's mixture of peoples had a hand in what Archimedes became. Here I have presented the story of Trinacria to the best of my knowledge, so that the truth may come to light.

---

[2] Triremes – an ancient warship with three banks of oars.

BOOK I

Visiting The Ancestral Homeland

Entrance to Akrai Archeological Park

Uncle Raffaele and my cousins At Greek Theater in Akrai
Visited in 1974

Uncle Raffaele and my wife, Ruth
At Greek Theater in Akrai
Visited in 1976

CHAPTER 2

Palazzolo Acreide (1974 AD)

It was the summer. I was finally on my way back home on leave. I had been teaching physics in Kenya for two years with the US Peace Corps. Before I left the States, it had been a volatile time in the US during both High School and University. There had been assassinations, race riots and war protests. The world seemed in so much turmoil. I had two years of respite in a mountain village teaching motivated students. There, I felt truly alive for the first time in my twenty-four years. I will return to that mountain village to teach when school starts again.

Now, however, I was on a quest. Before going home to the States, I would try to fulfill a desire I had had since a child – to visit my grandfather's ancestral homeland. I was headed to visit my great uncle, Raffaele, my grandfather Sebastiano's youngest and last surviving brother. He was in his 80s which increased my impatience about getting there quickly. There had been limited contact between Raffaele and my deceased grandfather since the end of WWII. My grandfather had made the trip to Sicily in 1950 for the first time since he had immigrated to America in 1912. But that was the last contact between the American and Sicilian branches of the family.

Sebastiano had been instrumental in raising me. From an early age he had filled my mind with tales of this most wonderful part of the world. The very stones of Palazzolo Acreide, old Akrai (Ακραι), Sicily, became ingrained in my bones. The tales of his childhood and the legends of this Mediterranean gem were carved like Greek statues into the fabric of my mind. I could visualize the landscape of the village on the high plateau and the narrow road descending into Buscemi and the Anapo River valley below. These places were real to me, even though I had not even seen pictures. I imagined the sparkling white ruins of the Greek theater on the acropolis above the present town. I could smell the incense and food at the religious festivals, the lemon grove around my great grandmother's house, and the succulent apricots plucked from the trees. Now, finally, I was looking forward to adding reality to this imagined paradise.

Though I would have wished otherwise, I had felt separated from my siblings in my childhood. I was the eldest and the only one in my family to remember what Sebastiano and the rest of the extended family told me about the old country. I did not know why I had such love for this unseen place, or what was drawing me here so strongly, but to me it was as real as the New York subway tracks or the Italian festivals on Arthur Avenue. I always knew that someday I would make the pilgrimage back in honor of my grandfather. The plan never left me, but only grew as I studied Mediterranean history. The Minoans, Trojans, Greeks, and Romans were calling me.

Now I was almost there. As the plane swooped quickly down into Rome's Fiumicino, I could see the splendor of Rome spread below for the first time. My pulse raced as I thought of the amount of history in one place. Italy lay below!

The city just whetted my appetite for the journey to come. After a few days I boarded the train. In 12 hours including the crossing of the Straits of Messina I would be in Siracusa. As they loaded the train cars onto the ferry at the Straits of Messina, I thought of the myth of Odysseus at Scylla and Charybdis.

In Siracusa I boarded the bus to my ultimate destination: Palazzolo Acreide, the Akrai (Ακραι) of the Greeks, founded in

657 BC as an outpost to protect Siracusa, the largest urban center in the Greek world.

The bus left State Road and began the ride up the twisting road to the town which rises 2200 feet above sea level. The air was already cooler. As we entered the town the names of the roads flashed by etched on the stone sides of the building – Via Nazionale, Via IV Novembre, Via Italia, Via Antonello da Messina, Via Iudica, Via Scipione l'Africano -indicating the varied inheritance of this town.

I was finally here. The bus stopped at the main plaza in front of the Café Sicilia and across from the Commune Palazzolo Acreide, the town hall. In the hot afternoon, the only people outdoors were some old men sitting at a café bar. *"Scussi, signore, dove è Via Apollonia?"* (Pardon, sir. Where is Via Apollonia?)

One of the men pointed up a narrow alley leading from the square. *"La. Cammina su. Chi cerchi?"* (There. Walk up. Who are you looking for?)

"Cerco mio zio, Raffaele Miano. Lo conosci?" (My uncle. Do you know him?)

"Ma, Si! Americano, tutti lo conoscemmo! E un buon amico. #12. Benvenuto!" (But yes! American, we all know him! He is a good friend. #12. Welcome!)

I walked the few blocks up the winding street as directed. My eyes were filled with the facades of baroque churches and historic houses. I later found out that this was the historic district of the town that had been inhabited for centuries, but that most had been rebuilt after the destructive quake of 1695.

My knock on the door of #12 Via Apollonia began my quest to learn more about my ancestors and the history of this place.

CHAPTER 3

A Time Of Decision (1974 AD)

I rang the doorbell. My cousin Crocetta looked down from the balcony above, and yelled, *"Il Americano è arrivato! Senti, tutti! É arrivato!* (The American has arrived! Listen, all! He has arrived!)"

The time with my uncle and cousins was a trip back in time. Meeting them was like being back in New York City with grandparents, great-aunts, and great-uncles, most who had died many years previous. From that moment, I was at home.

One day, Uncle Raffaele took me to visit the Greek ruins on the acropolis above the town. The Akrai of antiquity. It was just a short walk from his house. My eyes widened as I first looked upon the well-preserved Greek theater that could still hold 500-600 spectators. There was also a group of well-preserved ruins: a smaller theater-like structure, the Bouleuterion, for city council assemblies, and the base of the Aphrodision, a temple of Aphrodite which faced east toward the valley below and to Mt. Etna's plume in the distance. The base of the hill had tombs cut into the rock face. These were called the Santoni. They had carved figures of Cybele and other deities where the ancients performed the rites of their mysteries. As I wandered, I could imagine my Grandfather Sebastiano's childhood, as he played among the ruins. Did he realize the antiquity of the place or was it just a place to freely run and jump upon the theater steps? I was awed and inspired at this part of our shared heritage.

Near the tombs, Uncle Raffaele called me over to a man

working near one of the caves, *"Venni qui.* (Come here) I would like for you to meet a friend."

"Si, Zio."

"This is Enzo. He is an archeologist working at the site. He speaks better English than I and I believe he will give you a better tour."

"*Ciao,* Enzo. Piacere. Glad to meet you."

"Likewise. Welcome to Akrai. I am sure you are happy to meet Raffaele and the family. He tells me you are the first American relative to visit since your Grandfather Sebastiano's visit, so long ago. You will be returning to Kenya after your holiday?"

"Yes, I return to teach in the autumn. So, what is your work?"

"Right now, I have been studying the caves here and in Pantalica. Our team has been working for quite a while."

"It must be fascinating work. I am in awe of all the history in this small place."

"Yes, small now, but it was quite an important place in ancient times. It helped protect Siracusa, the greatest city in antiquity. The aqueduct carrying water to that great city originated not far from here. The Anapo, a river of myth, lies just there, in the valley below."

"I am so fortunate to meet you. Are you finding any of interesting new discoveries?

"Yes, we have found much over the years. We have reconstructed the Aphrodision, at least on paper. But, most recently, we have made an earth-shattering discovery. We have found pictograms and writing of the ancient people who resided near here even before the Greeks. These caves are right here below the acropolis. We are trying to date and decipher them. The most interesting so far is in one apparently small cave, which has led us to a surprising find. There are two inscriptions, one in Ancient Greek which we can read and comprehend, and another that appears to be in the language of the Siculi, Siculian, the Italic tribe that lived here before the Greeks arrived. Hopefully it will help us to translate the Siculi language."

"That seems like it would be a great breakthrough! Will you be working here for a while?"

"For at least this week. Then I must return to the university, but we will continue coming back until our work is done. Of course, provided we continue to receive funding. Would you be interested in coming back in the morning? It's late now. I could give you a tour of that cave and other interesting places."

"*Grazie.* I would be delighted. If it's not too much trouble."

"Not at all. See you tomorrow here at eight before it gets too hot."

"*Si. A domani!* (Tomorrow) Ciao!"

CHAPTER 4

The Job (1974 AD)

Early the next morning I climbed the hill to meet Enzo. I was excited about getting a personal tour and seeing what was usually not available to most tourists.

"*Ciao*, Enzo! What will we be seeing today?"

"I have been working on a very interesting and important find. I will tell you about it because Raffaele has high regard for you, and I feel you will not divulge any of what I tell you until it becomes public knowledge. Our group is counting on submitting the papers and receiving grants to continue our work. Without that, many will have to leave the group."

"I certainly understand. You can rely on me to keep this confidential."

"So, we believe this is probably the most important find in centuries. If we are correct, our team will be able to find out about the history of Sicily and the western Mediterranean long before the arrival of the Greeks."

"Amazing. Enzo, what I have read of the tribes and migrations is very problematic and not based on written documentation. I am finding that written records are very sparse, just inscriptions on vases and some tombs. However, I do understand that the Siculi arrived later than the other peoples and that they were Indo-European and spoke a language like Latin."

"Vero. Correct. But now we think we have found a breakthrough to understanding the language completely. We have found great surprises at the back of the cave which I will show you. So far only our team has seen it, and only the officials are aware of it. The cave is closely guarded by carabinieri."

"Now I am more than intrigued! I can't wait to see it!"

And so, Enzo led me up a narrow gravel path along the hillside below the acropolis. We passed a carabinieri sitting in his car on the road below. Enzo waved and we proceeded into a small cave only about ten feet square. The opening was circular with a diameter of no more than three feet, so we had to crawl through. It was a burial chamber into which a niche was carved just large enough to place a body in a fetal position. Enzo explained that they had found no remains at all. The only find was a small ceramic jar containing ochre. Archeologists believe that it was for burial rites. Then he pointed above the niche.

"Guarda! Here are two inscriptions in Greek characters. However, both inscriptions are not Ancient Greek words. I have studied Greek and the small amount of Siculian that is now known. This was spoken here before 800 BC. But now, look below the niche. This inscription is in ancient Greek: 'Here Diogenes sleeps. He was a good and wealthy trader. His children place him here with great respect and hope his soul passes to joy into the Elysium[3]. Praise to the Palici[4].'"

"*Che meraviglio!* I am happy you trusted to show me this and that you could explain and translate. My knowledge of Greek extends only to letters and phonetics from what I gleaned from the equations of physics. But what of the writing above?"

"Well, that is why we believe this is a find of great importance. We believe that the inscription above is in Siculian with the same meaning as the Greek. It is the Rosetta Stone of Sicily!"

---

[3] Elysium – the Elysian Plains (Ηλυσιον Πεδιον) - the place for the righteous souls to rest after death also referred to as aldilá.

[4] Palici – Παλικοι - the twin gods that became two sacred Sicilian naphtha lakes where the people took oaths.

"Now I understand the guards standing on the road below. You have found the discovery of centuries. *Auguri,* Enzo! What a find!"

"Yes, I am truly humbled. But the find was pure serendipity. As children we played in these caves, even though it was forbidden. At that time our parents were only concerned about us coming to harm. We naughty children loved to play, what do you call it? Seek and hide?"

"Yes, yes, but we say hide and seek!"

"*Scussi,* there is more! Much, much more! Come."

Enzo now moved toward the dark inner part of the cave. Shining his torch, I could see that at the bottom, below and to the right of the niche, there seemed to be a large boulder. Enzo took the heavy stick he had been carrying and lodged it under the boulder. I helped him push as directed and it rolled away like a wheel.

"I am glad you are of a typical Sicilian stature like me – nimble and not too large to fit through this tiny opening! Now, follow me. Crawl through the hole and you will see more marvels."

Enzo went through first illuminating the way. Once inside an enormous spacious room opened in front of us. I could also see that there was even more to see in the passageways beyond. Slowly, my eyes adjusted to the dim light, and I was astounded at what appeared all around me!

"This is like an Egyptian tomb! The walls are alive with pictograms and writing to explain them! You will be famous."

"We believe that the walls are like an historical journal of Sicily. We are slowly beginning to decipher the writing. It will take years. There are nine rooms as large as this. It is slow going, but the painted figures are helping. "See here!" Enzo exclaimed, pointing to a diagram, "this is an example of the boat raft the Siculi used to cross from Calabria by way of the straits. The writing tells us that they began their journey in the far north in what we believe is somewhere in Hungary. And look here. This is a reference to Troy and the tribe called Elymi and, there, they mention Minos and Daedalus!"

I responded with amazement. "So, what we know so far about ancient Sicily is confirmed? That much of Homer and Greek mythology is accurate?"

"Well, we are hopeful, but there is still a lot to check scientifically. They used an ink made with charcoal. There are pieces left behind. The charcoal that we find here is being carbon dated, and we have pottery fragments and chippings from flint blades to try to date. They also have Greek dates in some of the caves. The scribe who calls himself Luxo, dated happenings from the first Olympic Games, 776 BC!"

"Enzo, I will follow your discoveries closely. You have added fuel to the spark that I already have ingrained in me about Akrai! I am interested in learning the history of this place and my ancestors. When I return from Africa in the coming years, I will certainly stop to get updates."

Enzo replied, "I have been thinking. I have a proposition for you. I know you are very interested, and I need help with putting this story together for the public. I will be writing my results in journals, but I need someone who can tell the story so that common people will read it with interest. I would prefer a sort of novel, not a dull history. We need to give life to each character that is outlined here. Of course, it must be in English. Would you consider writing the story of our ancient land once we complete our research?"

I was silent for a while. I was a bit overwhelmed, but also excited. "You have more than tempted me. I would say yes, but it will depend on when you will be finished, and whether I will have the time and resources."

"Certainly, *capisco*. But think about it, will you?"

"I will sleep on it and let you know as soon as I can."

And with that a new world opened. I tentatively accepted but didn't know how it would fit in to my life quite yet. That was 1974. After many years of work, Enzo and his team presented the completed work in the year 2000. The caves would remain under close guard. He gave me copies of his published journals plus copious notes which the team had taken. The work seemed daunting, but I wanted to do it. Enzo insisted there was no time frame since he had already received the highest honor for Italian archeology, a Gold Medal. He became famous by this international recognition. But where to begin?

THE MUSE (2000AD)

I decided that before I would start looking at the cave transcriptions in Enzo's notes, I would do background research into the geology and geography of the island. I had collected quite a few tomes for my library and decided I would begin there. I decided to get an early night.

I fell asleep and had sweet dreams. I dreamt of my long dead grandfather Sebastiano and his brother Raffaele leading me through the streets of the town of Akrai. Turning a corner, we saw an old man dressed as a Hellene[5] and my uncle said, *"Questo e un buon amico mio!* (This is a good friend of mine.) *Parlataci.* (Speak to him.)"

"Ciao, seniore!"

"Ciao, parliamo in Inglese?"

"Yes, I am here to learn about the island and this village."

"Then let me help you. I know a great deal about its history. I have lived most of my life in this area."

"Who are you? And why are you dressed as an Hellene from long ago?"

"I will tell you in good time, but now let me begin with the myth of creation. You will be surprised and, also enchanted."

And so slowly his story unfolded, and I listened with an eager heart to the mysterious man whose mere presence had captured my curiosity! Now, he was about to stir my imagination with his tale.

---

[5] Hellene – ancient Greek

"Long ago, at the center of the warm sea, there were two small islands. There were mountains and fertile land on the larger north island. The other was a white rocky island.

"Each evening the sky god, Ouranos, used his power to cover the earth and block the sun. Each night this god covered the goddess of the Earth. Over the eons Earth, Gaia, bore him many children. He was not a loving father and hated each one of his children.

"Gaia had finally had enough. She called upon her children, 'Which of you will relieve us of this tyrant?'

"Only Kronos answered her call. 'Mother, how can I help you?'

"'Take this giant sickle which I have fashioned and use it to destroy Ouranos!'

"'Mother, do not worry for I control the seasons and time and will know when to strike!'

"So, one evening as a cold rain fell upon the land and sea, Ouranos was blind to all except Gaia, whose luring sexuality filled his eyes with lust. As he descended to cover Gaia, Kronos gathered all his strength and power to lift the giant sickle and remove Ouranos' creative parts. This castration led to an enormous flood which filled the sea between the two islands with a flood of foam!

"Mother, I have done your will. See how Ouranos foam fills the sea, but what should I do with this giant sickle?'

"Bury it on the tip of the northern island. We will call that place Zancle[6] to commemorate your extraordinary deed!'

"Now, the foam that was created swirled and swirled until a shape arose from the sea on a magnificent seashell. She was the goddess of fertility and love, a most beautiful maiden. She became known by many names throughout the earth, but we, the Hellenes, called her Aphrodite.

"Time passed. The son of Kronos promised Aphrodite to the

---

[6] Zancle – scythe – the former name of Messina whose harbor resembles a scythe.

god of fire and heat. Below the earth in his smithy, he, Hephaistos, sat. He took her to his hot underworld and married her. Her beauty was hidden in that sulfurous forge. Faithful she remained for eons but became more and more unhappy. It was not her world of beauty in this world of anvil, noise, and fire.

"One day she noticed the handsome and strong god of war, Ares. He was magnificent in her eyes. They made unending love concealed in one of the forge's caves.

"Nothing escapes the eyes of the gods! The god of the sun spoke to Hephaistos, 'Have you not noticed that your wife has broken her marriage vow? Under your very nose she lies with Ares!'

"Hephaistos' anger and jealousy blossomed! 'Aphrodite, return to the sea on your shell from whence you came! You have betrayed me! I will take another wife!'

"Hephaistos found Eithné, who also lived beneath the earth. They fed one another's anger. Her fire added to his, both in their passion for each other and their hatred of Aphrodite. It grew and grew, emerging from underground, deep below the sea. The sea boiled and bubbled between the two islands. Slowly the melted earth began rising and building. A huge mountain of lava, fire, and smoke grew and grew. It grew so large and high that it emerged from the sea to join the two islands together. A triangular land was created, with a mountain with an eye of fire connecting them, which can still be seen today. Trinacria was created from the forge of Hephaistos!

"But beautiful Aphrodite never forgot where she had been born, for she had a love for this land where she was created. She watched over it, protected it, and gave it fertility. The people repaid her by building altars and temples and giving her adoration and oblations for many, many years."

I awoke startled! The dream was so real. As if I had been there walking among the gods. Who was the stranger? As I drank my morning coffee, I dismissed the mysterious storyteller in my dream as a figment of my imagination as I engaged in Enzo's research.

I now started to incorporate the findings in the caves in Akrai inscribed in about 200 BC by looking at Enzo's notes and diagrams. As I started reading his notes and writings, my mind entered a new state of total absorption. I was not one to believe in mystical experiences, and if anything, the scientist in me was skeptical. But now in this altered state of mind, I was transported into the time of Daedalus and the ancient Sicilian tribes. The cave walls were written by the Siculo scribe Luxo, and I begin with his words. As the characters become alive in my mind, I saw them before me, and they helped move my pen.

As I stared at the page before me, I felt a hand on my shoulder.

"Salve! Let us begin our journey. This way into the world of almost 4000 years ago!

Come."

BOOK II

The Sicani And
The Minoans

1600-1300 BC

200 BC

Luxo – Siculi Scribe
Anax – *Sicani High Priest and Scribe*

1600 BC

Aide (also known as Aelia)– *daughter of Cocalus marries Ari*
Ari – *warrior and son of Iko*
Ariadne – *Minos' daughter and lover of Theseus*
Cocalus – *King of Kamikos in Sicily*
Daedalus – *Minoan Demigod who escapes from Crete.*
Gorka – *chief of the native Sicani of Thapsos, Sicily*
Icarus – *Daedalus' son who flies too close to the sun*
Iko – *chief of the Iberian Sicani arriving in Thapsos*
Minervala – *daughter of Cocalus marries Daedalus*
Minos – *King of Crete*
Makatza – *Native Sicani warrior, son of Gorka*
Parsiphaë – *wife of Minos*

EARLY BRONZE AGE SICILY

Posted by ALLISON SCOLA *on* MAY 9, 2016

From the Museo Archeologico Paolo Orsi in Siracusa, this door slab with carved spiral, anthropomorphic motifs is from the early Bronze Age. It's dated to be from sometime between the 22nd and 15th century B.C. and was collected from a tomb in Castelluccio, an archaeological area between Noto and Palazzolo Acreida in southeastern Sicily. Yes, yes .. it's not just you .. scholars believe it to be a "diagrammatic representation of the sexual act."

Grotte Di Adaura
En.wikepedia.org
PALERMO-MUSEO-bjs.jpg

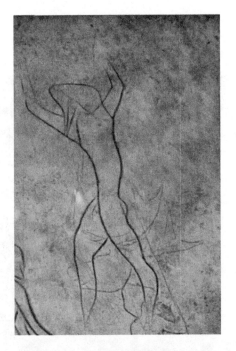

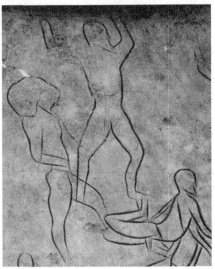

TWO DETAILS FROM 1000 BC
CAVE DRAWINGS

CHAPTER 5

Cave I, Wall 1 (Circa 1600 BC)

DAEDALUS

INSCRIPTION A

I, Luxo, the scribe of the Siculi, have lived here above the Anapo in the village which the Hellenes[7] named Ακραι[8]. Though I consider myself a Siculo, my ancestors tell a tale of mixed heritage. Many of my forebears were here long before the Siculi crossed the Straights. Sicani, Minoans, Mycenean, Elymi, all were in my heritage.

I was tasked by my Rēks[9], or King, to write the story of Trinacria. I gathered our myths and legends, our songs, and epic poems, I spoke with our elders and those of the Sicani and Elymi. I am recording as I was told of their exploits and adventures.

I am writing on the walls of these hidden caves, because in my many years of life I have seen the violence of nature and of men. Even now a bloody war has been fought against Carthage by Rome. We have become a province of that Roman Empire, but there is still much resistance. Even our great mother city, Siracusa, the largest and wealthiest in our world, has fought against the Romans. To the chagrin and disappointment of

---

[7] Hellenes – Greeks
[8] Ακραι - Akrai – Palazzolo Acreide
[9] Rēks – Indo-European title for the leader, king, or ruler. It is the root of the Latin, Rex.

many in Siracusa, including myself, it has lost, and a Roman General sits on the throne of that great city.

I am completing this now in the Roman year of 552 a.U.c.[10] in our new Roman Calendar, or 143.5 OΛ[10] in the Hellenic Calendar. I begin with the famous Daedalus, the Minoan from Crete. He is the first thread which begins the tapestry which I will weave to show how the culture and the people of Trinacria, or Sicania, have developed.

In this first cave, I record the early history of the Sicani, the first inhabitants of the island. Aphrodite, the mother goddess of fertility, led me to an old Sicanian, Anax, who possessed old tablets on which he had set down the story of his people in an ancient Phoenician script which he translated for me. He swore on the goddess that all is true and right.

I, Luxo, and my scribes have spent our years recording what we have learned. As my 80th year on this earth approaches, I am about to complete my task. Persephone, the goddess of the underworld protected me and inspired me to complete this grand work. She has promised to protect it in these caves, her underground palace for all to find in the future, so that they may know the greatness of our people, the Siculi, who first brought iron and the horse to this fertile land.

Anax began with the story of Kamikos, one of the larger of the Sicani settlements, when Daedalus arrived unexpectedly. Anax, by the grace of Erik, whom we call Aphrodite, presented me with these tablets and has translated what is contained in them. I, Luxo, have transcribed them from Anax's own words onto these cave walls so that all who come here can read and learn. Read and learn for we swear on the truth of what we write!

All PRAISE AND ADDORATION TO ADRANO, APHRODITE, AND KORE!

---

[10] a.U.c. - Anno Urbis conditae or OΛ - Olympiads - 202 BC

The Sicani elder began to relate the story of his people to the youngsters gathered around him in the palace court.

"We Sicani have lived in this triangular land for as long as we can remember. The land was verdant and forested with many strange beasts who now are long gone. Our forefathers tell of beasts[11] larger than horses with long trunks and large ears like boat sails. They stood as high as trees. Other large aquatic animals[12] like small grey-black boats submerged in lakes and rivers with huge square teeth and oval mouths. They mostly foraged on water plants during the day but came on land at night and could trample a man. Their legs were like tree trunks! One most feared was the one-eyed beast who men swore lived on the slopes of the mountain of the fire God, Aed. And there were heavy-set, bearded men, who lived in caves and only used stone tools. Some of our men captured their women to satisfy their lust, for the women were fierce and the men enjoyed having power over them. But mostly these people were reclusive and hid in the caves in the forest.

"Even though we have always been here, we do remember some of our tribe singing of a voyage from the south, from a place the Hellenes[13] call Libya[14]. They arrived much later than the original Sicani. They sang of starting their journey far to the west in a place later called Ιβηρια (Iberia). But we could understand their tongue, for it was almost the same as ours.

"Our clans were never large, 20-30 of us living in round huts in scattered places throughout Trinacria. In the southeast near the Anapo, Irminio, and Acate rivers we occupied the seacoast in places like Thapsos and Kamikos, and later, especially used

---

[11] Prehistoric elephant
[12] Prehistoric hippo
[13] Hellenes – I will use this term to refer to the Greeks, since that is how they referred to themselves.
[14] Libya - Λιβυη in Greek

the caves in Pantalica[15] for gatherings of all our clans for religious festivals.

"We fashioned tools from stone and bone, from obsidian from Lipari[16], which our seamen visited. They also brought back copper from the east from the isle the Egyptians call, Alashiya (Cyprus). It was a useful metal which we worked into tools and ornaments. We also carved rock for tombs and for houses. Thus, some of our homes were made of stone, even though most of us still lived in huts of wood and thatch. Men who called themselves Minoan, Mycenaean, and still others from further east brought us objects which helped us better survive, especially a way to make our copper stronger by mixing it with tin. They called it bronze. We traded our grain for tin. Our cousins in Iberia brought us goods in exchange for bronze objects, which we learned to forge for ourselves.

"We learned to build larger stone buildings and temples as our settlements grew. We built towns by the sea on high ground, protecting them with walls and ditches. We learned the use of the spinning lathe and kiln for making better, harder pots. We even made the pots more decorative by drawing and inscribing on them.

"Our largest towns were called Kamikos and Thapsos. In these places clans joined together for protection and chose a warrior chief whom they now called king. Our councils lost power and the king's word became dominant.

"We lived with the traders and the few newcomers from the east and west, traded for novel objects and we provided goods which we could procure here and from the west of the island.

---

[15] Pantalica – an area near both Siracusa and Akrai that has been inhabited since pre-historic times where the Anapo River forms gorges and many caves. I am using the more recent name for the area.

[16] Lipari - Λιπαρα in Greek. The largest island in the Aeolian group north of Sicily.

They were mostly men who came and sometimes chose wives among our women and established families. These new settlers lived with us as equals.

"Kamikos[17]was built of stone quarried from caves long ago. King Cocalus has reigned here for the last twenty years."

As the elder completed his history, the King came into the court.

"I, Cocalus, King of Kamikos, do proclaim Daedalus royal architect of Kamikos. Daedalus we all are grateful that the God Apollo chose to bring you here. We wish you to feel that this is your new home. I hope you will honor us with some of your work."

"Lord King, highest monarch of Trinacria, I am thankful and honored by your welcome and protection. If it is your will, I will build a temple to Apollo as an homage to the great god."

"Yes, that would be fitting as your first act as a new citizen of Kamikos. Later we will speak of other projects which I have in mind. But now I wish you to tell the court and the citizens of your adventures and how Apollo favored us among all other states."

"My tale, citizens begins in the far-off island of Crete, in the realm of the Minoans. We Minoans are a refined and cultured people who value fine things. We spend our time developing our art, music, and architecture. We have traded with far off places and have had small outposts here and even as far as Lipari, where we have obtained the best and finest obsidian and ores for our blades.

"However, a curse has befallen our people under the evil Minos and his beautiful, but evil, wife, Pasiphaë. They are the reason I arrived in such an unconventional way. Some of you witnessed it and were astounded. I created wings of feathers and wax to escape my imprisonment. I arrived alone, but in grief for my son, Icarus, who in foolishness and enjoyment flew too close to Apollo's disk

---

[17] Kamikos - town that was to the north of present Akragas, Agrigento.

and perished. He fell like a flaming meteor into the sea. But the wind carried me to this sunny island where Cocalus graciously gave me refuge.

"But now, let me go back to my history in Minoa, and tell you of our fall from grace.

"Minos, himself, was ruled by loathsome desires of wealth and power. He wished all to admire him, so he prayed, 'Poseidon, show me your favor. Send me a snow-white bull which I will sacrifice to you.' Yet, when the bull arrived Minos sacrificed another bull, for he greatly admired the snowy beast, as did Pasiphaë, his wife. She, a woman of evil lust, formed an unnatural bond with the beautiful beast and asked me to form a wooden cow into which she would climb. The bull seeing the cow, of course, exquisitely fashioned by me, mated with the cow.

"This unnatural pairing had a most terrible issue - the dangerous Minotaur! Nursed by Pasiphaë, it grew, and all of Knossos fell under their evil spell. Its ravenous appetite could not be controlled, it fed upon all human flesh!

"In desperation, Minos consulted the oracle at Delphi who decreed: 'Create a great labyrinth to house the creature, or all your children will be its sustenance!'

"Minos summoned me, 'Daedalus, you must use your skills to create a maze from which this creature may never escape. Build it in the caves below the city and tell no one the plan. Execute all who work upon it, so that no one may know its secrets. Go now and do my will with haste!'

"This order was a daunting task, but I proceeded with the help of Icarus, my son. The labyrinth stretched throughout the entire kingdom. But the King had no empathy in his blackest heart, so he imprisoned us both, so that none would know the secrets of the labyrinth. The bull still raged underground, and the earth shook as he banged against the walls as he searched for an escape.

And as much as he tried, he remained contained and trapped. His overheated breath escaped from a huge fumarole at Thera, reminding all people of his power. Mother Pasiphaë still held him in her putrid heart and gave it offerings of appeasement, children, and slaves to satisfy its unsatiable desires. Underground in the labyrinth as far as Akrotiri, the bull roamed scaring residents who ran to the sea for safety.

"But my mind never ceased searching for a way to escape. We were given birds and fowl to prepare for our meager fare and I collected their bones and feathers in the cloth in which they arrived. Icarus and I spent endless nights weaving and sewing them into large wings, held together with the wax of candles. Their entrails we used to fashion ropes.

"Late one night we were ready. We attached the wings to our backs and hoped that the plan would work. I first had Icarus try, for he was young and strong. 'Flap your wings with all your might! Flap, harder, Flap!' I cried. Slowly his feet left the ground, and as he lifted himself above the jail, he reached the open window and was airborne. Higher and higher he climbed and was free! I followed, but it took me longer and my strength was almost gone, until above the city I caught the wind, and both of us were carried over the sea and beyond.

"And so, we flew for days, but Icarus, my darling boy, played on his wings. He soared and dived and glided, made circles in the sky. I enjoyed watching as I fought with my arms which ached. But then, on a hot and sunny day, he soared higher and higher, close to Apollo who was angered, for Icarus thought he was a god. The wax melted, and my beloved fell headlong into the sea!

"In my grief I pushed onward, for though my heart was heavy, I knew that the tale of the Minotaur must be told and recorded to prevent this tragedy from afflicting men again.

"In two more days, I spotted the triangular island, that I knew was called by some Trinacria, and by others Sicania. I dived downward. Then I saw this fine city with cultivated fields, and so here I landed in blessed Kamikos, to be greeted by your gracious King."

The King spoke as the newcomer paused. "Daedalus, though I, myself, saw your arrival with great astonishment, I thought you were a messenger of the gods. But now I know that you in fact were helped by Apollo who saved you from the evil Minos. I was not aware of this evil in Minoa, and we will assist you in all your needs."

"Gracious Lord, I thank you and will be at your service for as long as I live. But beware, for I fear Minos' anger travels far"

"So, in fact, King Minos was enraged by our escape. He searched over his entire Thalassocracy[18] to find me. From city to city, he traveled presenting a riddle: *I offer one-thousand drachmas to any who can thread a string through a spiral seashell.* This in fact was devised to find me, for he knew only I had the solution.

"The rest of the story is known by you Lord and your court. But I will go on so it may be recorded for posterity.

"When Minos arrived here, your gracious King wined and dined him with all the hospitality that your people are known for. But he had a wise plan. King Cocalus fetched me to his private rooms to find the answer to the riddle. I of course knew the solution which I presented to Cocalus.

"When Minos arrived, he brought Cocalus a present, 'Cocalus, here is a present for your gracious hospitality. These types of Oleasters[19] have come to us from the East. We have begun groves in our kingdom. The fruit can be prepared with salt and are of a bitter but interesting flavor and provide our workers and warriors with energy and are easy to carry. They also can be pressed into

---

[18] Thalassocracy – maritime kingdom or maritime supremacy.
[19] A more domesticated olive tree as distinct from the wild olive which grows throughout the Mediterranean.

a rich oil for eating or for smoothing skin.'

"Your King responded graciously, 'Thank you. They are much appreciated.'

"Minos bowed and then the King presented my solution. "I was told by my erudite assistant that the solution is remarkably simple. Take a thin thread and tie it around the body of an ant. Place the ant at one end of the shell where you wish the thread to enter, and a drop of honey where you wish it to pass through. The little worker will seek a feast, passing the thread where you desire.'

"At once, Minos knew. 'This man can be no other than Daedalus, who escaped from my prison. He must be jailed at once!'

"Cocalus, being in conspiracy with me, had me carried off as a prisoner, to my sumptuous quarters where I enjoyed food, wine, and the company of many beautiful ladies.

"Cocalus, in his wisdom approached Minos. 'My dear Lord, you have travelled far. I have had a bath and unctions prepared for you. My daughters will attend you while you bathe.'

"'Thank you Cocalus, I do need to rest.'

"Once Minos was relaxed in his bath, the daughters, Aide and Minervala, entered. Aide, the younger was a shy brunette with green eyes. Her sister was taller, dark haired and assertive. Aide washed his face with warm cloths, while the Minervala cut his neck with a very sharp knife, ending the reign of the evil Minos forever.

"I was happy and free in Kamikos. My first business is to start planning the temple to Apollo."

But before this, there was much more that would change Daedalus' life!

THE MUSE (2000 AD)

As I wrote that last line visualizing the construction of Apollo's temple, I was present in that ancient world. Enzo's notes and the photos of the pictures on the cave walls were in front of me. My overwhelmed and tired mind led me into a very deep sleep. As I slept, it was as if I were walking among the citizens of Kamikos. Then a distant figure appeared. He was an older man. I could not see his face. He was tall, walked upright, and had white hair. At first, I thought he might be my Uncle Raffaele. I dismissed that impression almost immediately as the man approached, dressed in the manner of ancient Hellenes[20]. At this distance I could only see what appeared to be a long rod embroidered on his white garment stretching from the lower left part to the upper right shoulder. It had a triangle supporting it one third of the way from the bottom. What a strange decoration!

As I stared, I recognized my mysterious stranger.

"Who comes?" I enquired.

"I am your friend from the past, from very long ago. I see you enjoyed the myth of creation. It awakened your creativity. Daedalus now lives as he once did. I have waited a very long time to tell a worthy one of my people and how I came to be. Will you allow me to be your muse? Will you allow me to travel with you on this your journey in which you seem to be so engrossed?"

"Who are you? You seem to be someone I may have known? You have a familiarity about you."

---

[20] Hellenes - Greeks

"Many think they know of me, but I was waiting for the right person. You have shown extreme interest in this project, and I am grateful to you. I think we are connected in more ways than you now can imagine. You will see."

"Won't you tell me your name, or where you are from?"

"For now, be satisfied that I will lead you to the truth, for that was my sole purpose in my work throughout my life. In time I will reveal more. Do you wish me to accompany you? This story you have embarked upon is a long one. It will take time and effort to find the truth and weave the complete tapestry. Right now, it will seem to you as discordant parts of a quilt. But I am here to help you construct the whole which will be the sum of its parts."

"Certainly, I feel that I need assistance on this quest, but why are you interested in it?"

"Because I have a personal stake in seeing that the truth finally be told about this ancient land, this Trinacria, but a small island which from the beginning played a large roll in history. The story will also reveal how mankind progresses or how he fails, how the just and the evil interact. I hope mankind will learn, that like Trinacria, there is no pure race. We all, from the beginning are mixtures of many peoples, many customs, many beliefs. Arrogance is what destroys mankind. We will meet one of our most erudite citizens who lived long before me and spent much time on this island. He claimed that all change comes from the eternal battle between Love and Strife. In the end, we hope Love will win, but it is never certain. Trinacria certainly has seen much of both! We have much to do before we get to him. You have barely begun your task!"

"You have convinced me that your assistance will be of great value. How will I know when or how to call upon you?"

"Do not concern yourself with such minor details. I will be here when you need me. Do not fret!"

"So then, let us begin! I will await you, my Muse!"

CHAPTER 6

CAVE 1, WALL 2 (CIRCA 1600 BC)

DAEDULUS' WEDDING

Cocalus, dressed in his leather pleated kilt made a powerful entrance. King Cocalus spoke in the strong voice of a leader. "Citizens of Kamikos. Today a great tyrant has met his end! King Minos is dead. We will have a feast in two days to celebrate our good fortune and the freedom of Daedalus who will assist us in building a better life. Let us also honor Aide and Minervala who helped accomplish this great deed. All citizens are invited."

Daedalus was shocked and overwhelmed. "Sire, you truly are a wise and great King and I thank you for giving me my freedom. I have already begun plans on the great temple to honor Apollo, who spared me from so many terrors. The site you have selected truly has the best location on the hilltop for it has a superb view of the rising sun. Apollo will be pleased!"

"I give you complete reign over the workers and the men of the rock quarry. You may ask them for any materials. Use the captured Minoan seamen as your slaves to do the work. Now relax so that you will be well rested for the days of enjoyment. Minervala will see to your comfort. Now take your leave."

"Sire, until the feast then. Thank you."

The feast began in front of the Kings home. It was a large structure built as a round house of wood and wattle with a finely thatched roof. It was like those of his subjects, only larger with many smaller surrounding structures constructed in similar ways. The center was open to the air with a hearth for the colder seasons. Now, being summer, woven mats were set out in the stone courtyard in front of the palace. Pillows were arranged around the mats and people were gathering. The buildings were not as finely constructed as Daedalus was used to in Minoa. There were no stone structures, except for the Temple to the Earth Mother at the far end of the courtyard. It was made of stone pillars with a thatched roof. Stone blocks rose only half-way up the walls. He immediately saw how he could improve both buildings and the palace. They would complement the new Temple.

"Good day, Daedalus. I hope you are well rested."

"O, Minervala, I did not see you enter. You do look especially lovely today. I wish to thank you for your bravery. It must have been quite difficult for you to put an end to Minos! I admire your courage."

Minervala said, blushing, "Thank you. Sicani women do not shirk from responsibility. We have been taught to guard our children and how to protect ourselves with knives and stone clubs. Our men respect our courage."

"You are both beautiful and strong. You have made me an admirer!" Daedalus reached to gently take her hand. She allowed him.

"You are being most gracious. I have tried to dress myself like the figures on the vases of Minoa. We have many lovely things from your country. The ladies depicted are most beautiful, svelte, and elegant. Look here at this one on this vase. She is my favorite. I have copied her on the pots that I make and have even inscribed the circular wavelike pattern at the top. My favorites are the blue porpoises I painted! I have even done my own hair in the style of these women. I think they are beautiful. It's just that we Sicani women do not have the tall slender bodies. We are more substantial."

"Your art is truly as good as anything I have seen in Minoa! Truly a work of art. As are you. Your figure appeals to me. You needn't fret or be envious of these figures!"

"My maid worked very hard to raise and curl my hair. They copied the dress and hair from a painting I have always admired on the great urn in the palace."

"They have done a splendid job. But you needn't go to all that trouble. You are lovely in your Sicani dress."

"I wish to please you. So, do you think the dress is an authentic copy?"

"It is exquisite. You are exquisite! You would be at home in Minos' palace, but I am so grateful for what you and your younger sister, Aide, did for me. You were very brave! I am indebted to you."

"There is no debt. We were afraid that you would come to harm! That you would be taken away to Minos! We had to do everything in our power to prevent this. When my father suggested the task, we embraced it with determination. We did not wish you to come to harm. You are a gift of Apollo and have the physique of a god. We did it not just for our father, but also, for ourselves."

"How can I ever repay you?"

"Your presence gives us honor and your Temple will bless our homes."

"I insist that you sit with me at the feast tonight. I want to hear every detail of the story of the Minotaur and Parsiphaë[21] and of her unbelievable lustful appetite for the bull. We Sicani women can also be lustful, but only for strong, virile men. We do not have that particular lust for bulls!"

"And I, Minervala, have been attracted to you ever since we met."

"When I saw you descend as a god from the sky, I was in awe.

---

[21] Minos' wife who had relations with the white bull and fathered the Minotaur

Then my heart missed a beat when I saw how handsome you were standing in front of my father."

"When you first spoke, I was impressed with your intelligence and confidence. Then, after Minos' slaying, I was amazed at your bravery and courage. I am truly honored to be in your presence."

"I have always appreciated that my father has treated me and Aide as equals. I don't often see other men treating their women as equals. They respect them as mothers of their children but act more like they are their servants. They do not respect their ideas. My father is a very wise man. He has provided for my education and for my sister's. We are learning your alphabet so we might scribe the history of our tribe and all the occurrences of late. My secret passion is composing love songs and other ballads.

"Ever since my father Cocalus lost his only son, he wishes each of us to find a husband who will rule wisely. Our leaders are not always selected by bloodline, but it helps. Our people choose their leader. We have started to call him King, as you do."

"I already look upon you as a good friend. I look forward to deepening our relationship. I hope you will want to share some of your love poems with me."

"I would be glad to do so!"

They stood silently for quite a long time under a huge tree near one of the caves on the hill below the town. A field of golden wheat was swaying in the gentle breeze. It was a most perfect day.

"Look, Minervala, how the sun light plays on the grain. It dances in the wind. The gods have blessed me! They carried me here on angels' wings. It has been a miracle to have brought me here to you!"

"And they have blessed me too!"

Their eyes were drawn to each other, and they remained silent for quite a while, enjoying each other's company. Each was happy, but neither knew how to proceed. They were each tied to the customs of their respective peoples and there were strict procedures of courtship. Each knew in their heart that there was more than friendship here.

Minervala finally placed her hand on his shoulder and spoke, "You are a great man, and I am very fond of you, but we must be careful. I feel like we have much in common, but we must go slowly. We must find a way to approach the King. Later."

"I feel drawn to you as to no other. Certainly, we must wait, but at this moment I wish to fashion wings for both of us to fly to the moon. Forgive me, but Eros' arrow has pierced my heart!"

"As he has mine! The feast begins. Let us go."

The next day, Minervala wished to show Daedalus some of the great island. She had her slaves prepare food in baskets. Her lady attendant and two male slaves were to accompany her and Daedalus to the seaside. Each had a donkey to ride and one packed with provisions. They began early the next morning before the heat of the early summer day and headed for the Platani River basin, following the cool flowing water until they came to the sea. Cocalus had arranged a small, thatched cabin to be built a few meters from the sea and the river's outlet. The slaves entered and cleaned and arranged the cabin.

"This is perfect Minervala! I have flown over the sea but have not spent time near it since leaving Minoa."

Daedalus walked to the river and stared down toward the sea.

Walking up behind him, Minervala placed her hand on his back, to get Daedalus' attention.

"I see you are deep in thought. I hope this is pleasing to you. Rest while the servants prepare some refreshment."

Daedalus walked along the river's mouth and turned to the wide, open beach. He found a large rock and sat staring at the sea. He lost track of time, as he stared at the rolling waves, the white caps, and the blue green of the Mediterranean. It was so like the sea he had grown to know and love in Minoa.

"There you are! The food is ready, and the rooms have been prepared for the evening."

"Sorry, Minervala. I am distracted and still in mourning for my lost son! Every morning I see him soaring in the sky, so light, so filled with joy. Then I see his wings aflame, and him falling, falling eternally into Poseidon's realm! I awake panting and sobbing. Icarus was truly beautiful to behold, young and manly."

"Daedalus, I know it is hard. We want to remember those lost, always thinking on how they have enriched our lives. They are now part of the universe, and we honor them in our thoughts. Try not to dwell on your loss. I too have lost. My mother was taken early in childbirth. They all dwell now in a better world, without pain and suffering. We will all rejoin them someday. That is why we take such care to inter our dead in the caves on the side of the hills, facing the Platani."

"You are right. I must look at the future, and I must share that with you! I was feeling homesick, not only for my lost Icarus, but for all I left. The sea, the same sea reminds me that we are all united no matter how far we venture."

"Yes, I love being near the sea. It cleanses us with it waves. And when I look at you, I see a very handsome, strong, and wise man whom I wish to know better, and with whom I wish to spend my time."

"You flatter me. I am nearly twice your age!"

"That is not a concern of mine. I just wish for someone who understands and cares for me.
"Unions forever blessed,
When minds communicate
Merely with a glance
No words can ever enunciate
Love's trance
Uniting hearts!"

"Minervala, my love, you are truly gifted! I wish to ask the King for your hand. I would do it as soon as we return!"

"Daedalus, I would be honored to be your wife, but let us wait. My father is preoccupied these days with all that has happened. We will stay here a few days and then wait for the right time. Soon my love, soon. I will suggest the appropriate time. Let us be off now to our refreshments and our rest."

A year after the feast, Cocalus agreed that the two should wed. According to the rights of the Sicani, Minervala was dressed in a cone shaped white skirt from waist to her ankles. It was decorated with two graceful, parallel, golden chevron designs. The top consisted of blue sleeves and blue midriff. In the Minoan fashion, her lovely young breasts were visible amid the blue. These colors signified both the sea and Aphrodite. A thin veil covered her face allowing her dark hair to flow down her back, with a large curl beside each ear. Daedalus, bare-chested, wore his short blue and white Minoan kilt. In the typical fashion the hem was just above the knees, but curved so that it was lower on one side. He had a circular headdress fashioned of copper and studded with amber beads. Large bird feathers in blue and white were fastened to the top headdress and stood high and waved in the breeze. A narrow red sash was slung from his shoulder to his waist, to signify he was saved by the sun god, Apollo.

They entered the temple dedicated to both Apollo and Aphrodite. It was a man-made cave facing the river Platani, situated so that at the summer solstice the sun's rays illuminated the altar located deeply into the interior. At sunrise the priest held up his feathered staff and waited. The bride and the groom entered and faced the altar. At the precise moment of illumination by the sun, the altar stone shone brightly orange, with small crystals reflecting the light throughout the temple. At that same instant, the priest lowered the staff proclaiming that Apollo and Erik, the Sicani name for Aphrodite, had blessed the union because the light had had no obstruction from clouds. The priest and the people left singing praise to the gods while Minervala and Daedalus entered the inner sanctum.

"Minervala, your beauty shines like that of Erik! I am overjoyed that we have finally arrived at this point. It seems I have waited an entire lifetime!"

"Daedalus, I must reveal a secret to you before we go any further. I have another gift. A gift of seeing. Last night I saw you arrayed in your wings, and you took me in your arms, and we flew high, very high! I feared that we might meet the same fate as your beloved Icarus. But lo, we arrived on Apollo's doorstep, and he spoke to us. 'Minervala and Daedalus you will be blest with my light and knowledge and so will your children, your children's children, and all who proceed from your sacred union. Blest be you, but make sure you teach them to honor me, the truth, and the good. Return now to the earth and live!' I awoke in a state of bliss"

"We are truly blest by the sun. Let us embrace and fulfill our destiny!"

Inside there were mats and pillows, food, and drink. Minervala lit the oil lamps. She slowly removed her garments while she danced around the central fire. The flickering light added to her naked beauty. Daedalus was awestruck. He always thought she was one of the most beautiful women he had ever seen, but now he was breathless. He undid his kilt. He approached the swaying beauty. He saw her ruby red lips and then his met hers. They kissed and swayed into the night, consummating the union.

The fruit of this union would be many. Their progeny would have great influence on Trinacria.

CHAPTER 7

CAVE 1, WALL 3 (CIRCA 1600 BC)

THE EFFECTS OF THE MINOTAUR'S DEFEAT

INSCRIPTION B

I, Luxo, was glad to learn and write of the happy marriage between Daedalus and Minervala. Life resumed as normal in Kamikos as Daedalus started overseeing the construction of Apollo's Temple. King Minos' death and his evil reign were almost forgotten. Fear left the people of Kamikos as they tended their livestock and fields.

Minervala was sitting at her loom, while the children played in the courtyard. Suddenly, the earth began shaking violently. She ran out to get the children. She saw Daedalus running from the temple mount toward home.

"Daedalus," she shouted, "Come quickly, the children!" She had managed to round up the youngest, but the older one was too quick for her.

"I see him! I have him. Come into the open so you will be safe if the buildings fall!"

As they looked at the sky, an enormous cloud rose far in the east. Higher and higher, until it blackened the entire sky. Darkness descended on the world for three days.

"What is happening? Will the sun return?"

"The gods have been angered, Minervala. I fear that Apollo's temple needs to be completed more quickly. As soon as some light returns, I must get the slaves to work more rapidly!"

People wondered if the end of the world was here. Kamikos, as well as all Trinacria, were gripped in fear. But as suddenly as the darkness fell, a very strong sirocco began to blow and pushed the cloud to the north. As it blew stronger and stronger, the people watched the cloud rise and push north, north of Kamikos, north of the smoking mountain, until it was only a dark strip on the horizon. All breathed in relief and slowly all returned as it was.

After a few weeks, Daedalus' Temple was finally taking shape, and he arranged to take Minervala and the children back to the sea where they had so many good memories.

"Prepare for our outing," Minervala told her servants. "We go to the sea for a few days. The heat of this summer is intense, and the children will enjoy the sea. Be ready at sunrise."

So, the next day the small caravan began the journey as before. By the afternoon they could see the waves from the hills and were at their cabin by late afternoon.

"Daedalus, how I love it here! Even with the sirocco, the coolness of the sea makes me feel alive!"

As they sat on the sand, they saw a sail on the eastern horizon. Then more appeared.

"Look! Look! So many boats! They are loaded with people!"

"Yes, Minervala, and they are standing shoulder to shoulder! This is not an invasion! These are escaping!"

"Look! Look how some cling to the ropes. Some hang on the sides of the ships! Women and children! Poor, poor suffering creatures!"

"I see now that most of these are dressed as Minoans! Come, let us greet them."

The first boat pulled in not far from the beach and people began swimming and wading toward the shore. They looked hungry and exhausted.

Minervala called Vacho, the head servant. "Vacho, tell the others to bring as much water and bread as we have. Send two other servants back to Kamikos and tell the King that we have hundreds of starving refugees here on the beach. If you leave now, you can get there by dusk. Go quickly. Tell the King to send food and warriors to help transport these poor creatures to Kamikos. Go, go quickly!"

Daedalus approached one of the first young men who came ashore. He recognized him as being a high-ranking soldier by his dress. He wore the typical blue, knee length, kilt which curved lower to a point on one side of the right leg. It had a white stripe across the bottom. The round conical hat rose to a point to which three long plumes were attached. Daedalus had no doubt that he was a countryman, and an important one at that.

"Hail, I am Daedalus of Kamikos. I see that you must be from Minoa!"

The visitor bowed. "Hail, thank you Sir for giving us refuge! I am amazed that you speak our language perfectly! My name is Aranare. I was captain of the King's guard in Knossos! But we have suffered an unbelievable catastrophe[22]. It overcame us so quickly, and so many, many perished. Only these you see coming ashore have survived. We have been at sea for many months looking for refuge. But pray, before I tell you more, may I have some water?" With this he fell on the sand exhausted.

The servants and Minervala did the best they could to make sure each received water from the clear flowing Platani which was close by. The servants were busy baking quick breads and

---

[22] Thera, Scientists believe that the huge Minoan volcano of Thera exploded around 1600 BC in one of the largest explosive events in recent history.

Minervala made sure each had a small morsel until the morning, when she hoped reinforcements from Kamikos would arrive with provisions.

The next morning, Aranare woke early. He seemed very fit and awake.

"Sir Daedalus, again I thank you. We all thank you. But how is it that you speak our tongue?"

"O, that is a long and intricate tale. I will tell you more later. But in short, I too served Minos, but you may have been too young to remember. I escaped and found myself a place here among welcoming people and have made a life here. Minervala, my wife, is daughter to Cocalus, King of Kamikos. But tell me now, how is it so many are on these vessels? And what occurred back home to send you so far?"

Aranare became agitated as he spoke. His eyes were very wide, "Sir, we were attending to our lives, our duties, when in an instant the earth shook violently. The palace servants ran out and told us that the brave Athenian, Theseus, had slain the Minotaur with the help of the beautiful Ariadne. They escaped on a boat waiting for them and sailed back to Athens. The quake was the beast's dying death throws. But then, Poseidon, already angered by Minos' poor sacrifice, rose from the depths. He rose from the crater of the volcano and released the catastrophe. Half of the island was thrown into the air, creating a great black cloud which rose to the heavens, blocking the sun. The black cloud seemed to cover the Earth."

"We too saw the cloud and we were dark for three days. Luckily the sirocco came and saved us, blowing it north!"

Daedalus could see that recalling the trauma was not easy for Aranare, for he was raising his hands and swaying as he recalled his experience. "We too were fortunate to be able to sail away from Minos to safety just before the final explosion. But we had to endure enormous wind and waves at sea. The great explosion which you saw on the horizon was Thera being pulverized and thrown into the sky. The entire kingdom of Minoa and almost all its inhabitants are no more. The gods of the underworld had conspired with Poseidon to unleash the terrible power from the mountain in Thera. All our achievements, our art, and our citizens were buried in rock, ash, and earth! All for the evilness of our King. Only a few escaped and all that remain of Knossos were the few Minoans who are on these ships, or those residing or trading in Lipari, Trinacria, or Etruria."

Daedalus placed his hand on the visitor's shoulder. "Aranare, welcome to our land. Do not fear Minos any longer, for he was slain here. Rest now and once the guards arrive with provisions, we will head up to Kamikos where you all may begin a new life and help teach our ways to the Sicani."

"We are grateful for your hospitality. Blessed be Astarte, guardian of women, and Thalassa, who controls and stills the sea, bringing us to safety!"

INSCRIPTION β

I, Luxo, now record from Anax's Sicani inscriptions of the movements of the Daedalus' descendants. When Daedalus and Minervala's children were grown, they decided to move with them to Thapsos on the southeastern coast, not far from Siracusa's eventual location. They journeyed along the coast to the very important trading center and fortified town on a narrow strip of land near the sea. There they would be at the center of the evolving story of the most important settlement of the Minoan-Sicani in early Trinacria.

THE MUSE (2000 AD)

The arrival of the Minoans completed the first part of the history and set out the first thread of the tapestry which Luxo was weaving. The next cave led me to other Sicani, but I was not sure how to proceed with developing the characters. As I fell asleep in my chair, the tall, lean man approached, this time carrying a rod like the one embroidered on his chiton.[23]

"Salve! You have been working a great deal."

"Yes, friend, but I am confused because I do not know where this story is going?"

"I realize that you have only the few inscribed facts on the walls and still much was not recorded of the Sicani. But that is why I am here."

"So, you will assist me in finding the right words?"

"My purpose is for the truth to be revealed clearly after all these millennia. Much of the mystery of the Sicani had been removed from history. I will first take you to see the arrival of another early group of Sicani. Come. Follow me!"

I arose and walked out the door and I was suddenly in a completely different world!

When I awoke, I began translating Enzo's notes, but with a deeper understanding of what Luxo had written. My hand moved as if guided by my new-found friend.

---

[23] Chiton – a tunic that fastens at the shoulder, with one arm and shoulder left bare.

CHAPTER 8

CAVE 2, WALL 1 (CIRCA 1600 BC)

THE SICANI VOYAGES

INSCRIPTION Γ

I, Luxo, of the Siculi, record verbatim on this cave wall what Anax, the high priest of the Sicani, told me of their origins and what he showed me of the Sicani tablets. Following is the translation of the first Sicani tablet of the arrival of the Iberian Sicani. Anax began as follows.

I, Anax, record on these tablets in the writing of the Phoenicians, how some of our brother Sicani came to live in Trinacria.

Our first arrival is clothed in mystery. Some say that we have been here since the beginning of the world. As far as the elders remember, others of our ancestors left a land of cold in the north. Some went to Iberia, and others to where the Ligurians now reside. They are our close relatives. Our tribesmen migrated here at different times from the north. They traveled far, even to Libya. The Sicanian tongue was the language spoken in Libya and in Iberia. There is even a Sicano river in Iberia, and people who trade from that area look like us Sicani. Other epics tell of us arriving by sea, crossing from Libya, and intermixing with some of the inhabitants that lived in the hills. We traded with Libya, Iberia, and Malta in the west and with Troy, Anatolia, Minoa, and Mycenae, in the east. Sicani ancestors built the huge stone temples and megaliths in Malta. Many of these traders and visitors remained here and became interwoven in the Sicani fabric.

So, this has always been our land. Our language is not related to that of the Siculi or Elymi. The Siculi language is like that of the Latine, or Oscan, or others in Italia. I will recount the epic of the arrival of one group of Sicani as it has been sung by our elders for generations.

The day was a cool spring day with a slight sea breeze on the Libyan coast. The men were gathered on the shore in the early morning. Some were in small boats using nets to bring in the catch. Others were repairing sails or using pitch to fill the cracks between the planks of the boats.

"Ari, prepare for tomorrow!"

"Yes, Iko, the boats are loaded, and the people will be ready at dawn with the outgoing tide."

"We have favorable weather at this time of year for our voyage to the triangular island."

"Aye, it has been a long journey from our home along the Sicano river in Iberia to Libya. The winter here has been mild, and so now all is ready for the final journey. I miss our home, but not the dry weather and our struggle to keep our crops watered and healthy. Our cattle and goats had little to eat for years. It was time to move on."

"Our traders tell us that this island is a vast and almost empty land, especially good for growing emmer[24] and farro[25]. The fish, especially the great tuna, fill the waters of the nearby sea. If this be true, our people will flourish!"

"I look forward to a better time."

"Ari, will our cousins meet us on the eastern coast?"

---

[24] Awned wheat, emmer is einkorn wheat one of the earliest forms. A tetraploid wild variety.

[25] Farro is one of three hulled wheat species: emmer, spelt, einkorn. It cannot be thrashed.

"Yes, that is the plan. They were to head for the island of flint and obsidian which is known as Lipari. They will carry as much as they can for our use to make tools and for trade. If all goes well, they might already have arrived."

Aeolus, the god of wind, favored them, and they arrived at the southern coast of Trinacria in half a day. Now they would follow the coast east to a small settlement called Thapsos where a small community of the Sicani had established a fortification. They were the original inhabitants of the island but spoke a language close to that of the boat people from Libya. It was a famous place where people from east and west traded.

"Ari, I see the harbor! I see the fortifications! Look to the northeast!"

"Bai (yes)! Signal the others to head toward land. It is a fine harbor."

"We can see the huts and some people working on the shore."

As they approached, they saw that some men were looking at the boats and were aware of who they were by the markings on their sails. Some were waving. Ari and the others were elated by the fact that they had found the Thapsos they had heard about from the older sailors. Ari felt proud that now he could better provide for his family because of the lucrative trade in amber, alabaster, and metal. The copper, tin, and gold they brought from the north of Iberia would provide them with trading advantages. They now saw the characteristic round huts, like those they had left in Iberia. But they also saw the stone walls surrounding the peninsula of Thapsos. A very small isthmus connected it to the mainland, making it a perfect fortification. They were happy to finally again be among their own.

Upon reaching the dock they were greeted by the bare-chested chieftain in his white pleated kilt. He wore a wide shoulder strap across his chest which held his sword with its hilt decorated in amber beads. He had a gold necklace fashioned in the style of the Minoans. Next to him was another younger man also royally dressed. Ari and Iko were impressed.

"Welcome to Thapsos! I am Gorka, grand chieftain. The traders from Malta have told us to expect more of you Iberian Sicani who wish to settle in Trinacria. We welcome you if you will follow our dictates and live with us in peace. Later we will speak of where you may settle. Now come, rest, and eat."

Iko, the head of the group of emigres, bowed to the chief and kissed the hilt of his sword as was the tradition of respect to a leader or elder. "I am Chief Iko, and here stands, Ari, my son and trusted chief warrior. We come in peace, great Chief Gorka. We have heard much of this wondrous island, and its fertility. I and our brothers wish to help you build and extend the settlement. Thank you for accepting us."

Ari looked at his father, Iko, and whispered, "Who is the other stately man standing near the Chief?"

Iko shook his head, "I assume it is a son. We will find out soon."

Chief Iko, Ari, and the other men of importance followed Gorka to his circular hut. There were cushions of lamb's wool set out in the paved courtyard. They were invited to sit.

Iko was the first to speak. "It has been three years since you met with our kinsmen who came here from Lipari bringing obsidian. We were grateful to hear that you invited our clan to settle here in Thapsos."

"Yes, and we are happy that you all have arrived safely after such a long and strenuous journey. Did you all survive?" Gorka looked concerned.

"It was arduous. None of us were lost at sea but some uncivilized tribes attacked us while we were camped on the coast of Libya. Three warriors and one woman died in the attack, and others suffered minor injuries."

"We thank Erik (Aphrodite), the mother goddess, for your low losses. Now you can feel safe here. We have not suffered an attack since we built this settlement many years ago. We have many places to escape in the hills, and toward the great Mountain of Eithné (Etna). You have much to see that will amaze you. At night Eithné will light the east, and at times provide a spectacular demonstration of her power. The Fire God, Aed, protects us, because he elicits fear in all who wish to attack our shores. The cyclops below the fire mountain instills fear in them from landing but he does not disturb us. We offer sacrifices to appease Aed, and he keeps the cyclops away from us." Then, Gorka puffed out his chest in pride. "I have not presented my son, Makatza (wild one)," pointing to the man whom Ari had asked about. "He is a strong and fearless warrior. I believe he and Iko will learn from each other and be fine future leaders."

As some of Iko's men came up the path with baskets, Iko spoke, "Gorka, we have brought fine flint, copper and tin from Iberia. We hope you will accept our gift."

"It is accepted with humbleness. You are gracious to have brought so much on your long journey. Now let us eat. Our men will help with the unloading of your ships. The women will care for you and your children. We will help you settle and feed your people. Let us feast and drink and sleep for you can now rest without any cares. Welcome. Welcome!"

"Erik (Aphrodite) smiles on us."

As they sat drinking the strong wine which King Gorka had shared with the arrivals, an older but athletic-looking man dressed in a white skirt with gold chain around his neck approached them. He too was dressed in the fashion of a Minoan. Gorka called out, "Iko! I would like you to meet our honored guest, King Cocalus of Kamikos. He has travelled many days to visit us. We are forming an alliance of Sicani in Trinacria against any future invaders. Though he is a Sicani, he has developed favorable relations with the traders of Minoa. He also has had a visitor who arrived from Minoa in a very unusual way. I will let him tell you himself. "

Iko and Ari rose to greet Cocalus. "Lord we are honored."

Cocalus looked directly into Iko's eyes. "I am always glad to see arrivals of our people from far off places. Welcome. I hope you will some day visit our fair settlement. It is inland. Follow the Platani river until you come to our acropolis."

"We would be honored."

Ari, genuflecting, "It is an honor."

"This is my son and respected warrior, Ari."

As Ari rose to his feet, he looked in the distance just beyond Cocalus. A most beautiful maiden, dressed exquisitely and differently from the rough brown tunics worn by the women of Thapsos. Her hair was high on her head with intricate gold thread woven in its strands. Long curls surrounded her huge eyes, made larger with dark black paint. Her dress was was long and cone shaped. She had colored markings on her arms. Ari had never seen such a majestic beauty.

"Young man. I see you are staring. That is my youngest daughter, Aide, Princess Aide. Her dress was designed after the style of Minoa, by my assistant and teacher, Daedalus, who arrived many years ago. He has improved our way of life immensely."

"Forgive me, Sire, but I have never seen any woman so beautiful and exquisitely attired. You are truly blessed."

"Now friends and guests," announced Gorka, "come in and sit, for the slaves are bringing our food. And Cocalus will fascinate us all with how he witnessed an unbelievable event that changed the course of Kamikos when Daedalus arrived on bird's wings!"

As Ari's eyes strayed from Aide and looked toward Gorka, Ari noticed that his son, Makatza, had a crazed, distant look in his eyes. Makatza rose and then walked away from the feast.

As they all arranged themselves in the inner court of the long house, Ari could not think of anything but Aide. He was infatuated. He was determined to have his father arrange a meeting. After all, he was the son of a chief. He, himself, might be chief one day. He was determined to have her as his wife.

CHAPTER 9

CAVE 2 - (CIRCA 1600 BC)

PASSAGEWAY WALL
MAKATZA

The Iberian Sicani under Iko assisted Chief Gorka to build a strong settlement in stone at Thapsos. The streets were paved with the stone. Some permanent buildings were constructed of tufa[26] from Etna. A wall across the isthmus protected the inland side of the town. The harbor welcomed trading ships from near and far.

King Cocalus had returned to Kamikos to oversee his kingdom, but Aide had remained with Minervala and Daedalus in Thapsos. Before he left, Gorka had approached Cocalus and strongly suggested that a match should be made between Aide and Makatza. Gorka was very interested in cementing a strong bond between the two kingdoms. However, Cocalus was noncommittal. He told Gorka that he would give his answer in due time and would send his answer though Minervala.

Daedalus had grown blind and feeble. His many children gave him the best of care in his old age, and he soon passed peacefully into the next life and was buried in the caves outside the town according to the Sicani rituals.

A friendship had blossomed between Ari and Aide. None of

---

[26] Tufa – a variety of porous limestone used for building, especially for vaulting because of it light weight.

this was missed by Makatza's jealous eyes. As the son of Gorka and a fearsome warrior, Makatza walked around Thapsos wielding his privilege. He would enter any household and demand the owner turn over livestock for his flocks. He would demand tribute from the traders before the items were registered with the officials. All bowed to him in fear. Even his father, Gorka, was bullied by this son. Now Makatza turned his eye on Aide. He lusted for her body, but even more wanted her so that he could cement his power. Having the daughter of Cocalus as his consort would ensure that no one questioned his authority once Gorka had passed. The time came sooner than he expected when Chief Gorka became ill with a disease that arrived on one of the trading ships from Egypt.

Now Makatza became chief, and his chest swelled with pride, and he turned his mind to how to secure absolute power. He began by turning the citizens of the small Thapsos against one another. He would stand in the marketplace and harangue against the Iberian Sicani and other groups that were visiting from neighboring villages.

"People of Thapsos, you are the rightful owners of this land. You are the descendants of the native Trinacrians who were born on this soil of Erik. Kamikos and Thapsos must share in our wealth. All others are here to serve us. Watch carefully, for they wish to take from us – to take our women, to rape our children. They will rob us of our land. Beware."

Each day there was vitriol in his speech, and it raised a hatred in the natives of Thapsos against the newcomers. Ari and his people were hurt by the insults but had little power to do anything but submit.

Aide was pleased to be with her sister. Minervala was happy for the companionship once her husband had died.

"Sister, it is so wonderful to have you and your children so close. I miss father, but you have provided me with a good home.

My life seems complete now. I have only one more hope — that Ari will ask to marry me and that I will have the joy of children like you did."

"Aide, my dearest sister, I too pray to Erik that she will give you that joy and that she will protect Ari from the hate being fostered by Makatza. I fear for him, and you, also. Do you see how he looks at you when you are in the marketplace? His eyes are filled with power and lust. His evil flows from his pores as sweat on a hot day. Notice how he instills hate in the citizens and how they listen to each word as the truth from the gods above. It is an infection which spreads like the plague."

"Yes, Minervala. I have seen this. What can we do?"

"I have had visions. I have seen him taking you to his bed and forcing himself on you. He tied your hands and feet and took you. Then he spoke in the marketplace and told the people you had agreed to marry him. This would ensure his supreme power through our father's blood. In my dream, I also saw bloodshed and violence in the streets."

"O! Dear Minervala. What shall we do? I fear that Ari will approach Makatza, and it will end badly!"

"We need to be vigilant with our eyes and ears. I will look into the future and plead with Erik."

One day Ari was working on the docks overseeing the unloading of a ship from Crete. It was loaded with colorful ceramics, with copper ingots from Cyprus, and gold blocks from Egypt. As he worked, Makatza approached him carrying his spear and large knife attached to his belt.

"Ari, pig of Iberia, what are you bringing ashore? Have you not checked with the overlord of trade?"

"Sir, all is in order. The overlord has marked the clay tablets with the symbols and quantity of the items."

"You lie, you slithering snake! You and your people need to be watched. You are stealing those gold blocks. They are not recorded!"

"No, Makatza, you are mistaken. I saw the overlord recording the twenty gold blocks. Are you accusing me of theft? Of dishonesty? I swear upon my father's grave that I am an honest man."

"I have watched you since the first day you arrived. I see you and Aide each day and see that you have ill intent to marry her and steal my kingdom. Now you even steal gold so you can pay for power. Captain, take this man to the caves and lock him up for being a deceitful liar, thief, and traitor to Thapsos. I will deal with him later. Take him away!"

"Makatza, justice shall reign, and your spirit shall wander throughout eternity for your hate mongering and cruelty."

"Take him now, or I will drive this knife through his heart. Away!"

When Aide heard of what had occurred at the docks, she ran to her sister. "Minervala, Minervala! I fear for Ari. He has been taken to the caves by that evil tyrant. He is bound and awaits the Chief's wrath! Whatever shall we do? Help, sister!"

Immediately, silently, Minervala went to her hearth where a caldron was boiling violently. Steam filled the room. She placed a light veil over her head and stared into the steam for what seemed to Aide an inordinate amount of time. Minervala's eyes fluttered, and her head nodded back and forth.

"Aide, Aide, I see that Makatza wishes to kill your Ari. He will accuse him of treachery to Thapsos and will raise the people against him before he slays him. This was his purpose all along. His jealousy of Ari and his lust for power drives him to take you. This is his plan."

"But sister, what is our plan? How can we end this evil that consumes all of us!"

"Erik has shown me a way. She has outlined a plan and a way

to victory. While I prepare, go, prepare a large pot of food for this evening, then rest to fortify yourself, and return here at nightfall. I will send my son to fetch the food. Pray to Erik that our plan will succeed. Go now dear sister, go!"

So as the sun set in the west, Aide dressed and headed for Minervala's house. There she saw that her sister had divided the food into three gourds, each with a different stripe of color around its neck.

"Erik has shown me the way! This gourd with the green stripe is for Ari. The red one, is for the guard near Ari's cave. The last black one is for Makatza. I will deliver that one myself. You will take the other two. Make sure you see to it that the green one goes to Ari!"

"Minervala, tell me what you have done to the food? I suspect we are about to commit a crime, which may turn out badly for all of us!"

"Know that I am righteous in my decision and Erik has emboldened me. Ari's dinner is unadulterated. The guard's gourd contains a sleeping potion which will render him incapable of deterring us from our goal."

"And the black stripped gourd? For Makatza?"

"It is laced with hemlock which will take him to the beyond. His evil soul will wander the hills and mountains of Trinacria and never find a resting place!"

"But how shall we proceed to ensure our success?"

"Listen to me carefully. I will take my food to Makatza and tell him it is a gift of congratulations since he ascended to his new position. I will tell him that I hope he will rule with justice. I will make sure he begins his meal, then I will excuse myself and await outside behind the trees. Once he has succumbed to the poison, I will enter and steal the keys to the door on Ari's cave."

"O, Minervala! That seems so very dangerous! What if he discovers the poison and calls his guards! He will kill you!"

"Aide, I am old and alone. Daedalus has been gone for over ten years. I have nothing to lose and much to gain. Besides, Erik has assured me that we women will succeed over the evilness of this man. I trust our Great Mother!"

"So be it. I am with you. But what would you have me do with the two gourds?"

"While I am at Makatza's place, go to the guard. Tell him you bring him and Ari some food. Give him the red marked gourd and go to the cave and give Ari his through the food hole at the top. Do not say anything to Ari, until you see the guard eat and doze. Then await my arrival. Is that clear?"

"It seems simple if it all goes according to plan. I will pray until the deed is done."

And so Minervala went to see Makatza.

"Woman, why have you come? I would rather see your sister! Soon she will be in my bed and by my side."

"Sir, this is the reason I have come. I have accepted the inevitable, and since you soon will be my brother in marriage, I have brought you an offering. I have prepared some delicacies for you – a sweet stew of shrimp and young fish with delicate herbs and honey. Since we will soon be family, you may eat our Kamikos fare often. I hope it pleases you. If not, I will prepare another food for you tomorrow, or Aide may and prepare it herself."

"Minervala, you have disarmed me! I was ready to complain to your father for the delaying of my marriage. I thought you had come to protest. But now I see you are resigned, and I will soon have Aide's body in my bed, and many children to carry on my line."

"Let us forget the past, now taste to see if it is to your liking."

Makatza took his spoon and tasted from the top of the gourd."

"It is exquisite! Woman, you have outdone yourself. It is sweet, yet sour and salty. I hope Aide's fare will be as good!"

"Do not concern yourself with Aide's cooking, for it is as good as her form and her sexual prowess! Now eat and I will withdraw. Tomorrow Aide will come to you."

"Thank you. Till the morrow."

And so Minervala hid in the trees while the evil one consumed the totality of the gourd. She heard the gourd and metal spoon fall to the ground. Carefully she peered through the rear window and saw that Makatza lay prostrate on the floor. He had fallen off his stool and was lying face down, his nose on the dirt floor. She entered silently and saw that the keys were hanging on a copper hook in the corner. Slowly she walked up to Makatza and tried to hear if he had breath. He seemed inert. She crept closer and placed her fingers near his nose and mouth. There was no breath. She then pushed on his belly and the body growled! She jumped back!

"Ay.....e!"

Then a putrid vomit exited his mouth, and she was sure he was gone. Quickly she grabbed the keys and ran to the cave.

"Minervala! I was afraid you were discovered. Erik be praised. Is all well."

"Yes, sister here are the keys. I see the guard sleeps."

"Yes, all is well here. Ari awaits. Let us go!"

The next day Thapsos was in a great turmoil. Makatza's body was discovered, but no one even dared to approach him. The guard had awoken, but he did not know what to do. Ari went to the marketplace in front of the Chief's hut. He went in and dragged Makatza's body out, placing it in front of the people.

"Citizens, here lies the man whom you called Chief. Some of you felt strong because he said you were the chosen people. Others despised him, for he spoke with hatred against your origins. We are a divided village, even though we are prosperous, and immigrants and traders bring us more wealth. Why have we descended into such depths? We are all sons and daughters of the gods and worship Erik and Apollo who give us both fertility and light. I propose a new Thapsos. One where we all share in the work of building a greater Thapsos. I was accused of treachery and lies by a man who treated his people with contempt and only wished to have power over all of you. I take full responsibility for his demise, and you may do with me as you wish, but you no longer need to feel subservient to Makatza!"

The people stared at each other in the main square of Thapsos. Their world had been turned up-side-down in a matter of hours. Then finally from a large stone where an old, bent, gray-haired Thapsian was sitting, a wise voice emerged. "My family has been on this island for generations. I have seen how low we have come. I will not condemn you for I too am tired of the division. I will support you as chief."

Then another spoke, "Ari for Chief!" Then a few more. Soon the whole town was crying, "Ari! Ari! Ari!"

The crowd pulled Makatza's body toward the sea and threw him on the rocks, and it was carried far from Thapsos.

"Aide! Minervala! I am so grateful! You have saved me and Thapsos."

Minervala looked at him and Aide. "It was not I, but Erik, our great goddess of love. She has once more overcome hate. And now you must do her will also."

"I knew that justice and love would prevail from the beginning. Erik has protected us through our voyages at sea and all the evil of Makatza. Aide, come here. I wish to be your husband if you will have me."

"Ari, it is my deepest wish, and it is also the will of the gods. Let it be!"

THE MUSE (2000 AD)

The tapestry that both my friend, the mysterious stranger, and Luxo had referred to, began to take shape in my mind. The inhabitants of Kamikos and Minos, together with the newly arrived Sicani, were intermingling and forming one people. I was happy to see people of courage among the first inhabitants. King Cocalus' daughters, Minervala and Aide, were strong women who learned how to deal with evil in a very patriarchal society. Ari, came from afar, but was a man of high principles. The evil of both Minos and Makatza was crushed by those strong women, and Ari would be a good leader.

I still wondered if my friend was just a figment of my imagination resulting from long hours of work and little sleep. Now, as I continued to read the transcriptions, my mind wandered again. I envisioned the exploding volcano of Thera on the island of Crete, bringing destruction to a great part of the Mediterranean world. It broke up the landmass creating the two islands where there was one, present day Crete and Santorini. Scientists had theorized that the explosion, like that of Krakatoa in the 1800s AD, led to climate changes and prolonged winters. They had postulated that a premature nuclear winter had befallen parts of Europe with devastating consequences when Knossos and Akrotiri were destroyed.

Again, that night I dosed. Suddenly I heard footsteps. Opening my eyes, I saw a figure wearing a white chiton[27] with black trim

---

[27] Chiton – a tunic that fastens at the shoulder, with one arm and shoulder left bare.

along the top and bottom hem. Along the bottom were embroidered tetrahedrons, cubes, octahedrons, and other three-dimensional objects. Why?

"Good evening weaver of tales! I see you have visited Thapsos in Luxo's cave writings. I like what you have written. You have given the Sicani personalities. There is much unknown about these inhabitants, but I know that they are a conglomerate of peoples who shared common ancestors. History might have taken quite a wrong turn if Makatza had survived, but Erik, our Aphrodite, had a hand in seeing that love was stronger than hate. You are on the right track in your descriptions."

"Thank you, master. Why are you here at this late hour?"

"We now need to journey to the far north for the next thread of the tapestry!"

When he said the far north, I tried to envision what he meant. I then thought of the early settlements in what is now the northern Balkans or Hungry.

"Come, do not delay! Follow me to a large settlement of an Indo-European tribe who later became the Siculi. Come!"

BOOK III

The Siculi

1600 - 1100 BC

Aed, Adar – *Fire God of the Sicani, Siculi, respectfully*
Adhrano – *unified name for the Fire God.*
Erik – *Sicani name for Aphrodite*

1600 BC

Bolani – *chief of the Proto-Siculi in central Europe*
Casso – *priest of Proto-Siculi*
Suko – *son of Bolani married to Fiani*

1300 BC

Thiago – *head warrior of Proto Siculi crossing to Sicily*
Veragri – *priestess of Proto Siculi*
Xavo – *chief of the Proto-Siculi crossing to Sicily*

1200 BC

Baltra – *Baltra descendent of Ari and Aide and chief of Sicani of Thapsos and Pantalica. Husband of Mara.*
Mara - African slave of royal descent who marries Baltra.
Mirax -Sicani lookout at Thapsos.
Shekelesh – *Sea People possibly related to the Siculi*
Zora – *Sicani head warrior*

1100 BC

Anu – *priest assigned as Kato's ancestor*

Carni – *chief warrior of the Siculi*

Inguma – *King of the Sicani in Pantalica, close to what was to become Akrai married to Itaja*

Itaja – *wife of Inguma descended from the legendary King Cocalus*

Kato – *Rēks of the Siculi who undergoes the ritual of rebirth of the Sicani and marries Usoa*

Rituli – *Rēks of the Siculi and father of Kato*

Sarax – *captured Sicani warrior*

Usoa – *King Inguma's daughter and married to Kato*

Zeru – *Sicani priest at the time of Kato and Usoa*

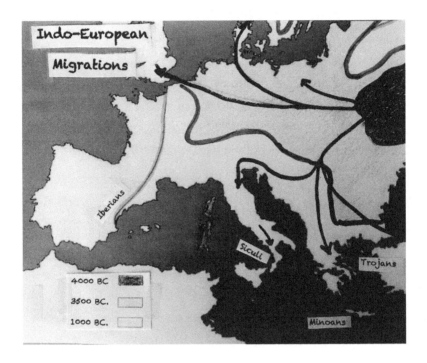

CHAPTER 10

Cave 2, WALL 2 AND 3 (CIRCA 1600 BCE)

THE SICULI

INSCRIPTION Δ

I, Luxo, the Siculo, living in Akrai in Trinacria now write on these walls of the journey of the Siculi from the far north as told to me by the elders through our epic poems and songs. Our trials and tribulations were many, but our joy of arriving in the land of the great Adhrano, whom we first called Adar, was great. He speaks to us in hot pools, and shooting springs, and in hot fire, in shaking earth, and in smoke and clouds from the great mountain. He is a great God that sweats and shakes! Our story begins in this land of cold winters in the far north where we lived near other tribes to whom we were related. Our story begins with two legendary figures, Suko, a brave warrior, and his father Bolani, the Chief.

Suko, a young handsome warrior, lived in a land of hills and in the far north, a land of forests rich in game. It was a fine summer day in the village. Suko was riding his new stallion. His tribe had mastered this art long ago when they were further east and met the fearsome men of the steppes. Eventually, these men pushed Suko's ancestors east, but they now had a new skill which would allow them to conquer new land.

Suko's horse was jet black with a white, elegant streak on his forehead. He had been broken-in only a few days. As Suko rode, he observed the great plenty which his people had coaxed from the land. He looked at the sheep and cattle that were now kept in pens near their village of timber and wattle huts. The fields of grain that they had learned to cultivate long ago were golden and ready to be harvested for the winter. The women were busy tending to the fires and the warriors were gathered talking of their hunts. It was early morning, and the sun was still low but the day was warm and clear.

Suddenly, out of nowhere, the Earth shook violently. The Earth God was taking his vengeance. Suko, the grandson of a respected elder of his tribe, was still young but had heard of spirits being released from the earth by angry gods. Neither he, nor any of his tribesmen, had ever experienced this before. A few of the elders remembered tales of such things from lands that their ancestors first had inhabited to the east. He thought to himself, *what is happening to cause such a rage? I must ride to my hut and family. What of my wife and children? Are they safe?*

In a while, the earth calmed. All were gathered at the center of the village. Their faces full of fear and wonder. The priests were busy consulting the auguries near their sacred rocks on the embankment above the town. They were looking at the entrails of a goat which they just had sacrificed to Adar.

The high priest, Casso, proclaimed in a loud voice for all to hear, "We must sacrifice an ox immediately. The entrails do not lie. There is evil about! Tomorrow, we will sacrifice a horse, and later hunt and slay an aurochs[28] to propitiate the Fire God who shakes. We bow to Adar! If this is not enough, we may have to sacrifice a virgin! We will continue to examine the signs."

---

[28] Aurochs – Bos primigenius – extinct wild ox of Europe from which cattle are probably descended. The last ones died out in Poland in 1627 AD.

There was mumbling among the people. No one remembered when there had been human sacrifice! Suko thought to himself, *These priests are using this to keep the people in fear to secure their own power. I fear for my own young daughter. I will not allow anyone's young girl to be sacrificed. I will speak to my father!*

Now Casso quickly prepared himself by covering his tall naked body with ocher and white ash. The white represented cleansing. He had an elaborate headdress of eagle feathers and a long staff whose head was of bone. It was carefully carved in the form of the sacred horse's head. The horse was worshiped as a sacred animal which gave them milk, mobility, and appeased the gods in sacrifice.

A white ox was brought to the altar in the holy site across the ravine surrounding the village. The far side of the ravine, which protected the village from intruders, had a high earthen embankment upon which the priests were gathered. From there they called to the people to gather. Just below the embankment was the temple, where the priests processed and began to surround the altar, a huge flat boulder within the temple.

The temple was circular. consisting of high wooden posts which had been cut from huge pine trees. Thick pine forests surrounded the village. The roof of the temple was thatched over wooden lintels. The sides were open so that the gods and spirits could pass through. In the center was a depression where a fire burned constantly representing the heat emanating from deep within the earth. God was in fire. Fire, like water, was a cleansing agent. Adar produced hot springs which sprang from below. The people used these to bathe themselves even in the coldest winter months when the sun ventured far to the south and the snow was as deep as a horse's shoulder. Just next to the fire pit was the large natural rock altar used for sacrifice.

At noon the ox was led in, and the people assembled. The temple filled to overflowing. The crowd extended outside the tree columns, for people from outlying areas were also concerned by the morning's events. Even some forest people from afar had arrived.

The sharp stone blade was readied, the ox's feet were tied, and a stout leather thong was around its neck and tied to two poles on either side of the altar. The ox's head was just above the large altar rock. The naked priests, covered in red-brown ocher and white ash, the colors of the Earth God, stood tall and ready.

They chanted the prayers. The people responded. The priest lifted the blade. Suddenly, before he could cut the artery, a strong unnatural wind arose from nowhere.

Someone shouted, "Look the heavens are falling! The southern sky! The Earth God is coming, rising from the earth!"

Casso looked over his shoulder and then yelled, "The Earth God is rising as a black cloud of vengeance! The transgression of the people surely is great. Seek safety in the caves!"

The people and the priests had to push into the wind to keep their balance. The ox continued his low-pitched bellow which grew louder as the wind became stronger. Birds were being thrown to the ground. All stared toward the south, from the direction where the wind was increasing. Large trees twisted and bent to the ground. The sky turned jet black on the horizon. The blackness rose higher and higher, closer, and closer!

The cloud, black as night, was rising in the shape of a giant mushroom. The black column, surrounded by white and gray clouds, expanded to fill the horizon. It was approaching at a speed that no one had ever experienced before. The people began to panic as they sought safety in the caves. People were pushing and some were trampled!

The priests yelled and encouraged the people to go into the lowest part of the ravine to the small caves. Within the hour the entire sky had blackened, the sun had disappeared, and night had fallen, despite that it was only a little past noon. Rocks, ash, and dust were pelting down and covering the earth. Everyone was terrified, and they began wondering if this were the end of time. Only the caves provided some protection.

Suko finally found his wife and children. "Fiani! I thought I had lost you all! Look, Fiani, how the black dust approaches us."

"Yes, husband, we find it difficult to breathe. It is entering the children's throats. See how they choke and gasp for air!"

"Here, rip this cloth and make a covering for our noses and throats. It may protect us from the worst."

Ash rained down as if the heat of the earth had been transferred to the sky. The fine dust even entered the caves. Within hours a blanket of ash covered everything, and the people all looked like the spirits of the dead. No one spoke and an eerie silence descended throughout the village.

As the wind ebbed and the ash subsided, the people began to exit the caves and look at each other in shock. No one knew what to expect. They all looked to the priests and elders for direction. But even they were at a loss. None had seen anything like this before, and there was nothing in their folklore to assist them in understanding. As one elder exited the cave, he was repeating again and again in a loud voice, the only voice among the unnatural silence. "Mercy, mercy! This is the revenge of Dégōm Dngu[29], the evil Earth God. Seek forgiveness all, seek forgiveness all! Mercy, mercy!......"

The people began to argue among themselves as to whether it was their transgression or of some other people's. They thanked the Earth spirits that they all seemed to have survived the immediate danger, but they were all full of fear. Even the priests did not know what to say, except that they must continue the sacrifice as soon as

---

[29] Proto-Indo-European "Dark Earth God," or God of the Underworld.

the temple area had been cleared. The day was still as dark as night.

Casso began ordering the people. "Gather wood and light fires around the temple. You, men, get some ladders and sweep the temple roof of ash before it collapses. Women, all of you there, begin sweeping the temple of ash! Get others to assist you. We must sacrifice as soon as we can."

Slowly, the weight of the debris on the temple roof was removed. The women used shovels made of hip bones of oxen to clear the piles of ash.

The priests completed the sacrifice of the ox in the somber eerie light of torches in the ash fog. They prayed to appease the Earth Mother, Dégōm Méhtēr, and Adar, the Fire God. They asked the sun god to return. The priests then dismissed the people. The tired mothers gathered their children and fed them cold porridge of milk and meal or anything they could find under the ash. Most of the huts had been destroyed. The exhausted populace found places to sleep wherever they could in the caves. Even the stars had disappeared. The village quieted into a dead silence.

The next day the sun did not show its face. It was still as dark as night, except for the very faint ribbon of light far to the east. This, too, soon also disappeared.

The high priest decided they needed to mark time with sand, for they knew it was dawn by the ribbon, but could not now follow the progression of the sun with its shadow. He placed the time gourd filled with sand on a shelf and placed a second gourd of the same size on the ground. Each gourd had a cork low, near the bottom. He called his two sons, Attico and Errico, "Keep watch on the sand! Remove the upper cork and now see how the sand falls slowly into the lower gourd. Do not sleep! Once the upper gourd empties, place a stick next to the appropriate mark on the etched stone which is there on the ground at the center of the temple. Then, switch the gourds. Place the lower filled gourd on the shelf and the upper gourd which had emptied below it on the ground and repeat the process. This is an important chore. Do not fail! You are like the sun, keeping time, until the daylight sky god, Dyēus Phter[30], again gifts us with his disk!"

Attico, the elder, responded, "Father, we will do your will. Do not fear."

In this way they could approximate noon and dusk because the sand was calibrated to one fourth of the daylight hours on the equinox. The sand flowed very slowly, and they were to watch that it did not stop flowing. They would use a sharp stick to unplug the hole if there was a problem and the sand stopped flowing.

The village remained dark for an entire week before the torrential rains began. The crops no longer green, already covered in ash and blown by the wind, now were swept away by the floods. The people were further afflicted by the damp cold which filled every corner of the village and the caves. Only the few dry, logs kept in the caves provided any warmth, even though it was summer.

After the second week the sun appeared faintly each day, but the cold continued. It was as if summer had ended, and winter had begun. It was so unnatural to have this cold rain so early! The solstice had been less than a month before, and now winter was approaching rapidly. At this point the elders and the priests conferred, for they needed to decide the future of the people. They discussed the approach of the black cloud. It had approached from the south and the east. Now every evening the sky was brighter, and the disk of the sun could be seen in the south and the west.

One afternoon, Suko's father, Bolani, the chief of the tribe and elder, called for a meeting of all elders and priests and leading warriors. "Men, we must decide what to do before the summer ends. As you see, our crops are gone, and our livestock have little

---

[30]   Dyēus Phter – The original Sky-Father or Day god of Indo-Europeans.

to eat. Our horses cannot forage and will lose their vitality shortly. We must act quickly."

Casso spoke up, "We cannot remain here any longer. This place has become cursed of the Gods. It is a forsaken, barren place. We must find a new place where the Earth Mother, Dégōm, goddess of fertility, will bless the land. First, we must sacrifice a virgin. Only her blood will appease the gods!"

Suko responded, "There will be no human sacrifice. This is not who we are. We value each of our tribespeople unless they have committed a taboo! As long as I have breath, I will not allow it. Yes, I do agree, we must find a place where our gods of fertility of the earth will show us a rich and bountiful place. I have noticed each night the sun appears at dusk in the southwest. Each night it burns brighter. Is it a sign?"

Chief Bolani then spoke. "As long as I am Chief, there will be no humans slain. But we must consider what Casso tells us."

Casso lifted his ceremonial horsehead stick which had rattles and feathers. He was carefully considering what power remained in his arsenal. If he demanded too strongly for a virginal sacrifice, he might be overruled by Bolani. After circling around the temple and shaking his rattle, he announced, "Yes, it is a sign, Bolani, do you see what I see? The gods have spoken to me from the heavens." Casso was staring southwest.

Bolani starring at the horizon spoke as if in meditation, "Yes, I see the sun god's disc surrounded by purple and yellow. He is showing us the way."

Suko asked softly, "Are we to migrate?"

Casso said in a loud voice so that all could hear, "Yes, if Bolani, the elders, and the warriors agree, then we begin immediately to prepare to migrate."

They looked over at the elders sitting at their place of honor on the large smooth rock and they all shook their heads in agreement.

One ancient man spoke, "We ourselves may not survive the ardors of the journey, but the young need a place which has fertility. We will begin the journey, even if we fail along the way. We will at least pass to the ancestors knowing that our children will live and prosper."

Bolani looked at them with wide eyes. A tear appeared on his strong face and flowed down the scar he had earned in battle when he was a novice warrior. He had seen many tribulations, as had the elders, and he was proud of the communal spirit now being so enthusiastically demonstrated. He was proud of his people.

Casso now asked, "What do you warriors say?"

One of the strongest warriors stood up and said, "We have been to the lands south and west, as far as the sea. Winter comes late in those places. And it goes quickly. There is much vacant land and forest beyond the high snow mountains. There is abundant grazing. Once at the sea, there is a long, narrow land which stretches very far south. We have not ventured far to the south, but the local tribes, who speak languages like ours, tell us that it goes on almost endlessly with sea on both sides. A vigorous and well-trained warrior can cross the narrow land and reach the sea on the other side in three or four days, and even shorter on horseback. It will take us longer with wagons. We might be able to travel across the narrow sea by boat. I suggest we begin as soon as possible. The closeness of the sea also provides the air with warmth and there are very fertile places."

Bolani replied, "Sounds like we all agree. If no one objects, we will begin preparations immediately."

Casso agreed. "I see no objection. Let us prepare!"

And so, they demonstrated what it meant to be a tribe. To put community over the liberty and independence which was part of the very being of these people. They realized without community and interpersonal relationships and commitment to greater good, there would be only tyranny of the powerful. Their common survival and shared responsibility would ensure that they would have the individual liberty which they each desired. All put the good of the whole before their individual comfort.

Most of the old would not survive such a treacherous journey, and some would be left behind alone, or with other peoples who would take them in. They began their preparations for the long trek to find a safe place away from Dégōm, the Earth God's destruction.

So, Bolani and Suko gathered the tribe. And with their flocks, their sheep, cattle, goats, oxen, horses and their goods on their backs, they headed west, skirting the mountains of snow touching the sky. Then they turned south to the sea where they crossed to warmer lands.

THE MUSE (2000 AD)

My mysterious stranger was still with me. He led me to the paintings on the cave walls.

"Look. These rafts depicted here are fighting the waves and the currents between the rock promontories.

"Look at these! Stare into the waves! They will transport you to that time when the tribe made a courageous decision. All will be revealed!"

"Who are you? I see the warriors and women getting on the boats with their horses and livestock! How can this be?"

What was happening to me? Who was this man? I was beginning to know Suko and the others more intimately than I could believe.

"Follow me!"

"I am so curious as to your identity. I feel very at home with you. It's as if I know of you from somewhere in the past. I will follow you, but why will you not tell me who you are?"

He was silent, but as he moved away, I followed, mesmerized, being pulled along by my great curiosity to find out more about these people whom I now cared for. I wished to see their tribulations and if they succeeded in their quest!

I could see an embroidered shape on the back of my Muse's chiton[31], for it was very warm and he had discarded his chlamys[32] which he had on before. The chiton was wringed in gold at the bottom below his knees and around his neck. On the back of this

---

[31] Chiton – a tunic that fastens at the shoulder, with one arm and shoulder left bare.
[32] Chlamys – a short cloak.

white garment was part of an embroidered circular object in black with a line radiating from the center in gold thread. There was a dot where they intersected. O! It was not a circle but a spiral starting at the center and spinning outward. The end of the spiral went off over his shoulder seemingly to infinity! I had seen it before! But where? I was so very curious about this man. Who was he?

CHAPTER 11

CAVE 3, WALL 1 AND 2 (CIRCA 1300 BCE)

THE CROSSING OF THE SICULI

INSCRIPTION E

I, Luxo, have recorded the wanderings of our tribe from afar and through Trinacria so that all may know the anger of Dégōm Dngu, the Earth God, who destroyed our homeland. Greedy people have long plundered the Earth which angered the Earth God. Men steal gold for vanity, copper for warriors to make tips for spears and arrows and obsidian to make knives for war. Tyrants arise who take away liberty and subject their people to ills or slavery. So, the Earth God spoke to our ancestral God Adar, our Adhrano God of Fire, and together they caused a mountain in the sea to explode with such rage that it destroyed half the earth. The people did not know the cause of destruction, only that the gods were furious. We know now that the kingdom of Minoa was destroyed because of the evil that lurked in the hearts of their leaders. Our people were not to blame, though they thought the gods were seeking vengeance. Even so, they survived and prospered.

I write this so that many generations hence people will know how we arrived in this beautiful land of abundance, with snow on the mountain of fire and palms by the sea. But there is more, much more which will have to wait for another day. I hope they will also learn not to plunder this earth which is a gift from the gods.

Here I continue the history of our migration. As we travelled south down the long narrow land, which the Hellenes now call Italia, where a warrior could cross from sea to sea in 2 or 3 days, we found a good place to settle. It was on the hill sides of one of Adhrano's mountains which mostly slept but rumbled from time to time. The land was rich, and our crops prospered.

We lived there in happiness for quite some time, and our population grew. Some clans even separated from us and formed new tribes. Some called themselves Latine, and others Campanie. But we the original seed continued to multiply forming a large population. We needed to find more land. There was pressure from these tribes and others like the Sabines, whom we fought from time to time. Now, we again began to think of leaving and trekking south as before.

After having left the far north, traveling past the mountains and reaching the sea, the Siculi slowly proceeded through the long, narrow land framed by sea on both sides. Eventually they arrived near a large mountain covered in white facing the west coast with a beautiful wide crescent bay rich in sea life. They scouted the hills and found interesting remnants of burned houses and trees and observed other destruction. Skirting these areas, they found some dark, rich soil which would be favorable to their crops not far from the sea. They decided to settle here, for it looked like they could prosper here.

Now, after so many years of nomadic existence, they settled in this land rich in olives and grapes.

Xavo was renowned for his strength and agility in battle. His great grandfather was Chief Italo, who had conquered the long narrow land all the way to the sea in the south. Italo descended from the great Bolani and his son, Suko, who first led the tribe away from the disaster in the cold north, leading them fearlessly into this long land of sunshine. They had become a powerful tribe. But lately there were disturbing signs.

Xavo had learned the complete history of his tribe as recounted in their epic poems and songs. He was the keeper of the tribe's lore and recited the verses whenever there was a festival, at harvest, or solstice, or at other important times.

"Thiago, what news do you bring from your explorations?"

"My, lord, Xavo, I have travelled far and to the land of some of our sister tribes, the Samnites, Oscans, and Campanians. They, like us, are becoming over-populated and looking for more land. I fear they are forming alliances to make war on us because we are in the most fertile land next to the sea and up into the highlands of the mountain. They envy the rich volcanic soil that the mountain has created and are jealous of our fruit trees and grapes."

"Do you think we can attack and overcome them by surprise?"

"My lord, we could overcome the Campanie alone, but if they are united with the others, we cannot win. We would be outnumbered ten to one! We also do not have enough copper blades and obsidian which we must obtain from Lipari. We are not able to find copper without trading with the east. They could easily cut off the trading vessels. There is not enough time to prepare a proper defense!"

Xavo looked toward the snow-covered mountain, for it was winter. He was silent for quite a time, then sent his runner for the high priestess, Veragri.

"Hear me, Veragri. The outlying tribes are preparing for war. You must consult the gods and look at the signs. What is the best course to follow that the gods will support?"

Veragri, a priestess who was blessed with the gift of seeing, was dressed in her wool cloak covered in colored feathers. It was of the softest white wool made from the sheep that inhabit the places high on the mountain. Her headdress was made of lynx fur and its tail hung over one shoulder. She held one of the antlers of those giant sheep which twisted in a spiral. Though she was a diminutive woman, she spoke in a commanding voice. As she spoke, she raised the antler and pointed at the mountain.

"Adar will be consulted. Dégōm, the Earth Mother, has been awake the last few days. There were low rumblings that only could be felt when my ear was on the ground. I will listen in the next few days and tell you the signs."

In the next few days there were quakes, and the sea was drawn outward, and then large waves hit parts of the shore. Smoke was seen venting from the sides of the mountain,

"My lord, I have observed and consulted the entrails of a sacrificed white horse," Veragri then changed to a most somber and authoritative tone. "Adar, our great Father, God of Fire, now speaks through me:

'Go south! You need to preserve your seed. You will be a great nation. But, here I, Adar, will bring the fire of war, and the fire of earth if you do not heed me. I have a place for you where you can honor me. Prepare to leave. Do not tempt me to unleash my fire and shaking. Leave! Leave now! Leave at once!'

As she said these words she trembled. With each word the trembling increased as she stuttered out her vision. "I have also looked at the horses' entrails! They, they, foretell many deaths if we stay here. Ah, ah, ah! I see, see a place, a very pleasant place, of springs right next to the water, a sea, an ocean. There, there, a beautiful young nymph is at play. There papyrus grows. I also see sacred colored twin lakes blessed by the gods!"

With this Veragri fell to the ground as if dead. Thiago ran to her and shook her to rouse her. After a time, she stood up and said in a low monotone, "This is the will of Adar!" She turned and left heading up the mountain to her place in the caves.

Xavo did not expect this direct order from Adar, but he knew he needed to act. "Thiago, prepare your warriors and the people to begin our journey. We must leave before the equinox so that we may arrive in the new land when Earth Mother readies the earth for planting grain."

After so many generations, the people again would be displaced. They journeyed for more than a month along the coast until they arrived at a narrow strip of land. Across the sea they could see another thin strip which rose in the west in high mountains.

Veragri, upon seeing this site across the blue-green sea, spoke again with authority:

"This is the place where Adar has led us! We must cross the sea! There is our safety!" She pointed her ram's antler across the sea to the outcropping of rocks on the other side of the straight.

Xavo and Thiago climbed some high rocks and looked out at the churning sea below. They saw the high point across. In a calm sea they could row in no more than an hour. But many of the tribe feared the sea. They were a pastoral people. They looked at each other and wondered how they would move all these people across. They were almost overcome, but then Thiago had a thought.

"Xavo, some of the slaves we captured from our skirmishes in the north were seafarers. We also have traders that go to Lipari and Iberia. They are few but have ships and know how to build them. Let us engage them in construction and all the people will follow their directives."

"That is a good plan. Thiago, we must prepare boats and rafts. They must be sturdy and have many oars. Have the woodsmen go into the forest and cut trees and shape oars. Tell the boat builders to prepare their tools and the copper for fastening, Have the women prepare the pine pitch to seal the boats. We will camp here until the early spring. Then all should be ready. Go, now gather them, and tell them Xavo commands it!"

Though Xavo spoke with authority, he had much trepidation

of the crossing. He was hoping the sea would calm when they became ready.

Finally, the day arrived. The air was warm, and the wind relatively calm. In the dim light of pre-dawn, Xavo spoke first to Thiago, and then to all the people, "Thiago, are the boats and rafts loaded?"

"Yes, all is ready. The animals and goods are loaded, and the people are ready to cross."

"Good."

Xavo then turned and climbed a huge rock that faced where the people were gathered. Veragri was standing on the same stone. "My people listen to me. Heed your high priestess. She is petitioning the gods and praying for our safety. She will lead you in prayer before we leave. Today we continue our journey started many years ago by Bolani and Suko. We follow the command of our god, Adar, who has led us far and always protected his tribe. We are his people. We must be brave, for the crossing will be difficult. The rocks are sharp and the currents swift. We must each use our maximum strength at the oars. We have 30 boats and rafts, and we must all survive. Veragri will sacrifice a pure white goat, as a gift to the God of the Sea to keep us safe. Then we will begin our journey to the land of Adar!"

With great ceremony, Veragri, standing on a very high craggy rock overlooking the sea, raised her ram's antler above her head. She shook and rattled the rod and called on Adar. "Adar, Adar, we beseech you to protect and lead us. You came to me in my trance and promised a safe arrival in a new land. Here is the goat I promised you. It is of the purest white. Give us protection we implore, we beg you! God of the Sea, we implore you also. Give us a safe journey!"

The goat was being held by a young man who now held Veragri's staff. She raised her knife while the young man held the goat on the rock and placed the sacred staff across its neck. The eyes of the goat were transfixed on the young man while Veragri made a small incision across the jugular. The blood flowed down the rock and into the sea as the spirit of the goat was released into the universe. Some of the blood was collected in a small gourd.

When all life had left the animal, the young boy put it on his shoulders and took it to the women below. It was cleaned and roasted, and small pieces were distributed to all the members of the tribe. Veragri took the gourd and sprinkled some of the blood on each boat and raft, proclaiming, "This is the blood that we offer to Adar and to the God of the Sea. It will calm the sea and protect you in crossing the waters."

As the people looked out at the calm water with a few small waves, they felt confident that the crossing would be uneventful. The wind was barely blowing. As a precaution, the women and children had tied ropes around their waists and secured themselves to the low benches.

It was a mighty exodus. The boats held the women and children, small animals, plants, seeds, and household implements, and their household gods. Other boats carried the warriors, holding spears and bows with other goods stored in the lower reaches of the boat. The raft like boats held the horses and carts. Others had cows, still others pigs, sheep, or goats. Each was manned with enough rowers to speed the boats across the channel. One boat contained the priests, with the high priest, Veragri, carrying the sacred fire torch which needed to always remain lit. It would be used to light the sacred fire once they had built the temple to Adar in their new home. Other priests held special pots with glowing embers to reignite it in case of accident. It was the sign that Adar was with them.

Once they rounded the huge rocks, which later the Greeks would name Scylla, the rocking boats lulled them into a peaceful

state. It was extreme calm. They even told stories, laughed, and
joked. But after a while the oarsmen began feeling a strong current
pulling the boats northward. The captains ordered the drums
to beat faster, so that the oarsman would increase their speed.
The steersman was ordered to point the rudder southwest to
compensate so that the boat would be carried in the right direction.
In this way they could go more westerly, and not with the current.
It seemed an impossible job to pull away from this current which
grew stronger and stronger. The current ruled them, even though
the rudder was aimed almost due south!

Then, as they were clearly in sight of the beach, a mist lowered
from the cliffs like a woman's fingers and engulfed each boat.
Slowly each boat was left alone as the others disappeared and
they lost sight of one another. The fingers seemed to be pulling
them into the circling current which was more like a whirlpool
than anything they had ever experienced.

Thiago had made the crossing with some warriors some
months before to scout out a landing place. Though it was not
as calm a day, they had little problem in crossing since they had
begun further south on the mainland.

Now, he took charge, and yelled at the top of his lungs,
"Captains, pass on the order! Rudders, south! Row south!" Slowly,
you could hear the order being transferred, even though they
could see nothing but the swirling whirlpool. For a time, the
boats seemed motionless, not far from the shore, but stuck at sea.

Veragri now yelled in the boat closest to Thiago, "Adar,
powerful god of fire, lead us to safety! And you, God of the Sea,
powerful God of the Oceans, spare us! Receive this offering now!"

With that she slit the throat of her sacred dog with her knife
and threw it into the sea. "God of the sea, receive this sacrifice in
appeasement, and save us!"

Now rowing almost backward, they could feel the currents

hold lessening. Though the whirlpool now turned north, they were on the edge of its southwestern side, so it was pushing them toward the shore. As they approached, they saw rocks protruding on either side and had to steer right then left, then right to avoid crashing. One of the boats carrying some warriors crashed violently into the rock face. The men jumped and those that could swim tried to swim toward the others as the fog was lifting. Many perished but some survived. It was a tragic loss of some of the best young men of the tribe.

Now, the boats began gaining speed and reaching the shore. Exhausted, the men, even helped by some women, rowed for more than two hours, but made headway. The crossing Thiago had made in a bit more than one hour was taking the entire day. Progress was measured by inches, but finally the first boat, headed by Thiago, reached the shore of the island which would be their home for generations and generations. As the sun set in the west, the first Siculi had found their promised land.

Veragri, upon arrival, proclaimed. "We shall call this landing place ῾Σφαχ Σικελι᾿[33] ('SPHAX SIKULI') because it has given us peace after this horrendous journey and has saved us from the attack of the alliance of tribes."

INSCRIPTION E

Σφαχ Σικελι

---

[33] Σφαχ Σικελι- invented name from some other inscriptions that have been found in caves in Sicily for the land which gave the Siculi peace after their long trek from central Europe through Italy to Sicily.

THE MUSE (2000 AD)

Here I stopped writing and stared at the inscription in the notes. I remembered Enzo pointing out the following inscription in the Siculian language, but written in Greek letters, in one of the caves: Σικυλι Τερα Σφαχ (Siculi Land of Peace). I could see that Siculian was very much related to Latin.

I had reached the point where two of the three tribes had arrived on Trinacria, but still had a long way to go. How did the tribes interact? I was losing the thread that my friend had told me would construct a tapestry. I called out, "Friend where are you? I need your help to tell me how all this is connected!"

I looked out my window and saw a figure in the distance. This was a young man who wore a short chiton secured at the waist with a leather belt. He held a silver mirror in one hand and a dried leaf in another. He was aiming the mirror at the sun and directing the light toward the leaf which burst into flame! I knew who he was! But the friend that visited me before was very old. Were they one and the same? I opened the door and walked toward him, but as I approached him, the fog engulphed him and I was left alone.

I began reading Enzo's notes on the arrival of the Shekelesh and their interaction with the Sicani of Thapsos. These were the Sea Peoples whom the Egyptians fought and left the only written record. Still, no one knows who they were or where they came from. Some even say they were related to the Siculi.

What struck and fascinated me was Baltra's wife. My mind started working on their relationship and my pen was led into amazing places by my unknown friend!

CAVES IN PANTALICA
(Italia.com)

LA NECROPOLI DI PANTALICA (30 KM DA SIRACUSA)

By Gaetano Miano

Silenzio e poi silenzio sui dirupi:
Dormono tutti, Siculi e Sicani,
Nei loculi scavati fra le rupi
Che mente fan librar su mondi arcani.
Dentro gli avelli ad alvear disposti
Hanno i Defunti imperituro ermo,
In questa valle lugubre nascosti,
Spogli del tempo lor, da evi fermo.
Affidan lieve al vento lo stormire
Solo ginestre e qualche monco ulivo,
E in buia gola l'Anapo al fluire
Si cheta e spegne il mormorio giulivo,
Tal che vision d'orrida spelonca,
Attonito lo sguardo reca al core,
Al triste comparer dell'apra conca,
Pena, sgomento, incubo e timore,
Il raro Pellegrino avanza muto,
Errando come in terra e in aldilà,
Ed al pensier d'acume chiede aiuto,
Fra immagine smarrito e realtà.
Dormite o Gente il sonno della morte,
E il dir commosso d'ogni vostro vate
Implorazione sveli, calda e forte,
Che mai sian vostre Urne profanate.

THE NECROPOLIS OF PANTALIC

Translation by Joe Miano

Silence and more silence on the summit of the cliffs:
All sleep, Siculi and Sicani,
Within the excavated niches in the cliffs
Making minds hover on their mysterious worlds.
Inside the tombs like empty hives
Have the remote everlasting dead,
In this lugubrious valley, hidden
Spoils of their past, frozen in their time.
The broom and a few one-armed olives,
Give subtle trust to the storm winds
And in the dark gulley the flowing Anapo
Quiets herself and extinguishes her jovial murmur.
Then a vision of a horrid cave,
A stupefying glance brings to the heart
The sad appearance from the harsh basin below-
Grief, dismay, nightmares, and fear.
The rare Peregrine goes mutely forward
Wandering on earth as in the next world
Needing help to sharpen its wits
Between misled imagination and reality.
Sleep O People the dreams of the dead!
And may the moved worlds of your poets
Implore, hot and strong,
That never will your ashes be profaned.

CHAPTER 12

CAVE 3, WALLS 3 AND 4 (circa 1200 BC)

THE SEA PEOPLES

INSCRIPTION Z

I, Luxo, the Siculo, recorded the history of the Sicani as I found recorded in their own language on tablets and I was assisted by Anax, a faithful Sicani friend who had recorded history in his own language using the alphabet of the Phoenicians.

Baltra was chief of the Sicani who was married to a slave who was captured from a royal African family. They had a large community established at Thapsos, along the eastern coast. It had substantial stone buildings, paved streets, and walls across the isthmus to protect it. Now this is how they recorded the arrival of the Sea People, the Shekelesh, among others, and the Sicani flight to the caves. The caves were inland along the gorge of the Anapo in the Hyblaean Mountains[34]. It was a protected place with only one point of ingress, so it was a place protected from attack. Uncivilized tribes once inhabited this place since before our earliest memories and there is a source of the finest flint in the hills.

Baltra, the young chief of the clans of the Sicani, of the line of heroes from King Cocalus and Daedalus, through the union of

---

[34] Hyblaean Mountains – or Plateau is a group of hills and mountains in south-eastern Sicily just below what later became the Greek outpost of Akrai.

Ari from Iberia with Aide, princess of Kamikos ruled in Thapsos on the southeastern coast of Trinacria.

The people of Thapsos believed all the Sicani were one people. Some believed they had always lived on Trinacria and that others had arrived from these far-off places. The others arrived here from what is now called Iberia where there is a Sicano river. They came by way of Utica[35] and Malta. All shared language and gods and lived a peaceful existence on this large island of plenty. They traded with other Sicani clans of the island and with traders who arrived from the sea. This allowed them to use the abundance of the land to acquire tools of bronze, gold ornaments, and many other items. They raised cows and sheep for milk and obtained wool from sheep to make colorful, warm garments. The fertile soil produced a great quantity of grain and grapes. Many prospered from the abundance of the sea.

At the beginning these lands were still sparsely inhabited. A timid people of hunter-gatherers lived in the mountains and hills. These stout and hairy people at first kept apart from the Sicani, but occasionally some were captured. They made hearty slaves and some of the Sicani had children with the mountain people. Thapsos was the largest and most prosperous of the settlements.

But the peaceful existence was not to last. The earliest ballads of the Sicani tell of the horror that came from the sea. They tell of the arrival of the marauding tribes known as the Sea Peoples. They arrived at the southeastern shore of Sicania. They came to one of our finest settlements called Thapsos, fiercely and in great number. The Egyptians called them the Shekelesh.

Baltra looked out at the sea in Thapsos one morning to see a ship coming into port. He and his men were glad to see their own ship returning. Lately, there had been very few ships. He greeted

---

[35] Utica - Tunisia

his traders arriving from Lipari. "Hail, were you able to procure the tin and metal which we need?"

"Sir, we have tried. We even ventured as far as Sardinia. We barely escaped with our lives! Some of our friends hid us in caves while we observed the destruction. Some tribes of displaced peoples from Iberia are migrating in great numbers. They seem to speak a strange northern tongue. Our friends told us that they have been at war with tribes from further north who have taken over the mines of tin and gold. These refugees have had to leave but now have turned into marauders! They burn, pillage, and move on. Right now, Sardinia seems to be a place of refuge for them until they decide they have exhausted the free wealth. Our friends call them the Shardana. Other different tribes are joining with them called the Shekelesh. They speak an even different tongue."

"Do you believe they will attack us?"

"Sir, I do not know. But all the trade routes from east and west are disrupted. Soon we will not have enough copper or tin to make strong weapons. We have loaded our boats with obsidian from Lipari, but there is no metal to be had!"

"Then, we must prepare. Let us build our defense walls more strongly and decide how we will escape if need be. We have neither the men nor the arms to carry out a prolonged struggle. Thank you for your warning."

Peace settled onto Thapsos for two years, but there was only local trade with the close islands and with other parts of Trinacria. There was a scarcity of items, particularly metals. One day, however, some unknown traders arrived from the east.

The weather was cool for the autumn, but the sun shone brightly. The boat docked in the harbor and three weather worn sailors came forward. Baltra and some of his warriors stepped forward. "Welcome. I am Baltra, Chief of Thapsos. What brings you to the shores of our great island?"

The older man spoke first, "Hail, Sir. We have some items to trade. We have been at sea for quite some time and require drink and nourishment."

"Come, have feast with us while we negotiate the terms of trade."

All seemed well. Most spoke the same strange tongue which was not understandable to us. However, a few communicated in an old Minoan dialect which some of our Sicani from the west could comprehend.

In a few days, however, all seemed to change in an instant. Our lookouts spotted a few ships on the horizon, then a large flotilla. Mirax, the chief lookout, raised the alarm, "Men, warn the chief and the people. I fear that our guests are not here to trade, but to make war. There are many ships approaching!"

Zora, the chief warrior spoke up, "They will outnumber us if those ships are loaded with warriors, and we do not have time to call for other clans to assist us. We must evacuate to gather assistance from other clans!"

"I agree, the tribe's survival is at stake. Run and inform Baltra. I will remain here with these few lookouts until I hear from you."

Antax's face, though stoic, showed his concern. "Zora, tell Baltra to imprison the traders in caves and try to find out more from them."

The prisoners were questioned, but to no avail. Zora now calculated that these in fact were the Shardana, and they were planning to raid.

So, Zora ran to the Chief's palace and told Baltra of the coming storm. Baltra was quiet for a great while, then commanded, "Order the women, children, old and infirm to begin the journey into the highlands. Have them take what provisions they can carry and camp this evening in the forest. Tomorrow they are to continue to the place of caves where we honor the god of fire, Aed. The wind is turning, and the sea is rough, we have some time to prepare. They will not be able to land before it is dark. Have some warriors drive some of the animals toward the highlands. Let the others wander so they do not provide provision for the invaders when they land. Tomorrow we will set fire to the crops before the last of us leave. They will not try to follow through the inferno and unknown forested highlands. It will buy us valuable time. They will not find our place of hiding in Pantalica. These Sea People shall find nothing but burned huts and desolation! The traders have indicated that they plan to continue to Utica[36] and then go eastward toward Egypt. They have used the terms Shekelesh and Shardana in referring to their people. These are the Sea Peoples that our men encountered in Sardinia. We must prepare!"

The trek from the peninsula of Thapsos to the highland caves would take an athletic warrior about 10 hours, but it took a good two or three days for most of the clan.

When they finally arrived tired and hungry, the Chief addressed the people.

"I, Baltra, proclaim this will be our new home until the danger passes. These deserted caves shall be our homes and workshops. Let us build huts in the valley below by the river. I have sent some warriors to hunt game for our meal tonight while we rest and plan for our future until we see what the invaders have planned. I have sent runners to the other Sicani to inform them of the danger. The caves can be our refuge for now until we arrange our village. It is still early in the year, and women may begin planting in the fertile valley by the river.

"Mirax, station warriors on the heights to watch."

"I will give the order immediately. I have stationed others by the river in case some of the Shekelesh decide to follow the Anapo. This is a much more defensible position than by the sea. It was wise to bring us here, great Chief!"

---

[36] Utica – modern Tunisia

"I am glad of your approval. You have helped immeasurably in bringing our people to safety. I leave you in charge so I can attend to my family."

"Mara, are the children with your sister and mother?"

"Yes, husband, all are safe and secure in that lower cave. As we speak, the older boys gather wood for fires and are scouting for trees for our future huts. The girls have gone with some of the women to gather wild herbs and eatable berries. Others have gone to search for reeds by the river for the roofs of our huts."

"Good, Mara, you are a good and dedicated wife. We will stay in the cave until we have completed the huts. It is still warm, and we have a few months before the cold winds begin. I think if we plant, we still have time for a late harvest."

"Baltra, thank you for this decision to bring us here in safety and for not insisting on war with the invaders. There would have been too much death, and I was afraid of losing you!"

"Mirax has told me he saw many large animals on the boats of the invaders. The traders whom we captured said they are called horses, and that they are used in battle. They are fearsome creatures, and we would have been decimated."

"Do you believe the Sea People will venture inland?"

"Not right away, Mara. They will plunder the seaside villages, the crops, and remaining livestock. I am glad I ordered much of our crops burned. The Sea People will decide there is nothing for them in Thapsos and will find another village to plunder. I fear there will be much death for the unprepared. I hope that they will not decide to build settlements on our island. This would take them time. I think they only wish to take what is free to plunder. Meanwhile, we can be safe here until we see what they are planning."

"Yes, this is a good place far and hidden from the coast. The deep canyons and caves provide safe places. We may honor the gods here. We will survive. Our union was not a usual one, but our passion has turned to love and respect. I am grateful that you will protect us in this time of uncertainty."

As Baltra prepared the things that he had brought with him from the exodus, he began reminiscing of the time he first saw Mara. They had now been together for a very long time.

Baltra was very pleased with Mara's hard work and a life dedicated to him and his family. She had adapted to the Sicani way of life very well. So much happened since those early days. He was extremely grateful that Mara, his children, and his people were safe, and most especially that he had married Mara. She knew what he was thinking even before he spoke. He was lucky to find a soulmate.

As Baltra climbed up to the plateau, a strong breeze was carrying the pungent scent of the sea. Oh, how he missed the sea and his former home! He lived by the sea in Thapsos for many years. Suddenly, Baltra was once again a young warrior, son of the Chief, surveying the fields outside of Thapsos on the mainland on an early warm fall day. He smiled to himself as he remembered.

That fall day I had followed the path along the river basin where the long row of oleanders was blooming in red and yellow. Behind them was a row of evergreen tamarisks my ancestors had planted. Their wood provided our warriors with strong bows for hunting.

The golden wheat danced in the wind. My father's slaves reaped the grain with energy and precision. I was truly luckier than most men! Someday all my father's fields would be mine. But there in the distance, I saw an unusual sight! A beautiful young woman. Her black skin glistened like obsidian in the afternoon sun! She wore a bone and ivory necklace that contrasted with her skin. Her bright green and gold cloth was wrapped around her waist. She was so graceful as she swung the scythe across the grain! This black Aphrodite fascinated me. Who was she? I approached her.

"I am Baltra, son of Chief Ari, son of Iko. Who are you? I have not seen you before."

She responded, "Sire, I am called Mara. I am but 14. I have just been purchased by the overseer. I have been here but a fortnight. My mother is still with our previous owner. Though I am treated well here, I miss her terribly."

"Mara, I have watched you work. You do your work well. Where do you come from?"

She related her story of hardship as I listened attentively.

"We were captured while I was still a young child with my mother, father, and brothers.

"The Egyptians made war on our tribe far to the south where there is no ice or snow. My father was the great King of Kush[37]. When we lost the war, we were taken prisoners and taken to the city of Pharaoh. My father was executed and my mother, brothers, and I were sold to some people of the Levant. They put us on a great boat and sold us to some men in Thapsos. It has all been overwhelming!" Mara's eyes filled with tears as she remembered her parents and all she had had to surrender.

I never felt such intense pain for another person before. My heart was torn by such injustice.

"Mara, this is a very sad story. You are so very young. I too feel your loss. I will see if I can lighten your burden."

I spoke to my father, and he agreed to let Mara be my house slave.

She worked in my home and garden day in and day out. One day, I approached her again.

"Mara, are you happy with your station here?"

"Sire, you know it is not for me to be happy. I am a slave to do as you command. I do appreciate working in the house instead of the hot field."

---

[37] Habasat – Ethiopia

I asked her to accompany me on a short walk so that we could continue our conversation. She said she always did what I commanded. I was taken aback. I really wanted her to be happy and content, but we were still master and slave.

We walked in a field below covered in wild fennel and purple lavender. The air was sweet with the smells of the fall. The yellow brooms[38] swayed in the distance. We came to a large cork tree where I invited Mara to sit. She did so reluctantly. I asked, "So, Mara, you are a princess?"

"You don't believe me! But why should you? We had servants and gold jewelry. My home was built of bricks, and we had water flowing from the Nile into a large pool at the center of our home. My father ruled an army."

I hurt that she did not think I believed her. I blurted out, "O! But I do believe you"

As we sat looking at the beauty of nature on our left and the blue-green sea on our right we told each other about our lives, our families, and our dreams. She became comfortable in sharing her short, but eventful life. She taught me a few words in her language, and I recited some childhood ditties in mine. We were becoming friends.

I said, "Mara, I hope we can do this again and more often."

She bowed her head and said, "Sir, yes when I am finished with my chores."

"Please Mara, call me Baltra. If we are to be friends, we should do away with formalities."

"But, Sir, Baltra, how can this be. I am still your slave."

"Mara, perhaps this can change, perhaps I could see if my father will grant you freedom."

---

[38] Brooms - Broom trees grow along the coast of Sicily which have yellow flowers. Genus Cytisus.

"Baltra, my freedom is precious to me, but it must be granted with no strings attached."

The fall passed into winter and Mara spent more time inside my house. We talked freely and often. One cold day as I sat by the hearth, I asked Mara to join me. I began, "Now that we are better acquainted, I wish to know from you, Mara, do you think you have any feelings for me?"

She looked shocked. "Sire! You have been very good to me. You are handsome and strong. I like you very much."

"So, is there any way you would ever consider a change in your station, that is, would you consider marriage? It would be a marriage according to Sicani custom, not one of master and slave, but of cooperating husband and wife. It would be that way because I am son of a Chief and you are a princess. You would be granted your freedom to accept my proposal or not."

"Baltra, I respect you a great deal. You have been kind and gentlemanly when you could have had your way. I do have feelings for you, and I will think upon your proposal. Now I must finish my chores preparing the food."

Spring arrived quickly. My father agreed to free Mara. Once freed, she agreed to our marriage. Our wedding day was full of sunshine and the sweetness of the season. I was in awe of her regal beauty as she approached in a long emerald-green wedding dress. A golden, jeweled headband complemented her lovely, long, black, braided hair. At that moment I knew that the gods had meant us for each other. We embraced amid the yellow and blue Spring wildflowers. She smiled and looked deeply into my eyes and whispered, "I am home!" My heart skipped a beat!

A sudden clap of thunder brought Baltra back to the present and his duties. As he descended from the plateau, he thought to himself, *how quickly the years have passed, how our love and family have grown. Mara and our children carry themselves with pride as is the custom of kings and queens of royal blood. My boys have my stature, and all our children have her fine features. All the members of the tribe respect her.*

Then in the distance he saw Mirax approaching.

INSCRIPTION Z

I, Luxo, was told by the Sicani elder, Anax, that Baltra established a thriving community in Pantalica. Since there was a need for protection, he had the Anaktoron[39] built as a palace fortified by high walls. The elders chose to crown Baltra as king in the fashion of Cocalus of Kamikos.

"Mirax, we need to create weekly scouting parties to the surrounding areas above the Anapo and up to the mountain where the river begins. This will enable us to be warned if the Sea People are planning further incursions."

"Yes Sire, I will arrange it and let you know if we need to prepare. Your will is my command!"

"As of now I don't believe they will attempt anything, because we have little for them to plunder here and our position is one of strength."

INSCRIPTION H

Here I, Luxo, write that these Sicani of Thapsos remained in these highlands for at least six generations. The Shekelesh and other Sea People moved on, and the Sicani again expanded to the sea and filled the inland highlands, including where I now reside, Akrai. But one clear day my people, the Siculi, came from the east along the coast

---

[39] Anaktoron – A Mycenaean princely palace – A structure with many rectangular rooms constructed of large stone blocks. It may have been used in the Eleusinian Mysteries.

in great numbers and riding large horses. We were a brave people forged in the years of our long arduous trek from the cold interior of the continent and made strong by our fights with the Latine and Osci, and Campanie. We also possessed other advantages. Besides our bows and weapons of bronze, we had a new, incredibly strong metal called ferrum[40]! We drove off most of the Sicani to the north and west, those who remained were slaughtered or enslaved. The slaves helped us in establishing our new settlements. Some even formed strong bonds with us, adopted our ways, and mated with our men and women to foster a strong people. We learned from them and they from us. But that story will be told later. The entire southeast of the island slowly became ours.

---

[40] Ferrum – iron.

THE MUSE (2000 AD)

I kept thinking of the vision of the young boy whom I had seen. As I thought, I came to the realization that he was a younger manifestation of my old friend. I thought about the embroidery on his clothes. Suddenly, a knock on my door, roused me from my dream!

"Salve! My friend I am here to lead you through the next difficult cave. There is blood and war coming!"

"Salve, friend. But I need to know who you are. You have kept me in suspense long enough, and I believe I know some of the symbols on your dress. Now I can see the circle and the inscribed square on your Chlamys. Is it not the famous proof of the squaring of the circle? And last time your dress had a spiral stretching to infinity?"

"It is indeed. You have solved the riddle which I presented to you on my clothing."

"Was not my vision an image of you at an early age?

"Indeed, it was."

"You played with mirrors to set leaves on fire, a premonition of your fight against the Roman fleet!"

"I think you have guessed. Yes, I am Archimedes whose life was cut short by the Romans. I still had much to offer the world, and that is why I have returned now, to you. You will tell the great epic of our people who once rose high above all others, to be brought down by Rome and others who only took from us!"

"I am honored that one of the greatest minds who ever existed chose me to assist you. I know how much you have impacted the modern world in a multitude of areas: mathematics, physics, technology, and civilization!"

"Let us not waste time. There is much to do and learn, and my time in this world is limited. The gods have allowed me but a short time, before I return as Persephone did, but not to the underworld, but to Elysium. Let us continue."

CHAPTER 13

CAVE 4, WALL 1 (Circa 1100 BC)

The Siculi Conquest

INSCRIPTION Θ

I, Luxo, write on this wall of the adventures of my people once they arrived on Trinacria, after braving the horrors at the straights. Adar and the other gods had protected them. They had left the tribes that had driven them from the rich land of the volcano near the coast of Italia and the protected harbor. Now they had to set out again to find the best place for their people. But they knew this was their promised land, because Adar had given them the great volcano which was always to their right as they proceeded down the eastern coast.

At first, as they proceeded southwest in Trinacria, they found little habitation or resistance. They left small groups to establish outposts. But as they approached the valley of the Anapo in the south they began to find more Sicani. Some Sicani had returned from the caves in Pantalica. They had fled from the coast many generations before because of the raids. Now the danger of the Sea Peoples was long past, many Sicani had returned to the coast. The Siculi presented the Sicani with new dangers. Siculi fought the Sicani, and many slaves were taken. Other Sicani fled north and west, especially after seeing men on horseback. The horsemanship and weapons of ferrum of the Siculi were no match for the islanders.

At the mouth of the Anapo, the Siculi found a great harbor as they did in other settlements which were now abandoned. Particularly they found a very substantial settlement on the coast north of the Anapo which had been burned to the ground, and they saw many scattered remains of items of habitation. They eventually found out that this settlement was called Thapsos, by the Sicani.

So, they first settled on the coast and prospered. Generation after generation they increased in number and strength. They began sending scouts up the Anapo and other rivers to investigate for good grazing and farmland. They settled the heights of Akrai and looked with lustful eyes on the land between the mouths of the Irminio and Acate Rivers. Rituli was now the most powerful chief of the Siculi.

They still were divided into clans, but Rituli had stood out for his bravery and leadership. All respected him for he was descended from the great Siculi who had led the tribe safely to Trinacria. He was known as Rituli D'Bolani, so that people would all know his power proceeded from his great ancestor.

I, Luxo, write here the story of my impressive ancestor so that you may know that we have done much to make this island a fine place. Read. read, and learn! Praise to Adhrano!

Since the Siculi crossed the Straights, they began occupying the coast both north and south of the great smoking mountain. They arrived as far south as what had been the settlement of Thapsos. They began sending scouts to find what lay inland to the north and west.

Rituli now approached his scout, Carni, "What have you found on your last mission to the source of the Anapo?"

"Rituli, greetings! There is a mountain[41] where the river rises, and to the east many cliffs and caves. As we were secretly hiding

---

[41] Mt. Lauro just north of Akrai.

in the trees, we observed many Sicani in the area. They have great villages below the cliffs and guards on the heights. They also have a large stone building where an important man resides. We caught one of the Sicani and have taken him prisoner. He is now here. You may question him. His name is Sarax.

Carni brought Sarax in front of Rituli. "This is our chief. Down on your knees!"

Sarax had his hands bound behind his back and a rope tied around his ankles so that he could only shuffle along. The warrior behind Sarax pushed him down on his knees and pulled his hands upward so that the prisoner had to bow down.

"Answer what the chief asks or you will pay dearly!" Carni commanded.

"Who is your leader?" asked Rituli.

Sarax did not respond. The warrior pulled harder on his arms and the prisoner cried out,

"His name is Inguma, King Inguma."

"What is the great stone building we see in Pantalica?"

"It is called the Anaktoron. It is the King's residence."

"And what does your King's name mean in your language?"

"It is the name of one of our powerful gods, one who wields thunder, lightning, and destruction. Our King's power descends from the gods. The blood in his veins is the same as that of a Sicani queen from a place called Kamikos and the blood of a demi-god called Daedalus who arrived from the heavens on wings. His power is unequaled! Beware!"

At this Carni struck the prisoner on the head with a heavy stick so that he collapsed.

"Take him away," commanded Rituli. "Feed him bread and water when he wakes, and we will decide what to do with him later."

Two warriors dragged the prisoner away to a cave.

"Did you hear that, Carni?" Rituli laughing, "This is a myth they are telling us so we will fear their magic. I put no credence in this. We will conquer them, and I will take one of their daughters as a bride for my son, so he will inherit whatever power they have. I do not fear the Sicani. See how they have all fled. Most still live in caves!"

"Chief, I agree. When shall we pursue them?"

"Let us go slowly, there is no haste. Send some of our people to establish themselves in the heights close to that mountain of which you spoke, where the Anapo and other rivers begin. We shall wait a few years to prepare our warriors and raise more horses. They will not attack us. For now, send that man, Sarax, back when he wakes. Have him carry a message back to see if they wish to establish trade with us. Let them believe we wish to live in harmony. We will strike when they are comfortable with us!"

INSCRIPTION Θ

I, Luxo, spoke to Anax. He reported that the elders told him that Siculi and Sicani lived in peaceful coexistence for several years. That Rituli met with Inguma, the King of the Sicani of Pantalica, and set up exchanges of goods. I believe this meeting occurred some fifteen generations before the first arrival of the Greeks. Antax said it took place on a high plateau above the Anapo not far from the coast. I believe the meeting took place in this small Sicani settlement of what the Greeks now call Akrai. It was a neutral place half-way from either group's territory. It is the place where I now reside and where these caves are located in which I write the history of the island.

Rituli and Carni were pleased when the meeting day dawned. It was early spring, and the air was filled with sweetness from the scent of wildflowers, particularly the caper blossoms. The lowland plains were fragrant with the intoxicating licorice odor of the Oleasters, the Olives which the Sicani had cultivated from the time Minos brought the four original trees. The Sicani had found that they were an irreplaceable asset and now that the Siculi had control of these plains, he needed to find a way to preserve access. It was one of the items at the top of his mind.

King Inguma of the Sicani arrived on the heights above the Anapo on a donkey. The Sicani did not have the horses the Siculi carefully guarded. He was arrayed in the manner of his forebears in a white, short Chiton, with many pleats at the bottom, and a leather strap around his waist. He was still young and carried himself well. A leather band also crossed his chest, and a large gold medallion was held by a gold chain around his neck and fell at the center of his chest. The medallion was an unusual form: an anthropomorphic design containing two opposite spirals at the opening into two legs. The opening had two large spherical balls sitting in the opening. It appeared to be an abstract fertility symbol inspiring the act of creating life. Carni imagined it to be symbolizing the King's great accomplishments in the field of procreation.

Rituli had arrived the night before and was also dressed to create an aura of power. He wore a fine dark, soft leather kilt, with an open cape about his shoulder trimmed in a black fur. His belt buckle was a large round shiny bronze and iron medallion, and on his head, a gold band.

"Hail, Inguma. We are pleased that we can meet to establish terms of trade. Hopefully we will agree on something that will be beneficial to us both."

"Yes, Rituli. I have been waiting for this day. Though our settlements are far apart, I believe that as our tribes increase, contentions might arise."

"That may come to be, but, for now, let us feast and talk."

They sat outside the large round hut that was built on a high plateau above a wide rocky valley.[42] Below, the river ran swiftly between banks of trees and greenery. At dusk they could see far to the east where the river rose from a high mountain, later to be named Mt. Lauro. Even further away, light reflected from Adar's home which still was covered in white, and it let out puffs of smoke that rose in red rings, reflecting the fading sunlight.

Inguma stared at the red puffs of smoke coming from the far-off mountain and exclaimed, "Aed, whom you Sicani call Adar, certainly presents a beautiful, yet powerful, image as he sleeps and snores. He is what makes this land fertile, and yet terrifying."

"Inguma, let us decide on goods to exchange. We Siculi are fine fisherman. Each day our catch outstrips our need. The waters are rich in squid, shellfish, and white fish. We can deliver fruits of the sea to you, live or dry. We can transport them up the river to a place below the plateau, and your traders can meet us there. It is about half-way."

"Yes, we miss this for we once resided at Thapsos where we had fine homes built of brick and fine defensive walls. Then the Shekelesh came, plundered, and drove us to Pantalica."

"I know of these Sea People. We saw the destruction at Thapsos. It was a considerable settlement. Long ago we shared ancestors with the Shekelesh, but they were driven to wander and plunder by others who attacked them and drove them to the sea. We instead remained as herders and farmers far inland."

"I was not aware of your connection with them. However, let us speak of the present. We have a great deal of meat from our sheep and goats. There is fine grazing in the hills near the cliffs and mountains. We also have tin arriving from our brothers in

---

[42] This height is where the Greeks would eventually build the town of Akrai in the province of Siracusa. It sits with a commanding view of the surrounding country. To the east lies the sea and the harbor of Ortygia, Siracusa, to the northeast, lies Mt. Etna.

Iberia, and arsenic which we mine in the west of our land. Both are good to strengthen copper. You also have the secret of this new metal, ferrum. We each have much to benefit the other. Trading seems desirable to me, and you?"

"Indeed. Besides the source of metals in the caves, you Sicani also have precious stones from Adar's mountain. We also are interested in obtaining some of the yellow, soft rock which can be crushed into poisonous powder. It is prized by our priests and healers. It produces a foul odor and the reddish flame of the god of the underworld, Hades. Its foul odor drives away the evil spirits. We call it zolfo[43], Hades' breath. We can exchange amber from the Simento."

"Indeed, our women value those beads! And you also have many herbs and fruit that grow on the warmer coast."

Rituli then offered Inguma his cup to share, "Let us drink from this same cup to seal the deal of trade. You have been more cooperative than I expected. I feel we have established trust. Let our tradesmen continue to talk, and they can report back to us. If we are then in agreement of the details, we can have a ceremony of agreement. Does that meet with your approval?"

"You too have been a most gracious host. I expected that our differences would be greater than our similarities. I am glad we have an agreement and that both our peoples will benefit."

As they ate and enjoyed their drink, Inguma seemed to relax. He particularly enjoyed the Siculi girls' erotic dances. Then a bard began the recitation of the epic of the Siculi journey from the cold north and the crossing of the straights. Inguma was impressed.

The following day, after the tradesmen completed the details, they brought Rituli and Inguma two inscribed tablets of clay with the details of the trade. There were two tablets. Each had

---

[43] Zolfo - sulfur

a unique symbol indicating either Siculi or Sicani. Below were crude drawings of objects, like sheep, fish, symbols indicating tin or arsenic. Next to each where lines indicating a number. The two men were both pleased and agreed to the terms. Copies of each were made so that each tribe would have the terms to take with them.

As a sign of commitment, Inguma signaled one of his men standing far off. He went down the hill to a small hut where some Sicani were staying. He appeared a bit later followed by a woman in a striking garment. Her dress was in the shape of a cone from the waist down. It was golden brown but split in the front where a dark green fabric filled the space between her legs. She had large bulging sleeves but was open so that her young breasts were exposed, and a gold necklace graced her lovely long neck. Her hair was jet black and piled high on her head, and two curls on each side fell over her shoulders onto her breasts. As she approached closer, Rituli's son, Kato, stared as at an apparition. Tall for a Sicani, she was also svelte. She seemed to float, not walk, toward her father. As she drew closer, Kato could see her light blue, almost green eyes. He was enchanted as if by a goddess.

"Rituli, this is my eldest daughter, Usoa. She is princess of Pantalica. You see that we have learned much from the Minoans at Kamikos. She is dressed in their fashion. My informers tell me your first-born son still has not taken a wife. I have a proposition for you if you are willing to hear me."

The events of the day put Inguma into a very pensive and nostalgic mood. He remembered the elders' ballads. They sang of those lovely days by the sea, before the arrival of the Sea People over one-hundred years before. It was a time of peace and prosperity.

As he looked at Kato and Usoa he thought of the joy he had experienced when he first met his Itaja. The first time he saw Itaja he was awestruck. He was a young warrior back from a hunt of wild boar. He walked into the canyon of Pantalica, tired and brown, his body glistening in sweat on the hot summer day. Itaja was at the well. Her bare arms pulled the rope in rhythm of her song, a song of the longing of a woman who had not seen her warrior love in many months. Itaja wore a plain white shift. Her hair, tied with a blue ribbon, glistened in the sun as it swept back and forth with the song. She was Erik arisen from the sea.

He greeted her and she smiled. She told him she had just returned from Kamikos. She had been raised in Pantalica but had gone to live in Kamikos to be with a married sister who needed help with her children. Her earliest ancestors, Daedalus and Minervala, had moved to Thapsos generations before. Their descendants had lived there until the Sea People attacked and they immigrated with all the people to take refuge in Pantalica.

Itaja, herself, had been away in Kamikos for six years. She had returned to Pantalica because she had become homesick for her parents. Once she told Inguma who her parents were, he knew she was from a well-respected family. Inguma and Itaja spent many joyful married years together in Pantalica. They loved all their children, but Usoa was their favorite.

Chief Rituli rose and took Usoa's hand, "Welcome, Usoa! Your great beauty graces all of us." Pointing to some cushions he said, "Please sit and join us."

Her face reddened as she responded, "Thank you, sire. I am happy to be here."

Rituli turned to Inguma, "Now your proposition. Though at first unexpected, I can almost guess what it is. I see an agreement possible."

Inguma had prepared how he was to convince the Siculi. He began, "I have been watching Kato, as Usoa approached. I propose we seal our deal with the joining of our children. My daughter, Usoa, is of most noble birth. Her mother, Itaja, is descended from Daedalus, the god who arrived on the wings of a bird from ancient Minoa. He wed Minervala the daughter of King Cocalus of Kamikos. So, you see, Usoa comes from a most noble bloodline. She has many gifts besides beauty inherited from the gods, among which is a mastery of metal work. Notice the gold necklace she wears, which is of her own creation. Their union will ensure friendship and foster the unity of our peoples. It will give examples to other clans of our respected tribes. It will be a symbol of our unity rather than enmity."

Rituli's initial thoughts of the Sicani were slowly softening. "Yes, I agree that this will benefit our peoples, avoid conflict, and foster trust. I, too, have heard the tale of the flying demi-god! I am in full agreement of your proposition. Kato comes from a line of strong brave men, and fine horsemen. You have heard the bard tell our epic. We are descended from the great Bolani and his son Suko who led our people through the dark days when they thought the world was ending, and from Xavo and Thiago who led our people across the straights, and braved Charybdis and Scylla. This is a union which will lead to greatness and peace."

Though Rituli spoke words of peace, his mind was working. *This is an interesting turn of events! Yes, we will cooperate. Let them be lulled into thinking we are friends. Then we will strike when they are asleep. Now we will proceed peacefully until the time is right.*

Inguma thought for a while, then spoke. "As they unite, so will our Aed, and your Adar, both gods of earth and fire, become one god. And so will our Erik and your Aphrodite, become one. We will meet soon to celebrate a wedding and enjoy each other's company. We will prepare for Kato's induction into our tribe. I will let you know when we are ready after I consult the priests."

Inguma reflected upon the gods. "In the far west there is a high promontory and small temple dedicated to Erik. It is called

Eryx[44]. From hence, let the goddess be called Aphrodite, and the place Eryx. Do you both agree?"

"Yes." "Yes." Both Rituli and Kato replied almost in unison.

Then Rituli spoke. "As for our god of fire, let us form a new name that is similar and easier for both tongues. Adhrano. How does that suit you, Inguma?"

"It is pleasing to me. Let us then agree. Aphrodite and Adhrano will be the gods we share and Usoa and Kato will wed!"

"So be it. Until we see each other again."

On the return to the coast Rituli was rethinking his assessment of the Sicani, and Inguma especially. He had become a changed man. He had thought about conquering the Sicani, but now he was more interested in the wealth and peace that he and his people might enjoy. The populations were still sparse, and the land was large. For now, there would be peace.

His son, Kato, would enter the Sicani cult and intimately learn about this tribe. It would be better than war for now.

Once home Rituli consulted his priests. They went to one of the dolmens which they had found on the hills just above their settlement. No one knew who had built these huge rock structures, but the priests said they must have been constructed by the gods, and so now they used the flat stones as altars for sacrifice.

The priests sacrificed a young horse to Aphrodite to ensure that the decision of Kato and Usoa to wed was indeed the will of the gods, and that the goddess would bless the union with fertility. The sun set that day and the crops grew strong and abundantly. Rituli was confident that he had made the right choice for now.

---

[44] Eryx, the son of Aphrodite and King of the town by the same name. The town is on the western coast of Sicily on a high promontory dedicated to Aphrodite. Branchina proposes that the divine mother, Erik, was a Sicani deity from Celtic origins. Genesi di una terra primordiale www.adranoantida.it/?p=1045 7/6/2019 Francesco Branchina.

THE MUSE (2001AD)

"Archimedes, my friend, as I proceed deeper into each cave, through these notes, you take my mind deeper and deeper into these early cultures. It's as if I am living with them and among them! What is your power?"

"I have been given this gift from Aphrodite to open your mind and guide your pen. She has always loved this island where she was born. She has protected it and given it both human and creative fertility. I was quite a skeptic while on earth of what the priests led us to believe about the gods. But like all knowledge, I have found religion also imperfect. Death has opened a new reality. Men try to invent to understand that which is non-understandable. Mysteries fill the universe. Its entirety is connected. We are all made of stardust and that relationship makes us wish to know god. On earth we must speak of them as entities like us, but with supernatural powers. I believe you are now ready to venture deeply into the Sicani mysteries of life and death. The next cave will give you a new understanding.

"You will notice that the rites you will observe are not too different from Celtic rites. These rituals were carried out near Pantalica[45], but the wedding would take place in Innessa[46], a place

---

[45] A UNESCO World Heritage Site, the Necropolis of Pantalica is a collection of tombs cut of rock, and the remains of at least one stone structure, the Anaktoron. It is located 14 mi northwest of Siracusa at the junction of the Anapo and Calcinara rivers. Dates from the 13th Century BC.

[46] Innessa, later named Aitna, and Etna, 19 km from Catania, on the right bank of the river Simeto. An ancient Siculi settlement of both myth and history. It sometimes is identified with the town of Adrano and may have been also a Sicani place of worship.

dedicated to Adhrano. Innessa was about a day's journey on foot from Pantalica, where the Sicani now resided. The horses of the Siculi reduced the journey to a few hours. Are you ready to begin?"

"My friend, lead me on. I am apprehensive but excited about what I shall learn. Lead on!"

CHAPTER 14

CAVE 4, WALL 2 (circa 1100 BC)

THE CULT OF DEATH AND RESURECTION AND THE WEDDING

Inguma approached Kato, "You must take part in our tribe's ritual of manhood and purification before the Adhranhiti[47] would allow marriage to my daughter. Remember that our line goes back to the demigod Daedalus who arrived in Trinacria on bird's wings. In fact, Usoa is named in honor of the arduous flight. Her name means dove."

"I will do as you command because Usoa flew into my heart like a most beautiful bird. I will gladly slay the Cyclops if that would win me her hand."

"You surely have been smitten! And Usoa, also, is extremely happy with this union. She continues to fill my head with a list of all your qualities! O, young love! I remember my first glimpse of Itaja, but that was far in the past. You realize that this is unusual. Many times, we make unions only for political expediency, but this is one where we hope to accomplish political advantages to both our tribes, as well as happiness in your union. I feel that this union is in fact ordained by both Aed and Erik, whom now we

---

[47] Adhranhiti – the priests of the god Adhrano

call Adhrano and Aphrodite. She, the goddess of love! Aphrodite who was born in the foam in the midst of our land and continues to protect us! The priests will explain all to you and why the signs align with your union with my Usoa. You will begin the rituals the day after tomorrow to see if the gods accept you into our tribe."

"Thank you, lord. I am happy to serve."

"Come. I will introduce you to the great Adhranhiti, Zeru[48]. He will lead you through the rituals and we will see you on the day after tomorrow, the first day before the summer solstice.

Zeru was an ancient priest with long flowing white hair. His thin face was as if carved of wood with deep furrows which had seen many years and many disappointments. His garment was a rough brown cloth tied around his waist. He had many symbolic tattoos on his chest. Bones protruded from his skin on his thin legs and chest. One tattoo was a spiral Kato had noticed inscribed on many walls and on pottery. Kato was told that these were symbols of the god of the sun and represented the melding of opposites. On one arm the inverted triangle, which Kato now knew, represented Trinacria, and on the other a large bull which he believed was reference to the wealth of the Sicani, which they held in cattle. Below the bull was a symbol of a man's body with the head of a large horned bull, the symbol of the minotaur. Kato assumed this represented their close connection with the Minoans in the past.

Zeru, though old, spoke in a very strong deep voice, "Kato, we are entering a most sacred time. Not only is it the solstice, but this year, we have a particularly propitious occurrence. It occurs only once in every score and ten years. There will be a full moon on the night of the solstice. Most have never observed this in their lifetimes. It is a time blessed by the gods for unions. Adhrano, god of fire, will mate with Aphrodite, the mother of fertility and

---

[48] Zeru – a Basque name meaning sky. Since little is known about the Sicani except that they migrated from Spain, I thought this was a good name for a priest.

beauty. If you are favored by the gods in the rites which we are to begin, both our tribes and people will be truly blessed!"

"Zeru, I will complete all the tasks you put upon me, for I wish to marry Usoa more than life!"

"So be it. Tomorrow evening, the night before the solstice, we will begin."

Kato rested and fortified himself with food the women brought to his hut. Zeru and the Adhranhiti arrived in the late afternoon before the day of solstice. It was bright and the air was warm but without the intense heat of the summer. They removed all his garments except for a white cloak and led him away to a remote part of the settlement outside the settled area of Pantalica. Kato was accompanied only by the priests, for this was a mystery for only Adhranhiti and initiates.

The Siculi also had rituals, beliefs like those of the Sicani. Kato had undergone the rituals of his tribe so he felt confident that all would go well. However, he still was a bit apprehensive.

They arrived at a high place where he could see the cone of Eithné[49], the nymph who fell in love with Adhrano, before giving birth to twins. The twins escaped the wrath of the fire god by turning into seals, and then into twin lakes, called the Palici[50].

They travelled for quite a while, climbing upward along a narrow path. Near the summit were caves in which dogs could be heard barking. The closer they came to the summit, the louder and greater was the roar.

Zeru, who was behind the line of Adhranhiti and Kato, yelled, "Kato, do not fear. These are the holy beasts of Adhrano. They guard the holy places!"

The high place was flat but surrounded by high cliffs of calcite

---

[49] Eithné – Etna – also daughter goddess of Balor.
[50] Palici may be derived from Balici, Bal, and Bel. These are gods that appear throughout pre-history from Mesopotamia to Celtic lands.

almost forming a complete circle. In the center was a large flat rock Kato assumed was an altar. The cliffs were not solid. There were many caves and tombs. But most striking were the carved archways through which one could look across the hills and valleys to the horizon. Some were high and broad, others low and tiny. They did not seem natural, but rather carved smoothly by man. At the summit of the hills were also stones piled in different places but in some sort of pattern. Kato was in awe.

What Kato was now to observe were rites which dated back millennia, to when the Sicani first arrived in this triangular land. Once they were near the central altar, Zeru began instructing Kato directly.

"We Sicani believe Anu, our first ancestor, was the first man. He was the first to enter this lovely abundant and green land and prospered. He died and entered the aldilá[51]. He opened the gates of both Earth, when created, and of the Sky, when he died. He became the God of Fury and Fire, like the sun, and was called by other names like Adr, or Aed, by our ancestors. Anu was the ancestors' God and our first ancestor. And now both our tribes agree to call him Adhrano. This holy place was selected by our ancestors from the earliest times."

Kato could now see the first temple. It had been carved from the living calcite in one of the many outcroppings in the area. It consisted of man-made carved arches at selected positions, forming almost a complete circle. They entered through a track which passed between the hills.

A large rock like an altar was at the center of the almost spherical line of outcroppings.

Zeru now caught up with Kato and explained, "We do not know how long these arches have been here. Our legends tell

---

[51]　Aldilá – the beyond

us that our first ancestors crafted them. Our epics tell of them coming from the north and travelling far before arriving. Some say their travels took them to Iberia, to Libya, and to Melite[52] before arriving here. Others claim they came by way of northern Italia[53]. Our rituals date back thousands of solar cycles. The large arches catch the first rays of the morning sun of the summer solstice and the last rays of the evening sun at the winter solstice. The smaller holes mark the equinoxes. They help us determine the times of planting or moving our herds. They inform us to know when to sacrifice for fertility or harvest. The smaller dips at the top of the rock outcroppings placed at almost regular intervals represent the movement of the full moon through the year. It tells us when Aphrodite tells Selene to block the sun to create night during the day. It also tells us when the full moon and the solstice occur on the same day and other important celestial events.

"Since your wedding is of great importance, we have chosen the day of the solstice for the ritual. The moon will also be full on the day of the solstice when the sun sets. That is when we will set off to meet Usoa."

Below, Kato could also see deep caves interspersed around the circle with very small openings. There was a large round hut at one end where some women were dressed in white shifts with a white head band. They were called the servants of Adhrano, for they served him night and day. They were waiting with food and drink for the travelers. The men were served and then the women withdrew down the path back to the village of Innessa.

That evening before the day of solstice, Kato was led to one of the small caves he had seen. A younger Adhranhiti led the way. This priest was assigned to Kato as his Anu, his Ancestor, who was to guide him in the ritual. He and Kato had to crawl on their

---

[52] Melite (Μελιτη) – from honey - Malta
[53] Liguria

bellies to enter the small opening of the cave. Once inside it was almost completely dark. The priest lit a torch. Kato looked around. He could see that the cave consisted of a large circular room with a domed ceiling. It had been carefully carved, and there were symbols on the walls and the ceiling. There was a small altar like rock on one side where offerings had been placed and incense burning in front of an image of Adhrano. The priest knelt and offered a prayer to the god of fire and fury.

He then was instructed to crawl through a second opening into a deeper cave, where a long smooth rock had been carved at the center. The priest placed a sheep skin on the stone. He told Kato to remove all his clothing. He was told to lie on the rock and place his head at the far end of the opening where there was a carved headstand. He positioned himself as he was told, head on the curved headstand, and feet pointing toward the opening. As he lay down in that position, he was able to see through the hole of the inner cave right to the outside where it was just dusk. The priest reminded him that he was to remain till daybreak and not leave the cave for any reason or the fury of Adhrano would visit him and the wedding would not proceed. Kato was only to emerge from the cave at first light. The Adhranhiti then took a clay chalice from a niche in the wall. He gave the cup to Kato and told him to drink deeply. It was a potion which would help him sleep. Kato did as he was told. The priest withdrew extinguishing all torches as the final light faded from the sky. Kato was left in the complete darkness to think and dream.

As Kato lay there and stared upward, he was only aware of the all-consuming darkness. He was filled with loneliness and fear. The utter lack of light was different than being in the forest at night when the stars shown bright even on the darkest of nights. In the villages there were always fires burning somewhere. It was a profound darkness that tested his very soul. He was spending the night in utter terror, not being able to tell whether beast or insect, bat, or snake, were crawling in the shadows ready to poison him. He was naked with no sword or knife. At first, he slept in fits and starts, trying to twist and turn in this uncomfortable bed. The night seemed interminable. Finally, the potion must have taken control and he fell into a deep sleep on his back. His dreams were filled with the symbols of Adhrano. He was travelling on the twisting helixes first in one direction, then another, falling, falling into the abyss. He finally saw that he had passed into the aldilá. He was one with the universe.

After what seemed a long time in the other world, he felt a warm spot on his forehead. It was like Usoa's warm hand was caressing him. Perhaps he was not dead. Perhaps it was only a dream. He called forth all his strength to force his eyes open. At first he could only blink, but it hurt to open them further. He must be in the presence of the fire of Adhrano! Fear gripped him again, but he remembered that he must overcome the trial if he was to marry. Finally, he summoned all his strength, opened his eyes, and sat up. He fell on his knees and prayed, asking Adhrano what he should do to assuage his wrath. He remembered that the Adhranhiti commanded him to leave at first light. He could only see the strong light and he crawled on his belly toward it, out of the first cave and into the second. He now could see Zeru, his Anu, and the other priests waiting for him with a white cloak with a golden belt and necklace with the symbols of Adhrano. They cheered in unison as he approached them, "He is risen! He has been led through the doors of the other world. He has returned from the aldilá. Adhrano be praised!"

Kato was covered in the cloak, then led away to be dressed as a Sicani warrior. He emerged from the dressing cave in the colorful flax kilt of a warrior. He had a leather strap across his chest and leather belt to which a bronze sword was attached. He wore the short white cloak on his shoulders with the gold belt attached loosely and the golden necklace on his neck.

A gold ring in the shape of an olive branch was placed on his head. He was ready to make the journey to the place of his marriage.

Zeru now spoke, "Kato, you have emerged from death to face all the tribulations of this life, a true warrior, and chief. We Sicani accept you Siculo as one of us since you have observed our most secret mysteries. You are bound not to tell anyone of these rites. Later you will swear to the Palici at the appropriate time. Now we are ready to begin our journey to the temple of Adhrano in Innessa. The journey would take a warrior two days on foot. We older priests take three or four. But since you Siculi have brought horses, we too now have learned to ride, and it has simplified our journey. Since it is still close to dawn, we should be able to arrive at nightfall. The horses and provisions are ready. The rest of the wedding participants left last week and are preparing a place for us. Let us begin our journey."

"I am glad our horses have made your lives easier. I look with great anticipation at visiting the most holy place of the God of Fire."

The Siculi had introduced horses into Trinacria when they first arrived. Their ancestors had learned the art of bareback riding from the time they were in the northern steppes. Lately they had introduced rope stirrups and bits. In recent years some Sicani had learned to ride horses but were not nearly as masterful. These changes reduced the time of the journeys substantially. The older priests still rode donkeys or were carried in wagons.

On the journey north to Innessa, Kato's Anu began describing why the place was holy.

"We are going to Innessa, where we adore Adhrano. The

goddess Innessa[54] joined with one-eyed Balor[55] to produce Eithné, the nymph who fell in love with Adhrano, giving birth to the Palici. In fear of their lives, the Palici twins transformed themselves into seals and swam away down the river Cian. Eventually the seals became the twin Palici lakes. I will tell you more when we visit those lakes later. Cian was another of Eithné's children. She is the river which divides in two branches, one of which became Cocalus, the King of Kamikos. Remember Cocalus is the ancestor of Usoa. The other branch is Lugh. He balances the spirals of left and right, dark and light. You have seen his inscriptions in the cave where you slept. This place creates a web which unites all Sicani."

Kato was concentrating on all that the Anu was telling him and thinking, *This land truly is a web of myths. Everywhere one turns at every place, there is a profound web of interwoven gods, goddesses, and nymphs!* Kato then replies to his Anu, "You are helping me understand much of the intricacies of your tribe. We too have always worshiped the Fire God, Adar, I mean Adhrano. When our ancestors left the north because of the darkness we called him Dyéws Phter, Daylight-Sky God. We also know about the twins by different names. Now that we have come to an agreement, our priests have seen that all these gods and myths are one and the same."

Once arriving at Innessa, the Adhranhiti, the Druid priests responsible for the upkeep and sacrifices, led Kato up the hill. Zeru followed behind. As they climbed Kato again heard the barking of dogs in the distance, the closer they came to the temple the louder they became, and he became concerned. The priest beside him said, "These are the Cirnechi hounds. They protect the sacred

---

[54] Innessa is associated with the Celtic goddess Lugh who joins with Balor to give birth to Eithné. The town of Innessa is associated by some as Adhrano, where the god was worshipped.
[55] The one-eyed mythical giant who wreaks destruction in Celtic mythology. Some studies have linked Siculi myths to original Celtic ones. They relate Balor to the Cyclops and place the myths occurring near present day Bronte.

precincts. Do not fear. They only attack thieves. They will escort us!'

As they drew closer the thousand Greyhounds followed them along the side of the path without a sound. They came to a flat place where a circular structure stood. It was much larger than the circular huts in the Sicani villages. It was built of strong, tall wooden poles from the forest which stood around the place. It had no walls, just a thatched roof, and a large flat rock at the center. In the distance the great cone of Eithné could be seen with smoke issuing from its summit. The puffs formed pleasing shapes in the sky, grey rings, and balls of smoke. The Adhranhiti were happy. It seemed the proceedings were pleasing Adhrano.

As Kato and the others drew closer to those already gathered in the temple, people met him with song, drum, and flute, singing, "He is risen like the first man. He has passed from earth to aldilá and back! He has come to our Usoa! Happy day! Praise to our Anu (Ancestors)!"

The priests then recited prayers and gave Kato a cup of sheep's milk to drink and led him to the altar where the sheep was sacrificed and where Usoa was waiting. She was in a cobalt blue shift representing the night sky and a long green head scarf trailing down her back. It represented the herbs and fertility of the earth. She had a garland of flowers around her head.

She was Erik (Aphrodite), the mother and goddess of fertility.

The couple held hands while a red cloth with a green stripe was bound around their joined hands. Red was the color of Adhrano, Kato's color, and green the color Demeter, Goddess of Fertility.

The priest recited a few words and then led the couple away to the union hut, prepared by the flowing stream down from the temple. It had been embellished with food and flowers for the mating couple. As they entered the hut, the full moon rose above Eithné, the princess who became a nymph.

There would be feasting and merriment for the next five

days. As part of the rites in unifying the royal households, single slaves and servants married members of the other tribe to cement the treaty Inguma and Rituli had agreed upon. Rituli took half his slaves and servants back to his settlement near Akrai, while Inguma and the other half returned to Pantalica, each satisfied that what they had done would cement peace for the near future. Rituli also took Usoa and her slaves with him, for the custom was for the women to become part of the husband's tribe. She would await the return of Kato.

Kato had one more rite to complete before he could return to his wife. Zeru and the others led the Siculi to the twin lakes of the Palici. They were Naftia[56] lakes. One was dark and ominous, the other clear. Upon arriving at the first lake, Zeru recited a prayer and then said, "Kato, repeat what I say: *By the dark waters of this lake all my profanity of spirit and heart will be washed away. I swear to this Palicus, the twins born of Adhrano and the nymph Thalia, that I will utter truth and never do anything to profane my spirit or the gods.*"

Kato repeated and took a cup of the water from the dark lake and placed it into the fire as an offering. It gave up a most putrid smell of zolfo (sulfur) with a cloud rising to heaven.

Then they moved to the second, clear lake. He repeated after Zeru, "I, Kato, ask this Palicus to give me true knowledge from the clear waters of this lake. May this twin give me clarity of mind to know and act on the truth. I swear that I will uphold my oath as long as I live."

The priest then wrote Kato's oath on a clay tablet. "Kato you must throw your oath into the clear lake. The Palici will decide if you are sincere. Beware that if they do not accept your oath, you will be blinded by the gods!"

---

[56] Naftia – naphtha, a flammable hydrocarbon which may escape from underwater deposits.

Kato took the tablet and flung it into the clear lake. At that moment the geyser erupted, supporting the tablet above the water. It did not sink.

"We see that the Palici have accepted the truth of your oath. Come we return to Akrai and Usoa. You have passed all the trials of the Sicani. Welcome warrior!"

With this the rituals were complete. Kato would return to his village of Akrai and live with his wife, Usoa, who would bear many children. Their progeny would carry the blood of many peoples. In them were united the original inhabitants of the island with the Sicani from Iberia, the Minoan descendants of Daedalus, and the Siculi newly arrived. They would populate not only the region of the Anapo but also spread to the coast and far inland.

BOOK IV

The Trojans

1100 BC

1100-1000 BC

Achilles – *Hero of the Trojan war, killer of Hector*

Anchises – *Trojan seduced by Aphrodite and father of Aeneas*

Aeneas – *Trojan son of Anchises and Goddess Aphrodite*

Ascanius – *son of Aeneas*

Egestes – *son of Egesta and the river god, Crinsus. Father of Solax and founder of the temple of Segesta*

Elymus – *Trojan who fled to Sicily for whom the Elymi are named. The natural-born brother of Aenaes*

Hector – *Trojan warrior killed by Achilles*

Inguma – *King of the Sicani in Pantalica, married to Itaja, and father of Usoa of Akrai*

Karisa – *daughter of Aenaes and wife of Solax, the Sicani*

Kato – *Siculi descended from Bolani who marries Usoa and undergoes ritual of the Sicani*

Odysseus – *King of Ithaca and legendary hero of Homer's poem*

Solax – *Sicani son of the Trojan Egestes*

Usoa – *daughter of the Sicani King Inguma and Itaja, the African princess and wife of Kato, Siculi chief*

CHAPTER 15

CAVE 4, WALL 3 (circa 1100 BC)

THE ARRIVAL OF THE TROJANS

INSCRIPTION I

I, Luxo, dedicate this cave to a people who arrived at almost the same time as my people. The Elymi arrived in Trinacria and settled the far west of the island. They had been driven from their lands by a terrible war and siege in the land of Anatolia some years before. They were wanderers for quite a while, first settling in Italy, before other warlike tribes drove them south to our island.

They found refuge in the sparsely populated northwest, in what is now Segesta and Eryx, the city of Erik, Aphrodite.

The men of Ilion, or Trojans, were taken off guard. After 10 years of siege, they assumed they were impregnable, but they failed to see how cunning were their adversaries and how internal jealousy could bring down a mighty people. When the huge horse, the symbol of Troy, appeared in front of the city gates, the people thought it was a gift of Athena and that the Hellenes had departed for their homeland. Before their return home, the Hellenes would dedicate this offering to Athena. This is to appease the Goddess for their destruction of her temple in Troy. The Trojans took the horse into the city. While they slept, a Hellene who was stowed away within the horse opened the gates of the city to the waiting Hellenic army. Destruction and death followed for the unaware Trojans.

Aeneas was the son of Anchises who was the mortal lover of Aphrodite. Zeus enraged by her infidelity struck Anchises with a thunderbolt which made him lame. Aphrodite had the River God cleanse Aeneas of his mortal nature and Aphrodite anointed him with ambrosia and nectar, making Aeneas a god.

But the Trojan Hector, slain by Achilles, appeared to Aeneas in a dream and warned him to flee, because all was lost in Troy and that he should take the gods of the house and hearth and his family to safety. So, he took his wife Creusa, their son Ascanius, his reluctant father, Anchises, and the rest of his family to Mt. Ida. A flame appearing over Ascanius' head, and a thunderclap provided by Zeus gave Aeneas confidence that it was the will of the gods. Aeneas had to carry the lame Anchises on his back. Creusa disappeared shortly after. Slowly Aeneas found there were many other refugees seeking protection. The next morning, he sees Creusa's ghost telling him to remarry, and when he sees the morning star rising above Mt. Ida, Aeneas knows that he must lead his people to a far-off land.

Aeneas found ships and set off for places unknown. Their long and circuitous voyage lasted many years. They stopped at the Rock of the Cyclopes in Trinacria and met a Hellene who had been abandoned by Odysseus. They then continued onward and found safe harbor in Libya where they stayed for quite a while. Finally, they set off again and stopped in Drepanum[57] on the western coast of Trinacria.

"Hail! I am Solax, son of our King. We welcome you if you come in peace. I see you are not prepared for war and come with your households. From where do you hail?"

---

[57] Drepanum – Trapani – a city of the northwestern coast of Sicily.

"My Lord, I am called Aeneas from Ilios. We have been at sea for many years after our home and city were devastated by the Hellenes. We are led by the gods to seek a new home. We touched upon your great island's shore at the rock of the Cyclops and were fed and greeted by Achaemenids, abandoned by Odysseus. We ask for refuge until we may continue our journey as the gods direct."

Solax awestruck, "By the grace of Erik, whom you call Aphrodite, we are pleased to welcome you and offer you and your households refuge. She protects us from atop the high mountain of Eryx. There we have her temple from where she watches over our town here below.

Once you are rested, we will make the pilgrimage to give her homage and thanks for your safe arrival."

"Certainly, we would be humbled by the act of adoration to Aphrodite who is my mother."

Solax fell to his knees in awe of Aeneas whom he now realized was also a god!

"I must now tell you who I am. I, Solax, am son of Egestes, son of Egesta of Troy and the river god, Crinsus. We are your countrymen! What we have is yours!"

And so, Aeneas, his son Ascanius and all the refugees stayed in Drepanum to rest and honor Aeneas father, Anchises. The people of Ilios and the Sicani feasted, recited their epics, and held funeral games to honor Anchises. Aeneas offered prizes as a sign of hospitality in the competitions of running, rowing, archery, and mock battles. But the Sicani were in awe of Iulus, Aeneas' son, who performed impressively on horseback for the Sicani had never seen horses, nor men upon them.

Now while the men were competing, the swift-footed goddess, Iris[58], conspired with Hera[59]. "Iris, we need to sow discord to

---

[58] Iris, the personification and control of the rainbow and light. A messenger of the gods, she could use light to form colored flames, etc.
[59] Hera, the guardian angel of women and female personification of life.

prevent these men from their voyage to Italia. Carthage is loyal to us, and Aeneas has already shown his dislike for our patroness, Dido, queen of Carthage."

Iris responded, "Yes, the women already are unhappy, for the men feast and have relations with the Sicani women. I will go to them and plant more discord. I will go as another Trojan woman and instigate them."

"Have them set fire to the boats, so they all will be stranded. We will avenge Carthage!"

Iris, in the guise of a poor Trojan woman, approached Karisa, daughter of Aeneas. "See how our men spend time in enjoyment, drunkenness, and lechery! We are left to cook and prepare their linens!"

"Yes, in Troy we had servants and slaves, and now all we look forward to is another long voyage, and perhaps another long stay in an unknown land. Where will we end up? Will we be led by the gods who do not care for us! We have become as slaves. We are tired."

"We can change our destiny. Listen. While they sleep and drink, we can prevent the departure. If they have no ships, they cannot leave, and we cannot voyage."

"Iris, what is in your evil mind? Are you suggesting sabotage?"

"Well, how do you suggest we stop the ships? Prevent them from departing?

"Fire is the dread of all sailors. I once saw lightening hit a mast, and the ship was ablaze in a short time. No one could save it."

Iris waited for the thought to sink into Karisa's head.

"We could carry our stoves to the ships in the early evening with the excuse that it will keep the food warm for the guards. While some of us distract the sailors, others can drop the embers in different places on the ships. By the time the ships are ablaze, we can be gone."

Iris thought, *I will use my powers to create flames of light that will engulf all the ships. The sailors will have no recourse but to let them burn!*

"Karisa, you are ingenious. Let us prepare the women. Only gather those you think will not tell their men. This is a plan hatched by the very gods!"

"Indeed, Iris, I think it will save us from more voyages!"

But the gods in their heaven war among themselves, and Aphrodite learned of Hera's and Iris' plan and came to Ascanius in his dream. His grandmother warned him of the women's sabotage but told him it was instigated by Hera who was patron of their enemy, Carthage. Ascanius was able to stop the evil plan, and told Aeneas, who called Karisa and the other women. "You have chosen a perverse remedy for your plight! Did you not realize the instigator Iris was none other than one sent by Hera! Shame on you and your friends!"

Karisa walked toward her father with confidence. "Father, forgive me, but we have reason for our discontent. We are tired of work and endless voyaging. We wish to remain in this fine land of sun and abundance. The Sicani are good to us."

Aeneas was taken unaware of how the women felt. "I realize that you have suffered much. I will allow those men and women who wish to remain to do so. As much as I would not want to lose you, I will respect your independence. It has always been our way in Ilios."

Karisa's face lightened. "We can make a good home here. Our grandmother Aphrodite guards us from her high place on Eryx. Also, father, Solax and I have spoken. He wishes me to be his wife. Other women have taken Sicani husbands. We wish to remain."

"So be it. I will make the journey to Eryx and offer thanksgiving. I am sure some of my men also wish to remain on this fair island. You will form a strong kingdom here. You will teach the Sicani our ways, and they will teach you theirs."

So, the Trojans lived in Drepanum for another two years. But the time approached when Aphrodite spoke to Aeneas. "My son, it is now time to complete the voyage which you have been created for. Italia awaits. Prepare, for the winds are favorable, and you are destined to achieve great feats and and found a great nation. Go with my protection!"

Aeneas called his Trojans together. "I have been to Eryx and have learned from the goddess that we must leave on the last leg of our journey. In a few days we leave for Italia. As I said before, I wish only willing settlers. Men and women who wish to remain are welcome to stay with our Sicani brothers. Egestes is happy to rule you as your king. Give him your loyalty and homage. Let me know your choice."

The sun shone bright in the early morning as the Trojans boarded the ships. As the sails were unfurled and the pleasant breeze filled them. There were many tears and crying as most believed they would never see family members and loved ones again. Aeneas was moved in seeing Karisa on the shore. But he was relieved to see the brave Solax standing behind her supporting her as she sobbed. Egestes and Elymus were sad to see the Trojans embark. Elymus was sad to see his brother, Aenaes depart. They had lost their father, Anchises, a few years before and now his brother was leaving for a far-off land. He was happy to have Karisa, his niece, and many of the Trojan women stay here in Trinacria. Together they would help forge strong colonies. Those who remained were ever more known as Elymi because of the towns founded by Elymus, the architect and builder, and because they came from Troy or Ilios[60].

Now some years passed and Solax's desire to voyage became stronger. He had always lived in Drepanum, but he wanted to

---

[60] Ilios - Ηλιοσ - the name of ancient Troy.

see other parts of this fabled Trinacria. He especially had heard of the wonders of Thapsos, the Rock of the Cyclopes, and Eithné, the great smoking mountain. He gathered others who wished to embark on an adventure. Solax took his wife, Karisa, all his children, and a boat full of settlers to points east. Aeneas' bother, the elderly Elymus, the great builder of the cities of Segesta and Eryx, also elected to go taking his entire family. They all hoped to settle in Thapsos.

THE MUSE (2001 AD)

My pen fell from my hand as I completed the last line of the arrival of the Trojans. My head then dropped to my desk into a deep sleep. Then not knowing whether I was awake or asleep, Archimedes was there to greet me!

"You see that the cave inscriptions continue to elaborate on Virgil's Aeneid. You are doing a fine job recording how some Trojans settled and mingled with the early Sicani. The next cave tells of the voyage of Trojans and Sicani to the east. Near the place of the Cyclops, they will meet with other peoples in the place later called Pantalica. Sleep now and rest. There is much, much more to reveal."

CHAPTER 16

CAVE 4, WALL 4 (circa 1100 BC)

IMIGRATION: SOLAX TO PANTALICA AND AKRAI

Solax's ship first arrived at the Rock of the Cyclops. There he was greeted by Achaemenids[61], the Hellene abandoned by Odysseus.

"Who goes there? I recognize your ship and the dress of these men. You are from my homeland. You are Trojans, are you not? I am Achaemenids. After Odysseus' men drove the spike into the one-eyed beast, I had no time to escape and was left behind. I was grateful for my life and have nothing more to fear from the blind Cyclops.

"We are Sicani and Trojans from Drepanum. I am Solax, son of Egestes. We are here on our voyage to Thapsos. Aeneas told us of his visit years ago and of your hospitality, and we wanted to see the great mountain."

"You are welcome to remain here if you wish, fellows of Ilios. I seem to remember the face of that fine lady near you. She was but a child when I saw Karisa with her father, Aeneas. How she has grown! Now, she is a beauty in flower."

"And she is my wife. We also have Elymus here with us who is the great architect. His magnificently designed cities and

---

[61] Achaemenids – a name meaning he who waits with affliction.

temples of Segesta and Eryx are even now being built in the west of Trinacria."

"Welcome all! Fair warning, my countrymen! You will not find a welcome in Thapsos. Since Aeneas' visit, this coast has suffered much from invasion. We first were attacked by the Shardana who came and plundered. The Sicani evacuated to the hills, so there were no casualties, but they have not repopulated the area near Thapsos. A few come to fish but return to the safety of the hills. Now, new Italic people known as the Siculi have invaded and taken up residence in Thapsos and now are extending their areas along the coast. King Inguma of the Sicani has moved his people into the highlands where Aed, now Adhrano, can protect them. It is a place of caves and religious rites."

"Can you lead us there? Can we go from here?"

"Yes, but it is an arduous journey. I hear from the local Sicani that Inguma has now just made peace with the Siculi and they trade. We shall see when we arrive if there in fact is peace. Remain here and gather your strength. The harbor is large, and your boats will be safe. But I will ask one favor in return."

"Anything in our power will be our pleasure to give you. Speak."

"My only desire is to be taken back to my home in Ithaca. When the Cyclops attacked us, I was separated from Odysseus, and could not speak for fear the beast would capture me. All the others escaped, leaving me behind."

"Achaemenids, the gods have not forsaken thee! After you leave us in Inguma's kingdom, I will have my men take you on their ships to Lipari where you may winter. There you will find traders headed back to Ithaca. Is that to your liking?"

"I would be most grateful. After you are rested, I will conduct you to Inguma's kingdom."

"Thank you, Achaemenids."

So, after a restful week they set out inland to visit Inguma. In three days, they arrived in the varied landscape of caves and hills, the smoking Eithné looming behind them, putting forth constant billows of smoke. Karisa was fearful. "Does the God constantly shake and smoke? Will he sometimes shoot fire to kill us?"

Achaemenids responded, "Do not fear him. The Adhranhiti offer constant sacrifice to appease him. They will take you to his temple guarded by the hounds. All will be well."

As they followed the river into the enclosed canyon, they were met by some men. "Who goes there? State your business."

Solax responded, for he spoke the western dialect of the Sicani, which he learned at the knees of his Sicani mother. "We come in peace, brothers. I am Solax of the Elymi from Drepanum. We come to speak with your King. We bring gifts from the west."

"Wait here while we inquire what we should do. I see a familiar face. Is that not one of Odysseus' men? Achaemenids?"

"It is I. I bring you my friends."

The guards went to King Inguma, who was elated that he had visitors from the far reaches of the Sicani kingdom. His mind was now opened to new possibilities. Perhaps, even uniting his kingdom with the west and creating an even stronger kingdom. He had already made inroads with the new Siculi. He was excited about the possibilities. "Guards bring the leaders here into the Anaktoron[62]. See that the others are fed and that accommodations are found. Go now!"

"Hail, King Inguma. We bring you felicitations and gifts from my father King Egestes."

"You are all most welcome to stay with us, but it might be more to your advantage to help my daughter's husband to establish a new village together with the Siculi on a high hill above the Anapo. My daughter, Usoa married Kato, a Siculo, to create a bond between

---

[62] Anaktoron, the princely palace in Pantalica built by the Sicani possibly with Mycenaean assistance. 1200 BC.

our two tribes. The place is not far. There is a wide view of the entire valley and on clear days, Eithné reveals herself."

Kato welcomed Solax and Karisa to his home. Usoa felt an almost immediate bond toward Karisa. This is how their long-lasting friendship began from the very first day.

And this is how the Elymi, Siculi, Sicani, and Minoans merged into a new group of people in the valley of the Anapo. Elymus helped with construction of the first small temple to Aphrodite, for she was a goddess close to the hearts of the people of Ilios. The village grew and prospered for hundreds of years. The people grew intelligent, for they combined the knowledge of the horse and iron from the Siculi with the seafaring of the Trojans, the love of beauty from the Minoans, and the knowledge of the land of the Sicani. These people thrived, safe from the invasions that plagued other parts of the mainland. Their descendants of this hill town would slowly spread down the Anapo, the Irminio, and the Acate, and fill the fertile hills which surrounded the heights of Eithné and Adhrano all the way to the lowlands of the coast. They called themselves Siculi, but they were a mix of people whose combined skills made them stronger and helped them better survive. The small settlement began from humble beginnings to eventually grow into the Hellene city of Akrai.

There was cooperation in the air. Trade was flourishing and the skills of each people increased as they learned from one another, bettering the life of all. Kato brought some of his men to the village on the acropolis. Usoa was instrumental in helping the women increase in the proficiency of their crafts.

First, Kato brought some of his workmen who were smelters to the valley below the acropolis and taught the Sicani how to make fires hotter. Taro, the master smelter and iron monger of the Siculi, began training two young Sicani, Lamax and Ajax. He taught them the secrets of ferrum.

"First, we must build a clay chimney called a bloomery. It will be in the shape of a cone with an opening at the top. There will be a rectangular opening at the bottom and some holes where we will introduce air." Taro was instructing the boys carefully while he started forming the bottom of the furnace with clay bricks. "Lamax, now you arrange the second layer!"

While Lamax carefully built the oven, Taro spoke to Ajax. "You go and collect dry sticks of wood. We must first have the clay dry and become hard. In a few days we will be ready."

Taro was happy with the two Sicani youngsters. They were careful and attentive. Once the furnace was complete, Ajax built a fire inside to harden the clay slowly.

"Taro, where will we get the ore to make the ferrum?"

"We have a supply which our people get with their trade from Elba, an island far to the north. Others bring it from the east. There is a supply chain, but it is not reliable. It has been disrupted for quite a while, but some of our brave seamen have found how to procure small amounts."

While they waited for the clay to harden, Taro was ready to start preparing the charcoal. "Ajax, we must build a pile of wood to make the charcoal. You and Lamax get the men and collect wood. We need lengths about as tall as a man and as wide as a leg. Also, many smaller branches."

Once collected they used a large wooden pole and stood it upright and placed stones in a ring around it, creating a small space for air. Now they piled the logs upright forming a cone around the central pole. They continued layer after layer as the cone grew outward.

"As you arrange the logs, use the smaller branches to fill in the gaps. When creating charcoal air is the enemy, but when making ferrum, air is our friend!" Taro continued.

"Now, cover the pile with damp leaves and grass. Then a layer of thick earth. Then we will light from below and let it burn, and burn, and burn slowly, until it is ready.

After 4 days of burning, the charcoal was ready. They had produced enough to smelt the iron.

The oven had hardened well. Charcoal was placed inside and lit.

"Ajax, take the ore in those baskets and use the hard grinding stones to smash it into small bits."

"Lamax, fill some baskets with charcoal. We will add a small bit of ore through the top of the furnace once the fire is hot, then a layer of charcoal. We will repeat the process from time to time."

"Now, Ajax, get the goat bellies and attach them to the holes at the bottom. Pump them to force air into the oven. Remember, air is the friend of ferrum."

The fire grew hotter and hotter, and a liquid like substance formed near the rectangular window at the bottom of the oven. They used bone scoops to push the liquid out into holes in the earth. As it cooled and hardened, they could see the magic ferrum forming."

Ajax, the younger boy called out, "Lamax, look the greyish metal forms before our eyes. We have done it, we have made ferrum!"

"Well done, well done!"

Kato also had some of his warriors teach a few of the Sicani to ride horses. They let some of the young boys play with a few young colts. Then Kato instructed the warriors to take some of the young Sicani men into the paddock and they taught them how to mount the horse bareback and hold onto the hair on the horse's neck. They circled the fenced area until both the men and the horses were comfortable with each other. Slowly they learned how to make bridles from bone, leather, and rope. The Siculi also had bridles made of bronze and iron, but these were so valuable that they were reserved for the best horsemen of their own tribe. The

Sicani were shown how to attach the bone in the horses' mouth and hold on to the reins when riding. In a few days they were enjoying riding into the fields and found the freedom exciting. It was so superior to riding stubborn asses. These stubborn creatures were not useful for going long distances quickly, whereas the horses would allow intercommunication between the Sicani east and west.

Usoa gathered some of the Siculi women proficient in weaving and dyeing cloth. Nura was highly skilled in the art of dyeing and fixing colors that would not wash out of the cloth. She was also a careful embroiderer. One day she was instructing Ajax's wife, Beraxi. "First you must learn how to find the correct stones to use to fix the colors. These are found near the rocky caves."

Nura took the women to the caves below the acropolis. She pointed to the reddish rocks in one area. "These contain good salts which help set red and brown colors. Beraxi, use the hammer to break some of these stones and place them in your basket. When we get back to the village, we will grind them with the hard stones and place the dust into water. After we strain the mixture, we will have the fixative."

Beraxi was impressed with Nura's knowledge. "Are these the only stones we will gather?"

"No, those greenish ones there and those that are brown also will work. We can sometimes also use common salt for fixing. Others are white like common salt, but you mustn't put them in your mouth. They are highly toxic! We once left a solution out overnight and our cats were found dead the next morning." Nura warned, "Beraxi and the others, beware!"

After an afternoon of gathering baskets of stones, they returned to the village. The next few days were spent preparing the fixatives. Nura also knew which were better for flax, wool, and other fibers.

Nura then put Murexi, Lamax's friend in charge of gathering the plants and animals for the dye preparation.

"Muraxi, attention! We can collect the ink from the gland of squid. This colors our yarn a deep, rich black. We then can use the squid for our dinner. We are lucky that the fishermen have brought us some just this morning!"

"Yes, Nura, we have used this before, but the color washes out after cleaning the cloth a few times!"

"But now with the fixative, it will hold fast! See this cloth. It is over two years old."

Murexi examined the cloth with awe. "It is still beautiful!"

"Now listen carefully to my list. The mucus of these snails in this bucket will give a deep purple; carrots can be boiled for orange, and artichokes, for deep green; red from beets or autumn leaves; brown from oak bark; and blue from a number of deep blue flowers, hyacinths in the spring and indigo later in the summer."

Muraxi was highly impressed at Nura's knowledge. She was happy to learn so that she could better instruct the other Sicani women. "Once we collect these items, what is our next step?"

"The liquids can be collected and used as is, or we can dilute them with water for a weaker color. The others must be boiled, and the water concentrated until we have the desired color intensity. Some of the fixatives will change the color. You will learn more as we start to color the yarn. First the fabrics will be soaked in solutions of one of the salts. Then the fabric will be placed in the dye and left to soak. Then removed and dried and washed repeatedly in the river until it does not bleed, and the correct color is obtained. Again, beware! Let the river run and do not bathe or drink the bleeding water until it has been washed clean by the current."

Muraxi and the other women were very glad to be learning. "Thank you, Nura, we are all grateful for instruction. We will be back tomorrow to work on our yarn."

"You all have worked hard. Go fix dinner for the men now. I

will see you tomorrow a little after dawn to continue."

Usoa, herself, was also skilled in pottery and carving. Her helper was Punoa. They gathered some of the Sicani potters, who were themselves quite skilled in using the wheel and in drying the pots in the kiln. However, their art of decoration was quite primitive in the view of Usoa.

Punoa told the group, "After you have formed the pot, you can take a brush and use one or more of the colors which the dyers have prepared. If you hold the brush steady, like this and move the wheel, you will have a complete circle which closes on itself. You can also carefully move the brush slightly and the wheel slowly and you can create a wave."

As she demonstrated, the Sicani women oohed and ahed as they saw the result of Punoa's work.

"You can do the same with different sticks of varying thicknesses and produce an incised marking."

In the meantime, Usoa was showing others how to paint figures and forms onto various pots.

At the end of the day the Sicani had all begun to understand how their pottery and jewelry could become more beautiful, and the unmarried women kept thinking how their dowery would be more valued than some others of their tribe.

Kato and Usoa, Solax and Karisa, their children, and grandchildren lived in peace in the small town on the acropolis which would become Akrai. A bond was being forged between the Sicani and Siculi. They were proud of how they were advancing the education and skills of the people of Akrai and the surrounding areas. Though their ancestors came from different places, they now were all proud to call themselves Siculi. Akrai was a settlement of the Siculi. Kato and Usoa were considered kind rulers because they had fostered cooperation among the people. Peace continued for many generations.

THE MUSE (2001 AD)

When I first looked upon this cave wall, I was dumbfounded. As I shined my flashlight on the wall the figures glowed back in technicolor! They were covered by the most colorful images I had yet seen in any cave in Sicily. One wall was a picture history filled with horses and primitive wagons depicting warriors driving out men, women, and children from their huts and villages. There were fires which appeared to be burning! They were as amazing as any I had seen in Minoa or Etruria. Some warriors had bound the hands and feet of women and were leading them away. Children were running after their mothers crying. The victors were dressed in bright colors and rode small horses toward what appeared to be the great smoking Etna. I turned to Enzo's notes with great interest.

Later, as I was sitting on my balcony looking out over the blue green Ionian Sea, I saw a man walking up from the beach. I knew he was Archimedes, for he was dressed as an ancient Greek and carried a scroll under his arm. I looked down and greeted him.

"My friend and great philosopher, how are you?"

"I am well, and I see you are working hard on your history."

"I am amazed at how much there is in these notes."

"Yes, you are doing an excellent job. Your writing is accurate and enticing."

"But you have not seen or read what I have written!"

"But I know. We spirits have our ways. I guide your pen with every stroke and inspire your mind."

"I see now. I understand why the prose flow almost effortlessly!"

"Continue my son, you are slowly entering the time of great happenings which will affect the entire world. I will visit again."

And he turned and sat at a table under the trees, unrolled his scroll, and started to draw diagrams of triangles. I returned to reading my notes.

BOOK V

Dutta And Letoni

900 BC

900 BC

Dutta D' Suko – *Siculi Rēks of Akrai who attacks the Sicani and takes the title Lord Duttone. Descended from Suko.*

Letoni – *Siculi Rēks of Akrai after Dutta. He is descended from Kato and Usoa.*

Talax – *captured Sicani King by Dutta.*

Tati – *Siculi Chief from the east of Trinacria.*

CHAPTER 17

CAVE 5, WALL 1 AND 2 (CIRCA 900 BC)

THE WARRIORS

INSCRIPTION K

I, Luxo, record in this cave the victory of the Siculi in southeastern Trinacria. There was bloodshed and suffering. The Siculi became impressed with their own power and strength so that they now wanted full control. Rituli and Kato's softening toward the Sicani did not last through the third generation. Their progeny gained in importance in all the towns and villages of the region. But that was not enough. Arrogance filled the hearts of one leader and some of the warriors. They were encouraged by the leader. The rulers of each place formed a loose confederation, but they mostly deferred to the ruler of what we now call Akrai. The Siculi lusted for more land and riches. Arrogance became a sickness. The war was started by Dutta, lord of future Akrai.

D utta finally made the decision to meet with all the chiefs of the Siculi. They were a loose confederation who all worshiped the Lord of Fire, but usually did not work cooperatively with one another. The fire in Dutta's heart burned like that of Adhrano and he was determined to transfer these embers into a fire which would burn in his warriors. This hatred filled almost the entire tribe. The gathering on the banks of the Anapo was set close to his home in Akrai. The day finally arrived, and he could see the chiefs all arriving on horseback.

"Fellow Siculi, we have prospered in this land since our forefather, Suko, led us here. Remember I am Dutta D'Suko. I share his blood and the fire in his soul. Many of us have the blood of Xavo, who led us through the straights against the evil demons. Others are the inheritors of Daedalus, the god who braved the winds and the sea. Still others have the blood of the brave Trojans who fought valiantly against the Hellenes but were fooled by a trick of the gods. We survived! We have multiplied and now we need more grazing land and homes for our new villagers. Most importantly we need to secure the holy places for our own priests. Let us seize Adhrano, Palici, Pantalica! Now is the time to act!"

Tati, a chief from the east spoke. "Hail, Dutta, so what are you asking? Are you calling for war? Are you asking us to shed blood for this cause of yours? Are you implying that it is also to be our cause?"

"Separately we cannot defeat them. All our clans acting together are invincible! We have the advantage of iron and the horse. If we wait, they will continue to learn, and the battles will be bloodier. Now is the time to act!"

"You speak reason, but our warriors are pleased with their lives and families as they are. What will they gain?"

"We do this for our children. They will have slaves and servants to increase their wealth. They will have the fertile valley of the Irminio! We must also be strong against those that now eye us from afar. The Phoenicians now come only to trade, but they already build large outposts in the west. The Elymi are in the north. Now is the time!"

"Let us talk among ourselves and we will decide tonight."

The chiefs withdrew to the banks of the river and spoke for a long time. Later that afternoon, Tati and the others returned to the meeting place.

"Hail Dutta, our warriors are ready. We placed stones in two jars and the outcome was forty-nine to one. We will join you. We have assembled all the warriors from the slopes of Eithné [63]to Thapsos and the banks of the Anapo. We are ready!"

Dutta now spoke. "Warriors what do you say? Fight or retreat?"

There was some rumbling, but then a sole voice yelled, "Fight!" Then another, and another and soon there was a resounding chorus of "Fight, Fight, Fight!"

In the distance Letoni, of the clan of Kato, stood pondering the decision. They all knew that he was the one discordant vote. He would fight for it was the will of his people. But his heart was heavy. He was a chief of lower Akrai and descended from Kato and Usoa who had joined together the Siculi and Sicani. They had lived in peace for generations. Now under Dutta a distant cousin, the desire for power and wealth had overcome the people's humanity. Letoni had married a Sicani from Adhrano who was descended from Daedalus. They had ten fine children and he wanted them to live in peace. But for now, his life had been decided by the tribe, and nothing could be done but fall in line. Dutta then approached his chief warrior. "Goro, you know our plan. We first head west driving the Sicani from the valleys of the Rivers Irminio and Acate. This is fertile land which we need for our grazing and farming. We take their women and children as slaves. Then we head to Innessa and drive the rest of the Sicani west. This will be our land."

"We have gone over the plan with all our men. Their horses are rested, the wagon wheels inspected, and the wagons filled with provisions. The bowmen have used the finest wood from

---

[63] Eithné - Etna

the forests of the mountain to make their bows and arrows with heads of ferrum. They are ready."

Chief Tati now decided he must make one more recommendation. "Men what do you say? Shall we appoint Dutta Rēks?" This was a name which meant leader of chiefs. Soon they all were shouting, "Rēks Dutta! Rēks Dutta! Rēks Dutta!"

"Thank you. I accept your appointment. I swear on the Twins that I will not forsake our cause. Good! We attack at the mouth of the Irminio at dawn."

Dutta had managed to persuade the chiefs with promises of power and wealth. Change was in the air. Dutta was inspired by the tales of the mythical Suko, who led the Siculi from the mainland in the days of darkness when they had believed the world was ending. His bravery enabled the tribe not only to survive, but to flourish. The warriors and the priests were also inspired by Adhrano, who blew smoke and ash into the air and sent a river of fiery red glowing, burning earth into the sea. Dutta was strongly built and athletic and possessed the fire of the mountain in his heart. Even though he shared the ancient blood of Minoa and that of the Sicani, he was first a Siculi. He regarded his tribe as the first among the others and he demanded complete loyalty. Loyalty first to himself, then to the tribe. But he was all important. Those who did not swear loyalty to him met immediate death. The Siculi honored him, bowed to him, did his will, but did so out of deep fear, for his revenge was swift and deadly. He considered himself a god because of his bloodline. His word was truth and there was no other. Loyalty to him, *Rēks* Dutta, came above all else.

And so, as dawn lit the eastern horizon, the Sicani rose to begin their normal routines of fishing and herding. They did not expect anything out of the ordinary. The women were preparing a horse stew for the men. At once a cry went up from the surrounding hilltops! "Warriors, warriors from the east!"

The women dropped their ladles. Dishes and pots dropped to the ground as they ran to pick up their young. They shouted, "Children, children, run, run to the hills. Warriors, attack, attack!"

The men ran to grab their bronze swords and the few iron ones which they had managed to pilfer from their Siculi neighbors. The Siculi warriors were brutal, for Dutta had filled their hearts with hatred and filled their minds with bigotry.

Just before the battle, Dutta had insighted his troops, "Men, warriors, today you do Adhrano's work. Our allegiance is to our old god whom we called Adar before we were contaminated with the Sicani. These animals, these Sicani, are here to rape our women and children, and to pillage our villages of our superior metals. We are the chosen race, chosen by Adar, to rule and to conquer. We are superior, for we have ferrum and horse skills. We need to rid our land of this pestilence that begins to infect us and will contaminate our children with their seed! Now to arms! To Arms! Destroy and conquer!"

The men were lifted to an extreme rage as they mounted their horses, prepared their weapons, and descended upon the unsuspecting Sicani with unbridled brutality. They not only killed but decapitated the bodies. Blood flowed to fill the streams in the valley. It was a massacre.

The women and children ran to the caves in the hills. The attack was swift and ruthless. They were no match for the iron swords, iron tipped arrows, and maces. The village was not large and those men that lost their weapons were tied up by the warriors that still followed the ancient code of battle. Not all the Siculi succumbed to brutality.

The women and children remaining in hiding were found and bound. Dutta himself satisfied himself with a few of the young girls cringing under some bushes. This made him feel more of a god. He knew of the gods' exploits and now felt that he was attaining greater heights. He felt power in every muscle of his being. Soon he would be master of Trinacria!

The Sicani hidden in the far caves escaped into the hills and forests to the north. They hoped they could reach the more secure places where the Sicani had larger settlements.

Letoni, who had cast the opposing vote, also fought, but he fought as a gallant warrior who showed mercy to those who lost their weapons and capitulated. The behavior of some of his fellow warriors sickened him. Letoni had always had a special devotion to Eleos[64]. He had inherited this love of the goddess from his ancestor Usoa who always carried her amulet around her neck. She had used her great skill to make it an exquisite representation of Eleos. It had been passed down through the generations. Letoni's mother had given it to him, and it adorned his chest. He must act, but how?

The Siculi pursued the fleeing Sicani for a few hours, then rested. Dutta gave the order that they now should consolidate their victory and posted guards in strategic places. The captured people were enslaved and were indentured to start building huts and rock houses for the new inhabitants who would soon arrive from the populous east. As the news spread north and west the Sicani began fleeing further beyond the mountains. By the end of the summer the two valleys and the land between the two rivers was now Siculi territory. Even the town of Adhrano on the slopes of the great smoking mountain now belonged to the Siculi.

The King of the Sicani, Talax, was under guard by the Siculi warriors. He decided that he must sue for peace so that no more land would be taken. Dutta agreed to see him in Akrai.

"Dutta, I had thought we had treaties from our forefathers to live peacefully. This was a surprise and a disappointment. I have nothing to offer you now but myself. Let us agree to peace. You

---

[64] Eleos -Ε'Λεοζ - the goddess of pity and mercy.

have taken much of our wealth, and many of my people. What more do you want from us?"

"Talax, I am satisfied with what we have done. We needed room to expand and workers to help us survive. You see our power. We are a superior race, and we will control your people to serve us. Already ships are seen on the horizon and traders come to establish centers. You have done nothing to prepare. I accept your peace if you will remain in the borders we have set. You must honor me as Rēks and pay tribute when you cross our land and when you trade with us. So, I have spoken, so it is."

"I am not happy, but I will agree. You may take me as hostage, but please let my family go west with my people."

"You may also go if you respect the new boundaries. You must do as I say and instruct your people as I command. Unless there is trouble, I will let your people be. In time, we may both be fighting a foreign foe."

Dutta now turned to the crowd of chieftains. "We have won a great victory. It is because the gods have honored me as one of their own. From now forward you may all address me as Lord Duttone, God of War. When you come into my presence you will all prostrate yourselves! So, it is proclaimed, so it is!"

Talax and his family prostrated themselves. "So be it. Lord Duttone!

"Let Adhrano and the Palici be witness to our agreement and strike either of us if we go against our oath.

Talax rose to his knees in front of Duttone, "I swear to uphold our words, great Lord!"

At that moment, an iron arrow crossed the sky and struct Lord Duttone in the neck. Blood spurted on all the prostrated Sicani, and Duttone fell squirming to the ground. All stared motionless. No one approached to help the proclaimed god, for they all expected Adhrano to come to Duttone's aid. He was dead in minutes.

Talax muttered under his breath, "Truly he thought he was a god!"

For a great while, no one moved. Then Tati was able to collect enough breath to step forward. "The great Lord is truly dead. You, soldiers, lift his body and take him to that house, there by the river. Women, clean the body. Prepare it for burial. Tomorrow, we will place him in the large cave in the manner of our tribe. Collect his sword, shield, and valuables to be placed beside him. All, now go and prepare for the solemn day! Go!"

No one saw who shot the arrow, and no one really cared to find the culprit. The chiefs would meet later that week to select a new chief, but they already had someone in mind who was more in line with their history and was the natural choice.

The leader of the guards approached Talax. "Duttone had agreed to set you free before he died. Go now. Take your family, and go, but leave your slaves and servants. Go in peace!"

After the mourning period for Duttone had passed, the chiefs met to select a new Rĕks. The council agreed that there had been too much bloodshed. Many brave warriors had been lost under Duttone's rule. Now that the Sicani had been driven from the eastern side of Trinacria out of the valleys of the Irminio, Acate, Anapo, and Simento, from the entire eastern coast, from Pantalica, and from the rich land surrounding Eithné[65], the Siculi only wished to live in peace. So, now, they looked for a leader of the house of Kato who was reasonable, powerful, and smart. They chose Letoni.

The warriors and members of the tribe were gathered. One respected old man spoke first, "Letoni, we wish you to be chief of the Siculi of Akrai and the Anapo valley. Lord Letoni, do you accept our decision?" The leader of the guards bowed as he spoke to Letoni.

---

[65] Eithné - Etna

"I accept your vote, but I will be called Rēks Letoni as my forebears have. As the chief of the most powerful clan, I also accept the responsibility of governing in cooperation with all the other clans of the Siculi. I wish us to live in peace. Praise Adhrano! All Praise!'

BOOK VI

THE GREEKS

735 - 480 BC

700-400 BC

Strategos – *general*
Gamoroi– *nobility*
Killichiroi – *commoners*
Rēks – *title for rulers of Akrai*
Oecist – *(Οικιστηζ) – founder of a colony*

735 BC

Actaeon – *handsome Corinthian youth attached by Archias*
Antigone - Hellene daughter of Archias
Archias – *Oecist (founder) of Siracusa from Corinth*
Azara – *wife of Rēks Iagu*
Iagu – *Siculi Rēks of Akrai marries Azara*
Loto – *Siculi son of Iagu and marries Antigone*
Marsu – *Loto's assistant*
Melissus – *Actaeon's father*
Nadda – *village woman translator for Loto*

664 -550 BC

Astrax – *Hellenized Siculi son of Iaxo and brother of Elox*
Daskon – *member of the Siracusan Gamoroi sent to establish Akrai*
Demetrius – *Hellene member of the Killichiroi class*
Elox – *Hellenized Siculi son of Iaxo*
Iaxo – *Hellenized Siculi Rēks of Akrai*
Menekolos – *member of the Siracusan Gamoroi sent to establish Akrai*
Naro – *Hellenized Siculi Rēks of Akrai, son of Loto and Antigone*

Menekolos – *member of the Siracusan Gamoroi sent to establish Akrai*

Tyro – *Hellene member of the Siracusan Gamoroi ruling council*

Zeno – *leader of the Gamoroi of Siracusa who has the idea to build of satellite cities like Akrai*

480 BC

Culox – *Hellenized Siculi Rēks of Akrai*

Dimioyrgos – *"Creator" descendent of Aeneas and Solax's daughter tasked with building the aqueduct to Siracusa*

Gelon I – *Hellene Tyrant of Siracusa*

Parmenedies – *Assistant architect to Dimioyrgos*

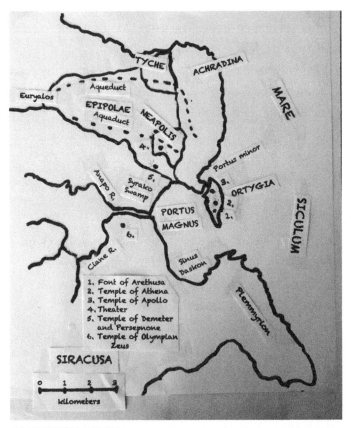

MAP OF SIRACUSA

FONTE ARETUSA
ORTIGIA HARBOR
(Inspirock.com)

ALLA FONTE ARETUSA
BY GAETANO MIANO

Fonte Aretusa che dal mare sorgi
in una conca di papiri cinta,
ove colombe ed anatre tu scorgi
all'acque fare cornice variopinta,
nel Mito contro il fiume Alfeo insorgi
che brama in corpo te, a lui avvinta;
al vento allor dell'Elide ti porgi
per sfuggirgli, nel mare giù sospinta.
E ricompari in terra d'Archimede
Con gentili sembianza di sorgente,
tu Ninfa, Naiade di stirpe erede.
Ma Alfeo, correndo il mar nel suo profondo,
riva di Ortigia bacia, fresca, aulente,
e dolce polla a te mesce giocondo.

Secondo la mitologia greca, la ninfa delle acque dolci d'Arcadia, Aretusa, per sfuggire al fiume Alfeo, si getto in mare dalle coste del monte Elide. Ricomparve in una piccola insenatura dell'isola di Ortigia, nel porto di Siracusa, sotto forma di fonte, ma Alfeo correndo sotto il mare, la raggiunse e mescolo le proprie acque alle sue, trasformandosi in una polla d'acqua dolce zampillante, detta occhio della Zillica.

AT THE FONT OF ARETUSA
TRANSLATED BY JOE MIANO

O Font of Aretusa, surging from the sea
Girdled in a papyrus shell
Framing doves and ducks artistically
In a splashing waters' spray.
Against the rising river, Alfeo
Craving your body's beauty capture –
The wind, Elide, arising, holds and hides you
And in the sea submerges you.
In Archimedes' land you reemerge
A gentle flowing spring –
You of Nymph and Naiad lineage.
But O! Alfeo running deeply through the sea
Ortygia's fresh and stately bank kisses
And with your waters joyfully mixes.

In Greek Mythology, the nymph of sweet water of Arcadia, Aretusa, to escape the river Alfeo (Alpheus) threw herself into the sea near Mt. Elide. She reappeared in a small creek on the Isle of Ortygia, near the sea in the port of Sicacusa in the form of a fountain, but Alfeo, running through the sea, rejoined her and mixed his waters, transforming them into a gushing sweet water spring right by the sea called the Eye of Zillica.

THE MUSE (2001 AD)

On another visit in the 1970s, Enzo had taken me down from the Acropolis of Akrai to see the river Anapo. It rises at Mt. Lauro just north of the town and meanders down to the coast to Siracusa.

It is a river of myth connected with Greece and the sea. But today Enzo was going to show me the aqueduct constructed by the Greeks in 480 BC to bring water to the great city of Siracusa, which one day would become the largest in the world. Most of the waterway was underground, but as it approached the great city near Neapolis, the inland part of Siracusa, we could see bridges of arches.

This day filled me with fascination, and I needed to find out more about the Greek architects and the building of Akrai, itself, begun in 664 BC to protect the northeast territory of Greek Siracusa, settled by the Corinthians in 734 BC. When the Greeks arrived, it was inhabited by the Siculi, and before that by the Sicani. I was anxious to get back to Enzo's notes to find out more. I waited for my friend to help me see this Akrai in each previous incarnation. Where was he?

Then suddenly, as formed out of dust, he was there before me.

"My friend, my friend! My excitement is heightened, for now my father's forbearers started arriving on this blessed island! They were a varied group. You will find explorers, adventurers, thieves, reprobates, philosophers, tyrants, and good men. But remember, they were not only my ancestors, but also yours! Come, follow quickly!"

CHAPTER 18

CAVE 5 (CIRCA 735 BC)

THE COMING OF THE GREEKS

INSCRIPTION A

I, Luxo, now am drawing upon our own Siculi elders and their legends at the time of the arrival of the first Hellenes. First, arriving near the base of Eithné[66] at a place which they later named Naxos, and shortly after, they arrived at the mouth of the Anapo, where we had a small settlement. The sailors arrived from Corinth and started to build an outpost on the isle of Ortigia, later the center of Siracusa. The island formed one side of the great protected harbor with only a small opening connected to the Ionian Sea. We did not oppose them for there were many and they arrived in various places along the coast. We first assumed that they wished to trade. We began fortifying our hilltop in Akrai and our villages on the Anapo and waited.

A t this time Rēks Iagu, Lord of the Siculi, currently ruled the region between the Anapo and the Irminio. His wife was called Azara. The Siculi were still organized into small independent chiefdoms, but Iagu was the most powerful. He ruled from the high hilltop fortress with of view of Etna to the northeast and

---

[66] Eithné - Etna

Thapsos and the sea to the east. All respected his wisdom and fair rule. He was descended from Rēks Letoni who was called 'The Good' and who came to power after the evil Duttone was shot to death by Letoni's arrow, so unexpectedly almost two hundred years before. But the legend lived in the memory of the elders. Letoni the Good brought stability and prosperity to the Siculi and treated both the Sicani and Elymi with fairness. Almost eight generations had passed since Letoni ruled.

Iagu held the inherited title of Rēks, which had been passed down from the time of Rituli. Rituli had formed a bond with the Sicani. His son Kato had married the Sicani Usoa, so their descendants shared the blood of the first inhabitants of Trinacria. Like Letoni, Iagu was a just fair ruler who consulted the other chiefs when decisions were needed involving all the regions. There still were skirmishes among the clans over territory, and with some Sicani, but in general peace reigned. On this fortified hilltop above the Anapo[67], the small wooden Temple of Aphrodite has stood ever since the time of Elymus, who had helped in its planning. The temple had a stone pediment with large wooden poles supporting the roof. The poles were cut from the nearby forest and were each 15 feet high. They were carved with the primitive Triskele, three spirals representing three legs. The Iberian Sicani had brought this symbol to Trinacria when they arrived. It represented three men striving to reach the sun. Later all the tribes of Trinacria had adopted it to represent the island, each of the three spirals in some representations, or three feet in others, representing the three capes of this triangular land. The spirals on this temple were three circulating feet with a circle representing the mountain of Eithné[68] in the center. From the wall to the roof, the temple was open to the air, as was the front

---

[67] Later called Akrai by the Hellenes
[68] Eithné - Etna

facing the great mountain. This was so the spirits of the ancestors and the gods could pass through. This was the belief of the Siculi in building their temples. Daedalus would have been proud of the temple's appearance and positioning.

Iagu summoned his faithful second in command, Loto, who had been at the coast watching the developments on the island from the mainland across from Ortygia[69]. Ortygia was the island where the Hellenes had begun their settlement. He also had spoken to some of the Siculi who lived on the coast and who had had brief encounters with the Hellenes. Iagu thought for a while and then told Loto, "We need to talk officially to these Hellenes. I wish to find out if they are here in peace or wish to conquer us."

Loto responded, "Iagu, I have been watching. The Hellenes have brought miners and masons. They are not only building wooden shelters, but now are beginning a large building. They have sent the miners and slaves they have captured to the caves on the mainland. Some are Sicani, but others our own Siculi! They are excavating stones from the caves on the mainland near the island and starting work on foundations. Maybe for a temple? The Hellenes have laid out cord making square shapes in the sand on the isle of Ortygia. They seem to be making a permanent village."

Iagu thought for a moment, then said, "Let us send some emissaries with the excuse of setting up trade to find out what their intentions may be. You go and take Marsu with you. Go as soon as you are ready. Take them some of our produce and wool, and the shiny stones from the mountain. Also take them some Aurichalcum[70] which we have received from Iberia by way of the Sicani."

---

[69] Ortygia - Ορτυγια - the name meaning quail which is the island on which the first Greeks settled and became the center of Siracusa.
[70] Aurichalcum - a rare ore Plato mentions containing platinum, tin, zinc, and copper.

Loto looked pleased with Iagu's decision. "We will leave first thing in the morning."

"Adhrano and Aphrodite guard you in your journey."

So, the two left early with three horses, one laden with sample items. It took them about four hours to arrive on the coast. They stopped on the mainland just across from the isle of Ortygia. They stopped at a small mixed village of Siculi and Sicani situated close to the marsh called Syrako[71]. These villagers reported that the Hellenes were peaceful and had come to them to barter for some fresh fruits and meat, exchanging metal coins, lovely pottery, and fine cloth. The Hellenes had captured and enslaved other locals from outlying areas who did not cooperate. For some reason, the foreigners were kind to the villagers near the Syrako. The head of the village sent Loto and Marsu to a village woman called Nadda, who was also an unmarried healer, herbalist, and seer.

Loto approached Nadda. "Good day, I understand from the headman that you are Nadda and know something of the Hellenes."

Nadda gave a cold stare at Loto. After a while, she said, "Yes, that is my name. And who are you?"

"I am called Loto, and this is my friend, Marsu. We come from the highlands and my chief, Rēks Iagu, needs to know about the Hellenes."

Nadda did not like being taken for an ordinary village woman and looked directly into Loto's eyes. "We, of course, have all heard of Iagu. He is respected and protects our lands. He drove some of the Sicani raiders from our lands in the time of my grandfather. Welcome to our small village. We have been watching the Hellenes for some time. I have learned the tongue of my ancestors, the Mycenaeans who were from Thapsos many generations ago. I have already spoken to the soldiers who came with some workmen to

---

[71] Συρακω, Syrako – the ancient name of the area where the name Siracusa derives. It means place of swamps.

mine rocks. They wish to build a temple to their sun god. He is called Apollo."

Loto looked at the old woman in awe. "I have heard of this god. The legend of our clan is that our leaders are descended from the mighty Daedalus who arrived here on wings. He worshiped this Apollo and built a temple to him in Kamikos."

Nadda then decided, "I can help you communicate with the soldiers who guard the mainland against all those who would venture to Ortygia. When I enter one of my trances, I see that they are not to be feared if we are cooperative. This may change in the future, but now they are still few, and perhaps we can gain their trust."

"So, Nadda, you will accompany us to meet the Hellenes?"

"Yes, Loto, but it is hot now. I will show you where you can rest with my brothers. We will leave once the sun drops lower."

In the evening, Loto, Marsu, and Nadda mounted their horses and set off for the short journey to the island. At the narrow inlet separating Ortygia from the mainland, they dismounted and saw that there were Corinthian soldiers standing near a rope ferry which they had built to cross the inlet. These Hellenes had arrived very recently and were busy building their settlement. One soldier approached Loto and spoke rapidly with authority. Nadda looked directly at the soldier and said in perfect Hellene, "Halt your speech! You think the whole world speaks your tongue? I am a local villager who has descended from some of the early Mycenaeans who came here long before even your great grandfather was alive. They first settled in Kamikos, the city of Daedalus. His family later migrated here to this coast. I too am a Hellene. Speak to me and I will translate. This is our land, and we welcome you, but you are here because we have allowed it. It is our hope we can learn from each other."

Loto and Marsu, from the small Siculi inland village, had

not seen Hellenes before. They could not understand, but they were amazed at the authority with which this woman spoke. They noticed that the soldier's face was in utter shock because he had not encountered anyone yet who could express themselves so eloquently in their dialect, let alone any woman. He shook his head in agreement then said, "I am Aegeus, the protector of our settlement. I am in charge and ordered to protect it from intruders by the will of the mighty Oecist[72] Archias, founder and colonizer of Ortygia, this quail shaped island. I am ordered to find out what business you might have in visiting us?"

"Loto and Marsu are here to inquire about setting up a trade between you, Corinthians, and the Siculi who live in the towns along the Anapo and Irminio valleys. Others of us live far upland near our sacred Adhrano. I am called Nadda and have been chosen to translate for Rēks Iagu, who is lord of this region. He rules from a hill town close to where the river Anapo rises. Loto is his trusted warrior and servant. We wish to cross to see your leader. You say he is Archias. Arrange this for us."

Aegeus said, "I will allow you to cross under guard. You must leave your horses here with us. We will see that they are cared for and fed. On Ortygia you will be led to a guest hut where you can spend the night while we speak to Archias."

Nadda responded, "Very well. This sounds like an agreeable arrangement to me. Let me ask Loto and see if he agrees."

After a short tete-a-tete with Marsu and Loto, she spoke up to Aegeus. "We three agree. Let us unload our goods and cross over."

"Nadda, I will have my men help you unload. Welcome to Ortygia."

Nadda, Loto, and Marsu were led to a small hut with hay spread on the floor. They placed their blankets down and were

---

[72] Oecist – the leader chosen to found a new city state by the leaders of the mother city state.

ready to sleep after the long trip, but a young woman, accompanied by two others carrying large crocks containing food, entered.

She spoke to Nadda in Hellene. "I am Antigone, the daughter of Archias. I am here to welcome you. You have traveled far and must be hungry. We have brought you lamb cooked with herbs in broth and mixed with faro. I hope it is to your liking. The other crock contains bread and sheep's cheese we call feta."

Nadda spoke. "Thank you, Antigone. This is Loto and there, Marsu. We are pleased for your welcoming us."

"Eat and rest now, and you will meet my father tomorrow evening. Sleep well. You have nothing to fear from us."

Loto stood staring at the beautiful Helene maiden. His mouth partially open.

Old Nadda looked at him disgustedly. "Close your mouth, young man. It does not suit you to dribble thus!"

Early the next morning the Siculi trade delegates rose early and walked by the sea. They had not seen this lovely part of Trinacria for many years. The moon-shaped crescent harbor was breathtaking to behold, and at the base of the island, a sweet water spring brought fresh water right by the sea. It was a holy place, and even the Siculi and Sicani had worshiped their gods there.

Loto spoke. "Nadda, thank you for all your help. I think you need to teach me Hellene so I can communicate with these men. I have a feeling that we will benefit from our mutual co-operation with them."

"Yes, Loto, they seem to be good people, but you must be strong. Speak to them with authority. After all, you are Iagu's son. Someday you will be leader."

Loto said, "I am learning. But you must not let them know who I am yet. We must first find out their intentions."

Nadda agreed. "I understand. There will be a time for that!"

As they sat by the cool spring surrounded by papyrus and the setting crescent moon above the sea, Antigone approached them.

Antigone spoke first. "I see you have found the most beautiful part of Ortygia! I come here often to meditate and think of the history and myths of my people, the Corinthians. I was sad to leave my beautiful Corinth, but now I have made peace with our leaving. We have travelled far and are trying to build a place of our own here."

Loto stared at Antigone as if for the first time. Her face was truly beautiful in the early dawn, reflecting the fading moonlight. Nadda interpreted as he spoke, "Yes, this is a fine place, and the water emanating from the spring cools the summer air."

Antigone responded, "Yes, this is truly a sacred place. It is called the font of Arethusa, the lovely nymph who lived in a place called Arcadia, close to my home, Corinth. One night as she was bathing in the river Alpheus, she had no idea he was a river god who flowed down from Elis[73] into the Ionian Sea. Upon seeing her great beauty, Alphaeus fell in love and began making advances. She fled wishing to remain chaste, for she was an attendant of Artemis (Diana), our goddess of the hunt. Artemis heard her prayers. The goddess turned her into a cloud so she could escape. As Arethusa began perspiring in fear, she melted into a fast-running stream which Artemis caused to run under the sea and resurface very far from Arcadia, here, in Ortygia, as an eternal spring."

"But what of Alpheus?" asked Nadda.

"Ah," remarked Antigone, "So, here the story shows how persistence changes feelings. Alpheus continued to pursue his love by flowing under the sea. Upon arriving here, he mingled his waters with hers! They now both inhabit these waters, sacred to lovers. Many find their soul mates here. It is a symbol of union. All love is blessed by the holy waters."

---

[73] Elis – the region in the western Peloponnese on the Greek mainland. On the same peninsula as Corinth.

"I see. Perhaps two people bathing in this water would find a common bond; would see each other in a different light?" Loto said coyly, shuffling his sandal in the sand.

"Perhaps, but I have bathed here many times," retorted Antigone, "and I have not noticed any change. But Arethusa's story continues in that she was an empathetic nymph. In flowing underground, she saw Persephone in Hades. Persephone told her mother, Demeter, and tried to persuade Demeter to help Persephone out of her predicament with Hades. Arethusa petitioned the goddess to help her daughter. She told Demeter that eternal winter would destroy mankind. There would be no love and no children. But that is another story."

Loto marveled at Antigone's poise and intelligence. He was enjoying himself but was also afraid of these new feelings. This woman was certainly different and enticing. He must get this out of his mind for there was business to pursue.

Antigone then suggested, "Let us retire now. I will come to you in the evening so we can meet the Oecist."

Nadda left Loto and went to sit by Marsu on the other side of the spring. Nadda, especially, was observing Loto and Antigone with her long nose raised in the air and squinty eyes. "Marsu, I hope Loto's infatuation does not prevent him from making a clear assessment of these colonizers. They seem peaceful now, but as their number grow, I foresee the destruction of our ways. We must take care!"

Early that evening, Antigone approached and led them to a large hut. They entered and she bowed to a man sitting in a large chair. Nadda and the others followed suit. "Siculi, this is Lord Archias, Oecist[74] of Ortygia. May I present, Loto, Marsu, and Nadda."

Archias acknowledged them and said "Welcome, you have

---

[74] Oecist – the founder of a colony

travelled a long way. I understand you come to establish trade. I would like to encourage trade with the local inhabitants for our mutual benefit. We will need many items and we have much to offer from the east. This seems a rich land with many benefits."

Loto spoke, and Nadda interpreted. "My lord, may I speak?" Archias, "Go on."

Loto began, "We have brought some goods for you and your men to inspect. They are just a sample of what we can offer you. We also have connections with the western people who trade with Iberia and Libya. I hope we can come to an arrangement."

Archias shook his head, "Yes, you can speak with my man who oversees trade, and we can later set the terms. But for now, I will show you what we intend. Follow me."

Archias took them through the town and showed them the beginning of the first large construction. It was to be the temple of Apollo at the center of the island. The layout was very large and around it, there were smaller squares. Archias indicated that these were houses for the nobles of the village, called the Gamoroi. It seemed to Loto that the Hellenes were here to stay.

The next day the Siculi spoke with the trade minister, and they set the terms of trade. As they were packing to return to Akrai, Antigone approached them. "I hope you have had a good stay and I wish you a safe journey back."

Loto responded, "Thank you. Yes, it was very profitable for us, and I hope for you."

"Loto, this is my first sea journey, and I am a long way from home. My mother died from a sickness before we left Corinth. It was not that long ago, and my father decided I should come with him to this place. Not many women came on this first voyage. More will be coming. Nadda, I hope you will visit me often. I will inform the guards that they should let you pass on the ferry any time you wish."

"Yes, thank you. I will be glad to visit you. I live close, near the delta."

"I will look forward to that, Nadda."

Loto stared at the young Antigone and could no longer resist his inclination to speak. "Antigone, I hope some time I can return and take you up the Anapo to my home. It is forested and beautiful. We could also venture close to Etna to give adoration to Adhrano, our god of fire and shaking."

"I would love to see your fine land. I will ask my father."

"Χαιρε!" (So long for now!) We must be off. It is a long way."

"Χαιρετε!"

Loto visited Ortygia many times bringing goods to trade. Each time he visited Antigone and they became more friendly. He began to realize that this was becoming improper, for it was the parents who arranged for the young to become familiar. One day he approached Archias and said, "I want to show Antigone some of our land. Do I have your permission to escort her to my home near the source of the Anapo and to the sacred caves of Pantalica[75] nearby and Mt. Lauro? Nadda and anyone else you may wish may accompany us."

"Loto, she is of noble blood, and you are just a commoner. I am not sure I can give my permission. I have noticed you visiting her each time you come to trade. She speaks of you often, and I am beginning to be concerned." Nadda was there to help translate, but Loto had learned quite a bit of Hellene over this first year of trading.

"Lord Archias. I have not been completely honest. Rēks Iagu has sent me to see if you truly come in peace. I am satisfied that you wish us no harm. We have extended our good faith toward you by our trade and friendship. Our blood line goes far back. Among our

---

[75] I have used this name for the caves for clarity. It was not named until the times of the Arabs, centuries later.

ancestors are powerful Sicani and Minoans. We descend directly from King Cocalus and the great inventor Daedalus. There have been very powerful chiefs among us. Since we now have known each other for over a year, I feel I owe you my complete honesty. I apologize if there was deception, but I was ordered by my father not to reveal who I was. Even now I break my word."

"So, you are Iagu's son! I felt there was more to you than a mere trader. I too needed to test you. There are many things in my past which I hide from the people here. I have not been the most honest and worthy of men, but now I try to be an example for my two daughters. We all are playthings of the gods! Now we can be on equal footing. I see your Hellene is improving."

"Yes, Nadda is helping me learn. I wish to also learn to read your script. Maybe there is a good teacher I can work with? And what of my request about Antigone accompanying us to my village which I see you have named Akrai. I understand it refers to the heights on which it was built?"

"Yes, indeed. It's meaning is 'peak'. You are so full of questions! Your mind is quick. Yes, there are scribes here who can teach you and I suppose a short trip can be arranged for Antigone. I will send some guards with you."

"And I will ask Nadda to accompany Antigone. They seem to be good friends."

"So be it."

"Thank you, Lord Archias!"

The entourage left Ortygia on a very lovely spring day. The rain had stopped, and the wildflowers had come out to greet the travelers. Marsu led the expedition on his brown horse. Loto followed with Antigone who rode a pure white stallion. She had a special garment made in black wrapped around her legs so that she could straddle the horse and wore a short blue cape over her shoulders. Her luxurious hair was tied into a long ponytail, and he thought she seemed the Goddess Athena riding her white stallion. She only lacked the hunter's bow. She was followed closely by Nadda and trailed by the two guards whom Archias had assigned as protectors.

They followed the course of the Anapo which wound gently on the plains. After about two hours they stopped for some refreshment of bread, cheese, and wine. The wine was a special variety that Loto had brought with him. It was made from grapes that grew near a small village just south of Syrako marsh.

They resumed their trek after they had rested. Now the plain gave way to rocky uplands.

As they trekked, Marsu and the captain of the guards, who had picked up enough of each other's languages, began a conversation. "What would entice someone like Archias to leave his homeland and establish a new settlement so far away? I understand he was a member of a Gamoroi (noble) family."

"Oh, my!" exclaimed the captain, "There is a story here, but I do not feel at total liberty to tell you all the details for it affects Antigone." He was silent for a while, thinking. Then he said, "However, it is quite general knowledge among the Hellenes in Ortygia. It will be only a matter of time before all know the story.

"Archias exiled himself voluntarily from Corinth. His behavior as a young man brought him to a very low status. I feel his choosing exile elevated him to the great man he is today. There are still some that hold his acts against him, but he has come here with his supporters. As a young man, he was foolish, like many of us, and he committed a great sin and an atrocity."

"My, my! I had no idea. He seems a good and fair ruler now. How did he learn his lesson?"

"It took a great while, caused much suffering, and the intervention of the gods! Let me begin at the beginning.

"When Archias was young he fell in love like so many of us

Hellenes did. His object of desire was a young, handsome, but modest, Corinthian named Actaeon. If only Archias had awakened to the fact that there was no way this love had any possibility of being returned or had this realization struck him in the beginning, he would have grown out of it and prospered.

"However, that was not to be. He was possessed by unreasonable, lustful desire. He conspired to get invited to the home of Melissus, Actaeon's father. Archais tried to abduct the young boy. In the melee that followed, Acteon was killed. Melissus' could not be consoled."

Marsu looked shocked. He could not believe that this was the Archais with whom he had supper and with whom they had agreeable trade deals. "Captain, I am more than shocked that the Oecist had so little control. Zeus save us!"

"But the story blackens, before there is some light! The next day Acteon's father, Melissus, so distraught and not in his right mind, went to Isthmia, east of Corinth, and climbed the heights to Poseidon's Temple. There he began invoking the God, "Poseidon, God of the deep and of storms, and of quakes! You mighty God of the Twelve! Hear me! I have been woefully wronged! My beloved son was taken in his youth! He was my favorite, and Archais slew him for his lust! Hear me, I seek vengeance for the wrong. I seek your wrath for his murder and dishonor. For this I give you my supreme sacrifice!'

"And with these final words, he threw himself from the heights to the rocks below."

Marsu was abreast of the captain, as their horses trotted along. His eyes were transfixed on the captain. "What tragedy! All this evil because of Archais. Is there any redemption?"

"Truly it is dark, but more is to come! But as we know, the gods are notorious in their punishments. Poseidon did not spare anyone from his wrath. All of Corinth suffered drought and famine for

nearly two years. That was how long it took for Archais to come
to his senses.

"Finally, realizing that all that had befallen Corinth, to his
family, and to his friends, Archias went up to Delphi to consult
the oracle.

'Archais, Archais!
Your transgression
Your lustful desire
Is a common one!
That was not sin.
But the greater sin
Was what drove you to lose control!
The act of destroying a soul,
One so young and innocent
Who wished you no harm,
The handsome, youngster, Actaeon!
And then your evil magnified
In causing the respected Melissus
To end his own life!
So now, to end this curse's strife:
Exile, exile, yourself!
So, now, the loss all Corinth has felt
Will be yours for evermore
By leaving this polis,
Seeing it no more!'

"So Archais gathered his wife and a group of his loyal friends,
along with a few possessions and sailed for Trinacria, a place as
far away from Corinth as he could imagine. Antigone was his last
born and was a joyful, energetic child. But, as they prepared to
leave, Archais' wife was overtaken by a dreadful plague, and he

had to bury her before boarding his ship. His loss now was total, except for his daughters. The story is known to you now, Marsu. They landed and founded Ortygia, which prospers. He and his two daughters are all he now has. The wrath of the gods took his wife, his home, and the respect of many in Corinth. He now shares the grief that Melissus and Acteon's family had felt. The gods' ways are mysterious, but there was justice."

"Captain, my heart is heavy, especially for Antigone. She seems a fine woman. Does she know the story of her father?"

"Yes, she heard it some time ago, and was saddened by it. But she is strong."

"I hope that is true. But Archais, though still young, seems a changed man."

"I believe he is. There was redemption. He is a good ruler.[76]"

So now Marsu understood what swords Antigone must have piercing her heart. Loto must know these hardships which she has endured. He was determined to find the right time to relay all this to Loto. With this heavy burden Marsu and the guard rode silently toward Akrai.

They reached the hills and mountains where the blue green clear river cut a gorge into the brown stone of the mountains. They now found the path which slowly climbed up the hills to their destination which was over 500 meters in height.

Antigone stopped and looked over the gorge to the crystal stream below. "O! how beautiful! It seems to be a place of the gods. I am so happy that you brought me here, Loto!"

"I am glad you like my homeland. It is rich in the gifts of nature. The name of our river, Anapo, means *swallowed up*. In many places it disappears underground as it searches for the

---

[76] Archais was killed by Telephus whom Archais had taken advantage of when he was but a boy. Telephus had pursued Archais from Corinth. Justice was served in the end.

sea. Anapo was our god of water who opposed the god of the underworld who kidnapped Persephone and Ciane. I think you call this god Hades. Hades turned Anapo into the river, which is swallowed up underground now and then, but he tries to escape! As you can see here. But he still retained his beauty. Thus, he remains forever young!"

"I wish to remain young forever! Like my mother who was taken from me when so young." She spoke of what she remembered of her mother. "My father keeps a medallion around his neck with her image. In my mind she remains the most beautiful creature I ever saw!"

"Antigone do not speak of death and sadness! You are such a beautiful woman. I am delighted you have come to meet my father."

As they rode, they spoke of their homelands, of what Antigone remembered of Corinth, as Loto pointed out his favorite places. Finally, they arrived in the small settlement high above the valley. Akrai sat on top of the high flat cliff overlooking the valley.

"Father, we have returned, and I have brought a friend. This is Oecist Archais' daughter, Antigone."

"Welcome to our village. We are pleased that you have made the long trip. My wife, Azara, and the women are waiting for you. Azara, this is Antigone. Take her to be refreshed. Antigone, our home is yours. Do not hesitate to ask for anything you need. Later we will dine and speak and become more acquainted. Azara, take Antigone to our quarters."

After they retired, Iagu approached Loto. "You should have told me you had planned a visit! Fortunately, my spies saw that you were returning with an entourage! Loto, if you were not so hard working and intelligent, I would have you whipped for disobedience. Now tell me of Antigone, she certainly is a young and beautiful woman!"

"Father, I spoke in haste to Archias, but I have had Antigone on my mind for as long as I have visited Ortygia. I wish I could ask for her hand, but do you think Archias might agree?"

"Son, you are descended from the gods. Do not be so humble. However, it is not for you to choose. You are forgetting our customs. It is I who decides whom you should marry!"

"But father, is it not to our political advantage to marry into the Hellenes? They certainly have come to stay. Now they occupy a small island, but more will come. Will they drive us out? We must think ahead!"

"You do speak with your head, even though you sometimes are ruled by other less reliable faculties! I agree that change is inevitable."

"Here is what we shall do. You must approach Archias and tell him of your ancestry and do not be retiring. The Hellenes respect manly virtues, and you are a strong warrior and an intelligent man. When you return to Ortygia, tell him that you speak with your father's blessing in asking for Antigone's hand. I will send gifts with you. We will speak of this later in detail. Now go, refresh yourself for dinner and show Antigone our modest temple and the views around this fine place. One day take her to Pantalica and to Adhrano's temple."

"Thank you, father. You have given me courage and hope. I will do as you say."

"Yes, you certainly have a way of bending my mind to yours."

And so it came to pass that both Rēks Iagu and Oecist Archais agreed to the marriage of their children. Antigone told Archias how much she cared for Loto and liked Akrai. The wedding took place in Ortygia overlooking the sea near the temple of Apollo which was rising behind them. Iagu and Archias became friends and the two peoples lived in harmony. Antigone had many children and Loto's line of Rēks continued for many generations, and the evil of Dutta had been put away for a time.

THE MUSE (2001 AD)

I had arrived at the point where written history and the writings of Luxo on the cave walls coincided. Would the cave inscriptions support what we know from the ancient Greek historians? I had a long day and decided to lie down on my bed for the night. I fell asleep, and then...

"I am here, my friend. I am still leading you. Follow me!"

"Yes, Archimedes! I am ready."

"My city begins to rise! But I have more connections to other parts of Trinacria than people are aware of. Come! We are entering the center of the city of Siracusa called Ortygia. See the Temple of Apollo. See how grand it is! And the buildings and houses have impressed the Siculi slaves and workmen who have helped build it. The poor were enslaved by the Corinthians, but the iron mongers and other craftsman were paid and resided in or near the city. The city is slowly spreading to the mainland. To the north on the mainland reaching toward Thapsos will rise the district of Achradina and further inland Tyche. To the southwest Neapolis will be constructed, and as you continue west the land rises to a high place which will be named Epipoli. The city has grown over the almost 100 years since the Hellenes arrived and will continue to expand and prosper."

"It truly is a beautiful place facing the harbors and the sea. I see the caves on the mainland which have been used to gather stone. One large cave I have visited many times. It is called the Ear of Dionysius."

"Yes, but that name came later. We are far from his time. Now the Gamoroi[77] rule the city. They agree that they need to protect their borders from other tribes and also from foreign invaders. The Carthaginians and others from the Levant have their sights fixed on the lands of western Trinacria. They will decide to build outposts. Follow me and I will take you there to help you visualize what Luxo tells you in the next cave.

"Sleep now and rest. We will continue another day."

I thought of the day in 1978 when Enzo took me down from the acropolis of Akrai to see the river Anapo. I had seen the river outside of Ortygia in Siracusa as it meandered on the coastal plain and exited to the sea. But here it was surrounded by verdant forest and flowed swiftly in the valley. It is a river of myth which connects Sicily with Ancient Greece. But today Enzo showed me the sites of the aqueduct. It was called the Galermi Aqueduct constructed by the tyrant Gelo in 480BC using Carthaginian slaves captured from the Punic War. It would bring fresh clean water from Mt. Lauro to what would become the largest city in the world.

It inspired me to learn more about this massive undertaking and about the architects that built the town of Greek Akrai (664BC) as an outpost to protect the source of water and to help protect the capital of the region. At this time the land was then occupied by the Siculi. How did they interact with the first Greek colonizers? I had much to read in the next few caves.

The Gamoroi had ruled Ortygia for a long period, but the poor and oppressed of the city who were of mixed Siculi and Greek blood became tired of oppression and rebelled. They called themselves Killichiroi[78] and founded the first democracy to rule Ortygia and the surrounding countryside which was called Siracusa[79], for there

---

[77] Γκαμεροι- Gamoroi – The nobles or land holders.
[78] Killichiroi – the lower class in the city.
[79] Siracusa derived from the prehistoric name Syrako, Suraku, Σιρακο meaning abundance of salt water or marsh.

were large marshes south of the city. However, in 485 BC, egged on by the Gamoroi, the Tyrant Gelon retook control.

I was particularly interested in what Luxo wrote about Akrai. When I visited with my Uncle Raffaele, only fragments of Aphrodite's Temple remained. Now I could see what Enzo found on the cave walls. The diagrams showed parts of an altar with scrolled relief, large pediments, and pieces of columns that lay on the ground. I marveled at the archeologists' detailed reconstructed plans made from the scattered ruins. The foundations of the temple were clearly visible. It was rectangular, 18.2 m by 39.5 m, six columns in the front and rear and thirteen on the longer sides. These columns formed a peritasis, or wide walkway, around the entire temple for the priests to process around the main room or cella. More columns formed a front porch or pronaos. The porch faced directly east toward Etna, the long side on an east west axis. Parts of the columns lay strewn about. They were almost a meter in diameter and the capital was of Doric form.[80]

At that moment I turned, and Archimedes was at my back. This time he was a young man in his prime. His brown eyes stared over my shoulder at the ruins. He had short dark hair in small curls and a kempt beard. He looked like the many statues and paintings I had seen of the ancient Greeks. He was lean, with broad shoulders, and wore the short, white tunic typical of the time. But again, a black belt and a black band around the collar. Near his right shoulder were symbols embroidered in a deep blue γ ζ''. Obviously not a Greek word. What was its meaning?

"My friend, let me show you the Akrai of my time. This temple of Aphrodite was magnificent. I visited it many times. Elox was a master craftsman who lived long before me. He had an intuitive grasp of form. He was a geometer whom I respected, and his mind's

---

[80] "Il Tempio di Afrodite di Akrai" L'Istituto Acrensi, Luigi Berbaò Brea

eye was that of an artist. There were few like him. Come with me and I will show you the marvels of Akrai. In your era, the Temple is only a pile of rocks, but in my day, it was a rose-colored splendor, with a great carved altar and a statue of Aphrodite and other gods. There were also smaller temples to other gods and goddesses. I will also show you the Aqueduct which was yet to be built. You will find out about it on the next cave wall. Follow me."

"Before we go – I am puzzled, puzzled about the symbols at your shoulder. I know it is not a word."

"Of course not! It is a number. It represents my early discovery in Alexandria of what you now call π. This is how we represented our number. γ[81] is the third number or your 3. The slashes represent fractions."

"I see! I see! ζ represents our 7 and the dashes places it in the denominator or 1/7! So, $\gamma \zeta''$ represents 3 and 1/7!"

"Very good. You would have made a good assistant. You catch on quickly. And now, let us proceed with the tour!"

---

[81] The Greek number system - Letters in the Greek alphabet were assigned to each number. γ (gamma) represents the number 3, ζ (zeta) represents 7, two ticks indicating placing the number in the denominator, hence ζ'' means 1/7.

CHAPTER 19

CAVE 6 (664 BC)

THE FOUNDING OF GREEK AKRAI

INSCRIPTION M

I, Luxo, will now describe the reason why this small town of the Siculi, close to the religious centers of both the Sicani and Siculi, was coveted by the Hellenes and became a site which was to play a major role in our early history.

In Ortygia, the Gamoroi now extended their rule around the island of Ortygia to the mainland and called the entire polis, Siracusa. They were of one mind that they needed to protect their new colony. The land around the island and its surrounding marsh rose as one ventured inland and was surrounded naturally by land which sloped upward to high hills and cliffs dotted with caves forming a crescent surrounding Siracusa. The land provided natural protection and boundaries around the growing city. The Anapo flowed through this land. It originated near Mt. Lauro and flowed through Pantalica and below the settlement of the Siculi on the high place which the Hellenes were to call Akrai. The city fathers needed outposts up in the hills to place watch towers. The most important was to guard the source of the Anapo and that was to be the outpost of Akrai. At this time, Akrai was ruled by Rēks Naro. His son was called Iaxo."

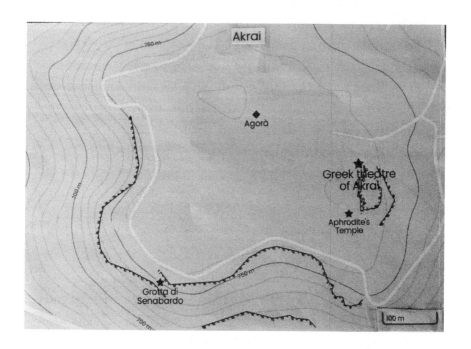

Z eno, the leader of the Gamoroi of Siracusa, called a council of members of the ruling class, "I have called you today to a most important meeting of strategy. As you are aware in the almost one hundred years since we arrived on these pleasant shores, the riches of this land have flowed into our city. The Siculi work the fields in the surrounding plains up into the hills of the Hyblaean Mountains that protect and surround our settlement. Our exports grow larger each year, and we trade with both east and west. But lately we see that we face threats not only from foreigners like the Carthaginians, but also from our fellow Hellenes who are establishing footholds alongside us. We must prepare!"

Tyro spoke his mind next, "The Carthaginians are in the far west and are divided from us by the mountains. Etna divides us from the eastern settlement. We have a strong navy. We are protected in our triangle by sea and the Hyblaean Mountains. Why do we need more protection?"

"Well spoken, Tyro. I concur that the gods favor us, so I will answer what you ask. Why should we not protect what the gods have bestowed? I know that we feel safe, but we do need outposts to warn us so we can defend ourselves if need be. I propose three new settlements. First, to guard our south, we will build the town of Helorus, for the Sun God and to guard our far western swamp, Kamarina, for the swamp nymph. Most importantly, in the far west on a promontory of the Hyblaean Plataeu, the Siculi town of Akrai. Akrai indicates a high place or peak. It overlooks the plains, the sacred Anapo, and Etna. It guards the northern boundary from the Sicani to the northwest and the Carthaginians to the west. If you agree, I would like to begin with the fortification of Akrai. It is now a friendly Siculi village surrounded by important sites that have been inhabited for many, many generations by these tribes. Their leaders are already tied to us by marriage. We have friendly and good trade relations from our founding.

The ruling family is known to me, and in fact there are ancient familial bonds through Archias' daughter, Antigone. As you are aware there are individual Siculi chiefs, but the man who has always had the greatest sway with the entire tribe has for many years resided in Akrai. Presently he is called Rēks Naro, he is the 4ᵗʰ great grandson of Antigone. I wish to send emissaries there to entice him to accept our pledge of protection. We shall build a fort there. There already exists a small temple to our mother, Aphrodite, queen of passion. It looks out at Etna. I now ask for comment from the governing council."

Tyro, old and wise, was first to respond. "As I said, I feel we have enough protection. We are well protected already and have a fresh source of spring water in the font of Arethusa right in Ortigia. It was provided by the gods! Do you not know their gift to us?"

"No, we young ones do not know. Wise, old, Tyro enlighten us. We need your wisdom," replied a young blond Gamoroi with a smirk.

Tyro took a deep breath to calm himself. With the desire to enlighten the youth, he said, "Know this, Zeno is intelligent and leads us Gamoroi with strength, yet it is good for you all to know our traditions. We here in Ortygia are blessed by the goddess of the hunt, Artemis, and Apollo, the sun god who shines on us each day. Leto gave birth to this godly pair and blessed this land right here in Siracusa. I will show you how the gods have always wished to protect our sacred land. In ancient times in the far-off land of our ancestors, the Peloponnese, Arethusa a young and beautiful virgin nymph was the desire of many a young Hellene. So, when Alpheus, son of the Ocean god, set eyes upon her, he was smitten and pursued her endlessly." And so, Tyro recited the myth which explained how the fresh water Font came to be so very close to the salty sea in the heart of the isle of Ortygia."

Zeno responded, "Well spoken, Tyro. I concur that the gods

favor us, so again I ask, should we not protect what the gods have bestowed?"

Tyro, in pensive wisdom finally spoke, "Citizens, though I am a philosopher of peace, I do agree that protection is always a preference to war. I concur with Zeno that we should begin this endeavor and build a fort in Akrai. For Akrai also guards the headwaters of the Anapo which flows into our harbor. We must protect its waters. It too has a significance to the gods. But that is another godly tale for another time!"

The young blond Gamoroi again spoke up, "Now, Zeno, your idea of first approaching the Rēks and building a fort on the heights sounds reasonable. Let us begin with this if the others agree."

"Aye."

"Yes."

"Agreed."

The responses came quickly. It seemed that the proposal was accepted.

Another Gamoroi then asked. "Who will take the proposal to Akrai? Who will oversee the building of the fort?"

Zeno spoke. "I would like Daskon and Menekolos to both take the proposal to Rēks Naro and then oversee the building. They have had much experience here in Ortigia in building our great temples and civic baths. What do you two say? Are you willing?"

Daskon responded. "Yes, I am willing. I see another advantage at beginning at Akrai. It overlooks the Anapo and very close to Mt. Lauro, where the Anapo begins and flows through Pantalica. We must protect the entire length of the fresh water to keep it clean at all costs. It is true that we have the natural spring of Arethusa, but we do not know if its waters originate from the Anapo."

Menekolos agreed. "Surely this is of utmost importance. I too will accept your appointment."

"Very good then. We have had a very productive meeting. Go

home and prepare for your journey and let me know as soon as you are ready to proceed with this important task. Good day all."

"Good day!"

"Good day!"

So came the unified responses.

In a few days a party of ten men headed by Daskon and Menekolos left Siracusa following the Anapo to the heights of Akrai. This was their first journey to the highlands, and they were awed by the deep valleys, the crystal water of the Anapo as it cut its gorges, the waterfalls, and the height of the town. They were greeted by Siculi warriors as they came close to the heights.

"Hail, Hellenes! Who do you seek and what is your business so far from your beloved Ortygia?"

"Hail. I am Daskon and we come to speak to your leader, Rēks Naro."

"I am called Iaxo and will be glad to lead you to his home. He lives near our temple of Aphrodite on the hill. But first, tell me if you come in peace."

"Iaxo, we come to ask your Rēks to join us in an endeavor of peace. Relay this to him. We will wait for an answer. Let us know when he is ready to receive us."

"Very well. It will not take long. My men will give you refreshment here while you wait."

"Thank you."

In less than a few minutes, Iaxo returned, for they were waiting just below the acropolis where the town was situated.

"Daskon, he will see you now and is preparing a place for you to spend the night. Follow me."

Slowly they followed the circular path around the acropolis, climbing higher and higher. At the top Daskon and the others were in awe of the panoramic view. It was almost a level hilltop with a high wooden temple at the center and circular huts arranged around it. One large hut with stone walls was in the figure 8 with many small round huts attached to it around the perimeter. They assumed this was Rēks' home.

Iaxo, pointing to the large hut, "This is the home of our Rēks. Wait at the door until he emerges to welcome you."

In a few minutes, Naro emerged. He was tall and well-built for a Siculi. He wore a dark orange flaxen kilt and a wide leather belt and strap across his bare shoulders and chest, which were highly tanned. A wide leather strap with colored markings surrounded his head. He had piercing brown eyes and Daskon guessed he was no older than twenty. He carried a large bone stick with a white horse's tail attached at the top.

Naro spoke in perfect Hellene, "Welcome to our Siculi village up here. As you see we have a fine view of our land, and Adhrano blesses us with the smoke of Etna in the distance. In the evening you will see her red hair rising to the sky!"

"We appreciate your hospitality, Lord Naro. We come in peace to discuss a treaty with you for our combined benefit. And we are pleased you speak our language so very beautifully."

"Thank you. It is a gift of my ancestor, the great princess Antigone, who came to us from Ortygia and demanded each generation learn both the voice and the alphabet of the Hellenes. Come now into my home. We have prepared some refreshment. Then we will talk."

And so, the bond was formed and Daskon and the others returned to Ortigia to prepare for the building of the fortifications of the village. From hence forward the town was named Akrai, which means high place. And slowly it would develop into an important outpost of the Ortygians, but always with many Siculi participating.

The Siculi continued to live as before and welcomed the Hellenes from whom they learned many things. The Hellenes also learned about the land and explored the surrounding countryside. The demand for olives, wheat, fruit, and meat increased as more Hellenes came to live and work there. This was added to the profits from trade with the growing colony of Siracusa. Akrai grew to become an important colony of the original city.

The Hellenes from Siracusa who came were mostly soldiers and guards, some brought their wives and children. They brought their Siculi and Sicani slaves, servants, and workers from the villages around Akrai and Pantalica. They were skilled in the cutting, carving, and using stone in building. Many soldiers took wives or concubines from the local population.

Slowly the town's plan took shape atop the promontory of Akrai and around the small Siculi temple to the goddess. The slaves carried stones from the surrounding hills to the top and built stone houses. These houses were built for the army who were to reside on the acropolis. A stone wall was constructed around the part of the mountain accessible on foot and a gate was built on the path into the town. The path passed by the temple and bisected the town, and was eventually paved with stone. Other paths were paved that led to the agora[82]. All the people were pleased with the improvements in the town. Akrai was taking its place among the leading colonies of Siracusa.

Almost one hundred years past when Elox, the youngest son of the Rēks Iaxo of Akrai, and grandson of Rēks Naro, had a prophetic dream. Aphrodite appeared and said, *"Elox, Elox you are not using your skills or your mind. I need a great Temple! You must build it!"*

"How can I build a Temple? I am a carver of stone and a seeer of the future."

Elox woke in a sweat.

---

[82] Agora – marketplace.

For a few days Elox went about doing his usual work of carving stones for houses and images of household gods for his fellow citizens of Akrai. However, the dream did not leave his head. He began carving a large stone in the image of the Great Mother. Day by day it grew grander and more beautiful. On a second stone, he began the image of Kore.

Each night the dream returned. He saw the beautiful image of the Great Mother. He saw how she had loved his ancestor, Anchises of Troy, and how she had helped Aeneas, Anchises' son, become a god. She had special care for his family throughout all these hundreds of years. Each night she also spoke to him, *"Elox, Elox, you are the seed of great men- not only Aeneas, but also of Elymus who built great temples and cities in the west, and for whom you are named. You have the blood of Egestes, another noble Trojan and of many Siculi and Sicani warriors and leaders. You must follow in their footsteps. You WILL build my temple. It will be different. You have the ability and the will within you! Build, build, build!"*

This time he woke in peace. The Mother of Love had bestowed on him desire. She was the goddess of passion. He already had the love of art, but now an all-consuming desire filled his being: To build the most beautiful temple in all Trinacria!

Days turned to months, and almost a year passed. Then, one day Astrax, Elox's brother saw some Hellenes approaching the city from below the acropolis of Akrai. He could see from their dress that they were Gamoroi, noblemen, from Siracusa. Astrax went out to meet them.

"Hail, lords, may I help you find your way in Akrai?"

"Thank you, we are come to inspect the fort and to speak to the Rēks. I am Demetrius."

"I am Astrax, his son. I can take you. Follow me."

"Very well."

As they climbed the hill to the fort and his father's home, Astrax began "This is the site of our small temple to Aphrodite. It is not very grand, but it is ancient. People have offered sacrifice here from ancient times. Before us the Sicani pledged to Erik, another name for our great mother of love."

"Yes, we have heard such. The Killichiroi who now rule Siracusa in what is called a democracy have sent us. They wish to fortify the acropolis of Akrai even further. They also believe we need to make sure the gods know we seek their protection. They have given us the commission and funds to build a more substantial temple. We have come to speak to the *Rēks* and the council. We will need builders and craftsmen."

Astrax could only stare at Demetrius with awed and surprised eyes. It took him quite a while to gather his thoughts. "You must truly have been sent by the gods! My brother, Elox, has been carving Aphrodite's image for over a year. Know that he is an artist and seeer. He has the blood of the mythical Egestes, the builder of the western settlement of Segesta, and of Elymus the son of Aeneas. Elox's mind lives with the gods. His rendering of our Great Mother grows more beautiful and detailed each day. He is gifted in visualization of stone monuments and buildings. You shall meet him soon."

So, the men climbed up to the acropolis, through the gate, following the road to the large stone house of the Rēks. After they had rested, Demetrius approached the young Elox who was sitting outside on a great stone peering at Etna, in the east, as she put white circular puffs which glowed red as the sun set. "Hail, Elox. Your brother tells me you are gifted in seeing and planning structures."

"My mind's eye can see great things! I see Temples here in this holy place. First a magnificent one to honor our great and beautiful Mother. She is the patron of procreation and fertility. But we must also honor others! We must build to Artemis and further down near the entrance, one to Kori[83], to honor the goddess who brings us springtime!"

"I see you have great aspirations for this place."

"Not only this, but I can see the future. I see an expanded agora[84], a theater, and a meeting place for our councilmen, a Bouleuterion[85]."

"So, you are a seer as well as a builder!"

Elox clarified, "With respect Demetrius, I have inheritance from the gods. My blood is the same that flowed through Aeneas and the great Elymus who built Eryx in the west, the holiest place to worship Aphrodite high above the sea, on a rocky precipice. My ancestors migrated to Thapsos from Eryx and Segesta, but they found it deserted because of the Sea Peoples invasion years before. So, they continued to migrate until they arrived in Pantalica and then to what is now Akrai, this safe and holy place. We have worshiped our mother here in the small temple, but she implores us to build a great home. I have already begun my project and was waiting for your arrival.

"Let me tell you of Eryx. Aphrodite's temple is amid the clouds which swirl constantly around her home. She appears to many mariners as they pass Eryx. I sailed there with my father when I was young, and I shall not forget the mystery of that place. When I climbed the mountain to her temple, a black cloud swirled above me, then it was infused with bright white light, and she appeared before me! She sat on an open seashell rising from the sea, and her naked body was milk white with a deep blue cloth streaming from her neck. I will never forget her words, *"Elox you are my youngest and most ardent believer. I will follow you and protect you. Do my will when I call upon you!"*

---

[83] Persephone
[84] Agora – the marketplace at the center of a city or town in Greek cities.
[85] Bouleuterion – a smaller Greek theater used for council meetings.

I descended the mountain in a daze. My father kept asking what was wrong, but I remained silent and kept this all stored deeply within."

"This confirms to us that our mission is truly the wish of the goddess. Did you know that we would come from Ortygia? How did you know?"

"In my dreams I was told by our Mother that the time was now. So, months ago I began carving a great stone with our Mother's image. It is almost complete. I am now starting to plan for Kore's idol. It is in my workshop."

Demetrius just stared at Elox with his mouth open.

"Sir, why do you appear stunned. I told you that this is the will of Aphrodite. Why are we delaying. We must begin to level the earth where the old temple sits! Let us begin."

And so, the great Demetrius, master builder of Ortigian temples, followed Elox into his workshop.

"This is my work. Aphrodite mother of love, of beauty, and passion! She has inspired me in this endeavor."

"Elox, this is very fine. It is a work that has more feeling than anything I have yet seen in Trinacria, or even Corinth. I am in awe of your talent. I will put you in charge as my assistant. Let me see what you envision for the Temple, and we will begin as soon as we agree."

Elox took his pointed stick and started to draw in the box of sand on his worktable. Slowly the plan for the base emerged. There were thirteen columns on each side running east to west. On the east side, facing Etna, there was a pronaos of six columns at the front, and six more some distance behind to form the entrance. The cella had three parts, a small vestibule, a larger cella, and a still larger inner sanctuary. It was a unique design.

Demetrius looked for a long time then commented, "This will truly be a work to be admired in the whole of the world. It is unique and its setting on this height will bring many pilgrims from Siracusa and the rest of Trinacria. You have more than convinced me of your ability and knowledge."

Within days, the slaves were assigned to excavate, mine stone, carve, and build the Aphrodision to their great Mother. Citizens of the town were placed over them to see that the work went according to plans. Once the building was completed, Elox's great carving of Aphrodite was placed in the cella. The carved image was what he had seen in Eryx, a milk-white representation sitting on a golden crescent seashell with a blue cloth around her neck, as if carried by the wind. Her golden hair also was long and wind-blown, and below the shell was a blue base with white, representing the sea foam from which she was created. And when the doors of the temple were open, she could look across to the east, to Etna, and the forge of Adhrano, for he still shook and sweated, producing glowing earth which as it cooled provided the rich fertility of the region. And with time the three temples would rise in Akrai. The trinity, the three goddesses, would overlook and bless this land: Aphrodite, goddess of passion, sexuality, and procreation; Artemis, goddess of the hunt, of the Moon, and of childbirth; and Kore, goddess of the spring, flowers, vegetation, and rebirth.

THE MUSE (2001 AD)

"Friend, come back to the present!"

"Yes, Archimedes, I lingered in the temple staring at Elox's statue. I am in awe of the workmanship! I have visited the ruins which now consist of the temple base and a few capitals. There is evidence of a statue of Aphrodite, but it disappeared long ago. How fortunate for me to behold it as it was! It is truly on a par with anything Michelangelo would create centuries later."

"Yes, Elox was a most gifted man, and his images were copied much later in statues and paintings to depict our Great Mother. This image has persisted into the present time. You, too, have a Great Mother of God, who sits on clouds and for whom blue is her favorite color! Do you not call her Mary?"

"I am beginning to see how all is connected into our present time."

"Now, my friend, let me tell you of our next adventure. "Akrai grew because of its location and its trade. Both Siculi and Hellenes prospered. People came from the surrounding villages to trade in its agora[86]. But soon it was to become much more important to Siracusa. Siracusa had been ruled since the time of its founding by the Gamoroi, the Hellene land holders. Later, however, the common people together with the Siculi rebelled and took control. They were called Killichiroi, and this was the first democracy in Siracusa. In 485 BC, Gelon the First[87] from Gela with the assistance of the Gamoroi conquered and took control of the city, and the democracy came to an end.

---

[86] Agora - marketplace
[87] Gelon the First - Ελων

CHAPTER 20

CAVE 7, WALL 1 (480 BC)

THE GALERMI AQUADUCT

Gelon approached Dimioyrgos[88] who was a descendent of the Trojan Aeneas and the daughter of the Sicani Solax. He had the blood of the gods and his engineering skills flowed from them.

"Our city state of Siracusa is expanding and needs a continuous supply of safe water. It has spread from the small island of Ortygia and now occupies a large portion of the mainland up to the heights which help protect us. I wish to engage you to find a source of water for our growing population. Your reputation is great and follows you throughout Trinacria. I am certain you can bring us Anapo water from Mt. Lauro to this thirsty city state before it gets contaminated by the Siculi villages and farms along the river. What say you?"

I would be honored to work on this project. This is a most enormous task and will require time and hundreds of slaves and workmen."

"You will have the men. We have captured many local tribesmen and we have indentured them to enrich our coffers. The Gamoroi have pledged their wealth and support us to keep the Killichiroi in check. They need clean water for their workhouses and homes."

---

[88] Dimioyrgos (Δημιουργoζ), meaning creator, the supposed architect of the first aqueduct in Siracusa. Gelon I was responsible for much of the improvements in the city.

"Then I will accept your commission if I can have my worthy assistant and colleague Parmenides to help me."

"You are free to hire whomever you believe can help complete the task quickly and efficiently. See my treasurer who will give you gold coins to begin your work. I have ordered some new coins struck with my image, so that all will know who now rules. I expect a work that will be the envy of the entire world! Go now and prepare."

Parmenides arrived at the foothills of Akrai and was met by a local citizen.

"Good day. I am Parmenides."

The local citizen greeted Parmenides. "Hail, I am called Culox. I have been sent down from Akrai to see why you are approaching our grazing lands with so many men?"

Parmenides replied, "We bring greetings from our great leader, Gelon. As you may know, Gelon now is tyrant of the city and of all the lands ruled by Siracusa. He has sent us to explore the Anapo to find a way to lead clean water to the great city. The city grows and thirsts."

"We in Akrai were distraught when the Killichiroi, the commoners, were dislodged from the city for we had many friends among them. Many were good Siculi. Many have been deported as slaves to other places. We have welcomed many refugees here. Our small city state of Akrai also grows. But now we have given our oaths and loyalty to Gelon. We only wish to live in peace and help protect Ortygia. We have many Hellenes in Akrai to protect this stronghold. Aphrodite protects us all, both Siculi and Hellene."

"Yes, Gelon has filled great Siracusa with many of his supporters. He has a strong following now. He has pledged to leave you undisturbed if you give him homage. We will not disturb your lives, for we are here only to fulfill his command to build a great waterway. We will need many helpers and workers to carry out the task once we have studied the land. Your population will continue to grow, and coins will flow into your coffers."

"This is certainly good news." Culox said relieved. "I am the son of our *Rēks*, and I will be glad to assist you in anything you need. I can offer you and your men accommodation for a few days while you study and measure."

"Good. Is the flow of the river constant? Is it clean?"

"Yes, the water is plentiful and untainted. As it flows toward your city it absorbs the waste of animals and people, but here it is still pristine."

Parmenides looked out toward close mountain. "I understand the river's source is at Mt. Lauro in the distance. Yes, I can take you there, and, also to Pantalica where the river forms a gorge. It is a place of holiness."

"Yes, I have heard that said. Tomorrow, we need to go to those heights and use our instruments to determine how far the water will fall in going to Ortygia. We plan to excavate tunnels which will conduct the water directly to Siracusa. This is a method used in our mother cities in Hellene. In this way the water will arrive unblemished. It is called an aqueduct."

"Will you take all the water? What will we be left with in Akrai? How can we agree?"

"Of course, the river's flow will remain. You will hardly detect any change, for we will build cisterns to collect the water before it runs down to Siracusa. I will explain as we proceed. We will also build an arm of the aqueduct for Akrai. Your slaves will no longer have to climb down to the rivers and streams to procure clean water."

"Let us go up to the acropolis. Once you are refreshed you can meet the *Rēks*, and we can discuss the details tomorrow."

"Thank you. We appreciate your assistance."

In the weeks that Parmenides and his men remained in Akrai,

he completed his measurements and made designs to take to Dimioyrgos. Within the coming months the excavation was begun. In three years, water began flowing underground to the heights at Epipolae, above the city of Siracusa. It would still take another year before the arched causeway led the water down to Ortigia. It was the first aqueduct in Trinacria.

Both Dimioyrgos and Parmenides settled in Akrai with their families. Culox, eventually became Rēks of Akrai. Being a descendent of Elox the great builder, Culox was named guardian of the waters. Together they controlled and protected the flow of the Anapo. Culox and his family and future descendants cared for the cleaning and upkeep of the underground system. In later years Culox would see to the building of a bath house for the people of Akrai. Clean water allowed more people, Hellenes, Siculi, and others to live within the town walls and the surroundings.

BOOK VII

Wars, Revolts, And Philosophers

460 - 340 BC

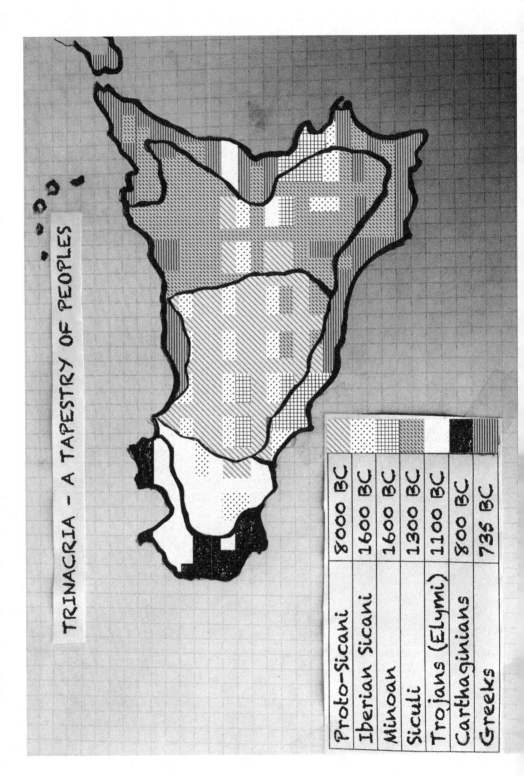

TRINACRIA – A TAPESTRY OF PEOPLES

Proto-Sicani	8000 BC
Iberian Sicani	1600 BC
Minoan	1600 BC
Siculi	1300 BC
Trojans (Elymi)	1100 BC
Carthaginians	800 BC
Greeks	735 BC

Strategos – *general*
Gamoroi – *nobility*
polis – *city state*
Killichiroi – *commoners*

500 BC's

Ducetius – *Siculi leader of the slave rebellion descended from Rēks
    Iagu*
Empedocles – *Philosopher of Akragas (polis near Siracusa)*
Gelon I – *Hellene Tyrant of Siracusa*
Pausanias – *Friend of Empedocles*
Timaeus – *Student of Akrai who follows Empedocles*

400 BC's

Rēks Culox – *Akrai ruler during the building of the Galermi
    Aquaduct*
Cassandra – *Hellenized Siculi granddaughter of Elox marries Ektor,
    the Athenian*
Demosthenes – *controlled the Athenian reinforcements*
Dionylsii – *Father and son tyrants of Siracusa during Platos visit -
    Dionysius I expanded Siracusa and built numerous monuments
    and temples. Dionysius I and his son Dionysius II*
Ektor – *Athenian warrior who marries Casandra*
Hermes – *Commander of the Siracusan military*
Hermocrates – *Democratic leader of Siracusa during the Athenian
    expedition*
Naydox – *Siracusan spy from Akrai who help rout the Athenians*
Turidox – *Siracusan spy from Akrai who help rout the Athenians*

The Generals – Strategos

Alcibiades – *the Athenian who changed sides many times- Charged with sacrilege, he fled Athens to Sparta and convinced Sparta to send Gylippus to help Siracusa*
Gylippus – *Spartan General, helping Siracusa*
Nicias – *Athenian General*
Sicanius – *Siracusan General*
Lamachus – *Admiral of the Athenian armada*

300 BC's

Alexandros – *Hellenized Siculi Rēks of Akrai son of Ektor. Marries Arete*
Arete – *Alexandros' wife from Akrai*

The Dionysii

Dionisius the Elder or I – *Siracusan tyrant fortified the city including the Eurialo Castle*
Dionysius the Younger or II – *son of Dionysius I who was more interested in Plato's philosophy than his father, Dionysius the Elder*
Dion – *A relative of the Dionysii who agreed with Plato's philosophy*
Doris of Locris – *the wife of Dionysius I*
Plato – *eminent philosopher who visited Siracusa three times*

THE MUSE (2001 AD)

I was sitting at my desk in deep thought, appreciating the tour my friend had given me. Though I had visited my grandfather's town many times and marveled at the ruins of the temple, it was an extraordinary gift to see it rebuilt and glistening in the sun with its rose-colored walls and carved relief which I had only seen fragments of in a museum. The statue of Aphrodite took my breath away. A fountain graced the agora of Akrai.

As I put down my pen for the night, I felt a hand on my shoulder. "Friend, we embark on a difficult period in the history of Trinacria. Let me lay an outline at your feet.

"But before I say more, remember that Luxo describes this history as a tapestry that he is weaving. We keep revisiting Akrai as different peoples visit or take up residence. Let us observe these women in the village weaving. Their full concentration is on the loom. They have tightly bound the unchanging warp to the frame, and then insert the woof so that a strong cloth is created. The strong warp of Trinacria were the original inhabitants and the Sicani who stretched tightly over the island. Through the ages, Siculi, Elymi, Hellenes and others inserted themselves peacefully or by force as the woof. Sometimes parts of the fabric were destroyed, but where they were bound to each other tightly, a stronger fabric was created, and the people flourished.

"So, as you continue your journey, there is a monotony. Just like the women who work the loom, one enters a trance. Warp and woof, over, under, back and forth, hand and foot, tightening the warp with the batten, all choreographed into a dance. Day in and day out, until the final cloth emerges: a beautiful, colored, and interesting tapestry. Like the different colored yarn, different groups continually approach the warp of Akrai. One after another, year in and year out, they climb to the acropolis. Each visitor brings a different colored thread, like that of the woof. Some leave just a fine thread or piece of one, but others stay and leave a lasting series of colors to enrich the fabric. Some are coarse wool or hemp, others fine silver or gold threads. The final product enriches the entire land. It will truly be a marvel to behold.

"Let us see what different hues will be added to this intricate lattice, how the shades and pigments will lighten or darken. Let us proceed with our adventure!

"Remember Dutta D'Suko of the Siculi? He had many illustrious forebearers, among them Daedalus, Suko, and Rituli. However, he met with an early death due to his enslavement of the Sicani in the southeast. He was a cruel and blood thirsty ruler who cared only for land, power, and fame. The arrow which pierced his neck was the will of Aphrodite the goddess of love and she saw to it that the title of Rēks passed to his good nephew, Letoni, who ruled the Siculi with justice and beneficence.

"By the late 400s BC Letoni's progeny were spread far and wide over the southeast. One descendent, Ducetius was born in the small village of Menai[89] and was to play a large role in the history of the region. Aphrodite was to choose him to right some of the wrong which evil men like Dutta had brought into the world."

I turned the page in Enzo's notes and found this inscription.

---

[89] Menai – Mineo, Sicily. about ten hours on foot north of Akrai.

CAVE VII WALL 2
(Circa - 460BC)

I, Luxo, now will write of strife and rebellion. Ducetius of Menai, called the Siculi Prince, was raised as Helene and taught the skills of a warrior. He was to rise far, and then fall as far, but he was to bring change. The tyranny of Gelon I and his brother Hiero had ended, and a Second Democracy was declared. The serfs or Killichiroi[90] were now in control having ended the rule of the tyrants. But there was strife with Catana[91]. And so, Ducetius went to the ruling counsel of Siracusa.

At the counsel he was empowered to fight for Siracusa. He liberated villages and freed the slaves. His following multiplied and his army grew powerful. When he reached the Lakes of the Palici, he founded a city where the former slaves could live in freedom. The central part of Sicily was liberated by Ducetius from Innessa and Adhrano to Akragas.

Now the Siracusan Counsel became concerned and decided to exile Ducetius to Corinth.

He was allowed to return after four years, and he founded the city of Kale Acte on the northern shore of Trinacria.

---

[90] Killichiroi - Κιλλικυριοι, in Greek – the serfs or lower class of a Greek city.
[91] Catana – present-day Catania.

THE MUSE

After reading this inscription about Ducetius, I fell asleep and immediately heard Archimedes speaking. "You have read the legacy of a great Siculi Prince. Though the area near Kale Acte had been inhabited by Siculi for hundreds of years, it was the first Helene polis[92] founded by a Siculi. Though most of the freed people were enslaved again in Akragas and Siracusa, Ducetius gave the slaves hope that they would one day be free and gave future people the hope of freedom during the Roman occupation. He had restored what Dutta D'Suko had destroyed by his wanton killing and enslavement of the Sicani. The desire for freedom became ingrained in the character of the people of Trinacria. It has continued up to your time, my friend.

"The next cave wall will deal with how a great man of Trinacria has dealt with this struggle in all men's lives. He called these opposites Love and Strife."

"Rest now, on the morrow we will begin another journey!"

I turned over and slept till the next day.

---

[92] Polis – Greek City State.

CHAPTER 21

CAVE 7 WALL 3 (CIRCA 494-434 BC)

AKRAI ENTERTAINS AN IMPORTANT VISITOR

INSCRIPTION Ξ

I, Luxo, know that many are familiar with the great philosophers of Hellene. When Gelon I was still tyrant of Siracusa, he heard of a new philosopher teaching in the neighboring polis of Akragas. He requested of Theron, the tyrant there and his ally, to send this sage to Siracusa. Empedocles of Akragas, visited Siracusa and Gelon became a strong believer in his philosophy. He then sent Empedocles to visit the satellites of Siracusa to educate the youth. Akrai was the last polis that he visited. His friend, Pausanias travelled with him.

Akrai welcomed Empedocles with open arms. The young gathered round this esteemed visitor. Timaeus, the eldest of the students approached him, "Welcome honored guest. We are all eager to hear your wisdom. It is not often that we have such erudition in our midst. I am Timaeus."

"Hail, young man, I come to tell you of my latest works. First let me tell you of my upbringing. My grandfather was also called Empedocles, a member of the Gamoroi, and was a victor in the ξα *Olympiad*[93]. He was a superb horseman. I believe he is descended from the gods, as am I!

"I have cured diseases and staved off epidemics, but now I am interested in reincarnation."

Timaeus queried, "Sir, do you believe you will return as another being?"

"I believe that most people will return, but I am different. I will tell you shortly why.

"First, I wish to detail my ideas of how the world came to be. All consists of an admixture of but four items which I identify with the gods: Zeus, Hera, Nestis, Aidoneus.

"Zeus is fire, power of purification.
Hera is air, weightless and invisible.
Nestis is water, refreshing and flowing.
Aidoneus is earth, grounding and fertile.
And in mixture, they reincarnate.
Water in a vessel on a glowing fire,
Transforms into ghostly air,
A cloud, a vapor.
Or pour her on glowing flames,
Then all that remains
Is quenched ash,
Cool grey earth!
Vanished is the liquid and the flame!
All change in water or vapor,
Fire or air,
All is mixture of the four,
Zeus, Hera, Nestis, and Aidoneus."

---

[93] The 61st Olympiad, or 536 BC.

Timaeus and the others were astounded by what seemed so transparent and how he effortlessly spoke in verse. He continued,

"Sicani and Siculi both
Have always known,
Two powers assist the four
In transformations!
In mixing of any of the four,
Be they earth or air,
Fire or water,
Or any other combination,
There are but two assistants
In this miraculous transformation:
Love is the power
Used in creation,
Strife, the cause of all destruction.
These opposites and these four
Account for all change,
That which is seen,
And that which is,
But is unseen!

Empedocles continued for quite some time, but then Timaeus again spoke. "Dear Sir, our leaders have prepared a dinner and a place for you to rest this evening. Pray tell. Where will you go on tomorrow."

"Tomorrow I must visit Etna, Adhrano's mountain and the source of Zeus' unending fire. As I told you, I am descended from the gods. I wish to bathe my eyes in the fiery glow. This is my destiny! To rise as a god. Follow me tomorrow and you will have a great reward."

They began the arduous journey early the next morning. It

took nearly the entire day for the climb became difficult for the old philosopher. Finally, they arrived close to the fiery craters high on the mountain. They could see small white clouds of smoke. They camped in a small valley as the cold of the night descended upon them. The cold, at first, was a relief after the long trek on this summer day. They could see snow higher up by the fiery crater. But as night fell, they began to shiver, and they had to huddle closer to the campfire. The young men wondered what was awaiting their master and them.

Early the following morning, Empedocles rose early and announced to the others that he was going to climb higher. The men followed him for a short while, but soon they were being struck by cinders. They stopped, but Empedocles continued. They watched while the god approached the crater and ash, hot cinders, and larger stones pelted him. The young men withdrew behind the rocky outcroppings to protect themselves. Empedocles knelt and implored Zeus.

"Father who rules all the gods, Great Zeus, you who are wise and fair, god of the sky and thunder, I have come to return to you so that I may return as a powerful god." He rose and walked proudly forward, holding his shoulders square, his head upright, and his chest puffed outward. He was taking the stance of the god he thought he was. "Hear me and watch as I sacrifice myself to your fire so that I may return to do your will!"

With those last words, he rose stepped to the edge of the crater, and threw himself over the edge. Down, down he went! As he fell the young men peered over their safe boulders. All they saw were streaks of fire, clouds of ash, and then a stroke of lightning and reverberating thunder. And then, and then, Timaeus yelled, "Zeus, Zeus has spoken. Look. Look, above the crater how Empedocles bronze sandal is lifted higher and higher, and now it falls. There. There it has struck the ground. It lies on the ground!"

One brave soul ran close to the sandal with a large branch and lifted the sandal, which caused the branch to start smoldering. He carried it down the mountain and brought it back to Akrai.

The young men hardly spoke on the return. They were exhausted, stunned, and disappointed.

Timaeus spoke as they entered Akrai, "A most erudite being was Empedocles, but one that like many is fooled by arrogance. His mind was filled with a gift of the gods, but as all foolish men, he assumed he was one of them. He thought that Zeus loved him, and that Love would recreate him, only to be met by its opposite, Strife. He will be respected for his knowledge but remembered for his foolishness. Fellow students, you cannot believe all that even a great teacher tells you!"

Timaeus and the others laid the one sandal in the Temple of Aphrodite, the goddess of Love, in Akrai. Pausanias brought the news to the Killichiroi in Siracusa and to Empedocles' family in Akragas within days. Timaeus heard many other famous men as they toured the region of Siracusa and spoke in the marketplace in Akrai.

THE MUSE (2001 AD)

As I read the incredible notes about Empedocles, I was stunned that the stories I had heard of Empedocles' demise always sounded like myth, but now the eyewitness accounts lent so much more credence to what I thought was pure invention. As I contemplated whether I should begin writing, I heard footsteps in the courtyard. I opened the blind, only to see my friend as a teenager dressed in a short white tunic with a black edge on the bottom and around the collar. He looked as if he were ready to attend school. He was tinkering with a silver toy-like object with a crank. A chain passed over a wheel and up a long crane-like rod. The top of the rod had a huge metal mouth with two jaws with sharp points. As he turned a wheel, the rod lowered, and the jaws opened. The claw grabbed onto rocks and other objects and raised them high. Then, releasing a lever, the rocks dropped to the ground. It was an amazing invention!

He could be no other than my good friend.

"Archimedes," I called, "What is that contraption?"

"I call it my giant claw. I hope someday to build one which can lift horses, men, or even ships."

I sat back down in awe! I had seen depictions of ships being destroyed by the Archimedean claw and now was present when the idea was born!

"Friend!" He called. "You have visited with a famous philosopher and seen his destructive end. There is more death and war where I will now take you, but you will also meet one of the greatest philosophers and men that has ever lived. We now enter the Siracusa and surroundings in what you label as 415 BC. Athens has been extending her reach and has grown arrogant in her power. Siracusa has become even larger in size and controls much of Trinacria. It was just a matter of time before the two became rivals. Come, follow, and be brave!"

CHAPTER 22

CAVE 7 WALL 4 (413 BC)

THE SICILIAN EXPEDITION

INSCRIPTION O

I, Luxo, know there was much written by Thucydides and others of the Sicilian Expedition, when Athens tried to conquer Siracusa. However, I have chosen to write from the eyewitness reports of two warriors of mixed Hellene and Siculi heritage. They were in the Siracusan army stationed in Akrai. They had risen from mere hoplites[94] because of their innate warrior and command abilities. Their testimony was written down by an Athenian called Ektor.

But first, let me describe the situation. The Athenians, allied with Corcyra[95] had arrived two years earlier. They arrived with a total of 134 triremes[96] and 130 supply ships combined from both poleis. With reinforcements they brought over a most formidable force – 10,100 hoplites, 500 archers, 700 slingers, 330 cavalry and almost 200 light infantry. The sea was filled from horizon to horizon with ships.

Siracusa, while the exact number of its ships and army were not known, was well defended by its standing armies, navy, and fortifications. It had a strong cavalry of over 1200 and over 100 triremes. Hermocrates, the Democratic leader of Siracusa, was allied with Sparta

---

[94] Hoplite – heavily armed infantry soldier of ancient Greece.
[95] Corcyra – present day Corfu.
[96] Triremes – an ancient warship with three banks of oars.

which provided 1000 men and Strategos[97] Gylippus (Γυλιππο⟨) to assist in the defense.

The great Athenian armada was led by Lamachus (Λαμαχο⟨), Nicias (Νικια⟨), and Alcibiades (Αλκιβιαδη⟨). Three different Strategos and three different strategies.

And the war continued on.

Hermes was the first in command of the Siracusan military.

"Listen, Hermocrates, the Athenians and their cavalry are in Segesta, waiting to attack. Others are wintering in Catania[98]. I believe we should attack them in Catania"

"Hermes, do you think we should take the offensive? Let us prepare to wreak destruction upon our enemies!"

However, the Athenian infantry boarded their ships and headed for a harbor called Leon, on the outskirts to the north of Siracusa and landed their cavalry and troops there. The Siracusans quickly headed back, and a vicious battle ensued. Siracusa was victorious and the Athenians headed back to Catania for the winter.

Hermocrates turned to Hermes. "We must become better prepared! Send envoys to Sparta and Corinth for reinforcements! We must build forts. Extra walls around the city! Fortify Akrai even further. We must streamline our command."

"I agree. We have too many competing generals. You of course must remain. Let us dismiss all fifteen generals, except for Heracleides and Sicanus. Sicanus can bring some of the warriors from the native tribes."

Meanwhile, Alcibiades, who had been dismissed by Athens, had gone to Sparta, and convinced Sparta to assist Siracusa. Sparta sent the great General Gylippus to help Siracusa.

---

[97] Strategos – an army leader, military general.
[98] Catania – I have used the present name for the Greek city state of Catana.

At this point Hermes reported to Hermocrates. "We have managed to understand the Athenian plan. They will surround us on land and by sea. But we have built impregnable defenses around our city. The walls and ditches are the greatest in the world. Akrai is guarding the aqueduct. There is good news that the Athenian attack has been repelled and Lamachus, the Athenian general, has been killed. However, the Athenians have entered the harbor!"

The democratic council met to consider the dire situation. They again reorganized the command. They replaced all the generals except Heracleides. The new commanders were now Eucles and Tellias. Hermocrates remained as titular head of the republic.

Hermocrates asked, "Hermes, what is the latest report?"

"Gylippus, the Spartan, and his men have defeated the Athenians on the heights of the city at Epipoli. Many have fallen to their deaths, but the walls have held. We have reports that the Athenian commander Nicias is ill."

"What is the plan for the harbor. The enemy ships are still clogging it!"

Hermes explained, "Gylippus is convincing other Sicilian city states to join us. And he has a plan for the harbor. I will report back."

While plans were under way, Demosthenes arrived with reinforcements from Athens. Another sea battle ensued in the harbor, but the Siracusans had devised their ingenious plan.

Hermes returned after the battle to report to Hermocrates. "After two days of sea battle in the harbor, our plan seems to have succeeded. We attacked the Athenian fleet and secured the chain boom across the harbor. There was no escape as they tried to flee! The Athenians could outmaneuver us on open sea, but they seemed helpless when hemmed in. We attacked again while they ate! They became frustrated when they saw we had the upper hand!"

"So, what now?"

Hermes continued, "Listen. This is our plan. We can now clearly see how we can maneuver them to our advantage. The Athenians will try to retreat. We will let them retreat but let us direct some of our Siculi men to dress in their Siculi costumes and infiltrate the Athenian ranks as spies. Have them fool the Athenians to think they are allied with them. Have them lead the Athenians to what they think are safe escape land routes. We will let them debark unmolested. They will try to pass overland to a safe place, but they are clueless as to the lay of our homeland. Our Siculi spies will be given orders to try to convince them to head toward places that they will believe are safe. However, they will be led to places that are to *our* advantage. Let us lead them along our rivers, along the valley of the Anapo, toward Akrai. Then, we will attack when we see fit. They will be in the deep gorges and valleys of the Anapo. We will have the advantage of being high up above them on the cliffs. We will have the superiority of the heights. What do you think?"

Hermocrates seemed pleased. "The plan is ingenious if we can carry it off."

"Well, I believe we can. In fact, I am confident."

So, while the fleet sat, there were new developments. Sparta was planning to attack Athens in its Hellenic homeland. Nicias was being recalled to Athens with his fleet to defend the mother city state. The gods were also favoring Siracusa.

Anxious Hermocrates asked, "Hermes, what is the latest news?"

"Praise the gods! We have another gift from Athena who protects us. I have just offered thanksgiving and sacrifice in the great temple which Gelon has constructed at the center of our great city. Nicias has decided to delay his departure since he saw the Lunar eclipse! These Athenians are a superstitious bunch, especially since their idols to Hermes were knocked down in their marketplace before they even started this adventure!"

Hermocrates looked pleased. "We will let them stew until they make their move. I imagine they will wait the 27 days for the next lunar cycle. I have confidence in my well-trained infantry."

Hermes agreed. "That is their plan. This is ours. We will attack before then! Gylippus is preparing."

The attack came on September 3.

"Hermocrates, we were victorious! We covered our ships decks with animal hides and the Athenian spears and arrows were useless. Their ships were trapped, and we pushed them to the shore. They are retreating by land, tired and hungry! They follow the direction of our spies!"

"Tell Gylippus we are proud of his defenses. We will honor him when this is all done. What about our spies?"

Hermes said, "The spies have convinced the Athenians to go where we have directed. We have told them to run into the wooded hills once our infantry and cavalry are nearby. I will go now to observe and will report back."

Now there were nearly 40,000 Athenian troops near the mouth of the Anapo river. There were skirmishes. Now the plan was to separate Nicias and Demosthenes' Athenians once they were on land. Meanwhile, our Siracusans went to the harbor and destroyed the Athenian fleet.

Gylippus and Hermes met with Hermocrates in Ortygia once the Athenians had landed, and their ships had been destroyed.

Hermocrates was glowing with pride as he saw Gylippus approaching. "Excellent! General Gylippus! I am impressed with how things are progressing. We are routing those dogs of Athens who had no right to invade our lands. Now, how do you intend to proceed?"

Gylippus in his casual and slow stammering manner began, "We will hide in the heights. That is in the heights of Akrai and Epipolae. I have sent men - I mean scouts to follow the Athenians.

I have placed my best, my very best scouts to command. They are ordered - no commanded - to send back dispatches. There are many woods, forests, and caves where our men - that is, our infantry and cavalry can hide - places where we can involve the infantry. We will rout these interlopers!"

"Gylippus," said Hermes, "What is the present location of the Athenians?"

"Nicias and Demosthenes have become - become separated in a small skirmish with our men."

Hermocrates, becoming impatient, "Yes, so where are they?"

Gylippus finally replied, "Our latest intelligence from our men - our spies is that - that Nicias is heading toward the Assinaro river."

Hermes, also wishing he would complete his thoughts, "And Demosthenes?"

Gylippus added, "He - Demosthense is being attacked now. Now, on the valley - in the valley of the Anapo - that is in the upper regions of the Anapo. O, what is that satellite city called? That fortified place with the acropolis? I recall now - Akrai. We have two men there in charge. They are Hellenes - or Hellenized Siculi - one by the name of Turi, I believe. No, no, his name ends in dox. Turidox is on the heights near Akrai. The other - the other even stranger by name - now, what is it? Something like Naiad? O, yes, Naydox that is. He is hidden in the trees, near their encampment. I have difficulty with these Siculi names. They are hard on my Spartan tongue."

Hermes looked at Gylippus and rolled his eyes at Hermocrates. They both were thinking the same thing. *How could such a brilliant General, one who could plan the defeat of the Athenian army and navy, be so slow in speech and have a so little command of names and places? They wondered how he ever communicated with his men. How could the slow, stuttering speech come from the same mind of a man with such brilliant battle strategies?*

Hermocrates was more than ready to end this conversation with the Spartan General.

"Hermes will accompany you and report back as soon as we know more. Thank you General. Your actions have saved our city. We will reward you generously!"

Hermocrates turning to Hermes, "I am relying on you. Go now and find out what you can. Bring me good news."

"Yes, sir. I will."

The final report was delivered to Hermocrates. It was reported word for word on the cave wall by Luxo as follows.

INSCRIPTION O

Naydox, one of the Siculi spies, spotted the troops heading up the road along the Anapo. That night they camped near the small village of Floridia. He informed the Siricusan hoplites[99] hiding in the undergrowth to let some troops pass. The following day, when half of the troops passed, the sign was given for the attack, driving some Athenians north, while the rest returned to the south. The Athenians were thus separated according to plan. Hermes was informed that the regulars at Akrai would come down to meet Demosthenes' Athenians. The Siracusans were also to bring the cavalry. However, they were to wait and not attack until they had an advantageous position.

Naydox called his troops together, "Men we must prevent the final half of the Athenians passage. It is imperative we divide them so that we may be victorious. Cavalry you are to start pursuit immediately at their center, and drive half of the Athenians south."

Arrows and spears started flying toward the center of the long

---

[99] Hoplites – infantry

train of Athenians. Seeing the cavalry, Nicias and his Athenians turned south, while Demosthenes' at the at the head of all troops continued with his Athenians to the north.

Naydox suggested, "Hermes, go back to Siracusa. Tell Hermocrates we have accomplished the division of the Athenian army. I will send a message once the rout is complete." So, Hermes left Naydox.

Nicias gathered his troops together once they had ventured far enough from the Siracusan onslaught and commanded, "Fellow Athenians, head for the southern river called Assinaro. You are tired and hungry. We can refresh ourselves there."

Meanwhile, Demosthenes with the northern group of Athenians almost reached the valley of the Anapo near Akrai, thinking that the fortress was full of Siculi loyal to Athens. He addressed his army. "Men, we have almost arrived. We must pass through this deep valley and up the escarpment to Akrai. We have been told that we are approaching the safety of the city on the acropolis."

Naydox, at the top of one of the cliffs, spotted the ragtag army approaching and called out to his men, "Akrai! Akrai!" He rallied his troops. "Siculi and Hellenes, our time for victory is here! Let us attack now."

The cavalry stationed near Akrai pushed some of the Athenians in one direction, while the rest of the cavalry stationed behind the rocks and trees, pushed them in another, separating Demosthenes' men into small groups. They were cornered because they were trapped by the high cliff walls on either side of the gorge. There was no escape. They were caught in the deep valley and the Siracusans had the advantage of the high ground. The number of casualties was great, and the rest were captured.

Naydox addressed the survivors. "Scoundrels, you came to subject us to tyranny from abroad and to end democracy which we have fought to have. Now it is your turn to lose your freedom. You will be our slaves. You will till our fields and harvest our olives and grain. You will enrich us, and you will be impoverished. You will be sold in the marketplace of Akrai with our goats and vegetables. I will keep your leaders for ransom as is the custom, but we will ask a high price of their rich Athenian fathers. Long live Siracusa! Long live Akrai!"

The prisoners were marched the remaining 14 kilometers to the caves surrounding Akrai, where they were kept until sold on the acropolis.

Meanwhile, Nicias' Athenians were slowly shuffling toward the Assinaro river. Many were collapsing from dehydration and hunger, for the days were still warm and sunny. The Spartan General Gylippus, his army, and the Siracusan cavalry and infantry were stationed on the opposite bank of the river. Turidox was watching and carefully noting their progress and reporting back to the General.

Suddenly, one of Nicias' foot soldiers saw the cool river bending not one-hundred yards away. He yelled, "Men, water, water. Let us run!"

This began a stampede which none of the leaders could prevent, even though they shouted, "Cease! Attention! Do not break rank!"

But it was impossible to stop the horde. The men were throwing themselves into the river, ripping off their uniforms and sandals, and drinking and bathing in the cool waters.

At that moment, Turidox gave the signal and the Siracusans were in the fray, horses and men were in the river. The waters turned red as the panicked Athenians tried to rush toward the shore to grab their weapons. It was too late. Most were cut down or lay drowning in the melee. It was a massacre.

The prisoners that remained alive, some severely wounded, were marched back to the Latomie, the caves on the outer edges of

Siracusa. They were kept there for many days in horrid conditions, and the dead rotting corpses and the sick lay among the living. The stench and filth were horrendously nauseating in the heat. The few remaining live Athenians were enslaved.

Turidox and Naydox were permanently stationed in Akrai. They were rewarded handsomely with promotion by General Gylippus. They were placed in Akrai as commanders.

The Spartan General Gylippus called them in to his headquarters before they left. "Congratulations are in order. You have protected - no saved many of our men by your keen - no astute knowledge of this place - I mean of the landforms - and and your ab - ability to get information to them - I mean the troops. You have helped rout - defeat the greatest power of the east - the eastern Mediterranean"

"Thank you, Sir!" responded Naydox.

Turidox agreed, "Yes, we are grateful. But we would not be here if it were not for your leadership. Do you return to Sparta?"

The general finally had become confident in pronouncing their names. "Indeed. Turidox and Naydox, you have excelled - done extremely well. Once we tally our losses - that is count the wounded and dead - we will load our ships. Only then, once we have lists, will we leave. The gods - your Siculi deities- as well as - as ours have smiled upon us and you. Go now back to your Akrai. Guard the slaves well. You may do with them as you wish. Do not put up with any of them - do not be timid - that is use force - the sword - or whip those that do not comply - that is obey! Thank you again."

"Go in peace, General. It has been an honor to know and work for you."

Turidox turned to Naydox, "We have earned a great honor. We return to Akrai as sole commanders. I am honored but concerned. Neither of us have the skills needed for documentation and missives. Our knowledge has many holes. Reading is not enough. We need more skills."

"I agree," said Naydox. We need to find a helper who will be loyal and have the skills and experience."

"Among the Athenians we captured, there was a commander who I saw writing on a parchment that he gave to a runner. Let us speak with him."

"Yes, let us see if he will return any favors which we grant him."

Later, at the caves in Akrai where the prisoners were being kept, they approached the man whom they had seen writing on the parchment by the Anapo. "You! Come here. We wish to speak with you. I am Turidox and this is Naydox. We are commanders of this Akrai, the city above on the acropolis. What is your name?"

"I am called Ektor. I oversaw my division, before we were routed by your cavalry. What do you want of me?"

Turidox studied the man. He looked at his disheveled leather skirt. He was bare chested and dirty. Dried blood streaked over his arms and legs. He had shaved his head and beard for the lice. He did not seem to be a commander, but Turidox saw beneath this. His eyes were still alive, and he was strong. "Ektor, I have seen you while I was observing your troops before you were captured. You wrote missives and I overheard your speech to your men. Your language was not ordinary. You spoke as a poet and educated man."

"Yes, Sir. My parents were wealthy merchants in Athens. They traded with Egypt for papyrus scrolls. We sold olive oil. I have seen the wonders of the Nile and the great pyramids.

In Athens I was schooled by Socrates, who opened my mind. Plato was a fellow disciple. He was at my side as we studied seated at Socrates' knee."

"With such an upbringing, why did you join in this invasion? Why did you put yourself in danger? Was it patriotism?"

"Though I loved the journey of the mind, I excelled in sport.

As you see even now after such trials, my body has not failed me. I trained for combat. Nicias and Lamachus inspired me. I loved Athens and was patriotic and moved to bring our way of life to all in the world. I was enticed."

"So, this now led you into slavery!"

"I was filled with the excitement of youth. I rose in the ranks. Now I realize that leaders have ulterior motives. I now have seen the greatness of Siracusa. That you have a democracy that is not unlike ours. That you are Hellenes like us and all you wish is to live in peace with your wives and children, which now I may never have. I do not hold my captivity against you. I would have done the same to you had you invaded my homeland. The gods lead us, we follow. Sometimes into the depths of hell."

"Ektor, no one can predict how fate and gods will trick us. Though I am not a strong believer in superstition, I have heard about the signs of the oracles. They warned you Athenians about this undertaking. The belief in the eclipse being taken by Nicias as a sign of doom prevented his escape and led to his death. We can either believe that the gods were on the side of Siracusa, or that their belief in superstition was pure stupidity that led to the Athenians' defeat."

"I agree. We never know how our life can change from one day to the next."

"So now, Ektor, you must serve me, an ordinary country commander of a small satellite city of Siracusa who can barely write! I am giving you a choice. I can leave you here to be sold in our agora[100] with the others, or you can come with me and be a loyal servant. We both will need help with many things that require a scribe. If you accept, you will be carefully watched until we are sure you are accepting your new position here. Man, what do you say to this?"

---

[100] Agora – marketplace

"Sir, I am grateful for this reprieve. I only thought that slavery or death would be my lot. I can give you my obedience and my loyalty. I have nothing against you or your people."

"I do not wish to punish you further, for I too am a warrior and respect your service. Come now with me. I will show you the bathhouse where you can wash, and we can give you some better garments. You can rest now. Later we will tend to our work and your duties. Agreed?"

"I can never thank you enough. Sirs. I thank you."

With this they climbed to the acropolis of Akrai, and Ektor was impressed with the city and especially the lovely temple to Aphrodite. He asked Turidox if after he bathed, he could offer a sacrifice to the goddess in thanksgiving. Turidox was impressed with this young Athenian.

More than a year passed, and Ektor continued to work faithfully for the commanders. One evening Naydox, Turidox, and three other men were gathered in Turidox's andron[101] for dinner. They were arranged around the room each on their own kline[102] while slaves brought in smoked fish with a dish of cabbage and carrots, followed by a course of cheese, bread, olives, and figs. When they were quite filled, slaves filled their goblets with fine red wine which had just been brought up from Turidox's vineyard near the Anapo. Turidox reclining on his left arm while lifting the goblet made a toast. "Friends! I wish to honor our trusted servant. Ektor has been with us for almost 18 months, and he has shown he is as faithful and dedicated to this place as any citizen born here. Let us toast him, then I have a proposition for all of you.

"Θυμοζ[103], Ektor!"

All raised their goblet and repeated, "Long Life!"

---

[101] Andron - male area of house
[102] Kline – long couches arranged around tables when eating.
[103] "Θυμοζ (Thumos) – Long Life.

"Now, gentleman, here is my thought. We have all served well in the war. We each have different experiences. Some we have shared, others are too difficult for us even to think about. I think for our children and for posterity we need to set them down in scrolls so that the great war where we have defeated one of the greatest civilizations must be remembered. What do you think?"

Naydox spoke next, "Yes, I too have thought that we must not forget this time. I think I may be reading your mind, friend."

"Yes. That is why I have made the toast. Ektor is eloquent in both speech and writing. Let us commission him with writing our stories of the war. How we fooled them into thinking the road to Akrai was safe, that this city was an ally. How we divided them in two and how they met their doom in the Assinaro."

"Great idea! If you all agree, we can call him in, ask him if he thinks he is up to the task. If so, we can toast him, and invite him to take a kline and join us. Agreed?' said Naydox.

All the men agreed. The slave was ordered to call Ektor in from the slave quarters.

"Sirs, you summoned me?"

Turidox responded, "Yes Ektor. We all wish to let you know that you have never failed us. We are extremely pleased with your work and loyalty. We now wish you to undertake a great task, but we need to know if you are up to this great undertaking. We need a scribe to record our experiences of the great war. We wish to include it in the archives of Akrai so our children and posterity will know how and why we fought. What say you?"

"I would consider it a great honor, Sirs. I enjoy using my abilities in this way."

"Good. I suggest we meet here a few times a week for dinner while you record our reminiscences. You may then join us in food and drink."

"I would like that very much. May I also ask if I may include what I have observed?"

"Of course! That would add to the interest. We are set then. Let us raise our goblets! Slave, pour one for Ektor! Θυμoζ, Ektor!"

All repeated. "Θυμoζ!" "Θυμoζ!" "Θυμoζ, Ektor!"

Ektor remained as Turidox's right hand man for 5 years and he had almost completed the three scrolls. *A Letter from two Hellenized Siculi and an Athenian: Athens' Last Days in Sicily* would be placed in the archives of Aphrodite's temple, and Ektor was completing copies to be taken to the mother city state of Siracusa. Turidox and the others were extremely pleased with both the contents and the beauty of his penmanship.

"Ektor, you have done a marvelous job. This tome will live for many years and enlighten many future generations. We have decided to reward you. After you complete the copy, we will grant you your freedom."

"Sir, Turidox! What a gift! I am so amazed and grateful."

"You may then do as you wish."

Part of Turidox's decision was based on the turn of events in Siracusa. Hermocrates had been the democratic leader throughout the war with Athens. Hermocrates had joined Sparta in her continued war with Athens. But now the Carthaginians had invaded Akragas, the neighboring city state, and factions in Siracusa had turned on him and assassinated General Hermocrates. Dionysius now ruled as Strategos Autokrator[104]. Akrai now might have less control over slaves if new rules were imposed. Ektor thought for a while. "Turidox, who will help you when I am free?

Turidox replied, "We may have to find another scribe. You must decide your path. You may return to Athens. You may remain in Akrai. Or you may continue to work for us."

"Athens is still at war. I have come to love this high place. I have many friends. I enjoy my work as scribe. I wish to continue

---

[104] Strategos Autokrator – a ruler with unquestioned and unbridled authority. The Dionysii were Tyrants who ruled Siracusa with an iron hand.

to work here."

"We would be pleased. You will be salaried. You may live in a small house we have on the outskirts below the walls. There are a few olive and fruit trees that will provide some sustenance. But do you not have a woman back home?"

"My parents are dead. I have no woman in Athens. I have made a fine friend in the marketplace. She sells lovely pots, and when I go to buy my ink and quills, I often speak with her, and I have purchased some tiny pots for my ink. She knows I am a slave and of my life. If I had the courage and the station in life, I would ask her parents for her hand. I know that marriages are arranged by the parents and she has not spoken of an intended."

"Perhaps I might help you. What is her name?"

"She is called Cassandra. She has very lovely dark hair and eyes. Her skin is amber. She shines brighter than her painted pots in the sunshine!"

"Surely you are smitten, man! I know the family. Her father also is a trader in olive oil, like yours! She has ancient and deep roots in Akrai and in Trinacria. She is descended from the fabled Rēks Culox who ruled when the aqueduct was built to Siracusa. There have been other gifted ancestors, both Helene and native. I will speak to her parents for you. I will tell them of your family."

"Your grace and helpfulness are most undeserved. I was your enemy!"

"Stop being foolish. You are free now. A citizen of Akrai. I am glad you will remain with us, grow your family, and help to teach our children to write and read as well as you do. You can also instruct them in what you learned from Socrates and others. We respect both your education and character in this, our home of Akrai. Now it is also your home."

"Thank you again. I will take my leave now. I have much to think about! Good evening, Sir."

THE MUSE (2001AD)

The notes and pictures of Cave Eight were filled with the details of the Sicilian Expedition, with particular attention paid to the actions of the two men from Akrai, Turidox and Naydox, and the Athenian, Ektor, who took up residence in Akrai. I turned the page to the third wall in the cave and was amazed at the next chapter in the life of Ektor. Suddenly, I heard noises in the garden. I assumed it was my friend, so I rose and walked to the garden.

"Salve!" I was greeted by my friend who now was middle aged. His beard was turning silver, but most of his hair was still dark. This time he was dressed as an infantryman. He was covered at his waist and shoulders by leather pteruges[105] which soldiers wore for protection. This time he had a much larger claw which he was using to lift large rocks and piling them atop one another. Then he used the claw to lift an enormous rock, and let it fall on the pile which it smashed to form tiny pebbles. *"Felix! Ego Successit!"* He yelled as I walked toward him.

"My friend, I see that you have succeeded in destroying the wall of stones. What are you practicing for?"

"Oh, I didn't see you. I was concentrating on my large claw. I am preparing for the Siege of Siracusa by the Romans. Oh, but that is much later, and we still have very important history to cover."

"Come now and follow me as the Athenian war is in the past, but

---

[105] Pteruges – leather strips like feathers that soldiers used to protect the upper part of the limbs, usually like a skirt

the intrigue continues in the court of the Dionysii[106]! We have orgies to attend, and a great visitor to observe. I think you will find his visit to Siracusa most fascinating, and it will add much knowledge to what you already know about him. Come!"

Orgies? I thought. I knew some of the decadence of those times, but never imagined that I would ever observe one in the flesh!

"Stop delaying, or we will be late!"

I grabbed my hat and ran out the door following him.

---

[106] Dionysii – A family of tyrants including Dionysius the Elder, Dionysius the Younger and Dion, among others. The dynasty ruled from (485-465 BC)

CHAPTER 23

CAVE 8, WALL 1 AND 2 (Early 300s BC)

ORGIES AND A GUEST

INSCRIPTION II

I, Luxo, now write of the court of the Dionysii, not only because it is historical, but also because it will relate to Akrai. Look upon this writing in which are included the observations of our citizens who went to the great court of Dionysius. Note the observations of these ordinary citizens as they behold what transpired in the court and the thoughts of the great guest that wrote what transpired in what is later called his Seventh Letter.

The Athenian Ektor and his Siculi wife, Cassandra, lived a quiet life in Akrai for many years. Ektor worked as scribe and oversaw his slaves as they tended the olive and fig trees, wheat, and livestock. Cassandra worked on her pots and oversaw the children. Five of their ten children survived into productive adulthood. Ektor remembered his tutelage under Socrates and the discussions he attended at the symposia when he was but a boy in Athens. He used the same method with his children and their friends. He helped form a gymnasium in Akrai for the older children. Many of his students later became teachers. His eldest was named Alexandros, and Ektor was most proud of the way Alexandros was developing.

Most of his children contributed to the development of Akrai as teachers and civil servants. Cassandra's family's influence was large, and her father's business had become very lucrative after the war. The disarray in and near Siracusa had increased the price of commodities, and they were doing very well.

Ektor was now in his 40s and enjoying fame. *A Letter from two Hellenized Siculi and an Athenian: Athens' Last Days in Sicily,* Ektor's compiled history of the war was read widely in many symposia throughout Trinacria. Alexandros had entered the guard battalion in Akrai and was training his body as well as he had trained his mind. He had even been to the Olympic Games to compete in the equestrian events.

As a very young man, Alexandros became a superior horseman and won the olive crown for arete[107] in Olympia. Siracusa was proud in being able to assert her prominence among all other city states in the games. Ektor was very proud of his son.

One day a messenger arrived in Akrai on horseback from the court of Dionysius I, the ruler of Siracusa. The scroll had the Tyrant's seal. Ektor called Turidox and the council together.

Rēks Turidox of Akrai was only a shadow of the man he had been. He was quite advanced in age. His fine warrior frame was bent, his bones were brittle, and he shuffled, rather than walked. He spent most of his days in the caldarium of the bathhouse to ease his joints. Naydox had taken over many of the Turidox's duties. Once all were gathered, Turidox gave Ektor permission to unseal the document. Ektor broke the seal and began reading.

---

[107] Arete – Excellence

INSCRIPTION π

I, the Strategos Autokrator[108] *of Siracusa, announce a great festival in our polis*[109]. *On the day of the full moon of the month of Artemisios*[110] *you are invited to send representatives to a symposium given by our honored guest, Plato. He is a renowned philosopher and teacher from Athens. He will lecture at court and there will be food and entertainment. Administrators and people of value are invited to attend. Respond promptly to this missive through the carrier that has brought this invitation.*

Strategos Autokrator Dionysius.

Turidox was the first to speak. "Certainly, this will be festive, but much too rich for my tired blood!"

Naydox, his second in command, was the next to chime in. "I must remain here to see to the running of the fort. In any case, I have been to one of his 'esteemed festivals' which go late into the night and the orgies continue on and on for days and days! I think we should send some of the younger members, and they can report back to us when they return"

Turidox called upon the members present at the meeting, "What does the council say? I propose we send three or four representatives."

"Yes," replied old Crodox, who was the most ancient councilman.

"Yes," replied Casandra's father.

It was followed by unanimous agreement.

Turidox said, "Ok I propose sending Ektor, who can return with a written report and his son Alexandros, since we are

---

[108] Strategos Autokrator – A title of tyrants meaning General and Sole Ruler.
[109] Polis – City State
[110] Artemisios – the seventh month of the Corinthian and Siracusan calendar. The year began in the autumn, so this would be March or April.

grooming him for the next Dioikitís[111] or what we still call Rēks here in Akrai. Who else shall we send?"

Crodox spoke up again, "Let us send two more. Our two youngest members, Gordox and Voluptox. They are both viral young men who would enjoy the pleasures of the court!"

Turidox concluded, "Well, if all are agreed, Ektor will write the acceptance and I will seal the scroll. Are there any objections?"

"No."

"No."

"Agreed."

So, the task was completed.

At the end of the discussion Turidox went to the desk where Ektor was completing writing the missive. "Ektor, as I remember you told me once that you knew this Plato. Is my feeble memory not correct?"

"No, your memory does not fail you. We were classmates together long ago in Socrates' symposia. I would doubt he remembers the oil merchant's son. Plato, on the other hand, was of noble birth."

"Well, you go and maybe he will remember you. It will be good for you to also take your son, Alexandros, who is well versed in philosophy thanks to your teaching. His Olympic triumph was only last year. I am sure Dionysius will remember Alexandros. I was serious about what I said about the next Rēks. I am not long for this world. My bones are weary. I have discussed this with the other members of the council. They unanimously agree that Alexandros is the best for this position. After all, he is descended from Rēks Elox through his mother, Cassandra. You might not know, but Elox was the designer of our Temple of Aphrodite here in Akrai. He also carved the great likeness of our Mother who

---

[111] Dioikitís - Διοικητηζ - Commander

graces that same temple. Have Alexandros speak with Dionysius if you get a chance. He will impress the Tyrant. Ah, I see you have completed the scroll. Wrap it and bring the candle. I will seal it with my ring."

Ektor handed the sealed scroll to Naydox. "Very well, Sir. I will take it to the messenger promptly. And again, thank you for everything."

As the men approached the palace in Ortygia, they were apprehensive, even though Ektor carried a scroll on which Turidox had put his seal. They knew that they would be stopped and questioned at the gate.

The entrance to this part of the palace had a line of almond and pistachio trees which had been a gift from Tyre when the Carthaginians from Lilybaeum in western Trinacria stopped to trade during the time of Hiero. The trees now provided a fragrant covered canopy to the entrance of the courtyard. Their names were announced by the guard at the gate of the Dionysian acropolis in Ortygia. The scribe sitting at a table checked their names, opened the scroll, and let them enter the courtyard.

The younger men's mouths remained open in awe as they stared at what was before them. They had never beheld such opulence, no such ostentation! As they entered, they marveled at the enormous number of attendees at the symposium. The courtyard was surrounded by a covered colonnade. Red and white Oleanders in large pots alternated on three sides of the perimeter of the square. The fourth side where they entered was planted with yellow Ginestra[112] (Broom trees). Kline[113] were arranged in groups of three around the yard. At one end among the Oleanders was a raised stage with two thrones and a podium. Two large date palms framed the thrones. Elaborate kline covered in purple with gold

---

[112] Ginestra – Broom trees
[113] Kline – eating couches

pillows were behind the thrones. Under the colonnades tables laden with dates, figs, dried meats, and honey breads were there for the guests to enjoy. There were spaces on the tables for other foods which they assumed would be brought out later. Bouquets of flowers lent a wonderful aroma to the entire courtyard which now was filling with hundreds of people from all over Trinacria.

Alexandros and his friends first noticed the entertainers. Young, svelte, naked girls were dancing at the center. African male drummers beat out the rhythm, while young blond men played lutes and pipes. The men from Akrai were conducted by a slave to a set of kline not far from the podium.

Alexandros, who was no more than nineteen, kept staring at the bounty and then at the men and women having orgies on their kline. "Father, this is certainly, certainly more than I expected. I had heard of his court being hedonistic, but seeing it is quite another thing! I feel quite provincial, but all this does excite me! I fear it is far from how you taught us to behave. Even our fertility festival on Kore's feast day seems quite tame compared to the court of Dionysius!"

"Son, yes. Religious festivals are in a different sphere from what goes on here. I also fear that this is not what my old schoolmate is comfortable with. Plato and I were taught at the feet of Socrates. He is a man of the mind, not of the passions. He believes in loyalty, friendship, and moderation. I am interested in hearing his speech, and even more interested in observing how our orgiastic Dionysius takes it. He is quick to anger. I fear for my friend."

As they sat their eyes revolved around the court. They observed that there were numerous representatives from the whole of Trinacria, even some Elymi that had travelled from Segesta, and other Hellenes from Italia. Though only in his forty's Plato was renowned across the entire world of Greater Hellas.

Once they all were settled, there was a fanfare of trumpets,

and Dionysius and his wife, Doris of Locris, led the procession
into the court with an entourage of nobles and guards. Slaves
carried large yellow umbrellas to shade the majesties from the sun.
Others had plumes of white ostrich feather fans to cool them. The
Tyrant Dionysius wore a short, white chiton, with a long golden
robe trimmed in a thin purple collar. His bejeweled crown was
of gold shaped into laurel leaves. His wife wore a blue stola of the
sheerest fabric, trimmed in gold at the bottom and collar, with a
gold belt. Her gold necklace had blue sapphires which diffracted
the sunlight as she moved. She wore a thin purple veil with a gold
crown to keep it in place. The crowd gave approving sighs as they
climbed the stairs to approach their thrones.

Dionysius began. "Fellow citizens, Hellenes, and guests,
welcome to the richest court in all of our Hellenic world. It is
good to see so many of you here from near and far. This is the
first symposium of our esteemed guest Plato the Athenian. He
will instruct us in the ways of high civilization. Listen so that we
may improve ourselves. We want him to know that even though
we have defeated the Athenians, we hold no grudge toward him.
Welcome him. Feel at home, my friend. We are eager to hear your
words."

With that he and his consort rose and were conducted to their
dark purple kline, behind the thrones. They were bedecked in
golden pillows. He went to his couch escorted by two very young
maids scantily dressed. Two young muscular guards sat on Doris'
kline. She reclined with her head on the shoulder of one, and her
feet being massaged by the other.

Plato took the podium. "What is happiness? Is it the fulfillment
of every carnal desire? To drink the mind into oblivion, forgetting
all cares? To fill one's belly, purge, and begin again? Or is true
happiness the result of good and loyal friendships? A home
with wife and children who fill our hearts with mirth and love? I

think you all know that the one is ephemeral and the latter, long lasting. Similarly, when we deal with the state, we must realize it is but an extension of relationships on a larger scale. Power, my friends, must be viewed as a potential means to higher good, not an end. Wisdom comes only through consistent, unrelenting study. Men crave stability in their lives, and good states and leaders provide stability. Competitive excess endangers that balance. Intemperate states will be plagued by constant flux. Oligarchy follows democracy. Democracy gives way to tyranny. Justice and law will then fall away! You can observe the last thirty years in my own Athens as an example. The decline led in the final times to the death of my beloved teacher, Socrates.

"So, in closing of this first lecture, I entreat you to start on the road to wisdom, for your State is truly a magnificent and beautiful place. I admire your great circular harbor, the lovely temples of Apollo and Athena, and the lovely fountain of Arethusa that brings blessed fresh water from Hellas! You are gifted by the gods. But your people require more than outward beauty. There needs to develop the wisdom to see inner beauty. My fellow Hellenes, you must develop your minds so that they can illuminate the world! You have had many examples in your illustrious past. Study and imitate them. Look as far back as you can from when Sappho, was exiled to this lovely isle and created her most beautiful lyric poetry, to Empedocles, of Akragas[114], Gorgias of Lentini, to Epicarmus the originator of comedy, to the great lawgiver, Charondas of Catana[115], Pythagoras' pupil, and so forth and so on! I hope to take you on this journey in future symposia, but it will require dedication and consistent work. Thank you for listening, and I hope I have moved you to learn more."

---

[114] Akragas – present day Agrigento, the sister city state of Siracusa, some 219 km from Siracusa, know for its great temples in the Valley of Temples.
[115] Catana – the Greek name for present day Catania

As he took his seat, there was rumbling among some of the audience. Dionysius, himself, looked distant and unimpressed. Doris continued to play with her guards throughout the talk.

Dion, the brother-in-law of Dionysius, on seeing that no one was going to speak, rose and went to the podium. "Thank you esteemed guest! Your words will be taken to heart by all of us. We look forward with anticipation to future lessons. Guests, I am sure that Dionysius wishes you all to enjoy the banquet. The slaves will serve the main courses shortly. Enjoy!"

Dion went over to Plato, and they shared a few words. He had met Plato earlier and was already a disciple.

Dionysius then motioned to Plato. "Thank you for your lecture, Sir. Though we do not agree with all your words, we do thank you for your thoughts, and look forward to more. Now go and mingle with the guests. Life is also meant to be enjoyed. We have arranged accommodations on the palace grounds not far from our quarters. We will share the garden. You will be conducted there after the festivities. Now relax and enjoy yourself. As you can see there is much to savor. Engage all your senses and ask for whatever is your pleasure."

As Plato descended from the dais, Ektor saw that Plato's eyes were staring in his direction. He wondered if Plato recognized him, even though it was more than 25 years ago that they had known each other. Young men change greatly in those years. Plato approached Ektor's kline and greeted him. "Χαιρε (Greetings). If I were in Athens, Sir, I would swear that you are someone I have known in the past. But it cannot be. We are so far from that city. But I place you with me at the Socratic School. Is that not correct?"

"Indeed, it is, Plato. We were taught together by the great man. I was so saddened when the news arrived of his demise. I am Ektor, son of the oil merchant."

"Certainly, now I remember you, Ektor. You also have a brilliant mind, and your character is beyond reproach. I have lost so many friends after the troubles in Athens and my flight to Megara. I see you too have immigrated."

"Well, that perhaps is not the correct term. I became a commander in the Athenian force which invaded Siracusa. After the defeat, I was captured by some men from Akrai, a much smaller city in the Siracusan sphere. It is but 230 Stadia[116] from here. I was a slave and scribe to the commander of the fort. He appreciated my work so much, that after 6 years he granted me my freedom. There still was so much chaos at home, and Akrai was such a peaceful place, that I choose to remain. I now have a family and am truly happy with my friendships. O, this is my son Alexandros, and two councilmen, Gordox and Voluptox. We were chosen to represent our Akrai."

"Pleased to meet you all. Hearing you speak, Ektor, I feel at home. I know you are not a native Siracusan for they mix in words with their speech that are foreign. I do not understand all they say."

"You will, Sir, they have many Siculi terms for items and idioms. Many words just change in their endings."

"Ektor, I remember well our discussions of what men see in the world, and what we philosophers see. After much thought. I plan on elaborating in my next thesis."

Next Alexandros timidly spoke. "Sir, I am most pleased to meet you. I enjoyed your words. After being here and observing what goes on in these halls of power, I especially am attuned to what you have intimated about happiness and stability. My father has touched upon these, but I wish to learn more. I am interested in putting philosophy to work in deeds. I am also interested in politics. I doubt our Autokrator will be receptive, but I certainly hope you can succeed for all our sakes."

---

[116] Stadia – a unit of distance. 1 km = 5.42 Stadia, hence 230 Stadia = 42 km

"Yes, I believe it will be more difficult than I first assumed. But Dion is my good friend. He is encouraging me to try and, also, to instruct Dionysius the younger."

"I wish you luck with that!" said Ektor, "I hear that the young man had given a feast where he was in a drunken orgiastic binge for 90 days!"

"Aphrodite save us! My task seems harder by the minute!"

"We must bid you adieu now, my friend. We need to start back to Akrai. There is much to do there. Alex must get back to his post. He is promoted to commander of the troops and will be Rēks of Akrai once Turidox, the present Rēks, resigns. It is a great honor for him, and for me, who has risen from a slave."

"Remember, Ektor, a slave can be happier than a tyrant. Look around you here. They are all slaves. You are a man of great worth and character as is your son. Go in peace."

"Thank you. I have tried. I wondered what you would think on seeing this court. Let me assure you that outside these precincts people are much more controlled. They go about their business trying to earn a livelihood and supporting their families. They honor the gods. Hopefully you will have time to meet some of these friendly Siracusans and Siculi. Maybe it will be possible for you to visit us in Akrai? Say in a month's time? I will ask Dion for you if you wish."

"Ah! Yes, of course. I would love to spend more time talking over old times. There is much to tell you about Socrates and our other classmates. I would also appreciate getting to know Alexandros better."

"Fine then. Let us speak to Dion together. Then perhaps you can also lecture to our people in Akrai?"

"I would find that a refreshing break from this!"

Before leaving, Ektor and Plato arranged with Dion that he would ask Dionysius.

At the beginning of the next month, Dionysius agreed to allow Plato to be escorted to Akrai and to remain for a few weeks. It took Dion a great deal of persuading because Plato was being kept under surveillance in his quarters right next to the Dionysius' home. Plato had undertaken the education of the younger Dionysius. He was unschooled except in the ways of excess by example from his father. However, Plato and Dion thought that the young man's character had the possibility of being molded. Many at court were worried that what the Athenians had not accomplished by force, they might accomplish through philosophy. Divided camps were forming to influence the Tyrant Dionysius.

Turidox had prepared a reception for Plato in Akrai. The great hall in Rēks Turidox's house was prepared. Food was served by the slaves. Lute and fife players performed. Members of the council and interested citizens were in attendance. It was a lowkey affair.

"Thank you for this. I feel at home already. I see why you stay here. It reminds me of the times we spent with Socrates. Athens, like Siracusa, has been through very difficult times. First the war took many men away, and the "Thirty Tyrants[117]" terrorized Athens. The war was lost to Sparta. Women lost their husbands or had to care for their wounded. Shortly after there was a coup d'état by the conservatives, followed by restoration of democracy by Alcibiades. People were confused and didn't know who to support to survive. Fear reigned. Some convinced Alcibiades that Socrates was destroying our youth and he turned against him. He spent his last days with us, his friends, before drinking the executioner's cup. We were all devastated. It was the saddest time in my life. His death made me rudderless. I had thought of entering politics to change all these catastrophes, but I became depressed and thought all was lost. I left for Megara."

---

[117] Thirty Tyrants – Spartan imposed oligarchy that ruled Athens after the Peloponnesian War.

"It must have been a most trying time," said Ektor, "I too have had times which I do not wish to live through again. At the end of the war in Siracusa, our army was left on land trying to find a way to escape. We had poor leaders who had not studied the land or the Siracusans. My contingent met the Siracusan cavalry, and I was almost killed, but the Goddess Athena saved my life. I was made a slave and kept in a cave. Again, the gods, smiled upon me. Turidox purchased me for he needed a scribe. After six years of servitude and writing the history of the war for him, I was given my freedom. I have remained in this idyllic place far from the excesses of the Mother State of Siracusa and its court."

"Yes, truly Dionysius' court is a most corrupt court, far worse than anything in Hellas. There is an excess of profligate wealth, which only leads to disaster. I have regained my will to turn philosophy into action, and there is hope that through Dion, I may be able to educate Dionysius the Younger. I hope I may be more successful with the son than I have been with the father."

"Dion is a good man and a loyal friend, but I do not trust the Dionysii. They will use what you teach them not for the good of the people, but for their own power and gratification. Beware my friend!"

Plato replied, " I am careful and will go only as far as I think is safe."

"Good," said Ektor, " I hope you will stay a while and teach in the marketplace here in Akrai. There are many young men who have heard of you and wish to know more. In the past we have had other enlightened visitors. I have heard tell Empedocles passed this way before meeting his dreadful end."

Plato was glad to have found so much agreement with his friend and replied, "He was one of the greatest. I would wish to see the great mountain and pay my respects to Empedocles. I have studied his writings. Trinacria has had great potential in its men of learning. It is its rulers who are depraved!"

"I will be glad to escort you to Etna. I will prepare for an excursion. But may I impose upon you once more?"

"Most certainly. Nothing you may ask is an imposition. You have treated me better than all the royalty of the Siracusan court."

"One more favor, then, " said Ektor. "Will you take Alexandros under your wing and teach him what you can in the time you are here? He has a fine mind."

"Certainly. You needn't ask. I have seen the light in his eyes. Maybe I will be able to influence a philosopher king after all!"

Plato's time in Akrai refreshed his soul. He spent the spring mornings walking in the fields below the acropolis among the wildflowers, fig, and olive groves. The time he spent clarified his thoughts about justice and the state. He realized that when there is friendship and loyalty, then justice reigns between you and your friend. How to formulate this between ruler and ruled?

He toured the many caves around the acropolis. He realized that this place had been inhabited for many, many generations, even before the arrival of the Hellenes.

"Ektor, what do you know of these caves? They seem to be everywhere."

"Before the arrival of the Hellenes, this was the territory of the Siculi, and before that, of the original Sicani, who now inhabit the west. The population here is the result of eons of intermarriage, even though now they all have adopted our ways and language. The peasants in the outlying areas and especially among the shepherds in the hills, still speak Siculian. It is related to the language of the Latins. They have many traditions which some still follow.

"The tradition of rebirth coming to them from the Sicani is the most fascinating. Not many still partake, but I was told that the young initiate is placed in a dark cave in the area to the east. It is a place of wonder with caves and deep gorges filled with clear water and hot springs. There in Pantalica the initiate is placed in a dark cave for the night. After drinking a potion, he his left and forbidden to leave until dawn. Drugged and in a stupor, he is blinded by the first sunlight that enters at dawn and is unaware of where he is. When he emerges, he is greeted by the priests as a person reborn, one who has seen his ancestral god. He is now accepted as a man of the cult."

"This certainly is fascinating. He has left the cave where there are only shadows, where there is not true knowledge, until he comes into the light and sees reality! Ektor, this is helping me formulate my next lecture. I think I will work on this image. It is just what I was looking for!"

Ektor returned to his work, and Plato sat on the temple steps looking out toward Etna.

He spent the rest of the day thinking and pondering about the cave.

The time soon came for Plato to leave Akrai. As he was about to leave, he encountered Alexandros. "Alexandros, I hope you wish to accompany me. Ektor believes you can profit from my teaching, but I will not agree, unless this is your will, and is deeply imbedded in your being."

"Teacher, I have no other desire than to be your disciple. I wish to learn how to be a better leader, for one day I may have great responsibility."

"Well spoken, Alex. I feel we will be able to learn much from each other."

As the years went by, Plato felt less and less welcomed at court. He was glad that he had visited Akrai when he did, because now, in Siracusa, he was practically a prisoner in Dionysius' palace in the acropolis of Ortigia. Dionysius had decided that Plato would not take offense in being enslaved. Plato had preached that any tyrant dominated by insatiable grasping remained a slave to his passions. Dionysisus wanted to keep Plato close. So, concluded Dionysius, Plato would be indifferent to his own slavery.

Finally, Plato had had enough.

"Alexandros, I need to escape this cage. I wish to return to Athens. Can you get word to some friends? If a ship could be found to sail to Italia, I could then cross to Hellas."

"Certainly, I will try."

Alexandros had arranged with a few of Plato's friends from the area and visitors from Italia to hire a trading vessel that was leaving shortly for Italia. However, when Alexandros arrived at the palace, the guard told him that Plato had been sold as a slave to one called, Horus, a jeweler. Alexandros and his friends went to Horus and bought Plato at an exorbitant price, but they were glad that they had found their dear friend. They were overjoyed that Plato was free. Plato was grateful for the good friends he had made in Siracusa. He bade them farewell and good life before he sailed off the very next day.

Ektor found that Plato had had a profound change on his son. He noticed that Alexandros now thought of ways that justice in Akrai could be improved. He often spoke of the ideas that Plato had planted in his head, and they began to blossom into acts. He was very proud of his son. Turidox's health finally gave out, and Alexandros was installed as Rēks, Commander of Akrai.

Arete, Alexandros' wife, played an important role in the governing of Akrai. Her excellent skill with pots which she had learned from Cassandra, Alexandros' mother, and her eye for art helped to decorate the temples and squares of Akrai. She also formed groups of women who met together to spin, weave, and sew garments. This not only increased their household earnings, but also made Akrai become known for its fine tailoring. Many of the aristocrats from Siracusa and beyond came to have their clothing, blankets, and sundries created to high perfection.

Though women of Hellas were reticent of making themselves public spectacles, Arete had inherited the presence and confidence of Sicani and Siculi women. She organized the women to help her with making Akrai a showcase and giving them a voice through her to Alexandros.

They had many children, among them Felox who would become the next ruler.

Dion had not given up on changing Siracusa. When Plato was in his sixth decade, Dion wrote to Plato, "*if ever all our hopes will be fulfilled of seeing the same persons at once philosophers and rulers of mighty states, you must act now!*"[118]

Plato did not wish to take on this voyage at his advanced age. He thought long and hard before answering. "*I [am] ultimately inclined to the view that if we were to ever attempt to realize our theories concerning laws and government, now is the time to undertake it.*"[119]

When Alexandros heard from Dion, he rushed to Siracusa to meet his friend. Much had changed. The young Dionysius had inherited the kingdom from his father. Alexandros, now much older, wished to show his friend that he had authority and was ruler of Akrai. As the ship pulled into the harbor, a golden royal chariot appeared. Plato was greeted by Dion and others. Plato was taken in this royal conveyance directly to young Dionysius' palace. After Dionysius sacrificed to the gods, Alexandros and Dion had a chance to speak with their teacher.

Alexandros was overwhelmed after so many years. "Welcome back, my dear friend! We are so glad you arrived safely."

"Thank you, Alexandros. Voyages become harder with age, but I am glad I made the journey. Glad to see you, and that you wear the cloak of authority for Akrai."

118 PLATO IN SICILY AEON.CO, web
119 Plato in Sicily Aeon

"Yes, I have much responsibility now. But I have taken your words to heart. Even though Akrai is small, Arete and I are trying to create a more just city. Arete is involving the women of the town and teaching them about happiness, justice, and friendship, as you have shown me. But we have far to go."

"It is in trying that we come to perfection. I applaud your attempts."

Then Dion broke in. "Yes, welcome. We are hopeful that the son of Dionysius has made a reformation in his character. We feel there is hope."

At the banquet the three men were impressed. There was none of the excess that had ruled the father.

Dion gave a glowing report as to how things had changed. "There are students of mathematics working in the halls of the palace and they have a passion for reasoning and philosophy. The younger Dionysius even shows gentleness and humanity in his dealings with men."

"It is gratifying that at least the outward signs are positive," observed Plato. "We will have to wait and see his motives." In his mind Plato also wondered about Dion's motives. *Was Dion using philosophy to persuade the younger Dionysius to step down? Was he planning to overthrow the young Tyrant? What have I stepped into?*

In his time away from Akrai, Plato had perfected his allegory of the cave. He would try to instruct Dion and Dionysius the Younger on his philosophy. Plato would speak to them about shadows and light to help them understand themselves. The Philosopher thought now was the perfect time to introduce this topic. He would begin with Dion and Alexandros.

After dinner Plato asked Dion and Alexandros to join him in the garden in the Acropolis of Ortygia. "Listen to my argument. We men exists as prisoners in a cave. It is as if a fire burns behind us. We only see the shadows cast and believe this is reality. However, if one of us were to escape into the sunlight, he is at first blinded by the brightness. But very slowly, gradually he views reality around him. He sees life in a deeper way. He now has seen the truth. He has gained true knowledge. But now, when he returns to the cave, none inside believe him. They even may think he is mad and wish his execution. His explanations are met with deep skepticism. He is a man alone, without friends. Do you now see the difficulty in our task?"

Dion and Alexandros nodded their heads in affirmation. "Truly," said Dion, "It is a great insight. But though Dionysius has changed, I am not sure how deep are the roots of his philosophy. Has he truly changed, or is he using it to secure and consolidate his power?"

Alexandros thought for a while, "Yes, he has seen the sunlight partially, but will he use it only to gratify himself. Only time and the study of his actions will let us know."

Dionysius looked out from his portico. He was looking at the three men speaking to each other and becoming concerned. "Plato, great teacher, come here and sit on my couch. You have spent too long a time away from me. I have missed you dearly during your absence. I hear your Academy is the talk of all Hellas. Students flock from the entire world. But I need you to be close to me. Now you will take up residence in the palace in the house in my garden. Siracusa needs you. Feel free to approach me whenever you wish. I consider you a close friend, a family member. I wish you to remain here with me permanently."

They discussed for the rest of the evening and Dionysius seemed pleased to have his friend return. Plato became afraid that he might again become a prisoner.

The following days were filled with intrigue. Lies spread through the court like fire. Powerful members of the court that were still skeptical of Athenians filled Dionysius head with calumny about Dion. These courtiers were convinced Dion was scheming with the Athenians, Carthaginians, and other enemies. At last, the young Dionysius could take no more. He called Dion and suggested they walk along the seashore. "Friend, I am glad we are having this time together. But now, I just have received some new information. There is a letter I have received that you were conspiring with the Carthaginians. They wish nothing else but to control our island and the richness of my realm! I know that you are not happy with my rule." Without giving him time to respond, he called out to the guards. "Arrest this man!" Dion was not prepared for so sudden a change.

"Dion, you are banished from Siracusa. I cannot trust you any longer. I should execute you, but your friends have interceded, and I still remember your friendship from the past. Go to Hellas and do not interfere in our court."

He commanded the guards, "Take him to the ship!"

The members of Dionysius' court were now ecstatic that Dion was gone and the courtiers influence on the Dionyusius would increase.

Alexandros did not realize that Dion was gone for a few weeks. When he heard he wrote a letter to him in Athens. Dion told him that he was at the Academy and had many friends who would assist him in returning and establishing an aristocratic government. Alexandros went to Siracusa to assist Plato whom he believed might be in danger.

However, Alexandros could not even see Plato because he was being kept in the acropolis next to Dionysius' apartments. Dionysius wanted to keep the philosopher very close.

Soon a war with Lucania and Taranto in Italia loomed on the horizon. Plato saw his chance and requested to go back to Athens before the shipping lanes became dangerous. Dionysius the younger agreed.

While in Athens, Dion schemed with members of the Academy and with Sparta and Corinth to return to Trinacria to depose Dionysius. Dion planned his return to Siracusa.

After Plato had been gone for a time, Dionysius the Younger continued to implore Plato to return one more time. Plato finally relented even though he was well over 70. This time Senocrates, Speuisippos, who was Plato's nephew, and other famous Athenians accompanied the great man. This time Plato decided to stay close to Dion in his mercenary camp outside the city. He would never agree to stay in the Tyrant Dionysius' acropolis again. However, Plato would try to heal the rift between Dion and Dionysius. As hard as he implored both men, it was to no avail. Dion became determined to use military force. Plato would have no part in this, and he decided to try to return to Athens.

Alexandros went to Ortygia to see Plato at Dionysius' palace. By this time the guards recognized him and allowed him to enter the garden where Plato was. He was glad to have time with the philosopher to gain more knowledge.

"Alexandros! How good to see you. Yes, it is good to see a friend. But I feel trapped and wish to return home. Will you help me?"

"Certainly!"

"I wish you to take a letter from me and see that it gets to Archita of Taranto in Italia. I will request he send a ship for me."

"Yes, I think it will be safer for you. I fear your very life is in danger. I understand that you and Teodota[120] were present in the garden when Dionysius wanted to capture and execute Eraclide[121] for his traitorous plans."

"Yes, it was difficult to persuade the impetuous and young Dionysius, but Teodota threw himself at Dionysius' feet and shed

---

[120] Teodota was Dionysius' uncle who pleaded for Eraclide.
[121] Eraclide, the General under Dionysius II who allied himself with Dion against Dionysius.

tears, pleading for his uncle, Eraclide. And I reminded Dionysius of the pact we made earlier to show kindness and mercy, the signs of benevolent rule. He has relented for now."

"Yes, you must leave. Write the letter now and I will see that it gets to Taranto. You see how Dionysius lusts for complete power. I will give you my goodbye now, for I need to return to Akrai and my family. Good dear teacher and friend, I will miss you. I hope this is not a farewell, but I fear things here are deteriorating quickly and Athens is a great distance. You have given me more than you ever realized. Go in peace, and know you leave many disciples here."

"I will miss you, Alexandros! You truly are a good man whose head is made for philosophy. Take what you have learned and try to create a just state in your most scenic home city. Let Akrai shine on its hill, so that men will know it is possible. The gods keep you safe!"

And so, they departed, each eventually reaching his home place, Plato to Athens and Alexandros to Akrai. Each had found that true and loyal friend who was an important part of Plato's foundation of justice and the beginning of a just state.

THE MUSE (2001 AD)

Plato's interactions with the Dionysii were mind blowing. I was still recoiling from the relationships and interactions among Ektor, Alexandros, and Plato. This further cemented the connection between Akrai, my ancestors' homeland, and the disciples of this famous philosopher. I wish I had learned this while my ancestors had been alive so that I could have shared this fascinating history. It had connected me even more strongly to my roots.

"Yes, I see that the revelations in the caves are opening your eyes to the interconnectedness of history. We tend to see history as something which happened long ago, but we don't realize that in a way it also happened to ourselves, all of us. It affected our ancestors, and through them, it affects us. It colors what we now believe as truth. What we do now will affect those who are to come. We and they enter the strands of the tapestry!"

"I see more clearly now, even though I seem to be speaking with an apparition!"

"No, no, young man! I am real. The gods have permitted me this gift, but we must move rapidly. I don't have much time left. First let me tell you of Timoleon, a great man from Corinth.

"Timoleon came to power in Siracusa. After Dion's death, Timoleon, the great leader and general, arrived from Corinth with enough forces to defeat Carthage. Siracusa's territory now increased so that most of the island was now in her control, including Selinunte and Erice on the west coast. Once established he introduced democracy, even though he favored the aristocrats. He provided a constitution to safeguard against tyranny and repopulated the cities of the island with immigrants and soldiers from Corinth, promising them land.[122]

"Now, follow me to Akrai!"

As he turned toward the door, I could see the back of his white pallium[123] trimmed in dark red. Down the back was the famous diagram which I had seen many times in school. A large sphere inscribed inside a cylinder of the same diameter outlined in the same dark red. It was his method of proving that the volume of the sphere is 2/3 that of the cylinder. I had known that since sixth grade, but to see it on Archimedes back was another matter!

I would follow him as long I could."

"I'm coming!"

---

[122] Timoleon ruled from 345-337 and comes to Siracusa with 60,000 Hellenes because Carthaginians were attempting to conquer the island. There was friction between new and old inhabitants. Akrai's building boon was fueled by the soldiers arriving from Corinth. The Oligarchy ruled from 337-317. This was called the Third Democracy. Agathocles rules from 317-289 and rescued large parts of the island from the Carthaginians. On his death bed he restores the Forth Democracy.

[123] Pallium – a large cloak.

BOOK VIII

Rome

340 - 212 BC

Strategos – *general Gamoroi – nobility Killichiroi – commoners*
Rēks – *Polemarchos - title of rulers of Akrai.*

300 BC's

Felox – *Rēks of Akrai, son of Alexandros*

289 BC

Agathocles – *Ruler of Siracusa for a short period during the marriage of Phidias and Liastrax*
Liastrax – *Hellenized Siculi daughter of Nolox from Akrai. Marries Phidias*
Nolox – *Hellenized Siculi Rēks of Akrai and grandson of Alexandros*
Phidias – *Hellenized Siculi mathematician of Siracusa, cousin of Hiero II, marries Liastrax, father of Archimedes*

278 BC's

Archimedes – *Hellenized Siculi son of Phidias and Liastrax*
Hector – *Hiero's war minister*
Hierocles – *Hellene noble whose illegitimate son was Hiero II, and through whom Phidias was related to Hiero II.*
Hiero II – *Hellene tyrant of Siracusa. Illegitimate son of Hierocles.*
Migru – *trusted slave of Archimedes*

260 – 212 BC

Eleni – *Archimedes' wife from Akrai*

Anax – *Keeper of the Sicani oral history which he transcribed for Luxo*

Hieronymus – *tyrant of Siracusa. He succeeded his grandfather, Hiero II, when he ascended the throne at 15 and was in power for only 13 months*

Luxo – *Hellenized Siculi scribe of Akrai who wrote on the cave walls*

Sevas – *the son of Archimedes' old age*

CHAPTER 24

CAVE 8 WALL 3 (340-250 BC)

AKRAI EXPANDS

INSCRIPTION P

I, Luxo, now record a turbulent time in the region of Siracusa, including Akrai. It was my father's and grandfather's time and much of what I record is of their remembrance. Siracusa was called a republic under Timoleon, the Corinthian general who defeated Athens. But the oligarchs remained a powerhouse. Then a rebellion of the people led to the Third Democracy which ruled for almost twenty years. The world was afire as the power of a new Macedonian general was spreading in the east. Though Akrai was at the periphery, it experienced a population boom as Timoleon had invited new Corinthian settlers. Almost 60,000 settled in the province.

Alexandros returned to Akrai after Plato had left Siracusa. Once at home he decided he needed to speak with his son. He had the servant tell Felox to meet him in the orchard outside of the walls. As they walked among the trees, Alexandros said, "Felox, my son, you have grown into a strong, intelligent young man. You have seen my disappointment at the inability of Plato to establish a philosopher king in Siracusa. My heart was torn when

I had to see Plato leave so downcast. I shall never see him again, but I have tried to foster a justice here in Akrai."

"Yes, father, this is now a fine example of justice and harmony. You have also improved the lives of our citizens by constructing the large cisterns supplying the continuous flow of clean water from the ancient aqueduct. Our bathhouse and fountains are always plentiful even in the heat of summer."

"Felox, I have tried to do my best. However, I still think upon my friend and what an irreplaceable sage we have lost. We are both elderly and I don't believe I will ever see him again."

"Father, you have much to be proud of, as I have said. You have also instilled in me the desire to follow in your footsteps, and I try to teach my children as you have done. Nolox already is being instructed by me in the mathematics of Pythagoras. I have made wooden forms for him to recognize how triangles can be joined to form rectangles and squares. He amazes me even at his early age of six."

"Son, I too am proud of you, and that is why I have asked you to come to me today. I know that I am close to leaving this world and joining that of the spirits. You must be strong, for I will propose to the council that you take my place when the time is right. Just remember to be just and surround yourself with trusted men who are loyal to our principles. It is imperative that you and your councilmen are loyal to our traditions and the principles which men like Plato have laid out. That is all I wish you to promise me."

"Father, you sadden me with this talk. You are still healthy and vibrant. But let me assure you that I will carry on what you have begun here in Akrai, and I will try to raise my children to do the same."

Plato's philosophy lived on in Alexandros. Alexandros had taken to heart the words of the philosopher: *Establishing true and loyal friendships is the foundation of justice.* Alexandros ruled

Akrai for twenty more years before this job was passed to his son Felox, who was unanimously confirmed by the council. Though he was not as philosophical as his father, Felox continued to rule in his father's fashion.

The town grew and prospered. The new Corinthians began a building boom which continued into the next century. A large theater holding seven hundred people was constructed during the reign of Nolox, Alexandros' grandson. In addition, a Bouleuterion[124] was built next to the theater in a semicircle which could hold as many as fifty people for council meetings and symposia.

These changes inspired a rich cultural life where philosophers, teachers, and plays could be held. This Akrai, this acropolis on the hill, had a rich, multiethnic population with deep roots.

The thoughts, skills, and heritage of the Minoans, Sicani, Siculi, Trojans, and Hellenes had constructed a woven marvel of strong, contrasting colors, yet hues which worked together to raise both the spiritual and material lives of the people of Akrai.

---

[124] Bouleuterion – a smaller theater that was used mostly for city council meetings.

CHAPTER 25

Cave 8, Wall 4

THE INTERREGNUM (289 BC)

INSCRIPTION Σ

I, Luxo, have come to the end of my story. The revolt in Siracusa tried to restore democracy but it brought uncertainty and fear. Then Agathocles ruled before a short democracy arose. It was during this turbulent period that Phidias and Liastrax married. Their story is the final weave in the tapestry. They had many children, but one was to achieve heights greater than any could have imagined. Phidias was an astronomer and closely related to Hiero II, the tyrant who later ruled Siracusa after the Interregnum of the three tyrants. Liastrax was descended from the great Trojan Egestes, builder of the great temples, as well as from Suko and Xavo, the Siculi who had crossed Skyla and Charybdis from Italia, and from Daedalus, who had flown from Minoa. Her blue blood was made rich and thick with that of brave men and women of creativity and invention. The stars and the gods aligned to produce a most creative human being, who would bring much change and knowledge to the world. No one else has achieved the heights in his field in the entire Hellenic world.

Phidias left Siracusa in early morning. He had calculated the solar eclipse to occur at noon in three days' time. He was taking his entourage to Akrai, for on that acropolis he would have a better view of this gift from the gods. Upon arriving he set up his instruments, the latest from the Library of Alexandria, that would try to measure the diameter of the moon as it crossed in front of the sun. Many calculations had been made of the diameter, size, and distance of the moon from the earth. Now Phidias wanted to verify some of those observations.

There had been much fear in the city when they heard of the approaching eclipse. Phidias knew that this was just the working of nature and tried to calm their fears. However, he also realized that myths and religion held a powerful sway on most people, and that science was regarded with suspicion and sorcery. Part of his job was to dispel this belief.

"Greetings Phidias, glad you have come. We are looking forward to your instructing us here in Akrai." Nolox came forward to welcome the astronomer. Nolox was a descendent of the Rēkses of Akrai. Since the time of the tyrants, they were now labeled Polemarchos, or Supreme Commander since the military outpost had become more important during these uncertain times.

Phidias greeted Nolox, "Hail, Rēks! We are glad to be here so we can have an unobstructed view of the heavenly bodies. This evening I would like to address the citizens as to what they will see and the precautions they should observe when the sun will hide its face. It is imperative that they understand that this is a natural occurrence that occurs often, but not in every place. In fact, this will not be seen in Akragas or Catana."

Nolox looked at Phidias with pride. "We are all honored that you have chosen Akrai to do your observations. Yes, you can come to the theater at sun-down and I will notify the people. They will be eager to hear your words. Our people are open to new ways of thinking. I remember my grandfather telling me about Plato's visit. He was a great man to have graced our small city. Once you have arranged things, come to my home, and have dinner."

Phidias smiled, "Thank you Polemarchos, I would be honored."

The discussions at dinner were very animated about the political situation and whether the forces of democracy would overturn Agathocles, or whether Hiero, Phidias' relative, would control the mother city of Siracusa to the south.

Polemarchos Nolox finally interrupted, "Enough of this fruitless talk. What will be, will be! I want to introduce you to my daughter, Liastrax. She has been learning the loom today and will be happy to have some distraction. After you see her, take her for a walk in our orchard. It is a beautiful warm evening, but a mild sea breeze is making the air light. The moon is new so take the torches with you to light the way."

Phidias bowed to the Polemarchos and said, "You are most gracious. I have been busy with my work these past weeks and will be happy for a change."

Nolox's wife entered with a tall slender young woman wearing a long flowing rose colored garment and a thin veil covering her face. "This is my daughter, Liastrax. She and her elder sister will show you the garden and the orchard. Go now and enjoy the evening."

"Good evening, Liastrax. I am pleased to make your acquaintance. How are you this evening?"

"I am well, Lord Phidias. I hear you will lecture us on the morrow about the celestial happenings."

"Yes. I am so glad I will have the opportunity to shed light on this great eclipse, which few people are privileged to see because it covers only a very few miles in extent."

"People here say that it foretells great catastrophe. Perhaps it is an omen of wars, plagues, floods?"

"These things occur without the moon or the sun. Just a few years ago Carthage was waging war with us and there had been no eclipse. Celestial events are just coincidences, not omens."

"I admire your strong faith in your philosophy. I wish I were more certain. I will be there at the symposium, even though it is frowned upon for women. The men in my family have always valued women's education, and I am most grateful. My parents admire the writings of Sappho, and it is said my ancestors knew her centuries past in Siracusa."

"Liastrax, you truly are an interesting woman. I hope to know you better."

"Let us enjoy the garden. Look, Etna smokes and the red fire rises from the summit!"

"The ancient Siculi believe that Adhrano, the God of Fire and Shaking, lives within Etna. They have a large temple on the slopes above guarded by one-thousand sacred hounds. Though I am neither a believer in gods nor myths, I would like to visit some-day."

"Perhaps we can venture there together? But for now, let's enjoy this lovely garden. Look here. These here are my favorite peaches, and they look ripe. Phidias, there! Reach for that very large one which has dew dripping from it and let us share it!"

Phidias stretched onto his toes and barely could claim the prize, but then placed it in Liastrax's delicate hand. Her long, beautiful fingers raised it to her mouth, while Phidias stared into her eyes. After a small bite, she raised the other side of the peach for Phidias to take. He took a bite as she did of the delicious fruit. They each ate, and the remainder fell to the ground, as their eyes met in a shared moment.

At that moment Liastrax's sister thought she should say something! "I am here as your chaperone, sister. Let us return now! Father awaits us." The sister took Liastrax's hand and led her away quickly back to the house. Phidias was left staring at Etna and wondering if there would be more than one eclipse in the following days.

The day of the eclipse began with a bright blue, cloudless sky and perfectly orange sun like the giant peach which they had shared the preceding evening. It rose above the smoking Etna and promised an eventful day.

"Phidias, what a beautiful day! The mornings are still cool, and Persephone has left the underworld! The green capers and red poppies fill the earth with their sweet fragrance."

"Yes, Liastrax, the world compliments your beauty today. I hope you are as excited as I am about the events we are about to witness. This is a first time for me also. Total eclipses are very rare occurrences, and most men never see even one.

"Phidias, I should not have acted that way, but I enjoyed being with you a great deal. It is as much my fault as yours. Anyway, my sister was there to remind us to behave, but I felt like a child. Let us not speak of it."

"Neither will I, but I so enjoyed our walk and time together last evening in the orchard.

Now, let us go up to the theater. I must prepare."

Phidias arranged his scientific instruments on the orchestra stage of the open-air theater. He was to study the progression of the moons shadow across the face of the sun, until totality, when the sun would be obscured.

"Liastrax, help me set up this angled table. It is angled so that it will catch the rays of the sun during the eclipse. I have turn keys on the lower legs so that I can raise it to follow the sun as it rises in the sky. The table has a small aperture in its center. I will aim it exactly at the sun, so that the shadow will project on the base, which is lined with papyrus. I can trace the sun and moon's shapes with this quill and ink. Hopefully, the moon's shadow with reveal whether it has the same apparent size as the sun when the eclipse is total."

"But why not look directly into the sun?" cried one of the

students sitting in the theatron just above the orchestra.

"Surely, son, you realize that you cannot look directly at the sun for even a short period on any day without your eyes tearing and becoming temporarily blinded. And the sun is so incredibly bright that you will not be able to see the moon's shadow until the entire sun is obscured. In Alexandria I learned that many people looking at eclipses were blinded for life, and then have accused the gods of treachery. And in any case, I could not record the size of the shadow by just looking. I need a record. Do not be foolish, young man!"

Liastrax, studied the apparatus. "So, seeing the shadow and drawing it, we can tell the radius of the moon as well as the sun and compare the relative sizes."

"Correct. Aristarchus claims there is no difference in their relative sizes. Hence, knowing the distances from the Earth to both the moon and the sun, calculated by other means, we can assume the sizes are in ratio to the distances. Any slight difference would yield a greater diameter of the sun, by the increased percentage which we will calculate."

As the multitude of Akrai gathered and stared at the apparatus, they were transfixed to see the shadow slowly grow and cover the disc of the sun. Phidias had carefully traced the entire circle of the sun and the slight crescent of the moon as it started to cover the sun's disc partially.

He then removed the papyrus, labelling it with A for the number one. He then removed that papyrus, adjusted the table's legs, for the sun had risen slightly higher in the sky, and repeated the procedure, which showed a larger crescent moon, labelling the accompanying papyrus B. He continued until the tenth papyrus, I, where the whole disc of the sun was covered by the moon. He continued in a similar fashion with ten more papyri until he labelled the final K. The twentieth diagram showed the sun's disc without any shadow. Daytime had returned to Akrai, and Phidias now had a precise record of the eclipse which he would take back to Siracusa to study and measure.

When he got to papyrus I, the moment of totality, all the brightness of the day vanished. He, Liastrax, and the crowd in the theater let out a collective "Ahh!"

Some called upon the gods, "Zeus, save us!" "Aphrodite, help us!" "Kore, return to us from the underworld!"

The birds started to sing, and small animals came out of the trees, and ripples of light moved like sparkling waves along the ground. Tiny images were seen on the ground repeating what Phidias was recording. Many people stared directly at the sun's image. Some people covered their heads and headed for home. Dogs barked.

But Phidias, Liastrax, and a few brave souls remained to finally look up and watch the corona burst forth from around the moon's shadow. They were all in awe, but Phidias yelled,

"Now, all, look away! You must not stare at the bright sun. Look instead at the shadow!"

All followed except for one poor soul, who kept staring. Finally, he looked away and cried, "I can see nothing! I am blind! Apollo has taken my sight!" He ran away stumbling down the theater's steps, when another man took his hand and led him away.

Phidias looked at Liastrax, "Some people do not listen to those of us who know of what we speak. They will remain blind or die in following their beliefs rather than good advice of philosophers!"

Liastrax replied, "I am sorry for Hippocrates. He is a good man but believes in every myth and god. But what the gods have showed us today is truly beautiful! It is as if Apollo has crowned Selene, the moon, with a beautiful crown of gold. I shall never forget the sight!"

"Oh, I shall never forget what we have seen today. The beauty of nature in indescribable and vanishes rapidly. Many will go away and forget and just go about their work-a-day lives. But I have dedicated my life to this work of understanding nature. I already see that Aristarchus was very close to being correct. But from the tenth outline I observe that the discs are not exactly equal. I will calculate the discrepancy. Aristarchus claims that the Sun is six and three-quarters to seven times the diameter of the earth. I will claim a larger number. See there is at least a one in ten larger disc surrounding the moon's shadow.

"I see that you have the drawings that will help you do a more precise calculation. I am impressed and in awe of your ability as much as I am of your character!"

"You honor me, Liastrax. You have become a dear friend, and I hope we can see each other again soon."

And so, the day was a great success in all spheres of Phidias' life, and Liastrax felt she had found not only a friend, but a man with whom she could live with and love. This friendship was fostered untypically, for it was an unusual occurrence in Hellenic custom. However, the people of Akrai shared the influence of many different tribes and peoples. Phidias returned many times to visit Nolox, and finally corralled the courage to ask him for his daughter's hand.

To Phidias' surprise, Nolox was pleased and honored. He was convinced that Hiero, Phidias' relative, would soon save Siracusa from democracy and restore the oligarchs. There would be no better position for his daughter than to be married to Phidias. Nolox accepted the offer and after the wedding Phidias would take Liastrax to Siracusa to start a family. He smiled to himself and was pleased.

The union was a happy one and within the year they had a son. Liastrax would have many other children. This boy grew up amidst his father's parents and aunts and uncles who doted on him.

He showed his intelligence from an early age, and as he grew, he was sent to the best tutors in Siracusa. The boy also met many of the leaders and intellectuals of the great city, for they often visited their home in Achradina.[125]

---

[125] Achradina – the northeastern district of Siracusa next to Ortygia on the coast.

CAVES BELOW THE AKRAI AKROPOLIS

CHAPTER 26

Cave 8, Wall 2

THE RITES OF KORE (289 BC)

W hen Phidias' first child had reached the age of two years, Liastrax asked Phidias if they could go to Akrai to visit her parents and show the child to them. So, one fine fall day they decided to take the short trip to her city. When they arrived, the people were getting ready for a great feast. After talking to the Polemarchos and her mother, Liastrax approached Phidias.

"Phidias, I know you and the gods are not friends, but my parents wish us to enter the mysteries of Kore. We have many ancient rites here in Akrai, as you do in Siracusa, but these mysteries are more intense and go back to the times of my Sicani and Siculi ancestors. It is an important rite of acceptance."

"I certainly understand. I too have been pressured at home, because of my relationship to Hiero. I will conform, but reluctantly, for I know that custom requires certain acceptances. I do not agree or believe, but I will accept for I do not wish to meet the fate of our beloved Socrates, who was accused of corrupting the youth of Athens. He was not a strong believer in the gods."

"Well said, my love. And besides, we will participate together."

So, at the appointed time of the new moon in the middle of Autumn, they both dressed in simple woolen cloaks died in black, with substantial hoods which almost covered their entire faces. The Autumn cold had already descended, so they were happy to have warm clothes. They met the other initiates and priests of

Kore in the agora, the central square and marketplace of Akrai. From there, they proceeded to the temple of Kore near the main gate, where the priest offered prayers and sacrifice. They then were led in Kore's hymn, as they continued down the hill to the caves below the city where the rites were to be conducted.

HYMN TO DEMETER

Praise our Queen! Our Mother!
Who rescued us from demise,
Fair-haired Demeter
Beautiful and wise!
Maiden Daughter, Kore
Danced upon the earth
Among crocus, violets, and capers
In sweet sea air and mirth.
Then a horrendous voice and thunder!
Father Zeus commanded Hades,
His underworldly brother:
"Abduct the maiden! Drag her under!"

Kore's soul with sorrow filled
Her heart full of grief, she sighed,
"I do not wish to go!"
Neither gods nor men heard Kore's cries.
Except Demeter, the Great Fruit Bearer.
She into veiled bird transformed
To search for Kore high and wide.

Bird Goddess now flies
As the days stretched to ten,

'Till Helios' chariot she spies.
He pities her for Hades' sin!
"I know, Demeter, where Kore was sent.
Come into my cart
Fly with me to the place of fate
To wait by this special well."
And there, in deep sorrow she wept and wept!
There dressed in black and veiled,
She seemed a forlorn old crone.

Came then Celeus' daughters four
Pitying her - so sad, so dark, so alone.
And so, Callidice and Callithoe,
And Cledisidice, and Demo
Took Demeter to their home.
And in the presence of the maidens four,
Chloe now appeared and bloomed,
As Demeter into Chloe transformed!
The house in divine Splendor filled,
Rousing Father Zeus,
Who ordered Iris and the gods:
"Entice our Queen to return to us!"

"No, no, to Eleusis I will not return
'Till by my side is Kore dear!"
So, Zeus decided to relent
"Hermes, quickly to Hades fly!"

"Hades!" Hermes called, "Take note
Kore must be released!
Men starve, and seeds fail to sprout!"
But Hades, full of wiles,

Turned to Kore in his lair,
A pomegranate offered her,
The trap, the snare,
Bondage and an everlasting tie!
Then and there he ravished Justice,
Goddess of Dry Fruits.
Now the earth would yearly die.

To Mother Demeter, Kore is given
Filling both with joy and gladness
Then overwhelming them with eternal sadness.
Mother Earth, Divine, knows now
Kore must each year to Hades go
Once earth completes her blooms
From the seeds which Kore sows.

Sing Praise to the Goddesses, two,
Birds chirp with varied melodies
For now, earth blooms anew.
Tall grasses sway in symphony,
Filled with buzzing bees,
While men reply in harmony,
"Returned are the Goddesses
Of bounty and thickest, sweetest honey."

But gloom on the horizon yearly sits.
Hades will reclaim his prize.
Kore must return to him,
Now, called Goddess of Destruction,
Persephone her name!

The cave was dark, lit only by a few candles arranged around the huge altar block. The altar stone was flat, large, and cold. Closest to the stone and to the left and right sat twelve young maidens, in very sheer, almost transparent dress, each marked with a sign of the zodiac. Liastrax turned to Phidias and whispered, "By Aphrodite, these young girls will be taken ill by this cold! I shiver just seeing them!"

Phidias sighed, "Ach! Religion! No wonder these mysteries are kept secret and we had to swear not to reveal the details! The girls probably have been laced with hot wine, or some potion! How else could they have the courage to come to this event, not knowing what may befall them!"

Once the initiates entered, they were directed to sit on stones arranged in a semi-circle around the altar. Once seated one of the priestesses of the Elysian Mysteries lit a standing torch behind the initiates so that shadows were cast upon the altar and the wall behind.

Suddenly from the dark recesses of the cave behind the altar stone, a large, tall, muscled figure jumped into the light so that his enormous shadow was cast upon the back wall. The terrified maidens and initiates gave out a terrified scream. Phidias and Liastrax looked at each other with wide eyes. The figure was barely clothed by a miniscule deep red loin cloth and covered in dark red with black symbols on his arms, legs, and chest. His long black beard came to a point on his chest, and he wore a golden crown which was laced with raised pointed stones in alternating black obsidian and red rubies forming Praise to our Queen, our Mother!

His movements created a flickering menagerie of shadow, which dizzied the audience with his magnified form. His black hair curled around his shoulders and two horns protruded from behind his ears. His large dark eyes reflected the candlelight in an ominous way. He carried a long golden bident[126] staff. His face was covered in white. He jumped upon the altar stone.

"I have come to steal the sun, to end the greenery, the growth of living things. Life must cease. I have come to satisfy my lust!"

He circled around the terrified virgins who sat transfixed, staring at the terrifying apparition.

He strolled about, jumping up and down from the altar stone, staring at each virgin. As he approached any one of them, they cowered. Finally, he came to rest among the three girls whose symbols were ♎ (Libra) ♏ (Scorpio) ♐ (Sagittarius).

"Why is he stopping there?" whispered Liastrax.

"I can only assume these are the three signs preceding winter, the time of death," replied Phidias.

He first took Libra's hand and held it to his nose, inhaling deeply, then dropping it as if poison. Then he had Sagittarius rise and placed his face right up against hers. She shook violently while he licked her ear, then pushed her away. She slithered to the ground whimpering.

Liastrax and Phidias looked at each other in disgust.

Then Hades grabbed Scorpio by the shoulders violently and placed her upon the altar, which was indented. The initiates could only see her shadow on the back wall of the cave. Before she lay down, the initiates could see her wide eyes filled with doom as she stared back at him.

"You will be my virgin bride. You will accompany me to my lair, you, Demeter's daughter, Kore! But first we must consummate the union. Ha, ha, ha, ha!"

He tore her shear garment away. The back wall was filled with Hades enormous form as he proceeded to rape the poor girl. She was silent and did not protest. People stared at the shadows in disbelief, but neither did any say a word.

---

[126] Bident – having two teeth – like a pitchfork but with only two tines. It is the symbol of Hades.

However, Phidias turned to Liastrax, "I cannot sit here any longer and be silent. This is a travesty and lacks all semblance of civilization!"

"Wait, Phidias, wait. If you speak up now, they will know you do not believe, and you will be mocked."

They reluctantly continued to watch the rite. When the rape was complete, the monster fell, exhausted upon Kore, then rose and spoke. "Scorpio, Kore, you are mine. We will now descend to the underworld and death will reign upon the Earth. You will not paint flowers any longer! Ha, ha, ha, ha!"

He lifted her upon his shoulders and carried her away and vanished as quickly as he appeared.

Then from another corner a matron appeared. She was beautifully dressed in a light green gown with a crown of white and yellow flowers. She carried her sheaf of wheat.

"That must be Demeter," whispered Liastrax.

"I am Demeter, mother of Kore. I have come to find my beloved. She was stolen from this Earth, which now lies dying. These flowers on my crown are the last. There will be no others, and the wheat will vanish from the earth. I must rescue her, or life will vanish. I have searched the world over and still have not found Kore. I will implore Father Zeus for remedy. Initiates, you must help, cry with me, pray, and plead with me. Drink the potions of mushroom broth set before you so that you may commune with the gods."

They all drank, Phidias and Liastrax also, but with great reluctance. They all fell into a deep hallucinogenic trance induced by the mushroom broth.

"Phidias, the room is turning! We are falling, falling deep within the earth. There is fire everywhere. Do you see?"

"Yes, I am here with you. Hold my hand. Do not fear, it is only a dream. Be brave. Look, there. There is Hades still cavorting with Scorpio. But look, Demeter approaches them."

"Hades, god of evilness and darkness! Father Zeus has commanded the release of my Kore. Release her! Come, daughter follow me to the world of life!"

Hades replied sirking, "Demeter, do not be in such haste. Let Kore finish her gift. I have given her the sweetest, most succulent pomegranate. See how she is enjoying each small bite!"

Demeter shouted, "Kore! No, no, do not eat one more morsel. Do not consume one more seed! Hades, you evil god! You have tricked her, for she who eats in this world must stay forever."

Kore dropped the remaining fruit.

Immediately, a deep voice reverberated in the cave. "I, Father Zeus, command that Kore must stay with Hades for six months, but she will be allowed the other six to refresh the world above. Hades, this is my will. You are to follow it. She will remain with you till Spring!"

Hades gave a wild howl which reverberated throughout the cave. "So, your will is my command, but I still have her for six months! My plan was not utterly foiled! She must return each Huakinthios (Υακινθιος), the month when the cold arrives above."

Hades put his hands on his waist and stared directly at Kore's mother. "Leave her here, Demeter, until the sun crosses higher in the sky. Then you can reclaim her for six months. I have many days of enjoyment remaining! Ha, ha, ha!"

"Hades you are a malevolent scoundrel! But be assured I will return in the Spring to rescue my daughter."

Demeter then addressed the initiates, "Men, Women, you have observed the treachery of Hades. Beware for yourselves. He can do even worse to you."

She then addressed Kore. "Daughter you were known as Κορη (Kore – young maiden), from now on I will address you as Περσεφονη (Persephone – bringer of destruction)!"

And with that, she turned and left in one direction, and

Hades carried Persephone off in another. The great torch was extinguished and only two candles remained on the altar giving off a very faint light. There was complete silence.

Phidias slowly emerged from his torpor. "Liastrax, come back, come back to me!"

Her eyelashes flickered as she tried to focus. "O, Phidias, what a horrendous nightmare!"

"'T'was no dream, my love! It was the all too real reenactment of the tale of winter. Come, let us leave this infernal place."

They rose and slowly exited the cave, walking up the road to the acropolis to her father's house.

"You realize we must return in Spring, to complete the initiation. We will then receive the scapula[127] of honor which signifies that we have taken part. Then all will know we have entered in the Elysian Mysteries. I am not looking forward to it, but I think that the worst is over."

"Let us put this into the back of our minds till then. We are here with your parents who are enjoying our first born. Let us be joyful for them."

In the Spring they returned to Akrai and descended into the same cave, but in the morning. The cave was flooded in light both from the entrance, but also from the circular hole above the altar. The hole had not been evident when they were there in the autumn. Demeter was standing by the altar dressed in her emerald-green gown, this time holding a large cornucopia filled with fruits and flowers. She wore a golden crown interspersed with laurel leaves. The altar had vases filled with the first bright flowers of spring in yellow and blue interspersed with green sprigs. A flutist played a merry tune.

---

[127] Scapula – a object of piety which hangs over the shoulders with a medal or picture which rests on the breast.

"Hades, Hades, I call you to fulfil the will of Zeus! Bring me Persephone!"

Hades slowly appeared from behind a wall pulling Persephone behind him. "Take her, madam, take the bringer of chaos, but know she must return. That is the bargain!"

Demeter took the poor thin maiden by the hand and gently led her toward the entrance of the cave. "Initiates, follow us to Kore's temple. Sing hymns for it is Spring. Take the flowers and throw petals before us, for the Earth is reborn today for another year! Be merry and sing! Give thanks to Zeus and all the gods who have bestowed graces upon you. Sing, sing!"

The crowd processed up to the Acropolis as other citizens joined the festivities. Drums, trumpets, and tambourines joined in the merriment. As they sang, and danced up the road, they gathered flowers and stopped to pray at Kore's temple, singing her hymn. The initiates were presented with the emerald-green scapulars[128] which were draped over their necks. They then proceeded to the agora processing around Aphrodite's temple where fires were cooking lamb, beef, and tables were filled with abundance. It was a day for merriment, for it was finally Spring!

Phidias turned to his wife. "Liastrax, this was the only enjoyable part of the entire ordeal! The Autumn rites have made me even less disposed to religion than I have ever been. I do not care to participate in any more devotions!"

"I agree. Let us make a pact to perform as few rites as we must, but never again any mysteries!"

"I profoundly agree. Our only mystery shall be our union and the other children which may ensue."

"Praise be to Aphrodite, the goddess of love!"

"Indeed, praise to Her!"

---

[128] Scapula – a object of piety which hangs over the shoulders with a medal or picture which rests on the breast.

THE MUSE (2001 AD)

Wow! Writing the story of the rites of Demeter from the transcription of the caves was shocking and eye opening. I had read of the Elysian Mysteries, and how very little was known about the secretive rites. But here, Luxo had decided to explicitly explain all! It showed me how much of these ancient rites were taken over into later days, and even survive into the present day in the church rites of Akrai. On many visits I had observed the *festas* dedicated to the Virgin or different saints. The processions, the spreading of flowers, walking on knees or barefoot, the prayers and hymns are all carryovers from ancient times. There are even other rites, in South America, where suffering and flagellation are parts of the program!

As I sat thinking and reading what was in cave nine, I seemed to remember the name Phidias from somewhere? But where? O, that was a very common Hellenic name, but Phidias was an astronomer. I had studied ancient astronomers in the history of science, but right now the name meant nothing. I went into the kitchen to prepare myself a cup of tea with hot milk before I retired for the evening. As I turned to grab the tea pot, I felt a presence. Turning, I saw him, but he was different. His back was turned to me. He was looking out the kitchen window. He was about the same height and not much thinner, except the belt around his waist on his short chlamys was drawn tightly, and he stood more erect with broader shoulders. His hair was jet-black, not white. Maybe it was another spirit?

At that moment he turned, and I saw a young man, perhaps in his late teens. But studying his face I knew. "Archimedes, it is you! You have returned to your youth! Have you made a deal with Aphrodite?"

"She watches over me, but we spirits may take many forms. I wished to show myself to you in my youth. The reason is that now you embark on the final journey with me. I will take you with me to my home and on my journeys. You will see the rich life I have had and the loved ones with whom I shared my short time on earth. I will not be here much longer, and for me this is the most important part. Do you not remember Phidias, the astronomer?"

"I have heard that name, but, but wait! Phidias is Archimedes' father, YOUR FATHER!"

"Yes, that is correct."

"So, this is where Luxo has led me, to your story. And there is a connection to Akrai! My grandfather's home village, but in the 19th and 20th C!"

"Yes, yes. We are connected. You are part of these men and women, of the Sicani, Siculi, Elymi, and Hellene! Artemis, goddess of the hunt, showed me your lineage. Once I knew your interest in history, science, and genealogy, we decided we would call upon you to be our voice."

"Now, put on a decent chlamys, not those strange two- legged things, and we will go! Come!"

CHAPTER 27

CAVE 9, WALL 1 (CIRCA 278 BC)

ARCHIMEDES

INSCRIPTION T

I, Luxo, have come to my final wall of the final cave. I have been leading you from the origins of our tribes to the final demise of Hellenic rule in Trinacria. As this is my eightieth year, I wish to complete my task before I must leave this realm for the next. It is with both happy and sad heart that I complete this story which ends in the greatest man to live upon this small island and who has contributed to the benefit of all men. I am sad that our independence is gone, but as Plato has told us, there are cycles in politics as there are in nature. Rome is here and grows more powerful each day. We have now made our bed with her, for better or worse. I hope that this story reminds you in your time that you will have days of democracy and independence, kings and philosopher kings, and most terrible tyrants. Love and Strife contend with each other endlessly. Take hope, my friends, for as Empedocles reminds us, the only constancy in life is change.

"Archimedes, your schooling is almost done here. Have you thought what you will do next?" Phidias was anxious for his son. He realized he was gifted, but he had seen this with other gifted students of his. When they enjoyed many things, they had difficulty settling, or never did."

"Father, I enjoy looking at the stars, and studying the theories of Aristarchus. I also am intrigued by the mathematics of Pythagoras and the geometry of Euclid. I too believe, as Aristarchus taught, that the Earth circles the sun, but I keep quiet about it, for not offending those that believe in the gods. But mostly, I am intrigued with Pythagoras and his theory of numbers. As you know I have worked on levers and studied ratios. I have yet much to learn. Right now, I am intrigued with the circle, the most perfect of all geometric shapes."

"My son, this is what I mean. You must choose now and proceed, or your life will be but a circle, forever circling upon yourself, and never coming to some endpoint!"

"Yes, father. You are very wise. Perhaps I need some wise teacher to help me on my road."

"Yes. I have inquired. Since Hiero took power, I have requested an audience. I know that Alexandria is the place for scholarship, and I know you are more than qualified to be at the great library where the world's greatest teachers hold their symposia. There is also the greatest accumulation of knowledge that the world has yet seen. We are grateful to the great Alexander for establishing the collection of scrolls. How would you like to attend?"

"Father, it would be the greatest opportunity! I would give anything to go to that great center. I might even study under the great Eratosthenes or even Aristarchus, himself, both of whom still are alive! I would give anything for this opportunity."

"So be it. We will approach Hiero."

So, father and son sought an audience which was granted them in Ortygia. Young Archimedes wore a short chiton with a wide black stripe on the bottom, the color of Siracusa.

His father wore a long grey chiton, with a white chlamys over his shoulder, pinned with symbol of the crescent moon. They were led into Hiero's throne room.

"Hail, my Lord and uncle. This is my son, Archimedes."

"Welcome. It has been a while since I have seen you, Phidias! Why do you make yourself so scarce? And I have never seen your son. Now you bring him grown, and handsome! Why now? Do you wish an appointment for him?"

"Your grace, no, not an appointment, but another type of favor. Young Archimedes is a brilliant youth. He has outpaced all the learning available in our great city. I believe he can be of future worth to Ortygia. I was hoping you could find it in your magnanimity to send him on to Alexandria, to the great library. There he might grow in knowledge and return to teach our young and help advise you in matters of learning or defense or public projects."

"Does the boy wish to go? Is he one to use this opportunity for the good, or will he drink, cavort, and play with the boys and maidens of Egypt? I understand the Egyptian maidens are trained in the arts of seduction! If I agree, I must have your word and his that he will use his time wisely, since he will be responsible to the State."

Archimedes stepped forward. "Lord Hiero do not think me bold if I speak. I am not one to cavort. I have used my sixteen years to better myself, to assist my father, and to work on scientific endeavors. See here. Observe this rod which is six pous[129] in length. If I place a brick of five mina[130] on one end and a fulcrum at the next mark[131] from the brick, then only one mina will be required to lift the heavier block when it is placed at the opposite end. The lengths and the distances are in proportion. This I discovered myself. I surmise that if you give me a place to stand, and a lever

---

[129] Pous- Hellenic measurement of length equal to 30.82 cm or 12.13 in.

[130] Mina- measurement of mass equal to 431g or 15.2 oz.

[131] Mark- the rod was divided into six segments. He placed the fulcrum at the fifth division, when the brick was at the sixth division.

strong and long enough, I could move the earth!"

Hiero stared. "You certainly do not lack for enthusiasm and self-assuredness. I like a man who speaks his mind. You must come again and demonstrate what you have described. I might have another problem for you concerning my crown and its value. Stay, I will describe my concern, and then you may return when you think you have the answer. And, yes, I will allow you to go to Alexandria. I am sending some trading vessels in the month of Theudasios[132]. I will arrange for your passage and funds for your study."

"Thank you, great Sir. I am most appreciative. I will not disappoint you!"

"Come closer now. I will describe my problem. I wish no one else to hear. I will whisper in your ear."

Archimedes had gleaned a great deal from his interactions with the intellectuals from all over the world in Alexandria. He had grown in knowledge and became an esteemed member of the library elite. As the time approached for his return to Trinacria, he became saddened. He was leaving all his esteemed friends including Conan of Samos with whom he worked, developing the mathematics of the conic-cross sections. He had met the esteemed Euclid who valued him immensely. Though he was setting sail with a downcast heart, he was now also looking forward to returning home. The time in Alexandria had filled his head with so many ideas and he was impatient to get started working on his own. Now that he had finished his studies he was also wanting more of a personal life and a family. He had had numerous friends and liaisons in Egypt, but now he wanted more of life.

The return journey was tedious and there were many storms during the voyage. But now he could see the isle of Ortygia and

---

[132] Theudasios - Θευδασιοζ - the month of June

the great harbor of Siracusa spread out on the horizon. It was one of the great harbors of the world. Ortygia's tip stuck out in the sea like a claw on one end of a great oval. The opposite end of the oval created an opening of less than seven stadia[133], providing protection for the anchored ships and the city. In fact, ever since the attack of Athens in the Peloponnesian War[134], a great chain could be stretched at the mouth of this harbor to prevent foreign attacks. The land army of Athens was defeated near the fortifications of Akrai[135]. And even Akrai, his mother's home, had played a great role in the defeat of one of the greatest cities in the world.

But that was in the past. Now Archimedes already had some ideas about defense that he would share with Hiero as soon as he was able to obtain an audience. Soon they had rounded the tip of Ortygia, and he could see the fabled Font of Arethusa whose source was in Hellas! The gods truly had blessed his homeland.

Archimedes stepped off the ship with his trusted Migru, a slave who had been with him from childhood and who had cared for him in Egypt. Migru considered himself a Sicani, whose ancestors had lived in Trinacria since time immemorial. In fact, he was descended from Inguma of Pantalica and was a relative to Dutta, whom he considered an evil aberration. He was glad that Dutta had been killed.[136] When the Siculi arrived, Migru's family was taken into slavery, and they were brought to a homestead below Akrai. They had worked the wheat fields and olive groves for the landholders. When the Hellenes arrived the owners changed, but they remained slaves, generation upon generation.

---

[133] About 4000 ft. (1 stadia=606.9 ft.)

[134] 415 BC

[135] 413 BC

[136] Dutta was the evil chief who considered himself Siculi even though he had Sicani blood and carried out a massacre of the Sicani until he was killed by Letoni, circa 900 BC.

As Archimedes and Migru waited for their goods to be unloaded from the ship, they walked along the Portus Magnus of Siracusa, Migru began revealing the secrets of his prior life.

"When I was born, the owner needed money and put me on the auction block in Akrai. I was only 10, but healthy and strong for my age. One of the wealthy oil merchants was ready to purchase me. He was an evil man who also owned large brothels both in Akrai and Siracusa. Both he and his wife were poking me, looking at my nakedness and making lewd comments. I was in great fear. Then a very lovely young girl and her father also asked my name. "What is the name of this young boy?"

The slave trader responded, "His name is Migru. He is from the lowlands. He is a good field worker. His family has tended wheat and olives. He is strong. We are asking two Siracusan silver drachmae."

At that instant the brothel keeper interrupted, "Four drachmae"

Now Liastrax looked outraged, "Father, you must bid higher. That poor boy!"

Her father spoke up, "We will give you six!"

At that point the brothel keeper looked angry, but he was already eying two other youngsters on the block, a boy about twelve and a girl about thirteen. When the trader heard no other bids, he turned to Liastrax and her father, "Sold to the beautiful young lady for six drachmae!"

Liastrax gave a sigh but was concerned about the other children on the block. "Father, can we do nothing about the others? That fat oil merchant is horrid."

"Liastrax, I cannot cross him further. He is powerful, and we cannot buy every slave in Trinacria! Come let us take Migru home and have him bathe."

Lisatrax's father went up to the slave, "I understand you are called Migru? You are now ours. Pick up your chlamys and come with us. I am Demetrax and this is my daughter Liastrax."

"Yes, that is my name. My parents are in the fields in the lowlands. I have never been separated from them."

Liastrax spoke to him kindly, "We are a good family of Akrai. We treat our slaves well. Do not worry. Come to our home and bathe. We will give you clean clothes. Your duties will include working in our orchard. We have many fruit trees to be tended. When there is no work there, you will assist the other slaves in household chores. We do not believe in harsh treatment, but my father will not stand for foolishness. We will give you time to visit your parents."

"Thank you, Madam. I am grateful not to have been taken by that evil man."

Archimedes had listened with great interest. In all those years together, he had never known how Migru had come to his family. All he knew was that he had come to Liastrax's family from Akrai. Migru, now looked at Archimedes, who looked truly astounded. "I had no idea how you came to us!"

"Yes, I was in your mother's household, when she married your father, Phidias brought us all to Siracusa. You were born after a year."

Though Migru was reliable and loyal, Archimedes now understood why Migru had a streak of temper and irritability. The Sicani never forgave the Siculi for driving them out of the southeast. Archimedes thought to himself *Migru is an asset since he has keen insights into how to copy my prototypes. I am a lucky man to have such a good and trusted servant.*

Once they had cleared customs, they hired an ass for their possessions and headed home. The boat had docked in the main harbor, but the city seemed different somehow. There were many mercenary soldiers in the harbor standing next to the Syracusan soldiers. There red insignias told Archimedes that they were

Romans. The other difference was the city itself. Hiero had continued his enormous building plans and the city was much larger. The walls were higher and thicker and the great new temple to Zeus could be seen in the distance. There seemed to be many new immigrants.

Archimedes hailed one of the Siracusan soldiers, "tell me, why so many foreigners? We have just arrived from Alexandria. This is our home."

"You may not have heard. We are at war. First, we were allied with Carthage, but now Hiero allies with Rome against Carthage! The Carthaginians captured Messana[137], controlling the straights. Rome retaliated and defeated Hannibal. Then those Carthaginian westerners captured Akragas. That was too close for Hiero! Now we are *amicus et socii*[138] with Rome! He says it is to keep our independence! Bah! Can anyone be independent from the northern barbarians!"

"Certainly, these are unexpected and troubling events. I have come home with the hope of helping Hiero defend the city. I had no idea it would be during a war. I am an engineer and need work," answered a confused looking Archimedes.

"Well, I'm sure you will find work. There is much to do. Our defenses and machines need repair. Go to the palace and speak with the office of war. Someone will assist you to enlist or find a job."

"Thank you, Sir, but I just want a job."

So, off they went northeast along the shore to the part of the city called Achradina, where Archimedes had grown up. As they approached the family house, Archimedes remembered the good times with Phidias. It was his father who had introduced him to geometry, the heaven's wonders, and machines. As he approached the door, the cook yelled, "Liastrax! Antra! All! Come,

---

[137] Messana, the old name for Messina on the tip of Sicily closest to Italy.

[138] amicus et socii - friends and confederates, a term of alliance to Rome.

come, Mendon[139] has returned! Archimedes, come here so I can hold you as I did long ago! You are so thin? We thought you must have died at sea! Your last letter was months ago. Come. I have some fish stew!"

"And who am I? Nothing?" Migru retorted.

"You're also welcome. Carry in the trunk and you also can have some stew."

Mendon was the affectionate name for Archimedes that was used when he was young. Soon his mother and sister were there to greet him.

"Where is father?"

Liastrax answered, "He is still teaching. He has had to work long hours to feed us since you left. But come now and tell us of your life."

They spent long hours together catching up on family matters and the rapidly changing political situation.

Archimedes rested, and after two days of eating and being with his family, he approached Phidias. "Father, I want to help defend the city. I have learned many things. My water screw was a great success, and I hope to sell some here to help with family expenses. But I have ideas to strengthen and make larger catapults. I also have worked on the design of a Crow. It can be used to pluck soldiers from the battlefield or upturn ships."

"Son, you amaze me even more since your return. Tomorrow we will go to Ortygia and speak to the officers in the War Department. I will also inquire to speak with Hiero. He remembers you with admiration. He often asks of you. I have kept him abreast of your studies. I am sure he will see us soon."

And it came to pass that after Archimedes returned from Alexandria, he was in the bathhouse where the slaves had filled the

---

[139] Mendon was a term of endearment, a nickname for Archimedes.

bath to the rim. When he lowered himself into the tub, the water overflowed. As he lowered himself further until even his head was under, more water left the tub. As he stepped out, he could determine the volume of his entire body, by noticing how much water was missing from the bath. He remembered what Hiero had whispered to him before he left for Alexandria. Forgetting himself entirely, he ran out of the bathhouse to his home yelling, "Eureka, Eureka, Father, I have found it! I have found the solution to Hiero's dilemma! I have found it!

"Son, but why are you running through Siracusa naked! Here take this cloak and wrap yourself! You are not in the gymnasium[140]! Now sit and tell me what you have found!"

His father agreed that his solution was worthy. Archimedes dressed, went to court, and proved to Hiero that he was defrauded. "Hiero, I will prove to you that your crown is not pure gold. Here, I have two identical vessels filled to the brim with water. They are placed in two larger containers which will collect the overflow of water. I have here a weight of pure gold identical and the same as the weight of your crown. I will submerge one in each vessel."

He let the gold sink into one and the crown into the other.

"Now, my assistants will collect the overflow into two identical glass measuring cups. We will then make the comparison. Look here. This represents the volume identical to that of the gold, and this other represents the volume identical to your crown."

"I see. The volume of the gold is much less!" Responded the Tyrant.

"Yes, my Lord. The volume of gold is almost half that of your crown. Knowing that gold is the heaviest of metals, there must be some inferior metals infused into your crown! I therefore claim

---

[140] Gymnasium - γυμνασιον - in ancient Greece it was a place of training facilities and competitions, a place for socializing and engaging in intellectual pursuits for adult male citizens, from gymnós – nude.

that you have been defrauded! The crown is not pure!"

There were exclamations of awe and whispers that circulated among the men standing at court.

"Archimedes, my boy, you have proved your worth! From now on you shall be one of my counselors. You will be rewarded handsomely! And, guards, go out and find the goldsmith! Bring him to me. I will have the crown of his head! That will be my reward!

"Come back next week when I will have more time to have an extended conversation with you, Mendon."

"Thank you, Sire."

In the time of Archimedes absence, the city had expanded, and a new theater was built in the new town on the outskirts of Siracusa called Neapolis, as well as an enormous altar to Zeus, 200 feet long, which Archimedes had noticed when he had just arrived. Ortigia sparkled, but the defenses along the walls and Eurialo fortifications needed mending. Hiero called Phidias and Archimedes to an audience to which he had also invited the war minister.

"My esteemed Archimedes. I have wondered about you often since you left for Alexandria. I was very impressed with your solution to whether I was defrauded! You have shown great enthusiasm in pursuing your studies. Phidias has told me how you have impressed all in Alexandria. You are to be congratulated in raising the admiration of our city, the greatest and largest polis in the Hellenic world! I see that you are well, and you look fine in your new clothes. Liastrax must have been spinning and sewing the entire time you were gone. I like the Siracusan black stripe at the bottom of your chlamys. I see also by your scapula[141] that you have been initiated into the rites of Demeter, like the rest of your family. You honor our city!"

---

[141] Scapula - - a object of piety which hangs over the shoulders with a medal or picture which rests on the breast.

"Thank you, Sire. I am glad to have returned but did not expect such a great difference and so many improvements. And, also, so much disturbance."

"It is true. We have had war and upsets. It is difficult to keep our independence. But we do have the strongest walls of any city in the world. Carthage wishes to capture and enslave us. Rome wants us to be a colony to increase her power and dominion. We are caught as though in a huge vice. Our civilization and our independence are most valuable to us, and I am trying to preserve this. I understand you are willing to assist us."

"Yes, Sire. I want to use my skills in engineering. I am a builder of machines. I believe I can help. In Alexandria I invented a water screw which can lift water to irrigate. I have plans to make some for our farmers." "Very good. We need productive farmers to feed our people and to insure a flow of funds into Siracusa's coffers. I would like you to meet Hector, my war minister. He will help you find your calling. Go with him now, and I will speak to Phidias a while."

Archimedes left with Hector and Hiero spoke with Phidias.

"Phidias, how is your family?"

"Sire, they are well, but I am not. I fear that I may be dying. Even this small excursion to your palace has eaten all my strength. I cannot keep any food in my belly. It is only a matter of time. I have not spoken to Archimedes yet, but my family knows."

"I am so sorry to hear this. I will send my physician to see you. At least he can alleviate any pain. Go home now and rest. I will have my slaves bring a palanquin to carry you home."

Hector was impressed with Archimedes. They spoke about the plans to defend the city and Archimedes proposed several ways to improve catapults and of his new inventions.

Hector first arranged for Archimedes to tour the borders of the city, and then had men accompany him to the satellite cities to see that they were fortified.

Archimedes was glad to spend some time out of the city, especially in Akrai, for this was his mother Liastrax's home. He had not been there since he was a small child. He barely remembered his mother's parents. There, he could see and stay with his relatives. While in the acropolis he was introduced to Eleni. Her parents had already spoken with Phidias, Archimedes father, about a possible union. However, Archimedes was unaware of any of these previous conspiracies. She was a lovely young girl who had known his father and mother and had heard Phidias lecture whenever he visited. She watched Archimedes as he instructed the soldiers in how to strengthen the walls around the acropolis. He had them construct an inner wall in a serpentine fashion and then fill it with rubble on the side near the main approach. She told Archimedes that as a young girl she learned a great deal about the heavens from Phidias. She was very interested in the movements of the planets. Archimedes and she spent many clear summer evenings together in the theater of Akrai. He would show her how to distinguish between the moveable stars. Tonight, Venus[142] shone brightly next to the full moon, and Jupiter at apex above sleeping acropolis. It was a most brilliant night. While Archimedes pointed here and there, she stared into his eyes. Finally, he met hers, and it dawned on him, *she is truly beautiful! I was impressed with her interest in the stars, but I also like everything about her. I have been blind. If I don't speak now, I will lose my opportunity.*

"Eleni, I have enjoyed our time together. I must return to Siracusa the day after tomorrow. But I will miss you and speaking with you each day. I know I am a lot older than you. I am already well past thirty years, and you are so young! But I was thinking, thinking of asking your father. I mean, asking you first, of course. Eleni, bright-eyed one, are you open? I mean would you consider?

---

[142] Venus – Hellenes would have used the names of their gods for the planets Aphrodite, and Jupiter, Zeus.

"Archimedes! You are normally most eloquent and knowledgeable. Get on with it!"

"Would you consider being my wife? There, I have said it!"

"I thought you would never ask. You are kind, very intelligent, a master of machines, but are so oblivious to life! Yes. Yes. Of course, I will be your wife. Go now. Tonight. Ask my father."

And so that was how Archimedes married Eleni, a descendent of the Siculi, the people who had crossed the dangerous straights from Italia on a day long, long, ago. But she also had Sicani ancestors who migrated from Thapsos before leaving the coast for Akrai.

After the marriage, they moved to the same home where Archimedes extended family lived in Achradina. Within the year, Phidias passed away. The time was a sad one for the family, but soon children voices warmed the house. Four came quickly, while Archimedes remained extraordinarily busy with inventing new ways to protect Siracusa and the surrounding satellite cities.

Archimedes met with General Hector in charge of defense who liked to use the diminutive, "Mendon, first we must fortify the Castle. Let us go."

So off they went to the heights above the city where the Eurialo Fortress was built by the first Dionysius to protect against the Carthaginian incursion. It was built on the heights of the Epipolae.

"I will not only make this impregnable but have an idea of a machine which can lift soldiers and siege engines from below when they try to storm the heights. I call it my "Crow". It uses pulleys and levers to drop down upon the men and grab them in its jaws."

"I will believe it when I see it!" retorted Hector.

"I have already left a prototype in Akrai, and the men there have already begun construction. I will do the same here. I also have an idea on how to set ships on fire from the hills around the harbor. I will demonstrate."

Hector just stared as Archimedes took two curved mirrors. They were like two halves of a hollowed melon but made of shiny metal. He placed some dry leaves and sticks on the ground and used the mirrors to aim the hot Trinacrian sun so that its rays were concentrated on the rubble. Within minutes they started smoking.

"See how the sun creates the warmth that causes the rubble to catch fire. I will construct large mirrors that will concentrate the suns heat onto the ships sails and we will see the fleets of our enemies go up in smoke!"

"You are truly gifted Mendon. I will give you what you need."

CHAPTER 28

Cave 9, Wall 2 (260 - 220 BC)

THE FIRST PUNIC WAR (264-241 BC)

INSCRIPTION Y

I, Luxo, am coming up to the end of my story. This is the final cave, full of sadness for me and my people. This war against Carthage began the loss of our independence, and our relegation to a small outpost of an empire. But there was also happiness in meeting men who helped me eloquently complete my story. Read, my friends, read these words and learn!

Appius Claudius Caudex of Rome invaded Trinacria. Siracusa first allied with Carthage while the Carthaginians who held Akragas captured Messana and controlled the Straights. Hiero saw the power of Rome and immediately switched and allied with Rome. Carthage continued to occupy the west of Trinacria for twenty-three more years. Later, the Romans captured Akragas and defeated Hannibal. Then, Gaius Lutatius Catulus defeated the last Carthaginian ship of Hanno. Trinacria became a province of Rome. As a concession the Lex Hieronica[143] was accepted by Rome in Trinacria. Siracusa and much of the island remained under Hiero's control.

---

[143] Lex Hieronica – the taxation system named after Hiero II in his kingdom which Rome allowed to remain in place after Sicily became a province of Rome

During this time Archimedes worked for Hicro and built a life for his family. His star rose as did his profits.

One evening while Archimedes and Eleni were sitting in the courtyard of their home, Eleni looked at her husband. "Archimedes how high has your star risen as you have worked hard! I am grateful for my life, our lives together. Is it time now that you let up on your work?"

"Eleni, I wish I could, but Siracusa depends on so many of my inventions. Some are complete and in use, but now I am working on a system of pulleys coupled together that will help with lifting large objects. It could be used on the docks to unload ships, on Hiero's building projects like the new theater in Neapolis, and to control war machines or bridges. Right now, the war is ending, but one never knows what is on the horizon. I also am involved with my mathematics. I am working on a theory of solids, parabolas, and circles. Squaring the circle has intrigued men since the time of Aristarchus and Pythagoras. If I could find the solution, I would feel as if I accomplished something great!"

"You have already accomplished great things and people all over the Hellenic world appreciate and know of you."

"I promise I will try to spend more time with the family, but I believe the answer to the circle is using smaller and smaller quantities, infinitesimally small ones. I am perplexed by the "how." Perhaps we can spend time going to the lovely beach each week now that it is summer. There is a very wonderful sandy place to the west near Netum, it is called Litore Netini."

"I am sure the children would be glad to be away from the intense heat. This season has truly been a challenge."

"Very well, Eleni, tell the slaves to prepare food for the journey. I will tell Migru to prepare the wagon and we can leave early in the morning. One day a week away from my concerns will be good for all of us"

"So be it. Thank you."

INSCRIPTION Φ

I Luxo, saw for myself how prosperous were the next twenty years for Siracusa. Hiero took advantage building an even greater city. Though autonomy was being eaten away bit by bit, the people, seeing prosperity, did not mind or notice their loss of control. After Carthage's first defeat, Sicily was annexed to Rome.[144] Trinacria became the first province of Rome. Things were to change even more when Carthage[145] invaded eastern Iberia. However, I am getting ahead of myself. First, Hiero saw every advantage in cultivating the powers of the East to entice more allies. So next he engaged Archimedes to design the largest ship of all time to be presented to Ptolemy, the king of Egypt.

Hiero commanded, "This must be the most marvelous ship to demonstrate to the East the power and riches of Siracusa. I wish it to contain a gymnasium, a library, and a temple."

After completion, it was loaded with thousands of tons of corn, salt fish, wool, and water for drinking and bathing. It was a marvel of antiquity. There was only one problem. It was in dry dock and could not be launched even with thousands of slaves.

"Archimedes, you have boasted, 'Give me a place to stand and I will move the Earth!' Therefore, build me a machine which will launch this great craft safely!"

So, the great inventor created a complex system of pulleys which were able to launch the great *"Siracusa[146]"* safely and send

---

[144]   241 BC – The Roman victory settled by the Treaty of Lutatius.
[145]   Carthage first invaded Iberia in 218 BC when Hannibal's army headed for Italy across the Alps.
[146]   *The Siracusa* – reportedly the largest transport ship of antiquity built in 240BC.

her on its way with 200 soldiers, its statues of Atlas, and its temple of Aphrodite!

Time passed swiftly for Archimedes as he became engrossed and lost in his work. It was Eleni who brought him back to the real world. He spent many happy hours with his family during the Interbellum period when peace seemed to have been attained. When Archimedes was in his fifties, long before Carthage invaded Iberia, Eleni gave birth to her fifth and last child.

"Archimedes, come see our youngest boy! We have four lovely children and now, this fifth, in the sweetness of our old age. See how he already walks, and it is hard to keep him quiet. He already uses longer words than his older brothers!" The older children have fine tutors. Is it not time now that you let up on your work to spend more time with Sevas?"

"Yes, at this time of peace, I will enjoy taking my youngest under my tutelage. I would like nothing better."

As the children grew, Eleni made sure she made time for Archimedes and the family to enjoy times at the seashore. It was the only way to ensure that he relaxed.

"Archimedes, help Sevas with his geometry. He told me he is having difficulty."

"Sevas, come here. Come with me to the beach and we will work out your problems on the sand and then we will enjoy a swim."

"Yes, father. That sounds like a better idea than working on these slates in this very hot house."

Eleni looked at Archimedes with a disapproving scowl. "You have a very soft spot for our last child. I think he uses every excuse to get you to take him for some enjoyment."

"Shoosh! I may not have much time left in this realm. You know that I am old, and my bones ache. Don't keep me from these final years of enjoyment."

"Don't speak like that. Go and enjoy the day. Come back to me both of you!"

The years seemed to fly as Archimedes and his son spent many hours together, both on lessons, as well as at the sea. Sevas grew into a healthy and intelligent young man.

One day Eleni could see the concern around his eyes as her husband approached. "Eleni, children, have you heard the latest news? I was at the docks today and heard that Rome is again at war. Hopefully this time it will remain far from us."

"Upon Eirene, Goddess of Peace! Let us hope we are not in the storm's eye this time," sighed Eleni.

Though Trinacria remained securely in Roman hands, everyone was concerned of the news that Hannibal had crossed the Alps headed for Rome. Then suddenly, Hiero[147] died, and with him the loyalty of Siracusa to Rome.

When Archimedes returned from his work inspecting the city walls, he announced, "The news is bleak. Hieronymus is now our tyrant. He is not a supporter of Rome, and he has gathered round him all that believe that it is to our benefit to ally with Carthage. He is speaking with Hannibal to arrange a treaty." Archimedes wide and wet eyes looked at Sevas.

The tall and handsome Sevas replied, "Father I do not know who or what is better for our city. We will have no independence, whether Carthage or Rome wins."

"I agree. We will suffer in any case."

This turmoil led Archimedes into deep thought. For a while he could not concentrate on geometry.

"Sevas, look here. I have squared the circle and will apply the same methods to parabolas and other figures. I call this my 'Method of Exhaustion.'"

"O, Father, please show me! I want to impress my tutor."

"Alright then, see here is a circle of diameter one which I will

---

[147] Hiero died in 215 BC

draw using this compass." He drew it in the sand outside their house. "Now let us inscribe and circumscribe regular hexagons. Do you remember how you were taught to use the compass?"

"Yes, father, that is a simple task!"

Sevas proceeded to draw a perfect hexagon within the circle where each side of equal length formed cords within the circle. Then he drew tangents on the outside of the circle at each point at the corners of the inner hexagon. It was a very carefully done figure.

"Well done, son! You are a fine geometer. Now, can you use your geometry to calculate the length of each side of both hexagons using the laws of triangles?"

"Indeed. That is quite simple. The inscribed triangle consists of six equilateral triangles.

Since the radius is of length one-half, each side is also one-half. That makes is perimeter, six-halves or three!"

"Very good. Now calculate the perimeter of the outer hexagon."

Sevas used what he had learned about angles and sides of triangles. Then, he calculated.

When he arrived at an answer, he reported, "Father, I find the perimeter of the larger circumscribed hexagon to be about three and three parts out of seven.[148]"

"Correct, son. Now, the circle's perimeter must lie between three, the inner hexagon's perimeter, and three and three parts out of seven, the outer hexagon.[149]"

"I agree Father. That would make the circles perimeter about three and three parts out of fourteen."

"Yes, son. That is our first approximation. Now, let's apply my

---

[148] Using the ratios of 30-60-90 triangles, one can find the length of half of one side of the circumscribed hexagon or about 0.2886, close to 2/7. Then the side is twice that value, and multiplying by six sides, one gets 24/7 or 3 and 3/7.

[149] Averaging 3, the inner hexagon with the outer, 3 and 3/7, one arrives at the first approximation of the circle's perimeter as 3 and 3/14.

method of exhaustion. We now circumscribe and inscribe regular polygons with more and more sides. Each time we get closer and closer to the perimeter of the circle which always lies between the two."

"Father, this is ingenious. I see what you're doing! More sides make the polygons closer and closer to the circle! At some point you are so close that you have its exact perimeter! What an ingenious idea!"

"Sevas, I have done this again and again and my best answer for the circle's perimeter of radius one is three and one part out of seven, or twenty-two parts out of seven[150].

"Father, this is brilliant. You impress me as always. I cannot wait until I can assist you and become a mathematician and engineer."

"You can begin to assist me soon. I have a plan to protect our family from the coming storm. I am sending your sisters to Akrai to be with your mother's family. Migru will conduct them there safely, then return to help us here. I think they will be safer if Siracusa falls to one side or the other. This will keep them from immediate danger. Your mother and I are old, and we do not want to be separated. Your older brothers and their families have already left a few days ago. You may also leave if you wish."

"No, Father, I wish to remain. I am young, but strong, and know how to wield a knife and a sword. I can also run fast if I need to escape, but most importantly I will take care of you and mother."

"Thank you, my child of old age! I will take care to inform you if danger is close. Remember, you can always escape by the inlet to the city walls where the Anapo flows. You can follow the river out of the city and then climb to Akrai. It is a difficult journey, but you are capable. I fear if something happens to me that your mother will have a hard time with the journey, but she must try. Promise me you will do your best."

---

[150] Or $\Pi = 3.1415$ or 3 and 1/7

"Yes, dear Father, I swear upon Aphrodite, the goddess of both Siracusa and Akrai. She will protect us. Do not worry. Perhaps all will be resolved for the better."

"I hope so, son. Now find Migru so I can tell him the plan.

THE MUSE (2001 AD)

"Archimedes, this is pulling at the strings of my heart, because I know how all this will end. You prepared for their safety, yet yours will end in sorrow!"

"No, no. At this point I had no idea of my end, but I was already old, and if I could involve my head in some mathematical problem, I never felt the ache in my bones. I had a most wonderful life and lived to see fantastic things. I met very famous kings and visited the most interesting places like Alexandria, when most people of the time rarely traveled more than 100 stadia[151] from their home. Do not pity me."

"I hope you know how I appreciate the visits of your spirit. You have enlightened me beyond imagining."

"I too have enjoyed our time together and showing you my world. Now, we must return for the final chapter. You will still learn a bit more, and then I must return for Charon's[152] boat awaits to take me back to Elysium.[153] I did not believe much in the gods when I was alive. Most of those stories I found entertaining myths which men invented. Now that I have crossed to the other side, I know that life continues. We use boats and fields to describe what is beyond the realm of human understanding but know this: Life continues in ways which you cannot imagine.

---

[151] Stadia – 1/8 of a mile or 185 meters, 100 stadia is about 12.5 miles or 18.5 km.
[152] Charon was the ferryman that carried the souls of the dead across the river Styx.
[153] Elysium - the part of Hades for good souls where the sun always shone. The other part was Tartarus where bad souls were punished. If the judges could not decide, they sent the soul back to the Asphodel Fields to just wait.

Again, do not sorrow, for there I will be joined to my family and loved ones, and, also, to all my ancestors of which you have written. The world is a fantastic place, but that which you yet have not seen, is beyond comprehension.

Let us go!"

CHAPTER 29

CAVE 9, WALL 3

THE FINAL DAYS (213-212 BC)

Migru appeared in the distance carrying a large basket of clothes drying in the sun. "Mendon, I come. I had to finish my chores."

"Yes, I need to speak to you of some important matters. I need you to prepare for the coming storm before the tide turns for the worse. Since Hieronymus has sided with Carthage, I fear the power of Rome. I want you to take my daughters and your family to Akrai to stay with Eleni's family. You are to remain with them, care for them, as if they were your own. You have been one of our family since you were a child. I have written this document to free you. Once you arrive and they are all safe, I have provided for you to have a small land holding below Akrai to farm for your family. You may live with them on the acropolis until you have earned enough to support yourself and build a home for your family on that land. This is in gratefulness for all the service you have rendered through my life."

"Sir, I will return to make sure you and Eleni are safe. I cannot leave you to the coming horrors!"

"No, you must not come back. I have no idea what will happen when the Romans arrive in Akrai. But there are many caves there, and if war and pillage come to you there, you may head for the hills or for Pantalica. I know you know the places there very well from when you were a child."

"Yes, I know the place well. If that is your will, I will honor it."

"Go now and prepare. I will tell my daughters. My sons have gone already and prepared for you. Artemis protect you!"

"And you my dear Mendon."

INSCRIPTION X

I, Luxo, followed the events closely from messengers who brought me news from the coast. This year was one of extreme turmoil in Ortygia. Gelon, Hiero's son ruled for less than one year. Then Hiero's grandson, Hieronymus took control. While Hieronymus was visiting another city, civil strife erupted between the pro-Roman and pro-Carthaginian factions. All Gelon's family, including Hieronymus were assassinated, and Siracusa allied with Carthage and now waited for the Roman assault. Hector remained war minister.

"Archimedes, take a tour of the walls and make sure all your large catapults are prepared.

The Romans march toward us even now. Have Sevas assist you. There is no time to waste. The Romans have assigned Marcus Claudius Marcellus. He is a formidable foe. We must prepare well.

"Also, inspect the Claws on the sea wall. I have lifted the chain in the harbor, but we must use the claws to grab ships and men if they come close to the walls. Our walls have held for 500 years, and they must not fail now!"

"Indeed, Sir, I am on my way."

When Archimedes completed his inspection, he returned to the War Minister's office. When Hector saw Archimedes, he approached Sevas. "Fetch your father and go home or go to the sea. The day is warm, we have inspected the ramparts, and you and your father need a rest. Tomorrow is the festival of Artemis, our patron and protector. All will celebrate to ask her blessings. Rest and pray. Go!"

So, Sevas took Archimedes home, which was two hundred meters from the sea in Achradina. The next day was the festival, but Archimedes told his son, "I need to work on the problem of the sphere, the spiral, and the circle. I will go to the beach to work."

"Father, I will remain here to complete my chores and will come to join you later."

"Very well."

INSCRIPTION Ψ

At this point, I, Luxo became disheartened. We were celebrating our festival, but the Romans took advantage of the lowering of defenses. Marcellus marched, breached the walls, entered Siracusa and the citadel in Ortygia. The next day he gave his men permission to loot. The city was sacked. There was rape and pillage and the citizens who had supported Carthage were carried off and enslaved.

Some time passed. Sevas completed his chores and readied himself to go to his father. He went to the garden and climbed a large tree on the beach to see where his father had gone. When Sevas saw that Archimedes, his beloved father, and the giant of Siracusa, was lying motionless on the ground, he ran to see. There his heart broke to see the bloody and slain Polymath. He ran back to fetch his mother, and they took Archimedes body home, to wash it and bury him on the family compound. Then Sevas, with tear-soaked eyes, honored his father's previous instructions.

"Mother, we must leave now before the soldiers return. Let us prepare a few food items and make our escape. Father has instructed me well. Come let us not delay one moment!"

"Sevas, I wish to remain here. This is my home. This is where my beloved lies. I wish to remain here and grieve! Let me be!"

"No, Mother, I cannot. I promised Father that I would care for you. And now that he is gone, I must keep you safe for us. Come, you can grieve as long as you wish, but you must be near your loved ones."

"Yes, Sevas, you are right. I will carry this grief on my shoulders as we proceed to the hills. You are your Father's son for sure. He would not like me to stay alone. Let us proceed."

So, two figures dressed in cloaks left at nightfall and followed the Anapo to the highlands and there found refuge with Eleni's family. They arrived on the acropolis at dawn as the sun shown in a clear blue sky, as Etna's white puffs rose in the distance.

THE MUSE (2001 AD)

"So, we have come full circle, Archimedes!"

"Yes, life is like that most perfect figure. But I have a final gem that is not written in the caves. My son Sevas and Eleni arrived unharmed in Akrai. Migru awaited them and all were saddened by my death whom they later would remember as the greatest scientist of antiquity. I believe they loved me very much and now I will again see them on my return to Elysium. So do not be sad for I am sure we will see each other again when it is your time.

"Now, Migru needed to have his papers of remission checked by the authorities so he could claim his land. He found a scribe to check whether the papers were in order since he could not read. All recommended Luxo, a very influential scribe who worked at the Questors Office. Let them speak to you themselves. Come!"

CHAPTER 30

THE SCRIBE LUXO (212 BC)

"Hail, my name is Migru, and I wish you to check some papers. I can pay you."

"And I am Luxo. You are a slave? What possible papers can you have?"

"I was the slave of Archimedes. Do you know his name? He is famous throughout the world, but here in this outpost, maybe you do not know him."

"You insult me and the citizens of this great Akrai before you even know who I am! Of course, I know this godlike man who has invented amazing things. He has lectured here, and I have seen him with my own eyes!"

"Well forgive me, Sir, but I have served this great man for his entire life, and he has now gone to be with the gods, for the Romans have slain him, and he lies in a cold grave in Siracusa."

"O what tragedy! His wife's ancestors still are here! Have they yet heard? O, what sorrow! What a loss! I had not heard of this tragedy. Forgive me. Now to your business."

"His relatives have been notified and his wife and children have come here for safety. They are all well but weary and disconsolate. When I left him, he gave me papers of manumission and a small plot near Akrai. I wish to know if all is in order, and who do I see to register."

Luxo looked at the papers carefully and made some sounds of affirmation. "Yes, yes, all is in order. I can show you where to go. But first, it says here you were purchased in Akrai years ago. Were you born here?"

"Yes, my ancestors were here from before the Siculi arrived. The ancestors went from Thapsos to Pantalica during the sea invasions, and then moved near the Anapo where the land was productive. We are of Sicani and Siculi blood line."

"And so am I. My family has the same tale of our ancestors."

"So, our trees have the same root."

"Come, I will help you. Please Migru, you must tell me more of the great man you served."

THE FINAL ENCOUNTER WITH THE MUSE
(2002 AD)

Migru filled Luxo's head with tales of Archimedes, and it was here that Luxo decided to begin writing on the cave walls. So as Rome stuck its claws deeper into Akrai and the surrounding regions, Luxo sought out his friend Antax and together they began the project of the caves to write the ancient history of Trinacria. Archimedes told me that they did not want any of the story of Trinacria to be lost.

"So now you know my story and all the great, good, and evil people of our island. I wished to let the world know of this because I have witnessed the horrors of almost 23 Centuries of the follies of men since I met my end. I had thought mankind would find a way to honor men of mind, loyal and principled as Plato had wished. However, those men of lower instincts and of greed, who seek only wealth and power, arise again and again, and the fight is endless. Love and Strife war and change is the only constant.

"You have seen Plato and other great men of centuries past – Buddha from the East, Jesus the Jew, Mohammed the Muslim, Men of Science and Art like Dante, Copernicus, DaVinci, Palladio, Galileo, Newton, and Einstein, political men of peace. But those who seek power and war arise and take the earth to destruction.

"Even your own democracy in the New World, born of the Enlightenment, with Jefferson, Franklin, and others has started to fail. Beware my son! This is my final advice before I leave. Disseminate this story of the history of this small Trinacria, because it is a microcosm of the history of the world. Learn from the evil of these past men. All truth is revealed on these walls. Remember this mystical city on the hill where men tried to establish justice. Remember Akrai. Read, learn, and beware. Goodbye my friend. I have enjoyed our time together. Now it is time for you to take up the torch!

"Farewell my dear friend. Go in peace and enjoy eternity!"

And as my eyes filled with tears, Archimedes turned and walked out my door and up the winding garden path. He was dressed as a noble Hellene in a white chiton with a black stripe around his collar and a black belt at his waste, in the colors of Siracusa. His grey hair blew in the wind. On his back was embroidered a sphere circumscribed by a cylinder in fine gold thread, perhaps his greatest contribution to civilization. It was spring and the garden path was framed by apricot trees blossoming in pink and white, and the petals were slowly drifting toward the ground. Persephone had returned. At the top he turned and waved, then slowly disappeared as the path descended. Looking up I saw Etna give up a halo of smoke, and one last blast of red fire. Then she was quiet.

This also opened my mind to emotions which had been dormant during the time I was occupied with researching and writing. As I remembered my dear friend, I thought of my Great-uncle Raffaele, whom I had met the first few times I had visited Palazzolo Acreide, the ancient Akrai. Now I realize he reminded me so much of Archimedes! I also thought of Enzo, the archeologist who first set me on this quest. Now, they both were long gone, but I was happy at the thought they too had met Mendon in the next life. I was grateful to them all.

For the last three years during which Archimedes visited me so many times, I had made a fine and dear friend. Now, alone, and sad, I wondered what was real and what was a dream. The reality of his absence filled my mind. He was gone. To me he was as real as anything I had experienced in life before. I would take his lessons to heart and proclaim and look for the truth in all things as Mendon had taught me. I look to the time I will rejoin him in Elysium. Good night my friends. Read and learn. Sleep well!

AFTERWORD

My visits to Sicily to meet my relatives inspired me to think about what life would be like on that island by the different people who settled there. The caves in Palazzolo Acreide, ancient Akrai, led me on a voyage into the past. Enzo is an invention of my imagination, but he helped me to find a way to create a story involving all these interesting tribes and people. Visit Sicily if you get a chance, You will not be disappointed!

ACKNOWLEDGEMENTS

I wish to thank the following mentors who helped me on my way.

My deceased cousin
Gaetano Miano,
physician and poet, who inspired me with his poetry.
His poems are collected in two volumes:
Abitare Nell'Anima
Cooperativa Universitaria Editrice Catanese di Magistero;
and
Dialugannu pi Ridiri e Pinzari
Libreria Minerva Editrice.

My friend, talented writer, and editor who gave me great pointers
on my manuscript,
Kika Dorsey.
https://www.kikadorsey.com

My colleagues from Casady School
Carolyn Horter, Merren Stewart, and Tom Stewart
who read through and corrected a multitude of errors and
discordant phrases.

My third cousin living in the beautiful city of Catania,
who graciously offered her watercolor of Etna for my cover.
Elena Cutrona.
www.elenacutrona.it

My wife who has stood beside me during the long hours of reading
and re-writing and who has always supported my work,
Ruth Miano.

BIRTH OF AN ISLAND

To understand this land and people, I began with the landforms that formed this mythical land. It has a unique geology which affects the inhabitants in their everyday life.

Trinacria lies on the boundary of the European and African plates. This has colored not only its geological history but its cultural development because of its location as a bridge between continents.

25 million years ago, three distinct landforms existed between Italy and Africa. Sicily was not yet one island, but a collection of small ones. First, the Hyblaean limestone plateau roughly in the area near Siracusa was an island lying in the southeast. Second, was the central-western part formed from land-derived sediments. And third, which was attached to the second, the limestone mountainous regions of the northwest near Palermo stretching to north of Messina. Both between and to the north of these regions there were deep marine basins, splitting the regions apart.

Then, around 700,000 years ago, the sea between the Hyblaean plateau and the north began to awaken. As the sea bubbled and waves grew in the normal quiet sea, lava began forming a land mass. Slowly a volcano's head appeared above the waters and started uniting the distinct islands into one landmass. Tectonic shifts raised the entire island, and land bridges connected the island for a time to the Italian mainland and Africa and to many of the present surrounding islands like Malta and Lipari. This allowed flora and fauna and humanoids to enter the new land mass.

The climate continued to change over the eons. As the ice grew over the Earth around 70,000 years ago, the sea lowered, in places as much as 120 feet. Land and land bridges disappeared and re-appeared. As cold winds blew from the north, more migrations followed to this new Eden where the sun shown more brightly, and warm blue-green waters reduced the bite of the cold.

Deer and mice, hippo and elephant crossed the bridges from Europe to the north and Africa in the south. Humans who formed stone tools crossed the isthmus and found numerous caves in which to work and dwell. Remains of some early species of hippos and small elephant have been found on the island

Looking to the north the inhabitants could see the smoke climbing from the sea toward the sky from Stromboli and looking toward the southeast they could see the huge smoking mountain of Etna which at times caused the earth to quake and copious lava to flow right into the sea. The environment shaped the people's gods, prayers, and poetry with a unique color.

Finally, about 10,000 years ago the island roughly attained its present form of a triangle, Trinacria, with the massive Etna still active, still affecting their everyday practices, still providing fertile ground, and resources.

The descendants of the original inhabitants would evolve further as the climate became yet warmer, and other peoples arrived by sea from east, west, north, and south. The triangle was a stepping-stone between continents and cultures, an island controlling the western Mediterranean, and a trading outpost connecting various far-flung regions. A small island, with a great legacy. This triangular island, Trinacria, was thrice blessed by its three landforms joined by Etna, the smoking candle at its center, all washed in blue-green seas. Again, thrice blessed by the three early tribes, the Sicani, the Siculi, and the Elymi. The triad was repeated, blessing the land three times three, when the early tribes were visited by the Greeks, and then the Romans.

This gave rise to the symbol of Sicily: the head of a Gorgon surrounded by three legs forming a wheel.

The early inhabitants would worship Etna as Adhrano, the fire god who sweats and shakes. They worshiped his progeny, the twins, the Palici, who resided in sulfurous and naphtha lakes. They paid homage to Persephone, the goddess of the underworld and her mother Demeter and father Poseidon, God of the deep. Later they sacrificed to other gods: Hephaestus, the god of fire and forges and sculpture, Apollo, God of sun and light, and Erik or Aphrodite, the Queen of Heaven, goddess of sexuality, fertility, and beauty.

Trinacria, a small place in an enormous world would have an inordinate effect on civilization and history. This is her story.

GODS AND SUPERNATURAL CREATURES

Aed – *Sicani God of fire – evolves into Adhrano*

Aeolus – *Greek God of the wind*

Adar – *Siculi God of fire and shaking – evolves into Adhrano*

Adhrano – *Trinacria's God of fire and shaking*

Alpheus – *pursues Arethusa and reunites with her in Ortigia.*

Aenaes – *Trojan hero and son of Aphrodite and Anchises*

Aphrodite - Greek goddess of love, fertility evolved from Erik

Apollo – *Sun God of the Greeks evolved from Dyēus Phter – Indo-European Daylight Sky God*

Arethusa – *nymph who flees Arcadia and arises in a spring in Ortigia near the port of Siracusa*

Artemis – *Greek goddess of the hunt, wilderness, animals, the moon, and chastity.*

Ciane (Cyanos) – *nymph meaning azure who tried to prevent the abduction of Persephone*

Dégōm – *Sicani evil Earth God*

Demeter – *Olympian goddess of agriculture who was the mother of Persephone*

Dyēus Phter – *Siculi Daylight Sky God – evolves into Apollo*

Erik – *Sicani goddess of love, fertility – evolves into Aphrodite*

Gaia – *Greek Goddess of the earth*

Hades – *Greek God of the underworld who abducts Persephone*

Hephaistos – *Greek God of blacksmiths and metal working.*

Hera – *Sister and wife of Zeus, goddess of women, marriage, childbirth, family.*

Iris – *Goddess of the rainbow and personal messenger of Hera*

Kore – *name of Persephone before her abduction meaning maiden.*

Kronos – *Greek God of time*

Leto – *A female Titan goddess, bride of Zeus, and mother of the twin gods Apollo and Artemis*

Ouranos – *Greek God of the sky*

Persephone – *Daughter of Demeter who was taken into the underworld by Hades. Kore's name is changed after she returns to the earth. Persephone means bringer of destruction and death.*

Poseidon – *Greek God of the Sea*

Thalassa – *controls the sea*

Zeus – *Greek father of the Gods*

PLACES AND RIVERS

Akrai – *Greek polis 30 km from Siracusa (current name Palazzolo Acreide)*

Catana – *Greek polis on coast 70 km from Siracusa*

Corinth – *Greek polis in Arcadia in mainland Greece*

Drepanum – *Trapani on the western coast of Trinacria*

Eithné – *Goddess and mountain of Etna*

Iberia – *Spain, where the Sicani are supposed to have originated*

Illios (Illion) – *Ancient Troy*

Kamikos – *Sicani town ruled by King Cocalus and where Daedalus arrives*

Knossos – *capital of Minoa in Crete*

Libya – *north Africa closest to Sicily*

Mt. Lauro – *mountain close to Akrai where the Anapo river rises*

Messéné – *Greek polis at the closest location to the Italian mainland (current name Messina)*

Naxos – *earliest settlement of Greeks in Sicily on the coast near Mt. Etna*

Ortygia – *the island off the coast of Siracusa where the Greeks first arrived to found Siracusa*

Palazzolo Acreide – *current name of Akrai and village of my ancestry*

Palici – *the place of the sacred lakes*

Polis (pl. Poleis) – *Greek city state*

Pantalica – *prehistoric site of caves and the Anaktoron close to Akrai*

Sicania – *ancient name of Sicily*

Siracusa – *Greek polis and largest of the world in the time of the Greeks*

Syrako – *the swamp land delta of the Anapo from which the polis*

Siracusa gets its name

Thapsos – *Sicani town north of Siracusa which was advanced for its time*

Thera – *Island that explodes near Crete*

Trinacria – *ancient name of Sicily*

RIVERS

Acate (Drillo)

Anapo

Assinaro

Ciane

Drillo (Acate)

Irminio

Platani

BIBLIOGRAPHY

Books

Benjamin, Sandra: *Sicily – 3000 years of Human History*. Hanover, NH. Steer Forth Press. 2006

Bierlein, JF: *Parallel Myths*. N.Y. Ballantine Books. 1994

Bradshaw, Gillian: *The Sand Reckoner*. N.Y. Tom Doherty Association, LLC.

Brea, Luigi Bernabó: *Il Tempio di Afrodite di Akrai*. Napoli, It. Cahiers du Centre Jean Bérnard. X ou;;vrage avec la collaboration de L'Instituto Studi Acrensi, Pallazzolo Acr. (SR). 2000

Cline, Eric H: *1177 BC, The Year Civilization Collapsed*. Princeton University Press. 2021

Funari, Salvatore; Eagar: *Myths and Customs in Greek and Roman Sicily*. Palermo, It. l986

Graf. Co.: *Syracuse Art History Landscape*. Italy. Ditta Co. 1986

Haywood, John: Freeman; Garwood; Toms: *Historical Atlas of the Ancient World*. Oxford. Andromeda Oxford, Ltd.1998

Hishfeld, Alan: *Eureka Man*. N.Y. Walker Publishing Co. 2009

Leighton, Robert: *Sicily Before History*. Ithaca, NY. Cornell U. Press. 1999

Lyon, Annabel: *The Golden Mean*. NY. Alfred A Kopf, Random House. 2009

Mallory, J.P.: *In Search of the Indo Europeans*. London. Thames and Hudson, Ltd. 1991.

Netz, Reviel; Noel: *The Archimedes Codex*. Philadelphia, PA. Da Capo Press (Perseus B. Group) 2007

Oxford: *Oxford Classical Greek Dictionary*. Oxford and NY. Oxford U. Press. Edited by Morwood and Taylor. 2002

Peet, Thomas Eric: *The Stone Age and the Bronze Age in Italy and Sicily*. London. Henry Frowde, U. of Oxford. 1909

Prichard, James Cowles: *Researches into the Physical History of Mankind*. London. Sherwood, Gilbert, and Piper. 1841

Articles

Hyde, Walter Woodburn: "The Volcanic History of Etna." Vol. 1, No. 6. Geographical Research. U. of Pennsylvania. JSTOR 1916 https://classics.richmond.edu/gallery/research-papers/CulturalInteractions.pdf

\Orefice, Zack; Story: "Cultural Interactions among Aegean Bronze Age Civilizations." 2009-11
https://classics.richmond.edu/gallery/research-papers/CulturalInteractions.pdf

Stampogidas, Nicholas (CHR); Marazzi; Massimiliano: "Sea routes – from Sidon to Huelva – 16th to 6th c.BC." Museum of Cycladic Art. Cultural Olympiad. Athens. 2003

Websites

Alio, Jaqueline: "Aphrodite, Astarte, and Venus." 7/15/21.
http://www.bestofsicily.com/mag/art412.htm

Ancientworld: "Syracuse." 7/10/21
http://ancientworld.hansotten.com/sicily/syracuse/

Brachina, DiFrancesco: "Adrano. L'Avo Dei Sicani." 5/11/21
https://www.miti3000.eu/adrano-l-avo/838-adrano-lavo-dei-sicani

Brachina, DiFrancesco:"Gli Dei Palici: Dicotomia del universo." 5/18/21
https://www.miti3000.eu/adrano-l-avo/869-gli-dei-palici-dicotomia-delluniverso

Brachina, DiFrancesco: "I Sicani: Hiberia e Trinacria – Adraño: Un Dio Indoeuropeo"
4/26/21. http://www.adranoantica.it/?p=1054

Brachina, DiFrancesco: "I Sicani: Le Origine e il Sito." 4/26/21.
https://www.miti3000.eu/mitologia-greca-mitologie-143/874-i-sicani-le-origini-e-il-sito.html

Brachina, DiFrancesco: "Sicans and Irish Celts." 5/11/21.
https://www.miti3000.eu/adrano-l-avo/895-sicani-e-celti-irlandesi

Brachina, DiFrancesco: "The Land of the Avo. The Sanctuary of Adrano. 5/11/21
https://www.miti3000.eu/adrano-l-avo/
nuove-ipotesi/76-avo-adrano/913-la-terra-dellavo-il-santuario-di-adrano

Cartwright, Mark: "Syracuse." 6/23/21
https://www.worldhistory.org/syracuse/

Calloway, Ewan: "Minoan Civilization Originated in Europe, Not Egypt." Scientific
American from Nature Magazine. 1/25/21.
https://www.scientificamerican.com/article/
minoan-civilization-origin-europe-not-egypt/

Celeste: "La Sicilia e la Colonizzazione Greca." 4/12/21.
http://www.celeste-ots.it/tematiche/distribuzione_tematiche/ tematiche15_sicilia_
greca_occidentale.htm

Cipolla, Gaetano: "Arba Sicula." 4/11/21
https://italicsmag.com/2020/07/25/sicily-and-greece/

Citizendium: "Journey of Aeneas." 6/20/21
en.citizendium.org/Journey_of_Aeneas

Conway, Robert Seymour: "1911 Encyclopedia Britanica/ Siculi. Vol.25. 3/12/21
https://www.enwikipedia.org/wiki/1911_Encyclopedia_Britanica/Siculi

Diazoma: "The Ancient Greek Theater of Akrai, Syracuse." 7/7/21.
https://diazoma.gr/en/press-releases/ancient-greek-theatre-akrai-syracuse/

DiFiliusapollinis: "Ipotesi e Ricercha sul Pantheon dei Siculi e Sulla Funzione religiosa
de Dio Adranos."
https://www.circolaoaletheia.worldpress.com/2016/09/15/ipotesi-e-ricercha-sul-
pantheon-dei-siculi-e-sulla-funzione-religiosa-del-dio-Adranos

Global Net: "Megara Hyblaea & Thapsos (SR)." 2/13/22.

  http://www.users.globalnet.co.uk/~loxias/sicily/megara.htm

Heritage: "Sicilian Wars." 10/29/20.

  https://www.heritage-history.com/index.

  php?c=resources&s=war-dir&f=wars_sicilian

History Files: "Siculi (Italics)." 10/24/20.

  https://www.historyfiles.co.uk/KingListsEurope/ItalySiculi.htm

Italian Academy: "Myth of Arethusa and Alpheus." 7/6/21

  https://www.theitalianacademy.com/portfolio-posts/myth-arethusa-alpheus/

Italy Guides: "Syracuse." 8/1/21

  italyguides.it/en/sicily/syracuse/eurialo_castle

Italy This Way: "History of Adrano, Legend of the God Adrano." 9/23/21

  italythisway.com

Italy Today: "Akrai." 1/16/21

  https://initalytoday.com/sicily/akrai/omdex.htm

Iudica, G: "La Antica citá di Acre (1819)." 7/4/21

  http://www.perseus.tufts.edu/hopper/text?doc=Perseus%3Atext%3A1999.04.0006%3

  Aentry%3Dakrai\

Jam Akram: "La Lingua dei Sikani." 4/23/22

  https://www.miti3000.it/mito/collabora/lingua_sikani.htm

Kessler, Peter: "Elymi (Italics)." 1/30/21

  www.historyfiles.co.uk/Kinglistseurope/ItalyElymi.htm.

Kessler, Peter; Salerno: "Sicani (Italy)." 1/30/21

  www.historyfiles.co.uk/Kinglistseurope/ItalySicani.htm.

Lases, Domus: "Sikels Who Really Were They?" 1/30/21

  www.saturniatellus.com/2020/12/sikels_who_really_were_they.

Livius.org: "Ducetius." 3/19/21

  https://www.livius.org/articles/person/ducetius/

Livius.org: "History of Syracuse." Vol. 1-5. 6/27/21

  www.ancientworld.hansotten.com/sicilu/syracuse

Macquire, Kelley: "The Minoans & Mycenaeans: Comparision of 2 Bronze Age

  Civilizations." 3/1/21

  https://www.worldhistory.org/article/1610/

  the-minoans--mycenaeans-comparison-of-two-bronze-a/

Mark, Joshua J.: "Inanna." 7/15/21.

  https://www.worldhistory.org/Inanna

Math.nyu.: "Royal Family of Syracuse." 10/5/21

  https://www.math.nyu.edu/~crorres/Archimedes/Family/FamilyIntro.html

Math.nyu: "Siege of Syracuse." 8/4/21

  https://www.math.nyu.edu/~crorres/Archimedes/Siege/Summary.html

Mormina, diEnzo: "Palazzolo Acreide." 7/5/2001.
   https://www.obmsnet.it/siracuisa/palazzolo.html
O"Connor, J.J.; Robertson: "Archimedes of Syracuse." 8/6/21
   https://mathshistory.st-andrews.ac.uk/Biographies/Archimedes/
Orsi, Paolo: "19th C Adventures of Paolo Orsi in Buscemi." 9/16/212
   https://www.italythisway.com/places/articles/buscemi-history.php
Picolo, Salvatore: "Bronze Age Sicily." 1/31/21
   https://www.worldhistory.org/article/1190/bronze-age-sicily/
Picolo, Salvatore: "The Dolmens of Sicily." 2/15/21
   https://ancient.eu/article/1148/the dolmens_of_Sicily/
Plato; Harward, J. (translator): "The Seventh Letter." 9/28/21
   https://classics.mit.edu/plato/seventh_letter.html
Religion.fandom.com: "Proto-Indo-European Religion." 6/15/21
   https://religion.fandom.com/wiki/Proto-Indo-European_religion
Roma Optima: "Aeneas, The Traitor of Troy." 6/20/21
   https://www.romaoptima.com/roman-empire/aeneas-the-traitor-of-troy
Roma Optima: "The Troy Games in Sicily in Virgil's Aeneid." 5/25/21
   https://www.romaoptima.com/roman-empire/
   the-troy-games-in-sicily-in-virgils-aeneid/
Romeo, Nick; Tewksbury: "Plato in Sicily." 9/23/21
   https://aeon.co/essays/when-philosopher-met-king-on-platos-italian-voyages
Saganawa's Club: "Le Prime Notizie Scritte Su Inessa." 9/25/21
   http://www.sganawa.org/book/export/html/916
Saks, David; Murray; Bunson: "List of Tyrants of Syracuse." 5/28/22.
   https://en.wikipedia.org/wiki/List_of_tyrants_of_Syracuse
Salerno, Vincenzo: "Ducetius." 7/20/21
   http://www.bestofsicily.com/mag/art226.htm
Salerno, Vincenzo: "Plato in Sicily." 4/11/21.
   http://www.bestofsicily.com/mag/art407.htm
Salerno, Vincenzo: "Sicilian Peoples: The Elymians." 1/27/21.
   http://www.bestofsicily.com/mag/art144.htm
Salerno, Vincenzo: "Sicilian Peoples: The Sicanians." 7/6/20.
   http://www.bestofsicily.com/mag/art141.htm
Simonetti, Davide: "Under the Sands - The past to the Present." 7/14/21
   https://underthesands.blogspot.com/2007/04/akrai.html
Societá Romana: "Archaic Italy: The Siculi." 7/6/20
   http://www.societasviaromana.net/Collegium_Historicum/siculi.php
Theoi.com: "Palikoi." 6/19/21.
   https://www.theoi.com/Georgikos/Palikoi.html
Trabia, Carlo: "Best of Sicily Magazine - Sicilian Neolithic Temple Builders." 2/5/21.

http://www.bestofsicily.com/mag/art294.htm

Verso, Tom: "Sicel-Sicilians and the Birth of Sicilian Culture." 10/16/14.

https.//bloggers.iitaly.org/bloggers/3872/sicel-sicilians-and-birth-sicilian-culture

wikipedia: "Adranus. 9/23/21.

https://en.wikipedia.org/wiki/Adranus

wikipedia: "Aetna." 7/17/21.

https://en.wikipedia.org/Aetna-(city)

wikipedia: "Akrai." 3/18/21.

https://en.wikipedia.org/Akrai

wikipedia: "Archimedes." 3/37/21.

https://en.wikipedia.org/wiki/Archimedes

wikipedia: "Castelluccio Culture." 9/5/21.

https://en.wikipedia.org/wiki/Castelluccio_culture

wikipedia: "Cyane." 7/14/20.

https://en.wikipedia.org/wiki/Cyane

wikipedia: "Daedalus." 1/27/21.

https://en.wikipedia.org/wiki/Daedalus

wikipedia: "Demeter." 4/14/21.

https://en.wikipedia.org/wiki/Demeter

wikipedia: "Elymus (mythology)." 6/26/21.

https://en.wikipedia.org/wiki/Elymus_(mythology)

wikipedia: "Eleusinian Mysteries." 10/6/21

https://en.wikipedia.org/wiki/Eleusinian_Mysteries

wikipedia: "Empedocles." 4/12/21.

https://en.wikipedia.org/wiki/Empedocles

wikipedia: "Galermi Aqueduct." 10/20/20

https://en.wikipedia.org/wiki/Galermi_Aqueduct

wikipedia: "Italic Peoples." 9/18/21

https://en.wikipedia.org/wiki/Italic_peoples

wikipedia: "Inessa." 8/19/21

https://it.wikipedia.org/wiki/Inessa

wikipedia: "List of Archeological Periods (Levant)." 3/23/21.

https://en.wikipedia.org/wiki/List_of_archaeological_periods_(Levant)

wikipedia: "List of Basque Mythological Figures." 5/11/21

https://en.wikipedia.org/wiki/List_of_Basque_mythological_figures

wikipedia: "List of the Fire Gods." 5/11/21.

https://en.wikipedia.org/wiki/List_of_fire_gods

wikipedia: " Minoa." 1/29/212

https://en.wikipedia.org/wiki/Minoa

wikipedia: "Minotaur." 1/26/21

https://en.wikipedia.org/wiki/Minotaur
wikipedia: "Monte Lauro." 10/25/20
   https://en.wikipedia.org/wiki/Monte_Lauro
wikipedia: "Necropolis of Pantalica." 10/20/20
   https://en.wikipedia.org/wiki/Necropolis_of_Pantalica
wikipedia: "Palazzolo Acreide." 7/27/20
   https://en.wikipedia.org/wiki/Palazzolo_Acreide
wikipedia: "Palike." 3/12/21.
   https://en.wikipedia.org/wiki/Palike
wikipedia: "Sicels." 10/20/20
   https://en.wikipedia.org/wiki/Sicels
wikipedia: "Le Prime Popolazione: Etoli ed Elidi." 7/10/21
   https://it.wikipedia.org/wiki/Leggenda_sulla_fondazione_di_Siracusa
wikipedia: "Sicilian Expedition." 9/13/21
   https://en.wikipedia.org/wiki/Sicilian_Expedition
wikipedia: "Siege of Syracuse (213-212 BC)." 3/17/21
   https://en.wikipedia.org/wiki/Siege_of_Syracuse_(213–212_BC
wikipedia: "Thapsos." 1/27/21.
   https://en.wikipedia.org/wiki/Thapsos
wikipedia: "Viaggi di Platone in Sicilia." 9/6/22
   https://it.wikipedia.org/wiki/Viaggi_di_Platone_in_Sicilia
wikiwand: "Anapo." 10/20/20. (access 3/19/210
   https://www.wikiwand.com/en/Anapo
wikiwand: "Le Prime Popolazione."
wikipedia: "Viaggi di Platone in Sicilia." 9/6/22
   https://it.wikipedia.org/wiki/Viaggi_di_Platone_in_Sicilia

Made in the USA
Coppell, TX
23 April 2024

31615951R00215